NORTH:
The Last Great Race
(Andi & North, Book 2)

Best Wishes,
Mettauer

Joan Mettauer

Cover photo of Inukshuk taken by award-winning photographer Krystal Tsuji in Rankin Inlet, Nunavut, Canada. Copyright © 2017 Krystal Tsuji. Instagram: @krystaltsuji

ISBN 13: 978-1545188644 (Paperback)
ISBN 10: 1545188645

1. *Fiction, Action & Adventure*

ALSO BY JOAN METTAUER

Diamonds in an Arctic Sky
(Andi & North, Book 1)

Honeymoon Bay
(Andi & North, Book 3)

After the Storm
(Andi & North, Book 4)

And for the Littles in your life,
The Adventures of Stripes the Gopher
(An early Readers Chapter Book)

~ For my grandson, Vince,
The newest member
Of our growing family ~

May your life be
One
Great
Adventure
After
Another

'The thrill is not just in running,

But in the courage to join the race'

Author Unknown

PROLOGUE

I start awake, my heart thudding painfully as I struggle to distinguish reality from nightmare. In my mind's eye, strands of hot scarlet dance and swirl with pristine, cold white, rising and falling and finally pooling in a shimmering pink, wet pool. Voices cried, a high-pitched keening. Were they human, or beast?

It all came back in a rush. I was in Anchorage, Alaska, laying alone on a strange bed, in a stranger's home. My lover and best friend had left days ago, determined to challenge himself and his dreams, intent on conquering a sometimes cruel and forbidding Mother Nature. Somewhere over Alaska's frozen, isolated expanse of land, ocean and mountain between Anchorage and Nome, the man I loved more than life itself was mushing in the Iditarod – The Last Great Race.

I had been blessed not only with my mother's green eyes, but her keenly intuitive nature, as well. Some called our gift the 'Sixth Sense'. This so-called 'gift' had been entertaining when I was younger – waking up and 'knowing' where my father's missing lighter was (between the sofa cushions), or walking to the telephone to call my mother, only to have it ring in my hands (my mother on the other end, of course). Always chalked up to coincidence, these events had once been entertaining. But as I grew and developed, so did my gift. I was now blessed with horribly accurate, uncanny dreams and insights into the future. It wouldn't be so bad if they were insights to joyful, happy events, but they weren't. I prayed that this time my nightmares were only just that – nightmares.

ONE

"COME HAW! COME HAW!" The musher guided his eight powerful sled dogs into a sharp left turn, each furry beast's lolling, pink tongue in sharp contrast to winter's monochromatic white palette. Snow and ice hissed beneath the skis of the light racing sled as it skimmed across the frozen ribbon of northern Canada's McKenzie River. Astride two runners protruding from the back of the sled's small cargo basket, the man's easy, relaxed stance could easily give a bystander the mistaken impression that mushing required little effort on the part of the dogs' human counterpart. His body moved in a continuous, yet seemingly effortless dance, perfectly synchronized with each bump and sway of the sled.

This particular musher was clad from head to foot in traditional Inuit winter garments: fur-trimmed caribou skin anorak, pants and kamiks. His hands gripped the sled's arched, wooden handle bar to maintain his balance and were sheathed in heavy animal skin mitts that extended to the crook of his elbow and were decorated with intricate beadwork. On anyone else, the time-honoured apparel, although warm and practical, would be deemed eccentric. On North Edward Charles Ruben, it looked regal.

North's team of spirited Canadian Eskimo dogs hurdled up the McKenzie River's gently sloping bank, effortlessly towing the sled and its passenger up and over the edge. The muscular, sleek dogs, their coats a rainbow of grey, black, brown and white, sensed they were near the end of their journey and began to yelp. The intensity and volume of their song strengthened as they dashed toward a small group of racing enthusiasts clustered near the finish line. Although the race was merely an impromptu, Saturday afternoon sporting event between friendly rivals, North's victorious shout resounded across the barren tundra when he slid over the finish line, capturing first place. His opponents may have entered today's contest merely for fun, but North Ruben had an agenda. These days, he took every sled dog race and each win seriously; each brought him another step closer to his lifelong dream of conquering the most grueling dog sled race in the world – The Iditarod.

Today's event was a relatively short two-hour run and many of the spectators chose to wait at the staging area since the race's slightly disorganized noon start. In an effort to ward off the inevitable chill of a January afternoon high above the Arctic Circle, they'd built smoking fires inside two 45-gallon steel barrels. The fires crackled and flared inside the lidless, rusted drums, releasing curls of dark grey, acrid smoke into the azure blue sky. Mitten-clad hands warmed over the smoldering fires, while mukluks and heavy, insulated boots stomped the hard-packed snow in an attempt to restore circulation to numb feet. Only the sturdiest of souls, many of whom warmed themselves from thermoses of hot coffee laced with whisky or Southern Comfort, braved a chilly minus 20-degree Celsius day for a bit of afternoon entertainment.

Once across the finish line North applied pressure to the sled brake, slowing his team's pace to a fast trot, then glanced back to check on the position of his closest competitor. His eyes grew wide and a slow smile spread on his cold, chapped lips. His closest opponent had already rounded the river's bend and was heading toward its bank. A cacophony of excited canine voices grew steadily louder, ringing through the otherwise tranquil, icy air. Shrouded inside the deep hood of a bright red Arctic parka, the musher's facial features were obscured in shadow. North laughed at the racer's determined, focused posture, his warm breath expelling a foggy cloud into the air. He knew those dogs, and he knew that musher. Intimately.

Still chuckling, North hopped off the runners and trotted beside it for a few seconds before calling the dogs to a stop. He set the snow hook to prevent his team from wandering away with the sled, pulled off his heavy mitts and tossed his hood back. Heavy black eyebrows drew one's gaze from a square jaw to thickly lashed, chocolate brown eyes. He scrubbed at his chilled face, restoring circulation to skin the colour of dark honey. The dogs, panting lightly from their exertion, were content to sit on their haunches or lie in the snow, waiting for their master's next move.

The second-place musher crossed the finish line with a jubilant cry and slid to a stop next to North. The dogs greeted each other with high whines and sharp yips, their feathered tails sending white flurries of snow swirling into the still air. Judging by the size of his grin, North was pleased to see the slight figure in red as she flew into his waiting arms. "I almost did it, North! I just about had you this time!" Andrea Ruben, North's bride of exactly seventeen days, pulled off her mitts and goggles and tossed the wolf-trimmed hood from her head, releasing a wave of gleaming, dark brown curls. Brilliant emerald green eyes sparkled over high cheekbones and a straight nose complemented by a subtle, upturned tip. She beamed at her new husband and raised rosy lips to his kiss.

Hoots and whistles erupted from the spectators when the newlyweds embraced; North hugged his bride tightly for a moment longer before releasing her. He took a step back and grasped her hand in a firm and formal shake. "Congratulations on running a spectacular race, Mrs. Ruben. You've become one hell of a good musher."

The spectators, led by a familiar voice, began to chant: "Go Andi! Go Andi! Go Andi!" Andrea Ruben, more often than not called 'Andi' by her family and friends, knew the instigator's voice well and would recognize it anywhere. She scanned the crowd and spotted Margo Thomas immediately; her best friend would have been hard to miss, standing at the front of the group in her red-trimmed bright blue parka, grinning from ear to ear and waving both arms in the air. They locked eyes, and Margo gave her a two-thumbs-up salute.

Arm in arm, the Rubens turned their attention back to the race, cheering enthusiastically when two more teams soon crossed the finish line within ten nerve-racking seconds of each other. They were followed a few minutes later by the final two competitors, concluding the informal event.

The Rubens spent a few minutes rehashing the highlights of the race with the other competitors and their cheering committees, then set to work unharnessing their respective teams. The well-conditioned animals showed no signs of exhaustion after the short twenty-five-kilometer race. In fact, they were barely warmed up and were eager to run again – to continue doing what they loved best. Although it was only 3:30 in the afternoon, 200 kilometres above Canada's Arctic Circle the late January sun was already sinking to the horizon. In twenty minutes another brief Arctic day would once again succumb to darkness.

The Rubens worked together efficiently, and soon all sixteen dogs were off the gangline, out of harness, had wolfed down a snack, and were comfortably ensconced in their respective cubicles on the back of North's brand-new baby – a 1997 Ford F350 dually. He started the truck and cranked up the heat. The mutts, sensing another adventure, poked furry heads through their porthole windows, creating a comical picture: two rows of busy black noses, erect ears and bright, inquisitive eyes peered from masked faces.

North ignored the dogs and lovingly patted the shining white hood of his new prized possession; he still hadn't tired of admiring the converted vehicle. In place of a standard cargo box, the truck's 3-meter-long custom bed boasted a large, double-decker plywood box which was divided into individual compartments to safely transport up to twenty animals. A narrow aisle ran down the center of the box, creating a convenient place to stow gear and food, and two sleds could be transported on its top. Within the spacious four-door super-crew cab, a converter system provided power for a small microwave to heat drinks and meals while they were on the road. North loved his new truck almost as much as he loved his new wife.

He had purchased the costly vehicle for the upcoming Alaskan Iditarod Trail Sled Dog Race, fondly known to the mushing crowd as *The Last Great Race*. This year's event was even more noteworthy than usual; it was the 25th running of the famous race. Special silver anniversary celebrations and media coverage were planned for Sunday, March 2, and for the first time in his life North was registered to compete. The mere thought of racing against the best mushers in the world, in the most demanding race known to man, often made his heart miss a beat. Not that he would admit his weakness to another living soul.

"I told Margo we'd meet them at The Brass Rail after we get the mutts settled at home," Andi said as she climbed into the high cab of the Ford. She knocked snow from her heavy white boots before pulling them into the vehicle's warm interior, well-aware of her husband's infatuation with the truck. He spent more time cleaning and polishing his new toy than she did on housework.

"Sounds good to me," North smiled. "I could definitely go for a cold beer and a burger."

"It sounds like most of this crowd is heading over too. They all want to hear more about the Iditarod."

North groaned, but his dark eyes glinted with pleasure. "God, you'd think I'd already won the bloody race, the way these guys have been carrying on." He shook his head solemnly, not quite succeeding to contain a crooked smile. "It's great to see they have some degree of faith in me, though, because I sure as hell don't."

"You're going to do *awesome*," Andi insisted. "I just know you're going to give the world a race to remember."

"Oh, I'm sure they'll remember me alright. They'll be laughing forever about the crazy Canuck who tried to run the Iditarod with a pack of slow working dogs."

They bounced along the trail leading from the river's edge to the highway, no more than two tire ruts in the packed snow. Andi reached for her seat belt. "I thought you had more faith in the dogs."

North signed. "I do. It's just that ..."

"What?"

His glance was brief, but long enough for Andi to see the doubt in his dark eyes. Doubt, and something else. "Maybe I am crazy. Maybe I should be raising Siberian Huskies, or Alaskan Malamutes, like everyone else. Dogs that can actually *run*. Nobody has ever attempted the Iditarod with a team of Canadian Eskimo Dogs before."

"So you'll be the first. I've never known you to doubt your team before, so why now?"

North shrugged. "Ah, I don't know." They'd reached the highway and bounced over a small snowbank deposited by a grader before hitting the pavement. "I love my dogs, don't get me wrong. You know I do. They can pull anything you harness them up to and go all day, but they're just not really built for speed. Or climbing, for that matter. I'm probably going to look like a fool in front of the best mushers in the world."

"Well, you can still scratch from the race if you really want to."

"I don't want to scratch."

Andi sighed in exasperation. "Well what *do* you want?"

"I want a beer."

TWO

There was standing room only in The Brass Rail pub when the Rubens walked into the popular downtown bar an hour later. They had both exchanged their heavy outer gear in favour of short, down jackets. At over six feet tall, North had no problem spotting Margo and the rest of their friends seated in a far corner. He grasped Andi's hand and headed in their direction, weaving between tables and milling bodies. Their slow passage through the smoky room reminded Andi of the evening two years earlier, when North had invited her to this same pub for Friday night drinks. She would never forget that memorable night ... she had fallen in love with the quiet, yet determined Inuit man who was destined to become her husband.

As she shadowed North through the noisy crowd, Andi spotted several familiar faces seated at one of the tables, the evidence of more than a few drinks on its cluttered surface. The men were all pilots, employed by Tuktu Aviation Services. She should know – she was their Flight Operations Manager, and had been their boss for the past four years. She'd loved almost every minute of those years. Her eyes turned unbidden to the long, gleaming mahogany bar set against the pub's side wall, remembering the three Tuktu employees who had mysteriously vanished two years earlier. The Brass Rail Pub had been one of their favourite drinking holes. Tonight, though, the ghosts of the infamous Captain James O'Neill, his co-pilot Hank Brister, and Tuktu's Chief Dispatcher, Jessica Hartman, were nowhere in sight.

The bar's lavish red-gold brass ornamentation, for which the pub was aptly named, glowed in the muted light, its rich lustre luring Andi's attention. Behind the high bar a vast array of intriguingly shaped liquor bottles burst with colour that rivalled even the most dazzling gems – emerald, sapphire, aquamarine, ruby, turquoise and smoky brown topaz. Strategically placed behind the bar on high rows of glass shelving, the bottles' flowing contours and hues reflected from the smoky mirrors behind them. Andi silently cursed the liquor industry for designing such seductively attractive vessels for their addictive, often lethal, contents.

Margo had saved them a couple of chairs at the long table; it looked like the Rubens were the last to arrive. "Thanks for saving us a seat," Andi smiled, draping her jacket over the back of the empty chair next to her friend. A burst of raucous laughter made her glance back; North had been ambushed by a couple of his buddies at the far end of their table.

"I thought you'd gotten lost," Margo laughed. She reached for a frosty beer mug. "What took you so long, or dare I ask?"

"Have you ever tried feeding twenty-four howling, hungry mutts?" Andi retorted, crossing her eyes in comic exasperation. "You're lucky we're here already. North dished out their food before we left for the race this morning, or we'd still be there cutting up bloody hunks of caribou or whatever it was he fed them today."

North finished a round of boisterous high-fives and squeezed into the empty seat beside his wife.

"Hey, there, North. Congrats on the win today." Margo toasted him with her mug and an infectious smile.

He slung an arm around Andi's shoulders. "Thanks," he smirked, giving her a squeeze. "The little woman here gave me a pretty good run for my money, though."

"Ha!" Andi exclaimed, tossing a few curls over her shoulder. "Little woman, my ass. I'm going to beat you one day, Ruben. Mark my words."

"It was a good race, guys," Margo said. "It's hard to believe you've been mushing for only a year, Andi."

"Eighteen months," she retorted.

"Whatever. Ya done good, and I'm proud of you."

Andi glanced around the table. "Where's Ken?"

"At work," Margo's lips twisted. "As usual."

Margo and Ken Thomas had been Andi's best friends for years – long before she'd moved to Inuvik. She'd met the couple in Yellowknife, and they had quickly become inseparable. Andi discovered that they were the kind of friends who stick together through thick and thin, through sorrow and joy. When the Thomases had relocated from Yellowknife to Inuvik four years ago, Andi had moved to the high Arctic settlement right behind them in hopes that escaping to the remote arctic town would help to numb the sorrow and pain of a deceased child and a broken marriage. Although she would never forget her sweet daughter, Natalie, lost at the tender age of three to a speeding truck on icy Yellowknife roads, moving to Inuvik had given Andi what she needed – a new start on life.

The move had also brought her new love. Andi gazed at her husband where he sprawled in the Brass Rail's deep leather club chair; marriage had done nothing to diminish her desire for him. Her heart still skipped a beat every time she glimpsed his heavily lashed, bottomless brown eyes, determined jawline and long, jet black hair. Even now, amidst a room full of friends and strangers, tingles of desire sparked through her veins. At forty-one years of age, North Ruben exuded virility. To his bride's dismay, his chiselled good looks and lean, muscular build, balanced by a calm demeanour and just the right touch of grey at his temples, still drew admiring glances from women of all ages.

Andi gnawed her lower lip, lost in thought until her reverie was broken by a sharp poke to her upper arm. "Why don't you save it for the bedroom," Margo teased. "You haven't heard a damn word I've said, have you?"

Andi stared at her with blank eyes.

North grinned. "Babe, she caught you staring at me with lust in your eyes again."

"Oh, stop it you guys! Can't a girl be left to reminisce in peace?" Andi retorted. But it was true ... she couldn't get enough of her impossibly sexy husband.

A frazzled waitress appeared with a heavily laden tray. She set a tall mug of dark beer in front of North, froth slipping down its icy sides. Andi unconsciously licked her lips and leaned marginally closer to the beer's yeasty, familiar aroma. Five years of Alcoholics Anonymous meetings hadn't quenched her thirst, nor her cravings; she rubbed the AA ring of fellowship on her finger, a habit she'd picked up years ago, when life itself had been almost too much to bear. Fashioned from silver and bearing the traditional AA logo of a triangle inside a circle, it was Andi's talisman; she wore the ring every day to remind herself that she wasn't alone in her struggle with alcohol. She took a deep breath and reached for her Club Soda.

Conversation around the table was, quite predictably, focused on North and the Iditarod. "Tell us more about the Iditarod," Charlie Alexie, one of North's oldest friends and also a competent musher, suggested.

"Yeah, how much money do you get if you win?" someone's girlfriend giggled, drawing a round of chuckles.

"Yeah, Ruben!" one of North's oldest friends shouted from the end of the table. "You going to share your winnings with us?"

North grinned. "I'll refrain from any comment about sharing my winnings. I'd have to run that by my financial adviser first." Smirks and chuckles rippled around the table. "So, the Iditarod starts on the first Saturday in March," North continued, "and only the first twenty racers to cross the finish line get a cash prize." He shrugged, shoulders straining the seams of his faded green and black plaid flannel shirt. "I'm not really doing it for the money, though." He brought his mug to his lips, then lowered it without taking a drink. "To be honest, I don't really expect to win, but if I do it will be a nice bonus."

"I'm really looking forward to the ceremonial start," Andi interjected when North paused to take a drink. "From what I understand, it's sort of a mock start to the race. They do it downtown on Anchorage's main street so everyone can get a good look at all of the mushers and dogs and take some pictures. It's more for the media and spectators than the contestants."

"So if you don't think you're going to win, why are you even doing it?" someone else asked.

"Why am I doing it?" North mused over the question for a moment while he swirled the last few drops of beer around in the bottom of his mug. "I guess it's because running the world-famous Iditarod is something I've wanted to do all my life. When I was a boy, back in Paulatuk, my dad would talk about the crazy people who went to Alaska and wasted time and money running their teams in some stupid race. He could never understand why they did it, since they weren't hunting for food or doing something useful. But I understood. Mushing is a ... a *passion*. I've dreamed about running the Iditarod for the past thirty years." North shook his head and toyed with his empty mug, making a circle of overlapping, wet rings on the surface of the dark, varnished table. "When I was in my late teens," he continued after a moment, "Dad bought his first snowmobile. He didn't have much use for the dogs after that, especially not for hunting. He got rid of them. It broke my heart." A shadow passed over the planes of North's bronzed face.

Andi reached for his hand where it lay clenched on his thigh, painfully aware that North's childhood memories were often dark and disturbing.

Two waitresses, their timing opportune, began delivering meals to their tables, drawing attention away from North and the Iditarod. Before his plate was empty, though, North's peers began peppering him with more questions. Between bites, he briefly described the Iditarod's two race routes – a northern one used on even-numbered years, a southern on odd. Each route was approximately 1700 kilometers and took ten days or longer to complete.

"It can get pretty fucking cold in Alaska," Charlie warned, a smear of ketchup on his chin. "I hope you're taking good gear."

"Yeah, it's going to be tough," North nodded. When he began to elaborate on the extreme, life-threatening weather and trail conditions he could expect to encounter during the long race, Andi lay her fork down next to the remnants of a burger and fries, her appetite having suddenly vanished. She studied her clasped hands where they lay in her lap.

"Why do they even have this race?" Charlie's girlfriend, Jodie, asked with a frown. "I agree with your dad. It seems a bit stupid."

North shrugged, tactfully ignoring her last comment. "It has an interesting history. Back in about 1925, there was a huge diphtheria epidemic in Nome. People were dropping left, right and center. The only way to get medicine to the isolated community was by dog team, and that's how they created the original dog sled trail to Nome."

"Are you taking Qannik?" Margo asked.

Andi's head shot up, and she shoved a strand of hair behind her ear. "Yes, we're *definitely* taking Qannik. I'm not leaving her at home. We're going to be gone for almost a month," she interjected before North had a chance to respond. Andi had bonded with the pure white Canadian Eskimo pup, whose name meant 'Snowflake' in Inuktitut, North's native language, when she was only ten weeks old. Their connection was strengthened after the pup witnessed and survived a horrific trauma – the senseless shooting deaths of three of her pack members, treasured dogs from North's own kennel. Andi closed her eyes for a moment, blocking out the gruesome memory of that fateful day.

"So you're both going to Alaska, I take it? I suppose you're driving that big truck you got now," Charlie chuckled. "Can you fit all of your supplies on it?"

North perked up. "Well, I'll take the sled and some stuff on the truck, but I'll also be sending a whole pile of food and gear to Anchorage in a few weeks. The race committee has a group of volunteer pilots they call the Iditarod Air Force. The IAF donate their time and their own aircraft to the Iditarod every year. They drop off bundles of food and gear for the mushers at different checkpoints, and fly any injured or dropped dogs back to Anchorage."

"Really? That's fantastic. Takes quite a load off your sled, eh?" Charlie laughed.

"Yup, it sure does." North stretched and rolled the kinks from his shoulders. "I have no idea how the mushers used to carry a month's worth of supplies with them back in the old days."

"I think they used to haul two sleds if they had to," Charlie replied. "I remember the stories my granddaddy used to tell us."

Andi yawned. "Ready to go home, Babe?" North asked softly. He reached under her long hair and encircled the back of her neck with his broad hand, massaging it gently.

"Yeah, I'm beat. It was a busy day."

"Party pooper!" Margo scolded. "It's only 6:30. You two get married, then all you want to do is go home and hop into bed. Have another beer, North."

North shook his head and grinned. "I'd love to, but I'd better not, Margo. I have some training to do tomorrow."

Andi was thankful for the room's dim lighting. Maybe there was a chance nobody saw the red stain that emblazoned her cheeks. Margo had read her mind; she wanted nothing more than to rush home to their cozy little cabin, strip off every shred of clothing and tumble into bed with her very hot-blooded man.

THREE

Andi pulled up to the Thomases' house the next Friday afternoon for one of Margo's famous TGIF parties. North sat in the passenger seat of her very dated Ford Country Squire station wagon, a Management Team perk courtesy of Tuktu Aviation. She'd nicknamed the travel-worn, rather cumbersome but reliable vehicle, 'The Land Yacht.'

They'd spent the afternoon in town, North at his native art gallery, The Qamutik, and Andi doing a few errands after lunching with a friend. The Qamutik was a treasure trove of northern artwork and handicrafts, from soapstone carvings, paintings and caribou-hair tuftings to handmade clothing and mukluks. North was also a competent photographer in his own right, and his beautifully framed work adorned the gallery's walls. Although The Qamutik was situated on Inuvik's main street and open to the public six days a week, most of its sales were made to private buyers, collectors and other galleries throughout Canada and the United States, as well as overseas. The thriving gallery provided North with a sizeable and steady income.

At the moment there was only one small flaw in North's otherwise perfect life: due to his recent, intense training schedule, he had very reluctantly begun to depend on his youngest sister, Ruby, to handle the day-to-day operations of the gallery. Ruby had only last year earned a Bachelor of Commerce degree from the University of Alberta in Edmonton. She was sharp as a whip, and although he didn't always understand or agree with her, North loved her dearly. Most of the time. Today wasn't one of those days. "Guess what Ruby told me?" he complained as Andi maneuvered the unwieldly car into the Thomas' driveway, nosing up to the rear bumper of Margo's van.

"What?"

"She's come up with another hair-brained scheme for the gallery. She says this one will *expand our clientele*," he mimicked in a high, soprano voice.

"What's her idea?"

"She's making a catalogue of some of our best pieces," he said, "the real expensive ones I guess. She's taking colour pictures and having it all printed up on shiny paper. Then she's going to mail the catalogues out to a bunch of places like art collectors and dealers. Some of our clients too."

"I think that's a fabulous idea," Andi frowned. "What don't you like about it?"

"Well," North shrugged, something he did on those rare occasions when he was stuck for words, "I've never used anything like that before, and the gallery's always done pretty well."

Andi patted his denim-clad leg. "And maybe it will do even better in the future. Trust her, North. Ruby knows what she's doing."

North harrumphed and opened the door. "It seems complicated. Change isn't always good."

They were early for Margo's famous 'Thank God It's Friday' party, an almost weekly event that the close-knit circle of friends and co-workers always looked forward to.

"I'm really ready for a beer," North declared. He jumped out of The Yacht and pulled a case of Canadian lager beer from the back seat.

"Just remember, you planned to do some training first thing tomorrow morning," Andi retorted, her words slicing through the cold air before she could swallow them back. Before the last syllable rolled off her tongue, she regretted her biting comment. She suddenly became absorbed with a loose thread hanging from her purple qiviut scarf, woven from soft muskox underwool.

"Yes, darling, I do remember," North laughed.

"I'm sorry," she murmured.

North lifted her chin, a glint in his bottomless, chocolate eyes. He kissed her crimson cheek. "Apology accepted. Let's go inside, Margo's probably waiting for us."

Margo Thomas' home was as familiar to Andi as her own. Before moving into North's cabin, she'd spent more time at the Thomases than her own rented duplex. She rapped on the front door twice, then walked in uninvited.

Margo poked her head through the archway between the living room and kitchen. She wore her golden-brown hair short and swept back from her face, and her hazel eyes sparkled perpetually. "Hi guys! Come on in. I'm just cutting up some snacks."

"I'll help you," Andi volunteered, shrugging out of her bulky red parka. She and North walked through the living room and into the spacious kitchen. Ken and two of Tuktu Aviation's aircraft engineers sat at a round, oak pedestal table, cans of beer and a bowl of peanuts before them.

"Ken, go put on some music," Margo ordered, waving a long butcher knife in the general direction of the living room.

"Yes, ma'am," Ken replied with a wry grin, promptly rising to his feet and ignoring the smirks of his co-workers.

"Put on Garth Brooks," Margo called to his retreating back.

Andi helped Margo prepare a tray of snacks. A steady stream of TGIF guests trailed through the front door, and before long the house was filled with laughter, the air thick with cigarette smoke.

Andi sipped her .5% alcohol beer and North tossed down a few bottles of the real thing while attempting to steer conversation away from his expedition to Alaska. When the front door swung open at 10 pm, releasing a frigid blast of air into the overwarm living room, Andi glanced up to see who the late arrival was. If not for the fact that she was already sitting on the living room floor, she may have fallen flat on her face.

"Surprise!" Ayame Saito, Andi's ex-dispatcher as well as a close friend, shouted as she burst through the doorway. A tall young man with close cropped, fiery red hair pushed the door closed behind them.

"Ayame! What are you doing here?" Andi shrieked, leaping to her feet. She raced to the door and hugged the young Japanese woman. Andi loved her friend dearly, but still hadn't completely forgiven her for choosing a career at NavCanada over one at Tuktu Aviation. Andi had offered Ayame the Chief Dispatcher's position when it was suddenly vacated by Jessica Hartman. At the time, Ayame was Tuktu's Assistant Dispatcher. After carefully considering her options, she eventually decided that she had to follow her heart ... and her heart wanted a career as a Flight Service Specialist. She was currently living in north-central Alberta, completing the airport tower unit of her training at the Edmonton International Airport.

With her arms still wrapped around her friend, Andi eyeballed the rather gangly stranger hovering by the door. "Hi, I'm Andrea Ruben," she said, extending a hand over Ayame's shoulder.

"Bruce Winters," he smiled and gripped her hand firmly. "I'm pleased to finally meet you. Heard a lot about you."

Andi frowned slightly.

"All good, of course." The timbre of the young man's voice caught her by surprise. Its deep, velvety baritone seemed in direct contrast to his aquiline, almost delicate features.

North materialized and lifted Ayame's slight figure into his arms, her small booted feet wind-milling above the floor.

"North, put me down!" Ayame squealed half-heartedly, betrayed by the twinkle of delight in her deep brown eyes. Ayame had come to appreciate and respect North's sincere, yet determined, disposition. Although he was unaware of the fact, Ayame had in the past repeatedly come to his defence whenever Princess Jessica had mocked North's one small imperfection – an overly long, pointed tooth that marred his otherwise perfect smile. The long incisor had earned him the nickname 'Fang'. Only North's closest friends ever called him by the name, and only then very rarely. Jessica Hartman was definitely *not* in that category, and when she'd used the moniker, it was always in an extremely derogatory manner. There had been no love lost between Andi's new husband and her former Chief Dispatcher.

"Nice to see you, sweetheart," North said, planting a fatherly kiss on the younger woman's round cheek before setting her on her feet again. "And who do we have here?" he asked, peering at Ayame's friend through slightly narrow, dark eyes.

"Bruce Winters." Ayame's escort stepped forward and introduced himself before Ayame had the opportunity to intervene.

"North Ruben. Glad to meet you." The two men took stock of each other for a moment, then, apparently satisfied with their assessments, smiled and shook hands.

Andi and Ayame exchanged a faintly amused glance. "Men!" Andi whispered in her friend's ear.

Margo strolled out of the kitchen, a frosty mug of beer in her hand. "You finally made it! I thought you'd never get here." Andi's brows knit together. Her bemused gaze flickered from Margo to Ayame and back again.

North and Bruce fled to the kitchen in search of alcohol. Andi tugged Ayame down the hallway to the spare bedroom, Margo close behind. "You have a *lot* of explaining to do," she said, peppering her friend with question after question. Ayame, given no opportunity to reply, merely laughed and shrugged her shoulders eloquently.

Andi turned to Margo. "What do you know about this? If you knew Ayame was coming to town, why didn't you tell me?" A pink blush highlighted her cheeks. Margo smiled smugly and took a sip of beer.

"We're just here for the weekend because Margo called and said she was throwing a 'Good Luck' party for you and North tonight," Ayame interjected when Andi finally took a breath.

"Oh God. The Iditarod," she said, realization dawning in her eyes.

Ayame laughed, a sweet, musical sound. "I thought it would be great to surprise you, and I've been wanting to visit for a while anyway. It's about time you met Bruce."

Andi turned accusing eyes to Margo. "I can't believe you didn't tell me she was coming!" she grumbled. "I would have fixed up the guest bedroom a little better."

"What guest bedroom?" Ayame asked.

"Oh, I guess you don't know yet," Andi beamed, any lingering trace of annoyance gone. "North built an addition on the cabin. Just wait 'til you see it! We have a second bedroom now, a huge den and another full bathroom."

"It's gorgeous," Margo piped in. "He did a fabulous job."

"Wow," Ayame beamed, "good for you. Does this mean we're staying at your place, then?"

"Of course." Andi's head bobbed up and down for a moment before she arched one eyebrow and smirked, "*You* can stay in the new bedroom and *Bruce* can sleep on the couch in the living room."

Margo cuffed Andi's arm and muttered, "Christ, Andi! Don't be such a damn prude."

The first strains of *My Maria*, Brooks & Dunn's new number one Country & Western hit, drifted down the hallway, luring the trio back to the living room.

Two hours later the party began to wind down, and soon only a handful of guests remained. As usual, they converged in the kitchen. North and Bruce were deep in conversation with Ken, Paul White and Walter McKerrel about the merits of equipping a DeHavilland DHC-6 Twin Otter aircraft with skis versus tundra tires when flying in the barren lands and far north. It turned out that Bruce, too, had been bitten by the aviation bug, and was currently finishing up his aircraft maintenance engineer, or AME for short, apprenticeship. Paul White was the sole proprietor and CEO of Tuktu Aviation, and Walter his Chief Pilot. Although Paul's wife, Carla was at his side, Lisette McKerrel was on duty at the hospital. North and Andi knew Lisette only too well; a Registered Nurse at Inuvik's Stanton General Hospital, Lisette had been one of the nurses in charge of North's care when a bullet nicked his shoulder two years earlier. The wound, though relatively shallow as far as firearm injuries go, had required a few stitches and an overnight stay in the hospital.

"Hey, Paul," Ayame interrupted. "Sorry to change the subject, but have you ever heard from Jessica or Jim?"

"Nah, not a word," Paul replied with a slow shake of his head. The temperature at the table dropped several degrees. Andi toyed with her drink, eyes fixated on the table; North reached for her hand and squeezed it gently.

Bruce cleared his throat. "Who are Jessica and Jim, if I may ask?" he inquired after an uncomfortable, pregnant pause.

When no one immediately replied, Paul took the plunge. "Jessica Hartman was my Chief Dispatcher at Tuktu Aviation for many years. Captain Jim O'Neill was one of our pilots. One of our *best* pilots, actually."

"I see," Bruce replied. Several seconds, later, when no further explanation appeared to be forthcoming, he tried again. "So – what happened to them?"

Paul let out a short sigh and tipped his beer back before continuing. "It's kind of long story, but to make it short, they both disappeared in the spring of 1995, along with Jim's co-pilot, Hank Brister. Hank had only been with us a few months."

"Really? Disappeared? Like, you mean, crashed?" Bruce's clear hazel eyes sparkled.

"No. No, nothing like that. They ... well, how should I put this?" Paul rubbed the dark stubble on his chin. "Andi discovered that the three of them, Jim, Jessica and Hank, were accomplices in a diamond smuggling ring. They were stealing uncut stones from one of our best clients – Pivot Lake Diamond Mine."

"Oh, man, that's brutal," Bruce whistled softly.

"Yeah, it sure was. Turned out they were in cahoots with one of the senior people out at the mine, a guy named Henrik Bruller. Bruller lifted the raw diamonds, then transferred them to O'Neill during our daily Twin Otter service trips to the mine. O'Neill passed them on to Jessica, who took them to Vancouver once a month or so and sold them to Bruller's underground contact there. It was quite the operation." Paul shook his head and took a few gulps of beer.

"So, what became of them?" Bruce asked, his voice low and conspiratorial. "What happened to these diamond thieves?"

"After Andi reported her suspicions to Sam Tavernese, the mine's CEO, he brought a team out from Toronto to apprehend them out at Pivot Lake." Paul glanced at North. "They caught them red-handed. North was part of all of that, so he can tell you more about it."

"They all ended up in jail, I take it?" Bruce asked.

Paul shook his head again, lips pursed. "Sam took Jim, Jessica and Hank back to Toronto. We never heard a thing after that. The whole thing was kept very hush-hush. Henrik Bruller died, though," he added. "He was shot while trying to escape."

It was North's turn to take a long drink. Paul hadn't mentioned the fact that it was a bullet from North's own rifle that had sent Bruller, the mine's Project Manager and master mind of the smuggling operation, to the hospital. Although he'd seemed to be recovering well, the man had unexpectedly died a few days later of complications after surgery. At least that was the story.

"Wicked!" Bruce chortled. Andi threw him a dark look, and Ayame gave him a jab with her elbow. "Sorry," he apologized meekly. "What I mean is, um ... that's a very interesting story."

"So when are you two love-birds going on a honeymoon?" Ayame asked, once again adeptly changing the subject.

"Right after the Iditarod is over," Andi replied before North had the chance to open his mouth. "We're going to a resort in Mexico. Probably two weeks in Cancun or Cozumel."

"No, we're not," North countered with a decisive shake of his head. "I've already told you that I did the Mexican resort thing once and I hated it. Way too boring."

"North!" Andi protested, "I really want to go to Mexico for our honeymoon."

"And I already told you, *I'm not going to a resort*. Final answer." He took a long draw from his beer.

"Hey you two," Paul, always the problem-solver, interjected with a mischievous grin. "If Andi wants to go to Mexico, but North doesn't want to do the resort thing, why don't you drive down with a travel trailer or a motorhome? Didn't you tell me that your brother in Port Alberni has one?" he asked, peering at Andi. His intelligent brown eyes sparkled behind frameless glasses.

"Yeah, Bryan has a motorhome of some kind," Andi said begrudgingly. "It's pretty small though. About twenty-four feet I think. Maybe twenty-six."

"There you go," Paul exclaimed. "Your problem is solved! It sounds like a love-nest on wheels if you ask me. It'd be the perfect size for touring down the Mexican Baja to Cabo San Lucas."

"Well I don't know," Andi muttered. "North probably doesn't even know how to drive a motorhome."

"Yeah, right! I can drive anything on wheels," North protested. "I'm game if you are, Babe."

"I'll think about it." Andi raised her arm and looked at her watch pointedly. "Well, I think it's time to get some beauty sleep, and our guests have had a long day."

"Yeah, you're right. You two ready to hit the road?" North turned to Ayame and Bruce.

"Definitely," Ayame replied with a yawn. "We rented a car at the airport, so we'll follow you guys. I can never find that secret road of yours."

"Let's drive Bruce by the Igloo Church on the way home," Andi suggested. "It will look beautiful under the full moon tonight."

They said their goodbyes and rounded up their coats. On the way out the door, a bewildered and somewhat apprehensive Bruce whispered in Ayame's ear, "What the hell is an igloo church? It sounds cold."

FOUR

North and Andi had married on January 2, 1997 in the historic 'Our Lady of Victory' church on Mackenzie Road, commonly referred to as 'The Igloo Church'. It was Inuvik's best-known landmark, and most photographed tourist attraction. It also happened to be the locale of the communities' Alcoholic Anonymous meetings, of which Andi was a regular attendee.

The two couples, hunched within their parkas against the bitter cold, left their vehicles idling in the church parking lot while they took a quick walk around the exterior of the unique, beautiful structure. An unrelenting wind had developed during the night, pushing frigid air down from the frozen Beaufort Sea. With the temperature hovering at minus forty Celsius, frostbite was guaranteed if skin was left exposed for more than a few minutes.

The round white church was painted to mimic an igloo, those unique Inuvialuit snow-houses of days gone by. Topped with an aluminum dome and adorned with sky-blue trim, art-work and steps, it was truly a sight to behold.

"I've never seen anything like this in my life," Bruce declared, raising his voice to be heard over the howling wind. "What's the story behind it?"

"The design was conceived by two Roman Catholic missionaries," Andi volunteered. She loved the old church, and had read volumes about its history. "It took about two years to build, and they completed construction in 1960, so it's not really that old. I think the most fascinating thing about it is the roof."

"Why is that?" Bruce asked, burying his hands deeper in his pockets.

"Under that silver dome they built a second one. The interior dome has twelve wooden arches representing the Apostles. The space *between* the two domes serves as a heat exchanger."

"That's amazing." Bruce shivered convulsively.

"The church is also unique because it's the only major building in town that's not built on wooden pilings. It's actually resting right on the ground, on a thick gravel bed to protect the permafrost from melting."

"What?" exclaimed Ayame, her voice muffled by several layers of her crimson pashmina scarf. "I never heard that before! How come I don't know that?" With her toque pulled low over her ears and scarf pulled up to cover her nose, only a sliver of skin and dark eyes were left exposed to the numbing wind.

Andi laughed. "It's not a well-known fact. Skeptics still claim that only divine intervention prevents the church from sinking into the ground."

"It's ... it's amazing," Bruce stuttered through chattering teeth. "We definitely have to come back and take some pictures. The folks back home aren't going to believe this."

"We'll do a full tour of town tomorrow, and you can get all the pictures you want," Ayame promised. She linked her arm through her boyfriend's and pulled him toward the waiting, warm cars. "But right now I'm freezing, so let's get going!"

Andi laughed. "You're turning soft on us, aren't you?"

"Yup, I'm a regular city slicker now," Ayame confirmed with a grimace as she tightened the loops of her long scarf. "You can keep this damn weather up here, where it belongs."

Twenty minutes later they pulled up to the Rubens' newly renovated home, situated a few kilometers north of Inuvik on Low road, just off the main highway between Inuvik and the airport. It was a quiet and secluded spot – the perfect location to raise and train a pack of rambunctious sled dogs. North secretly hoped that it would eventually become the perfect place to raise a family, too.

The mutts knew the sound of Andi's car, and although they were kenneled behind the house, their boisterous greeting pierced the crisp night air. The girls ran up three short steps to the narrow, covered porch, abandoning the men to the tasks of retrieving luggage and plugging in the block heaters for the cars. "Oh my god, this place is beautiful!" Ayame exclaimed when Andi ushered her into the house. From outside, the home looked like a rustic, roughly hewn wood cabin, but inside it was a masterpiece of colour, warmth and texture. Brightly patterned scatter rugs dotted the gleaming pine wood floors, and the home's completely open living, dining and kitchen floor plan gave it a spacious feeling. On one end of the large room an immense forest green braided rug lay beneath a long, dark brown leather sofa and matching love seat. A scarred, rectangular wooden coffee table lay between them, and a well-worn dark green La-Z-Boy leather recliner stood to one side. Numerous occasional tables and lamps were strategically placed throughout the room.

Each wall displayed stunning Native American paintings and drawings, and several pieces of exquisite soapstone and antler carvings were scattered around the room. Ayame spotted an inukshuk, a polar bear, a seal and a narwhale, but was immediately drawn to a sofa table that displayed one of Andi's favorite pieces – a single, cream coloured musk-ox horn. The end of the horn was crafted to resemble the stylized neck and head of a snow goose, then sanded down to expose its hidden black inner layers. The natural curve of the horn made the goose appear to be gazing over her own back, upon which a flock of three tiny geese, also carved from horn, rode. It was a very simple and elegant, yet powerful, piece of art.

"This is my very favourite," Andi said, leading Ayame across the room to a wooden corner display unit. The unit's muted recessed lighting illuminated the precious contents within, warming them with a golden glow that seemed to bring life to the priceless, inanimate objects. She picked up a small, dark green soapstone carving of a native woman clad in anorak and mukluks; in her arms she held a small child, similarly clad. Andi reverently caressed the carving's smooth, shiny surface for a moment before handing it to Ayame. "This one is called 'Mother with Child'," Andi's smile was radiant. "North gave it to me the day I told him I would marry him."

"It's beautiful," Ayame said, her voice rough with emotion. "I know it must mean a lot to you."

"Yes, it does," Andi chased a single tear from her cheek. "I love it."

Ayame wrapped an arm around her friend's shoulder and gave her a brief hug. "I'm so damn sorry I had to miss your wedding, honey. You know I would have been there if I could have. North's a good man." She was about to say more when the men blasted into the house on a breath of frosty air, each carrying a small suitcase.

"Who's ready for a night cap?" North grinned. He tossed his coat over a hook next to the door, kicked his frozen boots off, and then strode over to a large, footed world globe standing in one corner of the living room. He paused to ensure he had everyone's attention before giving the golden-brown globe a twirl, allowing the earth to spin on its axis for a few seconds. When he tugged on its top, the globe split open at the equator to reveal a well-stocked liquor cabinet within. North grinned and rubbed his hands together, whether to warm them, or in glee. It was hard to tell, given North's irrational obsession with his unique bar. Andi smiled and rolled her eyes at her husband's uncharacteristic, rather immature behavior.

"Sure. Got any scotch?" Bruce replied. He hung his coat next to the door, tweaking first his, then North's, to ensure they both hung perfectly balanced on their hooks, then neatly lined up all of the boots strewn on the rubber mat beneath it. He joined his host at the bar, and the two men immediately became absorbed in the intricacies and mechanics of North's favourite conversation piece.

"Nothing for me, thanks," Ayame yawned, "unless you feel like making some green tea?"

"Sure, I'll put some water on." Andi crossed to the kitchen sink and filled a kettle.

"When do we get to see the dogs?" Ayame asked, settling into one corner of the spacious sofa. She spread a multi-coloured throw over her legs. "I know Bruce is dying to see a real sled dog."

"We'll wait until morning," North said, pouring two hefty shots of neat scotch. "It sounds like they're starting to quieten down again." He compared the two glasses, eyeballing the portions, then straightened and grinned, scotch bottle still in hand. "And I tell you what. We'll do even better than *show* the dogs to you. How about we take you guys out for a sled ride?"

"Oh man, that would be just *awesome*," Bruce said with enthusiasm.

"YES!" Ayame shrieked. "I'd absolutely love that. I'm going with Andi."

"Right. Who was just complaining that they were freezing cold?" Andi snickered. "I'll have to outfit you with some proper clothes and boots before we go."

"Yeah, I've got some extra things that should fit you, too, Bruce." North nodded and handed a glass of scotch to Bruce. "The weatherman says this storm is going to blow itself out overnight. Tomorrow should be quite a bit warmer."

"Come with me, Ayame," Andi instructed. "While we're waiting for the water to boil, I'll show you the new addition and your bedroom. North can find a bedroll for Bruce."

Ayame frowned in consternation, then mouthed 'don't worry' at her bemused boyfriend before following Andi out of the room.

North, crystal highball glass in hand, dropped into his beloved, ancient La-Z-Boy, pulled up the footrest and sighed contentedly. Bruce settled onto the comfortable old sofa, his stockinged feet resting on the coffee table. They clinked glasses and savoured a few sips of the expensive liquor.

"So, tell me all of the down and dirty details of the Pivot Lake diamond heist," Bruce said, his eye sparkling. "What was your part in capturing the thieves?"

It appeared the two men were in for a long night.

FIVE

"I can't believe I'm finally here," North whispered in Andi's ear. Inside the banquet room of Anchorage's Alaska Hotel, the atmosphere sizzled with the energy of two hundred guests. Seated in groups of ten around round tables draped in white linen, the venue of the 1997 Iditarod Musher's Banquet was filled to capacity. Race contestants, handlers, family, friends, sponsors and fans from around the world gathered for the Iditarod Trail Sled Dog Race's Thursday evening kick-off event.

Andi and North, along with twenty sled dogs and a loaded truck, had arrived in Anchorage four days ago, late on Sunday, February 23. The long 2500-kilometer journey, which they quickly learned they had to convert to 1500 miles for the benefit of the locals, had taken three long days. The exhausting trip had taken longer than it should have, thanks to bad roads, blinding snow and dogs that needed frequent breaks to shake out and see to Mother Nature's call.

Their first night on the road was spent in Dawson City, Yukon Territory, from where they continued south and overnighted in Whitehorse. They made the long, long leg from Whitehorse west to Anchorage in one grueling fifteen-hour drive, and vowed they would stay on the road an extra day or two on the way back home. Had it been summer, their trip would have been 1000 kilometers shorter had they taken the famous 'Top of the World Highway' connecting Dawson City, Yukon to Tok, Alaska. But the scenic, high mountain road was only open from May to September, and even the Little Gold/Poker Creek international border crossing closed for the winter.

At precisely 6 pm the public address system crackled to life. "Could I have your attention, please? Attention, everyone!" The clamour of voices slowly subsided as all eyes turned to the front of the room, where a tall male figure stood behind a podium on a raised stage. His dark grey suit fit him like a well-worn glove, and his black shoes were buffed to a glowing brilliance. Pure white hair, worn in a short brush-cut, made a startling contrast to his deeply tanned skin. A ripple of expectancy ran through the warm, almost claustrophobic, air.

"I'd like to open tonight's event by welcoming you all to the 25th Silver Anniversary celebration of the Iditarod – *The Last Great Race*!" Cheers and whistles echoed throughout the room, its poor acoustics doing nothing to deafen the noise.

Andi and North Ruben, seated alongside North's nephew and dog handler, Eddie Ruben, joined in the rambunctious applause. Andi's gaze wandered over the crowd, and she unsuccessfully attempted to suppress a smile. For the most part, the Musher's Banquet attendees resembled those of any other large gathering; in her mind's eye she had expected to see a hundred varied versions of Grizzly Adams. Other than a slightly higher than average beard count, and the occasional fur-trimmed parka hanging over the back of a chair, the evening's guests appeared akin to those in any other North American city. She was disappointed that everyone appeared so *normal*.

Her eyes settled on a string of tables set up near the podium, where Iditarod race officials sat with Anchorage's mayor, Winston Irving. Seated next to Winston was his young and very beautiful niece, Stacy, who also happened to be North's Iditarider. Stacy had, in Andi's opinion, shown a great deal too much bosom at their Thursday 'Meet Your Musher' pizza lunch. Andi suppressed a small shudder, thankful that things weren't worse: Stacy could have been seated at *their* table tonight.

"My name is Chuck Evans, and I'll be your host for this momentous evening," the dynamic man behind the podium continued.

"I'd like to start by thanking each and every one of you for coming out tonight, and for contributing to the success of our anniversary celebrations. We have a wonderful program lined up for you, and a dinner you'll be talking about for months. Welcome, mushers!"

"As you all know," Chuck continued when the applause subsided, "this year we are celebrating the 25th running of the Iditarod. And with us tonight is a man I know you are all familiar with – The Father of the Iditarod Trail Sled Dog Race. Please join me in welcoming Mr. Bill Wrightway!" The crowd roared again, rising to a standing ovation as a slightly bent, weathered grey-haired man rose from a chair next to their host.

"If it weren't for the back breaking work and dedication of this hero standing beside me," Chuck continued, placing a gentle hand on Wrightway's sloping shoulder, "the Iditarod would never have become a reality. Since 1967, his dedication and devotion to long distance racing helped create the Iditarod, and make it the most prestigious dog sled race in the world. I'm pleased to announce that the powers that be have dedicated the 25th Anniversary of the Iditarod Trail Sled Race to this great man! I know you all join me in offering our most heartfelt thanks and congratulations." His last words were almost consumed by thunderous applause.

"Thank you folks, thank you," Wrightway said humbly, adjusting the microphone slightly to accommodate his stooped stance. "Seat yourselves back down again now." He waited a moment for the crowd to settle back into their seats before continuing. "I guess you're all here for the same reason I am. It's not for the prestige of winning the most renowned dog sled race in the world. And I know it's not for the exercise." A hushed murmur rippled through the rapt crowd. "And I know it's not for the money, 'cause many of you aren't even gonna finish this damn race." Throughout the room, heads nodded solemnly. "You're in this race because you love the feel of the runners under your feet. You love the harmony of a team of happy dogs. You love the feel of the wind on your face – it makes you feel *alive*. You're here tonight, and you'll be heading out to the great beyond on Sunday because YOU LOVE MUSHING!" The crowd erupted into a thunderous roar. Heavily booted feet pounded the floor, sending vibrations strong enough to chatter the glassware on top of the tables.

"Remember, winning is not important," the Father of the Iditarod continued when the cheering once again subsided. "Being on the trail with your dogs is what's important. When you quit hoping to win – *that's* when you get what you want. And now," Wrightway said with an impish grin, "I know all you good folks want to get to the most important part of tonight's agenda. Dinner!" Good-natured laughter and shouts of '*hear, hear!*' filled the room. "Well, it's gonna be a long night, so I'll step away from this damn microphone now and let us all get to the food. But I just want to say one more thing: good luck to you all, and may the best musher win."

"That guy is a legend," North said as he, Andi and Eddie rose with the crowd to honour the celebrated Iditarod hero with another standing ovation. "I'm sure he could show me a thing or two."

"If you get a chance, why don't you spend some time with him?" Andi suggested. "There's not many old timers around anymore. I'm sure he's got some fascinating stories to tell."

"Yeah, I will," North nodded. They took their seats again, and he rolled his empty beer bottle between his palms. "Sure wish I could have another one," he grimaced, "but I told myself two's my limit tonight. Hey look! Here comes our dinner."

"Fantastic. The smell of food's been driving me crazy."

Dinner was everything Chuck had promised, from the crisp salad to perfectly prepared AAA prime rib, Yorkshire pudding and Alaska king crab legs. While the diners completed their Baked Alaska dessert course, individual, decadent creations of chocolate and strawberry ice-cream and cake baked under a browned and sticky meringue, Chuck once again took the podium and advised that the most important event of the evening – the draw for a bib number – was about to begin.

The words had barely left Chuck's mouth when Andi sensed a change in the room's atmosphere; something akin to the sudden drop in air pressure before a violent summer storm. Her perceptive psyche detected traces of apprehension amongst the assembled competitors, and her sensitive ears began to tingle. But there was something else in the air, something infinitely more sinister than apprehension, that Andi couldn't quite identify. A cold shiver ran down her spine, leaving her feeling anxious and chilled in the overheated room. Andi's mother had blessed her with the extraordinary ability to perceive, through both her dreams and waking hours, events that had not yet happened. She often *knew* things she just shouldn't know. Some called her uncanny ability the 'Sixth Sense'. She just called it a questionable gift that had, for generations, been passed from mother to daughter, and today her intuitive nature had left her feeling unsettled.

She pushed her unfinished plate of Baked Alaska away, closed her eyes and took a few deep, steadying breaths. After a minute or two the uneasy feeling faded away; she opened her eyes and glanced at her husband, hoping her unease hadn't caught his attention. His dark eyes were riveted on the podium, the muscles in his square jaw rippling over clenched teeth. She leaned toward him and laid her hand on his rigid arm.

During the much-anticipated bib draw each competitor would be called upon to pick a number. That number would then become his or her race number for the duration of the Iditarod, and it also represented the competitor's starting position.

After an initial short ceremony during which Bill Wrightway was awarded the honor of being presented with bib number 1, competitors were called upon to draw their start numbers in the same order as they had registered for the race. When a petite young woman seated at the Rubens' table and dressed from head to toe in a shockingly bright shade of pink jumped up at Chuck's call, her run to the podium garnered a thundering round of applause from the audience. Evidently Rebecca Singleton was a favoured and well-liked contestant. Even though she'd pulled a disappointing bib number thirty-eight, she bestowed a brilliant smile upon North when she returned to their table, followed by a slow, almost conspiratorial wink.

North winced when Andi's booted toe connected with his calf, and he chose to ignore the daggers in her eyes. "I'd sure like to be near the front of the pack," he whispered instead, as musher after musher determined his or her fate, followed by a short speech.

North, having been somewhat undecided as to whether he and his team were actually prepared for the gruelling Iditarod, had not secured his spot in the race until several weeks after the registration had opened. He was, therefore, doomed to wait until all of the racers registered before him had drawn their bib numbers. The most coveted starting positions were joyously claimed. Bib numbers 2, 3, 6, 8, 10, 11 and 12 were already gone by the time North's name was called an hour after the commencement of the draw. Setting a determined smile on the shadowed planes of his face, he strode confidently to the front of the room. Back at their table, Andi twirled the silver AA ring on her right hand, simultaneously crossed the fingers of her left, and surreptitiously kept her eye on the cute blond across the table.

Behind the podium, Chuck held a finely crafted sealskin Eskimo mukluk, the unique vessel traditionally used to hold the Iditarod starting numbers. Tonight it had contained fifty-three numbered slips of paper; one for each entrant. Their host watched attentively as North dipped his hand into the boot. The crowd waited in hushed expectation as North passed his draw to Chuck. "Congratulations, North Ruben!" Chuck boomed. "You'll be wearing lucky bib number 9," he announced.

North beamed and gave the amassed crowd a triumphant thumbs-up salute. Chuck pushed the microphone into North's hand; it was time for the Canadian from Inuvik to say a few words to his fellow mushers.

"I'm honored to be here tonight," North began, "to stand before you as a rookie, and *with* you, as a contestant. This is my first, but I hope not my last, Iditarod. My team and I are from Inuvik, Northwest Territories, Canada, and the dogs I'm running are all purebred Canadian Eskimo Dogs." A hum rippled through the crowd, liberally accompanied by sceptical stares of disbelief; Siberian Huskies, Alaskan Huskies, Alaskan Malamutes, Chinooks, Samoyeds and any mix thereof were common contenders, but nobody had ever heard of a Canadian Eskimo Dog racing in the Iditarod before. North had apparently already drawn more attention than he had anticipated.

Studiously ignoring the ripple of surprise and disbelief running through the banquet room, he wound up his short speech. "I want to wish each and every one of my fellow competitors a safe race, and also thank my handler and nephew, Eddie Ruben – I couldn't have done this without your help, Eddie. And to my wife, Andrea, thank you for standing beside me and putting up with me, and for giving up so many months of your normal life to join me here today. I love you. Good luck, everyone."

Polite applause, raised eyebrows and hushed conversation followed North back to his table.

"Hey, boss, good speech," Eddie grinned, high-fiving his uncle before he had a chance to take his seat.

"Congratulations!" Andi's bright green eyes reflected the radiant smile on her face.

"Thanks, Babe." North grazed his lips over her cheek before reclaiming his chair.

When Rebecca rose and, on tip-toes, reached across the table for North's hand, Andi choked on the sip of coffee she'd been about to swallow. "Congratulations," she said. Her smile was angelic, her cobalt-blue eyes framed by soft, blond curls, her full hot-pink lips glistening. "I'm Becky. Welcome to the Iditarod, North, and good luck."

North responded with an easy grin and said "Thanks, Becky. Number nine's my lucky number, and I figure I'm gonna need all the help I can get."

"We mushers look out for each other on that long trail," Becky winked. "If you need anything   anything at all – just holler."

"Thanks," North grinned. "I hope I don't have to take you up on that offer."

A dark flush rose to Andi's cheeks. The sudden, intense stab of jealousy took her by surprise. She tried hard to curb her distrust of other women when it came to her husband. He had never, ever given her any reason to doubt his love, or his fidelity. She didn't want to turn into one of *those wives*, the kind that everyone shunned and husbands ended up hating. Rebecca Singleton was just being kind, like all northerners, Andi told herself.

The bib draw dragged on, and the evening grew late. Andi's mind continued to wander. She tried, unsuccessfully, to force all images of pink lips against dark skin out of her mind. *Maybe that's why I felt so unsettled earlier,* she thought, eyeing the woman in pink. *Who are you, Rebecca Singleton, and why do I have to worry about you? Are you going to give me a reason to be so stupidly jealous?*

Luckily, a fellow rookie seated across the table had engaged North in a hushed conversation. Andi had met the personable, though quiet musher at the Iditarider pizza lunch. She determinedly diverted her mind from illogical, jealous thoughts to the men's conversation. North had met Mats Pederson, a stout twenty-nine-year-old Norwegian, at the Rookie's Meeting held in December. It was a race rule that any contestant running the Iditarod for the first time had to meet certain requirements before being approved for the race: they were required to complete certain qualifying races; they needed confirmation that they demonstrated the necessary physical and mental aptitude and preparedness, as well as the necessary wilderness and mushing skills, to survive a gruelling 1000 mile race; they had to attend the rookie meeting; and they needed a letter from the Iditarod head veterinarian stating they had the skills to care for their dogs. There were twelve rookies starting the race this year, and forty-one experienced mushers who knew what the hell they were doing.

North nodded at Mats with a wry grin. "I guess us newbies are going to have a real steep learning curve."

"Oh yah, that's for sure," Mats smiled for the first time that evening, his perfectly even teeth a startling white slash behind a bushy, red-gold moustache and matching beard. "How many dogs did you bring?"

"Twenty, but one of them is only here to keep my wife company," North said with a smirk that brought a chuckle from the huge Norwegian and a playful slap on the back of his head from Andi.

"That young man beside you is my handler," North added, nodding at Eddie. "He's also my nephew, and he works magic with my dogs. They love him."

"Pleased to meet you Eddie," Mats said extending a paw-sized hand to the younger man. "I'm Mats, from Norway."

Eddie, normally an outgoing and vocal young man, was slightly overwhelmed with the events and managed only a weak smile and nod. North surmised that his young nephew would much rather be socializing with his own friends – three lads who had also made the long journey from Inuvik to Anchorage to provide moral support for their buddy – than spending a long, drawn-out evening with a room full of rowdy strangers.

"How many dogs do you have?" North asked.

"I didn't bring my own team. It's too far to bring them, and costs too much. I'm just starting out in the mushing world so I leased twenty-five good dogs from Wasilla, and been practicing with them for the past month. It's probably not long enough, but it's all I could afford to do. We'll see how it goes."

"Good luck, Mats. If I can do anything to help, just let me know," North said.

"Yeah, you too, North. We'll have to watch each other's backs, eh?"

"You got that right," North replied solemnly.

"So, you have Canadian Eskimo Dogs," Mats remarked in a low voice. "That's an unusual breed to race, from what I know about sled dogs. Good for you, and good luck," he added, before returning his attention back to the draw.

An hour later the Musher's Banquet drew to a close. Each racer had a start number (some contestants were happier with their places than others), and each musher had said a few words (some speeches were lengthier than others). North and Andi bid Mats, who had drawn bib number 22, a goodnight, and North waved at his new friend, Becky, before winding their way through the crowded room. Eddie caught up to them in the hotel lobby. It had been a long day, beginning with a 9 am Pre-Race meeting. The Musher's Banquet had dragged on past midnight, and they were all exhausted.

Andi spotted Stacy Singleton making a determined bee-line across the banquet room, headed in their direction. "Can we just take a quick walk before we go to bed?" Andi pleaded, tugging North toward the exit. "I really need to get some air and clear my head."

North hesitated only momentarily. "Yeah, sure. Some fresh air and exercise might help me sleep." Sleeping was something he'd been unable to do with any degree of success since arriving in Anchorage several days ago. "You up for a walk with us, Eddie?" Eddie Ruben was North's eldest sister's son, and like North, had been born and raised in Paulatuk, a small Inuit village on the shores of the Amundsen Gulf. Now living in Inuvik, Eddie had promptly dropped out of high school the minute he'd turned sixteen, much to his uncle's disapproval. Luckily, North had been able to secure the boy a job at an old friend's motor sports shop, where he'd immediately shown his affinity for mechanics. Eddie was now the head mechanic and had earned himself a job for life.

"Uh," Eddie stammered, blinking rapidly. He was a handsome lad, and, from all accounts, popular with the girls. "Uh, I think I'll go check on the dogs and give them a snack. Maybe meet up with the guys too."

North and Andi laughed. "Go ahead, Eddie," North chuckled. "Have some fun, but not too much, eh? Don't forget you have to feed the dogs at 6:00 tomorrow morning."

"You know I won't forget about them," Eddie laughed. "I'll see you both in the morning, okay?" Smiling now that he was released to his own agenda, Eddie punched North in the arm before fleeing through the hotel lobby and into the night.

Following on his heels, they were half a block from the hotel before North stopped in the middle of the sidewalk. "Hey, slow down," he chuckled. "The race doesn't start until Saturday." At a more sedate pace, Andi and North strolled hand-in-hand on Fourth Avenue, Saturday's venue for the 10 am ceremonial race start. The real race wouldn't begin until Sunday. This year the official restart of the Iditarod, normally held eighty kilometers north of Anchorage in the small community of Wasilla, would be held in Willow. Lack of snow had forced the Iditarod Committee to move the restart a further forty-five kilometers north. But tonight on Fourth Avenue there were signs of preparation everywhere including banners, flags, signage, visitors and news media. Every store window displayed winter clothing, mukluks, snowshoes, and racing memorabilia. Souvenirs, from cheap, tacky T-shirts, coffee mugs emblazoned with the head of a husky, and small imitation inukshuk molded from plaster to magnificent, expensive works of art from talented local artists were highly sought after by visitors and race enthusiasts alike.

Overhead, the Aurora Borealis blazed across the night sky in a dazzling display of dancing light. "Look at that, North!" Andi exclaimed, tipping her head back to drink in the breathtakingly beautiful display of dancing green, red and blue hues. "I never get tired of looking at the Northern Lights."

"And I never get tired of looking at you, Babe," North murmured, leaning down to nuzzle a particularly vulnerable soft spot just below Andi's left ear. "If you're done stargazing, how about we head back to our room and I'll show you some real fireworks?" The tip of North's tongue traced the contours of Andi's neck.

Andi signed and closed her eyes. "Do I have to worry about that blonde?" she whispered.

"What blonde? I didn't see any blonde," he blew in her ear, a barely-there gentle gust of warm air, then nuzzled her neck.

"What about your Iditarider? Do I have to worry about her?"

"Babe, you're talking crazy." He took her earlobe between his lips and sucked gently.

His touch drew a soft sigh from her lips.

"Ready to go back to our room?" North whispered.

Andi clutched North's arm and fought to steady her suddenly weak knees. A firestorm raced through her veins, settling like a warm ember in the base of her stomach.

Her voice, when she found it again, was husky. "Damn you, North Ruben! What are we waiting for?"

SIX

Although her eyes were still firmly closed, Andi simultaneously became aware of two things; the tantalizing, mouth-watering scent of brewing coffee, and the heat of North's tongue trailing down her belly. If it were a contest, she wasn't sure which would win first prize.

North's voice, muffled by the thick down duvet over his head, dragged her from a semi-comatose state to full awareness. "You awake yet, Babe?"

"Mmm ... sort of," she moaned, "but I'll fall asleep again if you stop now." North willingly returned to his task until she cried out and her long, lean body collapsed against the soft bed.

North fought his way out from under the covers and laid his head on his partner's breast, her heart beating loud and fast beneath his ear. They lay entwined in a tangle of sheets, their breathing loud in the muffled silence of the hotel room. When his heart slowed again, North planted a string of kisses up her long, dewy neck before landing on her lips. "Good morning, love," he whispered.

"Good morning to you too," Andi murmured. Her words were husky and slow, her mind still saturated with sexual gratification. A glimpse of brilliant green glinted from beneath heavy eyelids. "Where's my coffee?"

North rolled Andi's lean form onto her side and slapped her nicely rounded bottom lightly. "Is that any way to talk to a hard-working man so early in the morning?" he retorted.

Andi squealed and threw the duvet aside. "You're right. I'll get my own coffee." She slipped from the king-size bed and glided toward the miniature kitchenette, the room's plush, burnt-orange carpeting absorbing her light footsteps. A dim light burned over the tiny, bar sized sink, and in its muted glow North gazed appreciatively at his wife's soft curves, endless legs and beautifully tousled crown of mahogany hair.

"What time is it, anyway?" Andi asked, oblivious of the passion rising in her husband's dark eyes.

"Seven bells." North sat up and clicked the bedside lamp on. Andi, her large, brown nipples rigid, slid across the cool room and carefully set two cups of steaming coffee on the night stand, then crawled back into the warm bed. "I think there's just enough time for a quickie," he grinned.

Andi slid closer to her husband and rolled to her side so they lay facing each other. She traced the outlines of his face with gentle, reverent fingers, then pressed her lips to his. Her tongue slipped between his teeth, delving deeper, caressing the smooth, hot silk of his mouth.

His penis twitched against her belly, thickening and growing at her touch. She pushed him to his back and reached down to caress him, stilling his eager hands when they rose to explore her tender, swollen breasts. "I don't ever want to forget how you feel," she whispered, kissing his chin, his cheek, his eyes. Her lips moved to his neck, seeking that soft, warm spot beneath his ear. She nuzzled and licked her way down his trembling body, first encircling each nubby nipple with her lips, then flicking her tongue and sucking greedily. He moaned and wrapped his hands in her hair.

She moved lower, trailing a row of hot kisses over his taut belly until she reached his hard manhood. "I never want to forget how you taste."

Later she lay stretched out next to him, supporting herself on one elbow. One slim leg lay draped across his. North's eyes were closed; a faint sheen of perspiration still coated his skin. She lowered her lips to his neck. His pulse raced beneath her touch, his breathing laboured. She stared at him with hooded eyes until he sensed her brooding look and fought to open his.

"Promise me you won't *ever* leave me alone," she pleaded.

North wrapped his arms around his wife's trembling body and drew her close. Her silent tears dampened his chest; they clung to each other for long minutes. "I promise I will never, ever leave you," he whispered. "You don't have to worry. I'm too damn stubborn to die, and I love you too much to leave you."

Andi sniffled and brushed the tears from her cheeks. She lifted her head, smiled softly and whispered, "I love you, too." A hint of a smile graced her bruised lips. "I think our coffee might be cold."

"I don't really care about the damn coffee, it's horrible, anyway. I'd much rather have you." He cupped one full, firm breast, and then grinned, a flash of long incisor. "Can we do this tomorrow morning, too?"

"I don't know about that. I think you might need to save your energy for the race." Andi sat up and reached for their cups.

"Yeah, you're likely right," North frowned. He took a cautious sip and grimaced at the bitter taste of the inferior, cool brew. "I just hope that I'm up for all of this. Now that I'm here, and I've talked to some of the other mushers and hear how much training and preparation they've done, I don't think I have a hope in hell of winning this race."

"North, just being here is an amazing feat! You've said so yourself a hundred times – it's not about *winning* the Iditarod, it's about *racing* in it. It's all about being here and showing off your team. You've accomplished so much already . . . don't give up now!"

"I know, I know. You're right. It's just that sometimes I feel like maybe I really do want to *win* this damn race."

"If you don't win this year, there's always another time," Andi said consolingly, patting his hand. "We can always come back next year."

North nodded slowly, but looked sceptical.

"It's time for a shower," Andi declared. "I'd like to go downstairs as soon as we can and find a decent cup of coffee and some breakfast. How about you?"

"Yeah, I suppose."

Andi got out of bed and headed for the bathroom.

"Hey, wait for me, Babe. I'm right behind you."

She threw a sultry look over her shoulder. "Is that a promise, cowboy?"

After a very long, steamy shower and hearty breakfast, they drove the short distance from Anchorage to the Campbell Airstrip, where the musher's equipment and competing dogs were safely accommodated.

True to his word, Eddie had already fed the dogs, and was just getting ready to return to Anchorage when they arrived. His Inuvik friends, whom were likely still firmly ensconced in warm beds, had given Eddie their battered pickup truck to use for the early morning trip. Promising to meet up later, Eddie climbed up into the old Ford and rumbled off.

North and Andi spent the rest of the morning – the final day before Saturday's ceremonial start of the Iditarod – inspecting North's equipment, sled and harnesses and lines; everything had to be in perfect working order to meet the grueling challenges of the days ahead. From the equipment they moved on to the dogs themselves.

Late in the afternoon, North began aimless pacing. "Let's go back into Anchorage and see what else is happening downtown," Andi suggested. "Qannik can come too." Andi's favourite, the sociable, cunning young dog had also appointed herself as team mascot; she seemed especially pleased with her new hot-pink booties. The booties weren't really necessary for warmth, but Andi thought that they, along with Qannik's matching pink neck scarf, looked superbly cute on her fluffy white companion.

They parked on a side street and headed to Fourth Avenue, the staging area for Saturday's ceremonial race start. Qannik, a lead attached to her collar, trotted beside them, occasionally stopping to investigate something of interest. Bill Wrightway would kick off the ceremonial start and, followed by the rest of the Iditarod mushers, set an easy pace through the city to the short event's terminus at the Campbell Airstrip. The five-block race staging area on Fourth was already closed to vehicle traffic, bright orange mesh barriers in place to keep tomorrow's spectators safely on the sidewalks, and off the street. During the night, dump trucks would deposit a wide lane of stockpiled snow along the route. The organizers were lucky this year, as temperatures hovered well below freezing; the snow wouldn't melt before tomorrow morning.

"Let's grab a cup of coffee," North suggested.

"Good idea," Andi agreed. "I could use some caffeine."

While North was in JavaGenie getting their coffee, Andi caught herself daydreaming about tropical climes and their honeymoon plans. She had mixed feelings about the RV trip down the Baja; Mexico and its raging drug wars had been in the news too often of late. She wasn't sure she'd feel entirely safe traveling and camping in a country as volatile as Mexico but, despite her misgivings, she didn't want to spoil the trip for North.

She sighed and turned her attention to the bustling street. Event organizers were putting last minute touches on the first race checkpoint. Colourful flags representing the home countries and states of all competitors fluttered above the street in preparation for the ribbon cutting and ceremonial start tomorrow morning. Although there were a few flags she couldn't place, she easily recognized those of the United States, Alaska, Montana, Canada, Norway, France and Switzerland. She envisioned her husband taking his place among seasoned, world-famous competitors; the vision made her stomach flip. Not only would thousands of spectators be lining the street, the event would be televised world-wide; it was no wonder the poor man was nervous.

"Here you go, Babe," North's deep, melodious voice startled her from her reverie. She gratefully accepted the cardboard cup – anything to warm her frozen digits. "Let's keep walking," North suggested. "I'm too worked up to stand still."

Arm-in-arm they strolled up the length of the staging area and back again, drawing several curious and appreciative looks from the surprisingly large crowd milling around the street. But then, they were an extremely striking inter-racial couple, and North's chiseled good looks, regal demeanour and shiny, long black hair always attracted attention. A contented smile crossed Andi's lips, and she clutched her husband's arm a little tighter.

"Hey look!" North said suddenly, gesturing down the sidewalk to a small group of parka-clad young women. "Isn't that Stacy, my Iditarider?"

"Where?" Andi blurted, her words a little sharper than she'd intended.

North looked at her with a grin, and chuckled.

"What?" Andi demanded. "What are you laughing at?"

"You, Babe. You're jealous of my Iditarider."

"I am *not*," she snapped, her denial betrayed by flushed cheeks and pursed lips.

"Yeah, you are. But I think pink cheeks look pretty cute on you," North teased. He tugged at her arm, urging her down the street. "Hey Stacy!" he shouted, waving at the tall, blond young woman who had won the honor of riding in his sled on Saturday morning. "Wait up!"

An ingenious race devotee had recently devised a method for the Iditarod committee to raise much needed funds for the race. A public auction gave fans the opportunity to bid on a chance to participate in the fun and excitement of the Ceremonial Start, and ride in the sled of their favourite musher. They could also 'buy' their ride, but the cost was prohibitive for most individuals.

The winning bid for a ride in North's sled was Stacy Irving's, quite certainly funded by her affluent father or doting uncle. Stacy was twenty-one years old and a true Anchoragite. She was also, unfortunately for North, a knockout, vivacious, personable bundle of fun, and Andi was truly unhappy about the entire situation. When they'd met the young woman on Thursday, they'd learned that Stacy's family played an important part in Anchorage's history, and was very well-known in the area. Andi continued to bemoan the fact that the Irving family had such a beautiful, blond daughter.

When she'd questioned North about why Stacy had decided to choose him – a foreigner! – for her Iditaride, he had patiently pointed out that it was an honour, and she should be happy that he would be very much in the public eye because of it. Andi wasn't convinced.

"Hi, North!" Stacy waved enthusiastically. Qannik strained at the end of her leash, eager for any extra bit of attention. "Hey, everyone," Stacy said to her three companions. "This is North Ruben, from Canada. He's the musher I was telling you all about."

"Hi!" All three girls ogled North and giggled.

"Oh, and this is his wife, Andi," Stacy added. They dragged their eyes away from North only long enough to nod in her direction.

"I'm so glad we ran into you," Stacy gushed, entirely unfazed by Andi's frozen frown. "I've been telling my girlfriends *all* about you!"

"Well that must have been a pretty short story," North laughed. The girls were all uncommonly striking: Stacy's cobalt-blue eyes and platinum hair hinted at Scandinavian heritage, while two of her companions, petite twins with shoulder length, raven-black hair and espresso eyes, bore traces of Native North American ancestry, and the lilting voice of the fourth young woman, a tall carrot top with creamy, fair skin and blazing green eyes, much like Andi's, betrayed her recent Irish roots.

Qannik eagerly licked the girls' hands and nuzzled their pockets in search of a treat. They, in turn, gave the young dog some much appreciated attention. When North told them that Qannik was a purebred Canadian Eskimo Dog, a rare, endangered breed, they oohed and aahed over the bouncy white bundle of fur, and cameras were pulled out for a photo op with North and his 'rare dog.' Andi, standing to one side of the group, rolled her eyes and mumbled under her breath.

North continued to bestow his dazzling, toothy smile upon Stacy and her friends while they peppered him with questions about his sled dogs, life in Inuvik, and how he planned to win the Iditarod. After ten minutes, Andi could take no more of their starry-eyed smiles. Even Qannik, who had been abandoned in favour of North and was now being totally ignored, had tired of the visitors. She lay on the snowy sidewalk, her black nose resting on crossed white paws. Andi stamped her booted feet a few times and slapped her hands together.

"You getting cold, Babe?" North asked, finally noticing his wife's discomfort.

"Sort of. You about ready to go?" Andi's words were amiable enough, but the fire in her emerald eyes betrayed the smile on her lips.

"Gotta run," North announced to the unhappy girls, and after a protracted good-bye and Stacy's promise to 'see you bright and early tomorrow,' the Rubens made their escape from North's small fan club.

It was a frigid, long ride back to the Campbell Airstrip.

North had given Eddie the evening off to tear up the town with his buddies. After he and Andi fed the dogs their high-protein, energy laden dinner, they bedded them down for the night and hit a local steak house.

"Sorry about this afternoon," Andi apologized when they left the restaurant an hour later, their hunger assuaged by thick, sumptuous rib eyes. "I don't want our last day together to be ruined." She stopped in the middle of the sidewalk and tugged on her lover's arm, drawing a few curious glances from passersby. When North turned to look at her, she reached up and cupped his face with the palm of her hand. "You know I love you more than life itself, and it breaks my heart that I won't see you again for the next two weeks. Let's make the best of our last few hours together, okay?"

"Absolutely, Babe," North smiled, and kissed the palm of her hand. They strolled along the streets of downtown Anchorage, breathing in the excitement and festive air and talking about all the things they wanted to do during their Mexican honeymoon. As they neared their hotel, arms linked together, Andi's ears began to burn. She tried to ignore the icy threads of dread that settled around her heart, but the intensity and speed with which they grew left her breathless. She stumbled, remaining on her feet only by sheer determination. Seconds later, a black shadow slid past her eyes, bringing with it a sweet, fetid odor. The cloying stench saturated her senses – the scent of death was unmistakable. It was unforgettable. It brought with it heart shattering memories of pain and loss.

While the reek of death taunted her olfactory system, visions of intense, pure colour flickered before her mind's eye. First white, then red. White and red ... white and red.

Snow.

Blood.

Lots of blood.

Andi sobbed, and stumbled again. Only North's instant reaction prevented her from falling to her knees. "Andi! Babe, what's wrong?" he cried. "Are you alright?"

"I'll ... I'll be okay," she gasped. She doubled over and clutched her stomach. "Just ... just give me a minute."

"What's the matter?" North yelped. "Should I take you to the hospital?"

"No! No. It's only a stomach cramp," Andi lied. "I must have eaten too much. It'll go away."

She would never tell him the truth. He didn't need to know that she'd had the same kind of bone-chilling premonition in the past, just days before three of North's prized and cherished sled dogs had been senselessly gunned down in his own kennel. And as it had before, this premonition left her feeling chilled, unsettled and confused.

She hadn't been able to alter the deadly outcome then, and she couldn't now. She was cursed with knowledge over which she had no control, and it chilled her to the core of her soul. Who would die this time?

North didn't need to know the truth.

She drew several deep, calming breaths and pushed the putrid odor and shades of doom from her mind. Supported within North's steady arms, she slowly righted herself. She managed a weak smile and patted his hand. "Sorry, sweetheart. It was just a stomach cramp, but I think we'd better head back to the hotel."

North didn't need to know.

When they crawled into bed a little later, Andi made sure that the man she loved more than life itself would have plenty of warm memories to see him through the cold, lonely, and most certainly dangerous days and nights ahead.

She couldn't, though, prevent the visions and dreams that kept her awake and haunted her own restless slumber, leaving her anxious and exhausted the next morning.

White and red. White and red.
Snow and blood. Snow and blood.

SEVEN

"FIVE!"
"FOUR!"
"THREE!"
"TWO!"
"ONE!"
"GO!"

At exactly 10:17 am on Saturday, March 1, North Ruben's lifelong dream became a reality. After a long, slow procession behind eight other teams at the starting chute, the starter finally uttered the sweet, short word he was longing to hear. Before thousands of spectators, and proudly wearing bib number 9, he released the sled's snow brake and yelled *'HIKE!'* Anchorage's own sweetheart, Stacy Irving, sat proud and beaming in the sled basket, one gloved hand waving regally as the sled slid beneath the colourful, fluttering starting banner on Fourth Avenue.

Stacy was resplendent in a dazzling white parka trimmed with what could only be white mink. Her hair was piled high in a mass of golden curls, her smiling lips painted blood red. A long, emerald green scarf, the exact same shade as North's gear and the dogs' jackets, was looped around her neck, completing her stunning ensemble. Andi's blood boiled.

The Ceremonial Start of the 1997 25th Silver Anniversary Iditarod had begun a few minutes earlier, with speeches and a ribbon cutting ceremony. The first musher departed at 10:00, and this year Mr. Bill

Wrightway, the Father of the Iditarod, led the proceedings. The dedicated senior had earned the privilege to lead the proceedings wearing bib number 1.

With paws securely wrapped in bright emerald green booties, and wearing matching green jackets emblazoned with his sponsors' names and advertising, North's team of twelve Canadian Eskimo dogs were hard to miss. His own custom-made parka matched his dogs' jackets, and he gladly told anyone who cared to listen that he chose emerald green because it reminded him of his wife's mesmerizing eyes. He claimed that the unusual hue would bring him good luck during the long, cold, grueling days and nights he would face on the race trail. He had definitely scored some brownie points at home the day the new gear had arrived. Today, though, he may have lost a few, through no fault of his own.

Andi and a crowd of 10,000 fans, volunteers and race officials cheered him on amidst a volley of flashing cameras. Television crews and news reporters from around the world braved the frosty morning, filming and recording every second of the Ceremonial Start. The hardy reporters from the APRN (Alaska Public Radio Network) interviewed numerous competitors and spectators, relaying race coverage live to the rest of the world. Anchorage crackled with excitement and anticipation.

Although Andi was ecstatic and proud of her husband and his accomplishment – and yes, even qualifying for the Iditarod was a worthy accomplishment – she felt edgy and unsettled. Was it the disturbing presence of Anchorage's golden girl in North's sled, the blond, pink-clad musher, or the vision of white and red she couldn't quite seem to rid her mind of?

This day had long been North's dream, and then it became hers, too. She hastily brushed a stray tear from her cheek when North's nephew appeared at her side. Young Eddie adored sled dogs and mushing almost as much as his Uncle North did, and when North discovered their mutual love, he'd invited him to join his Iditarod team as his dog handler. It was a win-win situation for them both.

"Jesus, that woman is gorgeous," Eddie mumbled almost reverently.

Andi turned to follow the young man's dreamy gaze. *Stacy Irving!* Andi gritted her teeth. *Not him, too.* She cursed under her breath.

Eddie either sensed his aunt's stony look, or she'd spoken louder than she thought. "Uncle North's team looks great, doesn't it?" he commented tactfully.

Andi took a sip of her coffee, willing her quick flash of jealousy to subside. "Yes, they sure do. I can't believe we're actually here."

"This is the first time anyone from Inuvik has competed in this race," Eddie said, with something akin to awe in his voice. "I'd sure like to have my chance, one day."

"Really? I didn't know you had the same aspirations as your uncle. I hope you get to run it too."

"Yeah, so do I. Uncle North said he'd help me out, starting my own team and all. Once he really gets his breeding program going, he's going to give me a couple of pups in trade for me helping him out at the kennel." Eddie scuffed the snow with a booted foot. "I'd never be able to afford the dogs without his help."

"That's wonderful, Eddie. I'm sure he'll really appreciate your help. Has he mentioned that we're going on a holiday next month? Our honeymoon?"

"Yeah, he did. I'm going to look after the dogs for him. You're going to Mexico, eh? Lucky you."

"Yes, I'm really looking forward to it. But," Andi hesitated briefly, "but, I really wish we were going to a nice resort in Cancun or Cozumel instead of driving my brother's motorhome down Baja California." She sighed and took a cautious sip of steaming coffee.

"Ha! The RV trip will certainly be an adventure," Eddie laughed.

"Yeah, that's what I'm afraid of."

North and his golden Iditarider disappeared from view. Andi and Eddie watched a few more competitors begin their ceremonial run to the Campbell Airstrip before Eddie excused himself to look for his buddies.

"No problem," Andi said, glancing at her watch. "I'm going to go back to the hotel in a while, but I'll leave for the airstrip in about an hour. North should be done by noon."

"Okay, I'll meet you at your truck and go out to get the dogs unharnessed and stuff. Meet you at 11:30?"

"Sure, that would be great. See you then." The young man disappeared, quickly absorbed into the milling throng.

Walking down Anchorage's main thoroughfare on race day was a colourful, exhilarating experience. Andi hoped the activity and distractions would take her mind off the fact that Stacy and North would be spending the next two hours together. Alone.

A huge 'Iditarod Trail Start' banner hung across the street, flanked on either side with colourful flags from the mushers' home country or state, their bright red, white, yellow, green and blue fabric snapping in the light morning breeze. And of course Alaska's refreshingly unique state flag was everywhere. Eight gold stars, set against a dark blue background reminiscent of a night sky, represented The Big Dipper from the constellation Ursa Major, the Bear, and Polaris, the North Star. Andi pondered the Alaskan state flag as she strolled down the street; its depiction of Polaris, the almost stationary North Star used for celestial navigation by explorers and wanderers for centuries, would also be utilized by the Iditarod mushers. The flag's frequent presence was not only stunning, but also appropriate.

She headed to the Alaska Hotel, weaving her way around excited, expectant spectators waiting for that thrilling 'once in a lifetime moment' when their favourite competitor officially crossed the start line. The air was electric, charged with the energy of a thousand race enthusiasts. On both sides of the street, colourful red, white and blue 'Iditarod Trail *Alaska*' pennants, depicting the head of a Husky, hung from lamp posts and street lights. Everywhere one looked were images from Alaska's beloved Iditarod.

In her mind's eye, she traced North's route through the city: after beginning downtown, the competitors followed city streets, greenbelts and ski trails for a few kilometers before reaching a large, wooded park. Today's exhibition event would ultimately end at the Campbell Airstrip, eighteen kilometers from the city. Andi had confidence in both North and his team, and although many competitors said the noise and crowds of the day sometimes incited their dogs to a frenzy, she doubted that her husband would run into any difficulties. At least not today.

Andi's trust didn't extend to his Iditarider though. In her opinion, Stacy Irving exhibited too much interest in her handsome, oblivious husband, and she didn't trust the young woman one little bit. Images of bloody snow – images that had disrupted her sleep and continued to torment her psyche – kept popping into her head. What could they possibly mean? Was she that insanely jealous of a young woman her husband barely knew? Andi walked a little faster, her quirky ears twitching while her tormented thoughts left her feeling nervous and nauseous. She clutched her stomach and gently elbowed her way down the sidewalk, intent on returning to the warmth and tranquility of her hotel room.

Some of the sparkle had dimmed from her extraordinary day.

At 11:30 sharp, Eddie crawled into the passenger seat of North's big white Ford. Andi had already started the truck, giving the frost time to melt from the windshield without scraping it. "Hey, how you doing?" Eddie asked cheerfully. He gripped a slightly greasy paper bag from which emanated the unmistakable smell of a hamburger and fries. Her previous nausea had disappeared, and Andi eyed the bag hopefully; hamburgers of any kind were her favourite food.

"I know how much my uncle likes his cheeseburgers and fries," Eddie grinned. "I'm pretty sure he's gonna be starving by the time we get there."

Her hopes dashed, Andi smiled and took a sip of the extra-large coffee she'd picked up at JavaGenie. Another waited for her husband in the second cup holder. "That's very thoughtful of you, Eddie. I'm sure he'll appreciate it." She hadn't picked up a coffee for Eddie, as she knew he abhorred it.

They chatted about anything and everything during the drive to the Campbell Airstrip. From annoying relatives, to the tragic loss of Andi's mother to cancer, to Eddie's own hopes and dreams. Andi found the young man both a good listener and wise beyond his years. She briefly considered sharing her apprehensions with him, but quickly dismissed the idea as a bad one. One person short on sleep with dreams of blood-spattered snow was more than enough.

The drive to the Campbell Airstrip, delayed by barricaded roads and a high volume of traffic, took longer than expected. They were surprised to find that North had beat them to their destination. His team lay flopped and panting on the snow while North, a radiant Stacy Irving at his side and an immense grin plastered on his face, chatted with a small group of mushers, including Mats from Norway and Bill Wrightway. Wrightway, at age eighty, was the eldest and most experienced contestant in this year's event, having been the founder and principal promoter of the Iditarod Trail Sled Dog Race.

Although North's team was still in harness, the extra eight dogs, including Qannik, were securely chained within North's allotted kennel area. The moment Andi stepped out of the truck, the spoiled white dog commenced a high-pitched, keening howl, presumably intended to make Andi, who already felt guilty about leaving her best friend chained and abandoned with the rest of the pack, release her from the restraints. When she did, the spoiled dog ignored her and bounded over to greet her buddies. Team dogs were never left unrestrained at race events for fear of fight or flight, but Qannik was an exception. The young dog had developed few of the characteristics of the feistier racing animals, and seemed to have absolutely no desire to stray far from either Andi or North.

Eddie set to work unharnessing the team. His refusal of Andi's help left her free to join her husband and the growing crowd of mushers amassed around Bill Wrightway. She wound her way to North's side, studiously avoiding his Iditarider, who hovered at his opposite shoulder.

"You made it!" North beamed. His smile was by far the broadest she'd ever witnessed. He wrapped his arms around her and lifted her easily from her feet, hugging her hard before setting her back down.

"Congratulations, darling!" Andi's eyes shone with joy. "You've officially joined the ranks of Iditarod musher."

North laughed and wrapped an arm around her shoulder. They stood together, Stacy Irving making it a threesome, while Bill continued to regale them with tales of races gone by. Andi pushed down her unreasonable and as yet unfounded jealousy, determined to cherish every last moment she and her husband had together.

Half an hour later Bill announced he was 'too old and tired to continue this tomfoolery talking' and said his good byes to his fan club. North, Andi and Stacy wandered over to North's dogs. Eddie had removed the team's booties and jackets, checked their feet, fed them and settled each into their allotted sleeping area.

"Here, let me help you with that," Andi offered when Eddie went to get straw from the bales stacked near the kennel area. They made several trips, lugging armful after armful until each dog had fresh straw, which they immediately began stirring around to fluff into a comfortable bed.

North, meanwhile, was taking a few minutes to visit with each of his dogs. He sat next to each animal for a while, talking, stroking and whispering in their ears. They, in turn, grinned, panted and gazed at him with what could only be called love.

Andi couldn't help but notice that Stacy Irving looked at him with the same adoring eyes.

EIGHT

The day that North Ruben had waited for his entire life unfolded in the predawn hours of a cold Alaskan morning. He and Andi sat at a long, roughly hewn wooden table in a small restaurant on the edge of the tiny community of Willow, 125 kilometers north of Anchorage. They had relocated to the site of the race restart the previous evening. Luckily Andi had had the foresight to book two hotel rooms shortly after North had signed up for the Iditarod; there wasn't an empty room in the entire town.

"Remind me again why we had to get up at six o'clock," Andi yawned, her eyes slightly unfocused over the chipped rim of a heavy earthenware coffee mug. "It's still dark out."

"Sunrise is at 7:56, but official light starts thirty minutes earlier." North glanced at his watch, the lines between his eyes deeper than they had been the day before. "It's already 7:15, so it will officially be light in exactly eleven minutes."

Andi rolled her eyes and groaned in mock exasperation. North sensed movement beneath the table, and deftly shifted his shin out of reach of her booted foot. Andi's theatrics succeeded to break his concentrated frown. "You didn't seem to mind your wake-up call this morning, sweetheart," North grinned.

Andi had the decency to blush, and lowered her eyes as images of North's lips trailing across her breasts and down her belly flashed through her mind. Recalling the touch of her husband's skilful hands made her blood burn. "Well if I'm not mistaken, you enjoyed your wake-up call this morning too."

"You got that right, Babe. I think you gave me enough lovin' to last the next two weeks."

"Oh, North, I really hope it doesn't take that long to finish the race," Andi shuddered. "I can't stand the thought of you out there alone in the wilderness. What if something happens? What if you get hurt, or are in an accident?" The distress in her voice escalated with every question.

"We've gone through all of this before," North said calmly. He reached across the table and grasped Andi's hand. "There are fifty-two other racers this year, and we have to travel through twenty-two checkpoints before we hit Nome. I'm never going to be alone for long. And don't forget, I'll have my rifle with me at all times."

A lone tear trailed from Andi's eye. "I know. You keep telling me you'll be safe, but I still can't help worrying."

White and red. White and red.

Snow and blood. Snow and blood.

Andi hadn't mentioned her vision, or her haunting dreams. Although she had no intention of sharing them, the tragedy they foretold was never far from her thoughts. "Just promise me you'll be careful."

"I'll be alright, Babe!" North laughed. "And with any luck you'll be looking at my ugly mug in less than two weeks. I'm aiming at eleven days, if all goes well." Their breakfast arrived, and he withdrew his hand to scoop up his fork. Andi dropped her hand to her lap, and unconsciously twirled the silver AA ring on her finger.

Their chipper waitress, clad in a tight white uniform with a skirt three inches too short, set a massive plate of eggs, bacon, ham and hash-browns in front of North, and another with four slices of toast beside it. She smiled at him amiably. "There's ketchup, jam and peanut butter on the table. If you need anything else, hon, you just let me know." North returned her smile and nodded, his mouth already full of ham.

"I'll be right back with more coffee. And your granola," she added, glancing briefly at Andi. Andi glared at the back of her retreating brunette head before turning narrowed eyes on her husband, who tactfully ignored both women.

"It never stops, does it?" Andi muttered. She scowled in the waitress' direction again and drained her coffee mug. She was still two cups shy of a good mood.

"What's that, Babe?"

"Women! They all want you," Andi's clipped words carried both pride and indignation.

"Nah, they just think they want me," North said between mouthfuls. "Once they get to know me, they definitely don't want me. I'm too difficult to live with, too set in my ways. You know that."

Andi's granola and skim milk appeared, and their coffee cups were topped up. North determinedly refrained from making further eye contact with their chatty server, much to the young woman's dismay. She lingered by their table for a moment before drifting away.

"I know you're just saying that to make me feel better." Andi's mouth twisted into a sad smile. "You're actually the easiest person in the world to live with, and I do love you. I'll just be really glad when this race is over and we're back home safe and sound." She scooped up a spoonful of granola and chewed it slowly before dropping the spoon back in the bowl.

"Something the matter with your cereal?"

"No, the granola is fine. I'm not really hungry. I think I'm just nervous."

"Would you like some bacon, or ham? I have plenty to share."

"No, thanks," Andi shook her head. "But maybe I'll try a piece of toast."

He pushed the plate toward her.

"Aren't you nervous?" she asked, nibbling on a half slice of toasted brown bread. "If it was me, I'd be a basket case."

"I'm trying not to think about it. I know my dogs are ready, and I know that my equipment is top of the line and is in excellent condition.

I'm as prepared as I can be, so worrying isn't going to help one little bit. I'm more concerned about you right now."

"Oh, please don't worry about me. I'll be perfectly fine, but I'm really going to miss you."

"I'll miss you, too, Babe, but I'll be thinking about you all the way. You'll be right here, every minute." He thumped the breast pocket of his red plaid flannel shirt. Secreted in the pocket, encased in sealed plastic, was a picture of Andi. She had tucked it in the night before. "You'll be riding along with me every step of the way. Right next to my heart."

She managed a weak smile. "You're such a romantic. I guess that's why I love you so much."

North wiped his plate clean with the last triangle of toast, then glanced at his watch. "It's sunrise," he announced. Outside a bank of windows set along the restaurant's east wall, as if on cue, the charcoal grey pre-dawn sky began to lighten to slate. Moments later a thin orange-pink band of colour bloomed along the jagged mountain tops. Still hidden beyond the peaks, the sun began its daily debut. "Time to get going," North said, pushing back from the table. He was too preoccupied to appreciate the splendour of a winter morning. "I hope the kitchen has our food ready."

"Wait," Andi said. "I have something for you." She dug into her parka pocket and pulled out a small blue jewellery box, placing it in his outstretched hand.

"What's this?" he asked, his forehead creased.

"Open it."

North pulled off the lid. Nestled in a bed of white cotton lay a small silver Inukshuk pendant hanging from a heavy silver chain.

"It's a good luck charm," Andi said, her eyes bright again, unshed tears threatening. "To guide you back to me if you should lose your way."

"It's beautiful, Babe," North said solemnly, holding the amulet in his hand for a closer look. "I love it." He fastened the chain around his neck and dropped the one-inch long Inukshuk into the neckline of his white T-shirt. "And don't worry, Babe. I'll come back to you come hell or high water."

"You'd better. You're my soul mate."

North leaned over the table to cup her cheek. "And you're mine, Babe. But right now I have to get going or I'll be late."

While North paid their bill and collected his lunch – a thermos of coffee, four bacon and egg sandwiches, and a half dozen freshly baked banana-nut muffins – and a toasted Denver sandwich for Eddie, Andi stepped outside to absorb the morning's glorious explosion of colour. Mystical, multi-hued bands of soft light bathed the landscape, rapidly transforming everything below from a dull, dark grey to warm pink, gold and coral. Mother Nature's paint palette was having a fiesta on the wild canvas called Alaska.

"The starting checkpoint is sure busy," Andi commented when they drove up to the temporary headquarters of the Iditarod a few minutes later. A flurry of activity hummed around the small wooden shack; race officials, media and mushers all seemed to be in a rush to get the big day started. Exhaust from a dozen vehicles clouded the air, the foggy vapours adding to the surreal, frosty morning.

"I'll just be a minute," North said. He parked on the street, leaving the truck running. "I'm just going to run in and tell the race coordinator I'm here."

"Sure," Andi said. "I'll just wait here."

Five minutes later North returned, and they continued past the checkpoint to a nearby patch of vacant land dotted with small trees and scrub - the temporary home for 900 dogs who would hit the trail in less than two hours. To say that the air was filled with a cacophony of sound would be putting it very mildly; dogs howled, they sang, they barked, they yipped, and they moaned. The land resounded with their voices.

The staging area was already a beehive of activity. Mushers, handlers, and helpers thronged the area, as well as several news vans and a dozen reporters. From somewhere nearby came the distinctive *whop whop whop* of a helicopter.

North parked next to the old Ford pickup Eddie had borrowed from his buddy. His team, resting on their straw beds, recognized North's truck and began to yap and wail. Eddie, who had been peering into a large, steaming pot, smiled broadly and gave a jaunty wave.

"Let's just sit for a little while before we get out," Andi begged. She was reluctant to surrender their last few minutes of privacy. She slid across the bench seat and reached for his hand, wondering for the hundredth time if she should share her concerns. Should she warn him of ... of what? A bad feeling? Her nightmares?

They sat together quietly, listening to the slow *tick, tick, tick* of the truck's cooling engine. Beyond the line of scraggly jack pines surrounding them, the rugged beauty of The Alaska Range's snow-capped mountains was breathtaking. The rising sun illuminating their high peaks in a rare pink glow. "It's considered good luck to see those mountain peaks," Andi murmured, her words barely audible against the background of yapping dogs. "They're normally blanketed in clouds. Some visitors never even get a glimpse of them. This is a *very* good omen." She lay her head on his shoulder and ran a hand down his arm. He was tense, his muscles as hard as rock. She reached for his hand and brought it to her lips. It was too late to share her foreboding thoughts. "I'm going to miss you." Grief strangled her words.

North put his an around her shoulders and held her close. "I'll miss you too, Babe, but I'll be back. I promised, remember? And I never break a promise." It was daylight now; the sun, having lifted its face above the horizon, rose at a remarkable pace.

In just two short hours North would take his place at the official restart line. "I gotta get started," he said, too keyed up to notice the pallor of Andi's skin. He hopped out of the truck and walked around the front to open the passenger door. As she was climbing down from the high cab another wave of anxiety hit her; coffee rose from her stomach, sour and sharp. She gagged it back down, disguising her distress with a loud cough. By the time she closed the truck door, North was already standing beside Eddie. She hurried to catch up.

"Good morning!" Eddie called, shouting to be heard above the clamour created by 900 dogs.

"Brought you a sandwich and muffin," North said, tossing a paper bag in his direction. Eddie had foregone his own breakfast in order to get a head start on preparing the dogs' morning meal. "How are you making out?

"Good. I've already fed them and started another batch of food for your cooler." Sled dogs burn up to 10,000 calories a day while on the trail, and need quality food; North had created his own blend using a high-quality kibble, vitamins, fat, bonemeal and raw meat – usually beef, caribou, chicken or a blend of all three. Mixed with hot water, it provided all the nutrients, protein, energy, and liquid the dogs needed. His cooler would hold enough cooked dog food to last two meals, and keep it warm for twelve hours or longer; the dogs would be fed three or four times a day, plus be given several raw meat snacks. North would carry enough frozen meat and kibble in his sled bag to feed the dogs for at least two days, just in case he should he be delayed between checkpoints.

"You're a life saver, Eddie," North grinned.

"No problem, Uncle. You'll owe me," Eddie chuckled.

"Don't I know it! And knowing you, I'm sure you'll collect somehow."

As soon as their master had stepped from the truck, the intensity of his team's keening escalated. They knew, from other races, that their fun was about to start, and were getting impatient. Andi immediately freed Qannik, who raced around in circles, digging her snout into the snow and voicing either her pleasure at being released, or her displeasure at being held captive. It was impossible to tell.

Months later, back home in Inuvik, Andi would discover that one of the things she remembered most vividly about her experience at the Iditarod were the sounds. At every turn, and around every corner, there were sled dogs. And sled dogs were a noisy, vivacious and vocal bunch, silent only on those rare occasions when they were sound asleep. The clamour of hundreds of sled dogs coupled with the excited, sometimes anxious, and often accented voices of multi-national mushers, handlers and spectators, would always be paramount in her memory.

In addition to the sounds of the Iditarod, she was also astounded by the friendliness, comradery and genuine kindness of the gregarious group she came to think of as 'the people of the Iditarod.' Not only the mushers, but their support group – trainers, handlers, the Iditarod committee, sponsors, volunteers, and a multitude of others – enable *The Last Great Race* to become a tremendously successful reality, year after year after year. People of the north, Andi was learning, looked after each other. That was one of the reasons she loved the country so very much; you could always count on your neighbour and friends to come to your assistance in times of need, which was a quality sorely lacking amongst big city dwellers.

North had already begun to pull equipment out of the truck's various storage compartments. Andi grabbed a sleeping bag and North's small duffel bag of personal items and clothes, adding them to the axe, sheathed hunting knife, snowshoes, and bags of emerald green dog jackets, booties, and belly warmers already lying next to the racing sled.

"Have you decided how many dogs you're going to start with today?" Andi asked. Once away from the starting line, a musher was not permitted to introduce another dog to his string, and ultimately ended up with a dozen or fewer in harness by the end of the race. Race rules stipulated that at least six dogs must be on the towline when the team passed under the Burled Arch in Nome, the traditional finish line.

"Yup. It seems like everyone else is starting with sixteen, so I'll do the same. I'm putting Kia and Weasel in lead, and Nanuk and Suka in swing. Duska and Chica will start in wheel. I'm going to harness all of my original dogs, too – they deserve a chance at this as much as I do, after what happened." Well-trained sled dogs required a huge investment in a musher's time and effort, and were normally trained for specific tasks and positions. Lead dogs run in the front, and generally must be both intelligent and fast; mushers only use spoken commands to direct the dogs, and at times there appears to be ESP between a musher and a well-trained lead. Swing dogs run behind the leaders and help 'swing' the team in turns or corners, and wheel dogs, who tend to be heavier than the other dogs, are positioned directly in front of the sled and pull it out and around corners or trees.

"They certainly do deserve a chance at this," Andi agreed, thinking about Juno, North's treasured lead dog who lost his life in the senseless massacre at North's kennel. Juno would have been a powerful asset to the team today.

Eddie lugged the full cooler of warm dog food over and set it next to the sled, then made a second trip for the large metal cooker and pot, dog bowls and the long ladle used to scoop the food into the bowls. North would need all of the items to feed the dogs while on the trail. HEET, a liquid fuel, is poured into the bottom of the vented cooker and ignited, usually with a little straw thrown it to act as wicking. The aluminum pot, filled with snow or water, is then inserted into the cooker to warm. North would put the hot water to a variety of uses, such as making tea or instant coffee, warming his own frozen, sealed meals and drinks, and adding it to an insulated cooler of frozen meat and fat for the dogs. When the meat was thawed he would ladle servings into the dog bowls and add a cup or two of dry kibble.

Nine of the Canadian Eskimo dogs that North would hook to his sled today were from his original kennel, and had been with him for four years; Kia, Nanuk, Suka, Duska, Togo, Chinook, Ikkuma, Mika and

Chance. The balance of his team would be made up of new additions to his kennel – purebred Canadian Eskimo dogs he had purchased over the past two years. He had spent long, hard months of training to incorporate them into his team, as well as exercising abundant patience, something he never ran short of.

The only new member of his team that hadn't needed extensive training was Toffee. An exceptionally smart, four-year-old lead dog, Toffee had been raced by one of the few Canadian Eskimo Dog breeders in the world, and had come to his kennel fully trained. Toffee had cost him more than he cared to admit, even to himself, but she was worth every penny.

In 1995 a vicious, senseless shooting took the lives of three of North's prized dogs. It was a hard hit to his new kennel. The perpetrator of the gruesome killing had never been brought to justice, but North and Andi had a pretty good idea who was responsible. If they were right in their assumption that the late Henrik Bruller, Pivot Lake Diamond Mine's Project Manager and architect of the diamond smuggling ring, was behind the killing, the man had already met his own just demise. The loss of three fine, highly trained dogs had not only dampened North's hopes and dreams of competing in the 1997 Iditarod, but his breeding program as well.

While Andi finished unloading the truck, North sorted through the equipment and supplies. He gave everything a final inspection, marking each item off his checklist. Then he began to pack, the mound of food and equipment sitting on the snow gradually disappearing into the sled bag. When the sled bag was packed, North went back to the truck for one final item – his rifle – which also disappeared inside the sled bag. Eddie secured the cooler of warm dog food on the back of the sled under the seat, and the packing was done.

At 9:30 they began to ready the team. Eddie and Andi helped North put on the dogs' little green booties, fasten sixteen harnesses, and hook each rambunctious, eager animal to its designated position on the towline, or gangline as it was also called. A neckline was attached to each collar, then to the gangline, and a tugline ran from each harness to fasten behind the dog, securing each animal to two points on the long main gangline.

And then it was time to head to the starting line. North trotted behind the sled, with Eddie and Andi flanking the team, holding back the lunging, yapping dogs. Qannik, wearing her own pink booties and matching collar, trotted at Andi's side. The short trip to the starting line was one of the longest of North's life.

Andi and North said their last brief good bye as North waited in the starting lineup. He hugged her, kissed her and held her close. She clung to him, struggling to hide her fear and sorrow; she didn't want North's last memory of her to be of red-rimmed eyes and tears.

Flocks of people thronged the street, hovering around the start line, though not nearly as many as at the Ceremonial Start in Anchorage the day before. Neither were they quite as loud as they cheered for their favourite musher and team. Cameras still flashed, and reporters once again attempted to get a few last words from some of the departing mushers – the most popular and famous of the bunch.

At 10:17, following the departure of the first eight teams, it was North's turn to yell "*Hike!*" Andi and Eddie released the screaming, straining dogs. They leaped ahead, frantic to run. North ran beside the sled for a few seconds before hopping on the runners. He lifted a hand in farewell, a jaunty grin on his face, and then he was gone.

"I'm going to head back to the dog lot," Eddie said, turning away a few seconds later. "I'll start cleaning up and get the dogs ready to go."

Andi nodded, not trusting herself to speak and unable to draw more than a shallow breath. She stood rooted in place, her burning eyes boring into North's retreating back, reluctant to let him go. Qannik whined softly and nuzzled his mistress' gloved hand.

Musher number ten was pulling ahead, positioning at the starting line. Andi backed away, Qannik shadowing her every step. When

North's bright green parka disappeared from sight, Andi could no longer hold back her tears. She dropped to her knees and wrapped her arms around Qannik's soft, white neck. She closed her eyes and buried her face in her fur, drenching it with tears.

Had she betrayed the man she loved, she wondered for the hundredth time? Should she have said something? Told him about the black shadow of death that hovered over their lives? Told him about the cloying stench, the sweet, fetid odour of death that no amount of perfume could mask? She shivered, the horrific memories chilling her to the bone.

Her eyes were closed, yet she could still see the nauseating colour swirling before her eyes.

White and red. White and red.

Snow and blood. Snow and blood.

Andi Ruben said a silent prayer. *Please God. Please, please don't let it be North's blood.*

NINE

His world revolved around sixteen strong, eager dogs, a heavily loaded sled, and a biting wind in his face; an hour after his emotional send-off from Willow, North's mind focused on nothing but those three things. He was living his dream, running the Iditarod.

Checkpoints ran through his mind – the strange, unfamiliar names he had committed to memory: Knik, Yentna Station, Skwentna, Finger Lake, Rainy Pass, Rohn Roadhouse, Nikolai, McGrath, Takotna, Ophir, Iditarod, Shageluk, Anvik, Grayling, Eagle Island, Kaltag, Unalakleet, Shaktoolik, Koyuk, Elim, White Mountain, Safety, and finally Nome.

The checkpoints became little pieces of heaven, a place to sometimes visit with other mushers or find a steaming hot cup of coffee and its welcomed jolt of caffeine, or perhaps a hot meal. The mushers' drop bags containing supplies of dog and human food, HEET, spare equipment and sometimes even spare sleds had been positioned at the checkpoints about three weeks prior to the race by the Iditarod Air Force. Straw, used for dog bedding, was also available at most of the checkpoints, and some mushers even carried an armload or two tied to the top of their sled to use while camping on the trail.

For years North had fantasized about finishing the Iditarod and crossing the finish line in Nome. In his dreams, he passed beneath the famous Burled Arch amid a fanfare of flashing cameras and cheering spectators. He had visited the city of Nome years ago, and had stood in awe beneath the five-thousand-pound arch. Shaped from a single massive spruce log, it had been airlifted from Fairbanks to Nome in 1974. Volunteers had inscribed the words 'End of Iditarod Dog Race' on it, as well as the words 'Anchorage' on one end, 'Nome' on the other, and '1049 Miles'. Each season it was carefully moved from its summer resting place and placed over the finish line.

North allowed his team to run at will for the first few miles, and they were overjoyed to find themselves unfettered and free to test their power and seemingly endless endurance. The sky was clear, the sun shining, and the lead dogs followed the trail unerringly, needing little guidance from their master. The day had warmed to a mild minus ten Fahrenheit, and mushing conditions were perfect. North's mind was left to pursue its own race, slipping between checkpoints and gear and back again. Did he have everything he'd need until he reached the next checkpoint? Had he packed the spare batteries for his headlamp? A repair kit and spare runner plastic? Did he have his sleeping bag, the axe, hand warmers, and extra necklines and tugs? Had he packed enough booties, dog food and HEET? The list was endless.

North had spent hour upon hour over the past ten years reading everything he could get his hands on about the Iditarod, but nothing had prepared him for the horror stories he'd heard during the past week. Nobody wrote about those. It seemed that a rookie was doomed to hear the dire stories of disaster and death first-hand from those seasoned mushers who had run the long, demanding trail time and time again. Their grim tales had left a shadow – no, a *wall,* of doubt in his mind – was he really ready? Could he and his dogs endure the hardships they would surely encounter over the next eleven, twelve or thirteen days? He'd heard that some mushers actually lost their minds somewhere between Knik and Nome. And sometimes dogs died on the trail, trampled by an incensed moose, or dropping like a rock, cheated by their own weak hearts.

He tore his mind from thoughts of potential disaster and sank to the chair he'd attached to the back of the sled's runners. The chair's light aluminum frame housed the metal Coleman cooler. His snowshoes, inserted into specially designed slots in the chair frame, stood upright to form a makeshift backrest. A few mushers stood on their sled runners the entire race, but North knew he'd be grateful for the opportunity to rest his legs and feet.

He settled on the chair's padded seat and studied the rhythmic movements of his team's shoulders, their sinewy muscles rippling beneath glossy, thick fur. They pulled the racing sled effortlessly, sixteen bushy tails curled high in pure joy, happy to be doing what they loved best. His eyes rested briefly on his lead dogs, Kia and Weasel. He didn't know it yet, but during the coming days the two dogs would prove to be his savior, their instincts, intelligence and determination bailing him out of trouble time and time again. In the unlikely event that both Kia and Weasel became injured, he'd hitched two additional lead dogs to his sled today – Toffee and Kodiak. The compliant pair were presently content to run mid-team.

North knew that his sled dogs ran about ten miles per hour, and estimated it would take him approximately one hour and fifteen minutes to reach Knik, the next checkpoint on the trail, only fourteen miles from Willow. The distances between checkpoints were always measured in miles, given that the United States used the Imperial system of measurement. He, however, being Canadian, was accustomed to the Metric system, and found himself automatically trying to convert miles to kilometers and degrees Fahrenheit to Celsius; the trail from Anchorage to Nome was one thousand forty-nine miles, or just a little less than seventeen hundred kilometers. To make it easier on himself, North decided to think like an Alaskan for the duration of his time in the land known as 'The Last Frontier' – in miles, and degrees Fahrenheit.

Knik checkpoint, once a small mining community, was now nothing more than a one-cabin ghost town but on race day it buzzed with activity. Race enthusiasts and the media travelled from Anchorage or Willow by snowmobile or ski-equipped aircraft to give the mushers a final enthusiastic send-off. North stopped only long enough to sign the check-in sheet. Mushers were required to sign in at each checkpoint on the race route, to document their arrival.

The morning was still clear and cold, the dogs barely warmed up after their short run from Willow. They were screaming to run, leaping and straining against their harnesses. When North pulled the snow hook and yelled '*Hike!*' the sled bounded forward, its weight little burden for the combined pulling force of the strong team.

Eight mushers and approximately 125 sled dogs had already passed this way before them, and North's team was eager to follow their scent. A well-conditioned sled dog could easily run for periods of four to five hours, excluding short breaks, before requiring a meal and a longer four-to-five-hour rest. Some mushers ran their teams for considerably longer periods. Snow conditions and terrain, especially climbing, certainly affected their endurance, which was what concerned North more than anything. The terrain around Inuvik was mostly barren flatland, and his dogs weren't accustomed to hard climbing. They would, unfortunately, be doing a lot of it in the next three or four days. Their first, and possibly hardest challenge lay directly ahead – the rugged, imposing Alaska Range. It loomed to the east, about one hundred miles from Anchorage. Majestic Mount McKinley, the highest peak in North America at over 20,000 feet, rose before them, its snow-capped peaks deadly, magical and seductive. Even from a distance, the mountain range looked massive. It looked imposing, and utterly impossible.

Kia and Weasel needed no guidance. They followed the easy trail, packed down and clearly delineated by the paws and runners of the teams who ran ahead of them. North's mind was left free to wander, and he considered the imposing mountain range ahead, its tall white peaks in sharp contrast to the deep blue sky. There was no easy way around it; the Alaskan interior and Bering Sea coast lay beyond the range's blustery peaks and deep valleys.

The initial day and first hundred miles of the race between Willow and Skwentna took the mushers through an area known as 'Moose Alley', so named due to its heavy population of the massive beasts. When the ground is thick with snow, the moose had been known to use the pre-existing trails while foraging for food, often causing hazards for the dog teams. North's first impression was that Moose Alley didn't live up to its dire reputation. In fact, the soft, deep, unblemished snow and frosted evergreens looked like the background for a Hallmark Christmas card. He'd heard the tragic story more than once, though, about a female musher who had been attacked in the alley twelve years prior. The musher made a sharp turn and encountered a pregnant moose on the trail. The cow, taken by surprise, had attacked the team, killing two sled dogs and seriously injuring six others before another musher arrived twenty minutes later and was able to shoot it. That same year, three other teams had been chased off the trail by incensed moose. North stayed alert, determined to avoid any such encounter.

The stretch from Knik to Yentna Station was just over fifty miles. The trail was in constant use all winter by local mushers and snowmobilers, and was packed down and even rutted in places. The first thirty miles was an easy run over low evergreen and birch studded hills and a string of open swamps, where most mushers stopped briefly to snack and rest the dogs. North pulled up near a couple other teams. He'd met all of the contestants during the pre-race festivities over the past weeks, but couldn't put a name to their familiar faces.

The temperature had risen considerably during the day, and the sun shone bright and warm in the clear sky. Now that the wind was out of his face, North felt the heat of the sun and knew the dogs could too. Their heavy double coats could easily cause them to overheat on the trail, even in sub-zero temperatures. Depending on the weather, mushers were often forced to rest during the day, and run during the colder hours of night. He decided to search for a sheltered spot, feed the dogs and give them a break out of the heat of the day.

He pushed on, crossing the swamp and another lake before hitting a large, lightly treed area. The mixed stand of birch and cottonwood, though their branches were leafless, afforded a measure of protection from the sun. Another musher had already settled his dogs in the area, and was napping himself, and North opted to do the same. Leaving enough space between the teams to avoid any altercation, he swiftly tied the sled to a tree trunk and unhooked the dogs from the gangline, giving them more freedom of movement. He looked each dog over quickly, examining paws and palpitating shoulders for signs of soreness, then slid on their insulated jackets, something he would do every time they stopped to camp on the trail, or slept at a checkpoint.

The dogs eagerly gobbled down a ration of warm food then curled up in shallow hollows they pawed into the soft snow. With feathered tails brushing their cold, black noses they closed their eyes and drifted to sleep. North made a mental note to try and carry a chunk of straw with him when he left the next checkpoint, especially when he hit the cold interior.

He wolfed down a sandwich and muffin, washed down with a few gulps of strong, tepid coffee from his thermos, then spread his sleeping bag out in a patch of sunlight next to the sled. He crawled in, pulled the bag's goose down hood over his head, and dropped into oblivion for a few hours.

While North was sleeping, several mushers passed by on their way to Yentna Station. His dogs acknowledged their arrival with low growls and grumbles, then fell back to quiet slumber. It was late afternoon by the time he roused them again, and he was alone in the stand of trees. The sun had reached its apex and was covered by a veil of high, thin cloud, the air noticeably cooler again. After relieving himself against a scraggly spruce tree, he wolfed down a protein bar, gave the dogs a snack and fastened their harnesses to the gangline.

The dogs, after their long rest, were recuperated and eager to run again. Kia and Weasel set a brisk pace. As the miles fell behind them, North noticed that the snow began to deepen; there was much more than in Willow. He estimated that a good six or seven feet of the white stuff had fallen over the winter. He wasn't out of moose country yet – the infamous 'Moose Alley' extended all the way to Skwentna; he would have to remain especially vigilant when evening approached, and was glad that he'd had a jolt of caffeine. An encounter with an angry thousand-pound moose was the very last thing he needed. He'd made a promise to his wife to come home in once piece, and he fully intended to do just that.

The temperature continued to fall as he pushed through the late afternoon and evening, stopping only for a short break to snack the dogs, check paws and replace a few little green booties that were showing signs of wear. He let his lead dogs set their own pace, neither pushing them nor holding them back, and was happy enough with their speed. Nobody had passed him yet, which meant he couldn't be running too slowly in comparison to the other mushers.

Only once did he spy a moose, half hidden in the shadow of a copse of trees. The lone animal was well off the trail and posed no threat, merely turning a disinterested gaze as he and his team glided by. Nevertheless, he hoped he didn't come across any more of the massive beasts.

The trail continued to run through the trees for a few miles before beginning a slow descent to the heavily-treed Susitna River bottom, where they encountered one of the first real challenges of the day. The trail narrowed and twisted across a series of small, steeply banked channels before dropping fifteen feet to the river bottom. Someone had left the main trail, opting to weave their own way down the steep embankment; by the looks of the marks left in the snow, the musher and his sled had taken a nasty spill at the bottom. North followed the main trail, letting his trusty leads pick their sure-footed way down the steep drop to the river, glad that they had passed this obstacle during the last daylight hours.

An unexpected surprise met him on the winding, frozen Susitna River. Dozens of smoky bonfires blazed along the river's path, their flames bright and cheery in the failing light. Around each was clustered a handful of avid race fans and their brightly coloured snowmobiles. Their warmth and exuberance surprised North. Somehow, he hadn't expected to see so many faces this deep in the wilderness. They cheered and waved and pointed cameras in his direction, so he stopped for a few seconds to exchange quick greetings and pose for a picture with his team. The Alaskans seemed delighted and enthralled with his uncommon Canadian sled dogs.

He left the Susitna greeting committee behind, and continued along the river for a short stretch before veering off to follow the wider Yenta River. He was, by his best estimate, only an hour from the Yentna Station checkpoint. As the miles dropped behind them, the sun dipped behind the mountains. North reached into his sled bag and pulled out his headlamp, relieved that he'd remembered to put it on top of the gear at his last stop. He slipped the unit over his wool hat, adjusting the band so it fit snuggly, and tested the light; it shone from the middle of his forehead like an alien third eye, but was practical and easier than carrying a lantern or flashlight. He snapped the light off again to conserve its batteries, although he'd already stashed spares in an inner pocket of his parka, a trick he'd learned years ago after having a headlamp suddenly go dead on a dark trail. He'd had to fumble through his gear blindly for spare batteries, cursing his own stupidity. Since that day he'd made a mental note to always have his headlamp at hand *before* it got dark, and to keep a few batteries in his pocket. He'd definitely learned that lesson the hard way.

He didn't see the brightly lit Yentna Station checkpoint until he was almost upon it. Situated just around a bend in the river, the station was a popular tourist draw for wilderness enthusiasts. Today it was a beehive of activity, with several teams camped along the riverbank.

North signed in and presented his Veterinarian Notebook, usually just called the 'vet book', for inspection, then gladly accepted a cup of steaming coffee while the vet examined his team. At each checkpoint, mushers were required to present his or her vet book for examination by the veterinarian. Once in a while, if a musher was only very briefly passing in and out of a checkpoint, and at the discretion of the vet, a team may get passed through without an exam. It was regular practice, though, for a vet to examine each dog at each checkpoint, and make a notation in the musher's book to document the team's health along the trail. If a musher loses his vet book, he can't continue the race. If he forgets it at a checkpoint, he must return and retrieve the book, wasting valuable time. North's vet book was securely zipped in one of his parka's big pockets.

Unlike some mushers, North didn't begrudge the extra time spent waiting for the vet checks to be completed; his dog's good health and well-being was of utmost importance to him, and vital if he hoped to complete the gruelling race. Ten minutes after arriving at the checkpoint, with his dogs declared to be in perfect health, he pulled the sled's snow hook and continued his journey, bound for the next checkpoint – Skwentna.

TEN

The Skwentna checkpoint lay thirty-five miles ahead over trail that was reported to be some of the easiest in the race. The sky was clear of clouds and a million stars twinkled overhead, but the moon had not yet risen; when North switched off his headlamp, he could barely make out the shapes of his lead dogs. He flicked the light back on, more for his benefit than that of his team. Even without the assistance of his headlamp's bobbing beam, North knew the dogs would follow the dark trail unerringly. He trusted their keen sense of smell and sharp night vision. He, on the other hand, felt entirely too alone ... too *vulnerable* ... running a strange route in total darkness.

The trail followed the Yentna and Skwentna rivers and was an easy, uneventful run, as promised. Just after midnight on the first day of the race, North pulled into the checkpoint. They'd run a long stretch, and although it wasn't difficult, he regretted not stopping earlier and camping somewhere along the trail.

The tiny community of Skwentna was only forty minutes by air from Anchorage, making the checkpoint a favourite for the media, as well as friends and spectators, who flew in to follow the progress of the race. It was one of their last opportunities to report live coverage, and North had been warned that, especially during daylight hours, the checkpoint would be teeming with reporters and photographers itching to get an exclusive interview. Luckily, either the late hour or plunging mercury had kept the reporters asleep or indoors. He hoped he'd be able to slip away in the pre-dawn hours without arousing their interest.

The checkpoint cabin was located atop the high riverbank, light pouring from its two small front windows and smoke from its chimney. The time of day, or night, was meaningless on the Iditarod trail, and North wasn't surprised to find the checkpoint buzzing with activity. By the glow of the cabin lights and several small bonfires, he saw a half dozen teams bedded down on the frozen river, stretched out in long, parallel lines. Each dog was curled up on its own straw bed, and for the most part they ignored the new-comers. Although mushers, veterinarians and race volunteers went about the business of delivering straw and drop bags, examining dogs, cooking food, repacking sled bags or any one of the other hundred necessary tasks, they did so unobtrusively and in quiet tones. It helped that the abundant layer of snow seemed to absorb all sound, cushioning its sharp corners and rendering it faint and muted.

He stopped his team alongside a line of dogs bedded down on the ice and set the snow hook. His dogs were due a warm meal and a good five hours of sleep, and so was he. His stomach grumbled, reminding him he hadn't eaten for hours. The thought of another frozen bacon and egg sandwich held little appeal though, and he hoped the rumours were true and a pot of something hot and filling would be bubbling on the cabin stove.

North had just begun the task of releasing the dogs from the gangline when a squat figure suddenly appeared by his side. He wore a fur hat, and his mukluks were covered in silver-tipped, long brown fur that looked like it had once graced a grizzly bear's hide. "Welcome to Skwentna," the stranger said. His words were clipped, his voice low. "Don't think I've seen you around before." He held a small wooden clipboard in one hand, its bottom edge resting on his rotund belly.

"No, you haven't. I'm a rookie," North chuckled. "North Ruben."

"Ah, Ruben," the man, evidently a checker, muttered. He peered at the clipboard illuminated by his headlamp. "Canadian, right?"

"Yup, that's me."

"You the one running those funny Eskimo dogs?"

"Yup, that would be me."

"Heard about them. Nobody's ever raced them kind of dogs in Alaska before."

"That's probably right. We're making history, aren't we?" North laughed.

"So, from the looks of it you're staying a while?" His words were more a question than a statement.

"Yes, my dogs need food and a rest, and I need to pick up my drop bag."

"I'll send the vet down and someone with your bag and a load of straw. It's a fairly long hike. The name's Pearson." His chest seemed to inflate against the parka's already strained front zipper, then he jabbed a thumb in the direction of the cabin. "That's my cabin up there. Me and the wife been Skwentna checkers the past thirty years." His chest seemed to rise even higher, if that was at all possible. "I'm the postmaster hereabouts, too."

"Pleased to meet you Mr. Pearson," North smiled, "and I thank you for your help. Any chance of getting a bite of something hot to eat tonight, too?"

A smile crossed the taciturn man's lips for the first time. "You bet. Our Skwentna Sweeties have a hot pot on the stove day and night, and a table busting with more pies and cakes than you've ever seen." He laughed and patted his ample belly. "Trust me, they're pretty damn good cooks."

"Well I'm sold," North grinned. "I'll be up as soon as I get the dogs settled."

Pearson left, melding into the night as silently as he had appeared. North returned to his task, and had just released the last dog when his supplies and a generous bundle of straw arrived. He thanked the helper and distributed an armful of fresh, clean bedding to each dog. They were tired, and quieter than normal, but didn't waste any time wolfing down the last of the cooked food he dished out.

He left the dogs pawing and nosing their straw into a satisfactory bed and trudged up the steep trail to the cabin. The climb was well worth the effort; his own mother wouldn't have fussed over him more, and he made short work of two heaping bowls of hot moose stew, half a dozen baking powder biscuits and two slices of blueberry pie with only slightly more table manners than his mutts. When his stomach couldn't hold another bite, he poured another cup of coffee and, with the permission of the postmaster's waiflike wife, poured a couple of cups into his thermos. He spent ten minutes talking with the helpers and a few other mushers; he'd hoping to run into Mats, but there was no sign of the young Norwegian. It wasn't easy to leave the warmth and hospitality of the cabin in exchange for his cold campsite, but the arduous task of preparing another batch of dog food had to be tackled before he slept. If he didn't, he'd have no chance of slipping away in the morning without the team howling their displeasure and hunger.

Back at the campsite he dipped some water from a hole in the ice purposely kept open for the mushers, and set about cooking dog food. He dumped enough frozen meat and fat into the cooler for two meals, and set the pot of water on the cooker to heat. While the water warmed, he sorted through his drop bag and transferred the new supplies to his sled, then checked over every inch of harness and line for wear before turning to the sled and runners. He was glad to find everything still in perfect condition.

When the water was hot he poured it over the dog food in the cooler, then spread his sleeping bag out over a cushion of straw next to the closest bonfire and zipped himself in. His last conscious thoughts were of his bride. Was she lying in her comfortable, warm bed back in Nome, thinking about him? His burning, tired eyes stared into the fire's flickering red and orange flames, but his mind registered glimmering green eyes, flawless pale skin and lush, pink lips. Within minutes he slipped into deep, dreamless sleep.

Andi lay awake, staring at the dot of light that had forced its way between the drawn curtains to land on the pale blue wall at the foot of her bed. Not *her* bed; *the Shannon's guest bed.* She'd been tossing and turning for over an hour, her over-exhausted mind worrying about her husband's fate one minute, then furious that he'd talked her into staying with his old colleague from Toronto the next. Tom Shannon and his wife, Pat, were nice enough people, and certainly welcoming, but Andi felt the situation decidedly uncomfortable.

She was bone tired, but her eyes refused to close, though it was past midnight and she'd been awake since before 6 am. North's departure had drained her, sucking every last bit of energy she'd had on reserve. It had been all she could do to help Eddie pack up the bits and pieces of spare equipment North had left behind and then load the four remaining dogs into the truck.

Eddie had followed her back to Anchorage in his buddy's Ford. His friends were waiting for him at JavaGenie when they parked outside the coffee house.

"Well, good luck, Andi," Eddie said when they stood on the sidewalk saying their goodbyes. "Are you sure you're going to be alright getting the dogs settled at the new place?"

"Yes, of course," Andi said more bravely than she felt. "Thanks for all of your help these past few days, Eddie. We appreciate it so much."

"Well I'd better get going then. These guys want to hit the road."

"You drive safely and phone me when you get to our place. There're meals in the freezer and the pantry is full so just help yourself. You've got that phone number North gave you? Where I'll be staying?"

"Yes, I put it in my wallet. Don't worry about anything. I'll look after your place until you get back."

Andi gave Eddie a warm hug. "Here come your friends. I'll talk to you soon."

She waved the young trio off, then went into the coffee shop for a tall coffee to go before tackling the rather unnerving task of ensconcing herself and four sled dogs at a stranger's home. "Damn you, North," she cursed under her breath while she waited in line, drawing an indignant look from an elderly couple enjoying a coffee and scone.

She sat in the truck for a few minutes, sipping her coffee and steadying her nerves. By the time she arrived at the Shannon's home, she'd come up with a plan. She'd spend a night or two with the childless couple, but look for other accommodation – somewhere she wouldn't feel like she was being *babysat*. After all, her husband wasn't about to pop back to check on her, and what he didn't know, wouldn't hurt him.

North slipped away from Skwentna before dawn the next morning, his departure undetected save the sleepy, annoyed stares of neighbouring sled dogs disturbed from their slumber. Several mushers had left during the night, and others had arrived. He spotted the bright pink jackets Becky Singleton's sleeping dogs wore, but the petite, blond musher was nowhere in sight, and neither was his new friend, Mats Pederson.

The run to the next checkpoint, Finger Lake, was about forty-five miles and North planned to do it in one go, stopping twice for short breaks. Dawn was still three hours away, and once again his headlamp guided their way, its narrow beam lighting up small slivers of vast, dark wilderness. The trail followed the Skwentna River for a few miles, then ran up its left bank. They began a gradual uphill climb that would eventually lead them to Finger Lake, weaving through swamps and climbing up heavily wooded hills. After two hours North stopped the team and gave them a snack. He spent a few minutes massaging shoulders and legs, removed their booties and checked their feet and gave the gangline a cursory inspection. He stuffed yesterday's last sandwich and muffin into an inside pocket of his parka, hoping they would thaw out enough to be edible in an hour or two, and drank the dregs of last night's coffee from his thermos.

The trail continued to climb, crossing creeks and down through swamps. The night sky lightened so slowly North's mind barely registered the fact he could see the trail without the help of his headlamp. He crossed a small lake, the rising sun at his back, and the great Alaska Range looming ahead. The majestic, rugged mountains rose high over the dark green evergreens encircling the lake, their snow-covered slopes glowing an otherworldly, muted shade of violet-pink in dawn's first intense rays.

Finger Lake still lay an hour away when North stopped in a meadow to snack the dogs for the second time. The sun had already pushed its way into the sky; its warmth was more noticeable when he knelt beside the dogs, checking paws and massaging muscles. He was still at the task when the mutts started to whine. They turned their heads to stare back down the trail, ear alert and noses in the air. North stood up and saw another team emerging from the woods. He'd stopped at a widening of the trail, the snow trampled down for twenty or thirty feet on each side of it; others passing this way had evidently rested here as well. As the newcomer approached, North's team began to stir, barking and talking, excited to see another sign of life after four hours alone on the trail. The musher, an old-timer North remembered meeting at the banquet, flew by without stopping, urging his team on when they showed signs of slowing. He raised a hand in greeting and disappeared into the woods on the other side of the meadow.

It wasn't yet noon when North slid into Finger Lake, but the sun was already strong and warm; in another hour he would have had to remove the dogs' jackets. The checkpoint was, for lack of a better word, a zoo. He found a spot in the dog lot to bed down the team, but just barely. It appeared that every musher traveling before him had decided to make a long stop in Finger Lake too, and he knew why.

"This is a goddamn gong show," a growly voice muttered. North looked up and into a pair of icy, clear blue eyes. They peered from a weathered, lined face covered in a week's worth of grey stubble. "I never seen anything like this before," the old musher grumbled.

"I thought it would be busy here, but I didn't expect *that!*" North waved his gloved hand at an espresso stand set up fifty feet from the dog lot.

"Yeah, what the hell do we need that for? Probably just to make those city reporters happy." His tired blue eyes glared at the long row of ski-equipped planes lined up beside the ice-strip, which also happened to be just on the other side of the dog lot. North stood next to the old-timer, taking in the activity and sharing the old man's sentiment. Spectators dotted the lake like ants. Reporters had set up mobile stations and stuck microphones into the faces of anyone who had the misfortune to pass by. Some threaded their way through the resting dogs and mushers, trailing photographers laden with heavy, bulky cameras behind them.

"If I'd known it was going to be this bad, I would've stopped on the trail before I got here," North muttered. "I'll never get any sleep."

"Nope, you sure won't, sonny. Bruce Litman," the musher said with a nod.

"North Ruben."

"I see you're the one with those Eskimo dogs. Rookie from Canada, right?"

"Yup," North said with a sigh of resignation. If for nothing else, he would evidently be remembered for his unusual dogs.

Bruce nodded reflectively and eyed North's team for a long minute. "Watch out for the gorge," he warned.

"I've heard about it. You're talking about the Happy Valley Gorge, right?"

"Uh huh. Slow down before you hit it and stomp on your brake," the old timer warned.

"Okay, I'll watch for it. Thanks for the tip."

"Well, I'm gonna get my dogs settled and try to get a few winks myself," Bruce said, his last words all but drowned out by the whine of another approaching Cessna. He swore under his breath, a long string of expletives that made North's brow creep up, then turned to his dogs.

North began his long, laborious routine: check in, present vet book, put the dogs on the tether line, vet examination, put on their jackets, remove little green booties, check their paws, apply ointment if needed, replace booties, feed them, bed them down in piles of straw, cook up a new batch of food. The tasks were endless and exhausting.

It was well after 1 pm when North finally found time to indulge himself. He peered at Bruce intently until he was satisfied that the old curmudgeon, who had stretched out beside his sled, was fast asleep. Then he dug deep into a pocket for the small wad of cash he carried, and headed over to the espresso stand, intent on a double, or maybe even two.

ELEVEN

The stop at Finger Lake was a disaster. Aircraft landed and took off throughout the afternoon, buzzing by less than fifty feet from where North and the dogs were attempting to sleep. Mushers arrived and departed amongst a chorus of canine greetings. Neither North nor his mutts got more than a couple hours of sleep during their five-hour stop. He was hooking the team to the gangline and feeling more than a little disgruntled when he was ambushed by a rosy cheeked overachiever from one of the biggest U.S. television networks. The young reporter dove right in and began bombarding North with questions while his photographer slunk around, panning a heavy video camera over his dogs, sled, equipment and himself.

"Can you tell us something about your dogs, Mr. Ruben?" The young man said, holding a microphone to North's face.

"They're purebred Canadian Eskimo Dogs," North replied, resigned to the fact that he'd have to spend a few minutes with the media. Any exposure for the dying dog breed would be great, and because of the anniversary celebrations, there was a chance that the rest of the world might become aware of the plight of the Canadian Eskimo Dog. "I've got twenty-four of them, and am starting my own breeding program in Inuvik."

"I hear there's some speculation between the other mushers about whether or not your dogs can handle this race. Do you care to comment?"

"Of course they can handle it," North spat, realizing too late that his words may have come out just a bit too sharp. He took a breath and quickly reorganized his thoughts. "I've been working with Canadian Eskimo Dogs all my life," he continued in a steady voice, "and my father and grandfather before me did too. Canadian Eskimo Dogs are a strong, big-hearted breed with more stamina than most."

The reporter smiled encouragingly. "You're a rookie, correct?"

"Yes, I am."

"How are you finding the trail so far? Any problems out there you'd like to share with our audience?"

"No problems at all. So far the trails have been not much more difficult than the ones I run every day in Inuvik."

"The next leg to Rainy Pass is always a tough one. Are you ready for it?"

"Absolutely," North grinned. "I've had some coaching from one of the more experienced mushers, so I don't think I'll have a problem."

"Can you see yourself winning this race, Mr. Ruben?"

North hesitated, then looked directly into the camera lens. Its operator zoomed in on North's face. "I've dreamed about racing in the Iditarod all of my life," he said solemnly. "Whether I pass under the Burled Arch first, or claim the Red Lantern, doesn't really matter. What matters is that I'm thrilled to be here, and I'm honoured to join the few brave men and women who can call themselves Iditarod mushers. I'm going to run the best race of my life, and wish each and every competitor and team a safe trip to Nome."

The reporter looked at North speculatively, about to ask another question.

"Thanks for talking with me," North grinned broadly and waved at the camera, "but now I have a race to run. See you in Nome!" He turned away from the camera and returned to the task of hooking up the dogs. What he didn't know was that the network's editor would be taken with the short interview and footage on the Canadian rookie, and the piece would be the following day's lead story on Iditarod Silver Anniversary coverage. Within hours, a million viewers around the world would become entranced by North Ruben's captivating, slightly snaggle-toothed grin and his team of rare and endangered Canadian Eskimo Dogs.

When he hit the trail again it was slightly past 4 pm and the mercury was beginning to plunge. Both man and beast were tired and cranky, which was damn unlucky since the run to Rainy Pass was heralded to be a tough one. He'd been warned more than once about the Happy River Gorge, or Happy Canyon as some called it. North was confident of his own ability and his team's sure-footedness, though, and was mentally prepared for whatever the trail would throw at them. If all went according to plan, the run, which normally took between four to five hours, would put him into the Rainy Pass checkpoint just before nightfall. He was looking forward to a good meal and four or five hours of uninterrupted sleep.

The trail started out easy enough, running up a small ridge and along a nearby lake before beginning a longer, more challenging climb up a ravine. The dogs pulled hard on the steep and twisting ravine trail, heads down, heavily muscled shoulders straining against their harnesses. Where he could manage it, North jumped from the runners and trotted beside the sled, relieving the team from the burden of his own weight. When they cleared the ravine they ran along a mile long ridge and series of wooded shelves and swamps, very gradually dropping down to a heavily wooded area.

North pulled off the trail to give the dogs a short rest. He gave them each a snack and removed their little green booties, inspected paws, replaced the booties, massaged shoulders and legs and checked the tugs and harnesses, praising and fussing over each dog while he did so. He was rewarded with loving looks from soft, liquid eyes, low whines and the occasional gentle head bump. When the dogs were looked after he tossed a few handfuls of high-energy trail mix into his mouth and did a few jumping-jacks to get his blood circulating. He could feel the first nudge of exhaustion setting in, but was eager to hit the trail again and conquer the upcoming Happy River steps everyone seemed to dread. He was curious to see what all the fuss was about, and more than a little bit cynical about its degree of difficulty. After all, everyone seemed to make it down to the bottom of Happy River Gorge and survive to tell the tale.

The trail continued along the edge of a heavily forested incline and began to drop, becoming narrow and deep and passing through big timber. North slowed the team a little, the old timer's repeated warnings to 'watch your speed on the steps' echoing through his mind. The trail continued to drop and zigzag its way down the slope, twisting and plunging ever downward. North, heeding Bruce's warning, stomped on the brake when they began a headlong, slightly out of control plunge down a particularly steep hill that he thought must be the last of the three dreaded steps. *Piece of cake,* he thought when they reached the bottom unscathed. He released the brake and Kia and Weasel, totally unfazed by the challenging slope, bounded forward at full speed, fourteen willing and eager teammates at their heels.

North relaxed and spent a few seconds formulating the beginning of his own slightly patronizing Happy River Gorge tale in his head. He looked forward to telling whomever he met around the next cup of coffee or bonfire how very easy he'd found the dreaded steps, and grinned at his smug, self-satisfied thoughts. The blissful moment came to an abrupt end when North Ruben, veteran musher and seasoned arctic hunter awoke from his stupor and instantly realized that he'd made a dreadful mistake. Perhaps, even, a life-and-limb threatening mistake. He'd foolishly done what many rookies had done in the past, and would continue to do in the future; he had vastly underestimated the gorge.

'You have to be careful', they'd said. 'Stomp on the brake and watch your speed,' they'd warned. 'Watch your ass!' a particularly cynical old timer had advised, shaking a gnarled finger in his face. Nothing he'd heard, though, had really prepared North Ruben for his faceoff with Happy Canyon. Kia and Weasel barrelled unchecked toward what looked like the edge of a cliff. Two seconds later, North realized it *was* a cliff ... a damned steep one, and the trail *vanished* over its edge.

North's heart plunged when he saw nothing but dark blue sky over the cliff's white edge. Belatedly, he realized that what he'd moments ago thought was the *end* of the Happy River Steps, was really just the beginning. He prayed, a fleeting, unspoken word to God, that the steps wouldn't be the end of *him.*

Kia and Weasel continued to race toward the very edge of the earth, happy and eager to follow the trail and scent of the teams that had plunged down the precipice before them. North froze. His cheating muscles refused to cooperate with brain tissue that screamed *stop stop stop!* His lead dogs were two or three flying steps from the edge of the gorge when North came out of his stupor and stomped on the brake. The u-shaped metal bar dug in, slowing the sled a little, but not nearly enough for him to gain complete control of the team's downward plunge.

Kia and Weasel swung left and dropped off the face of the earth, followed by the other fourteen dogs in pairs, then the sled and finally their master, who wrapped his clumsy, uncooperative hands around the handlebar and hung on for dear life. Two hundred feet almost vertically below lay the white, frozen expanse of the Happy River. North heard a muffled, indistinct scream, one that sounded like it had passed through a body of water before bubbling to his ears. The terrorized musher didn't realize for some time that the cry of denial he'd heard came from his own tortured lungs.

The dogs had their head – they were in control and he at their mercy. He was merely a passenger along for the ride of his life. Seconds that felt like hours dragged by as the sled plunged headlong down the side of the gorge on the first of the Happy River Steps, nothing but air under its runners for long, nerve-racking seconds. Almost before it began, the narrow trail switched back on itself and the team executed a sharp turn to the right. North felt the sled begin to slide out from under him and threw his weight on the right runner to stabilize it. It wobbled briefly, then settled back onto two runners, pursuing the team along an impossibly narrow bench.

The dogs were running too fast, plunging headlong down the perilous trail, out of control. North hung on, crouched on the runners and clung to the handlebar. He knew he could do nothing to stop them now, and turned his focus to the twisty, steep trail, watching his lead dogs' twitching ears while he let the horror of the Happy River Steps play itself out. His wide, shell-shocked eyes were traitorous though, drawn left to stare stupidly down a sheer fifty-foot drop to the next shelf.

Left again, down the second harrowing step, then right to what would be the third and final step to The Happy River – the scariest step of them all, he remembered grimly. Down they flew, on a trail that instantly grew so narrow that the sled ran on the right runner only, the left flying free through the air. North leaned hard to the right, hugging the uphill side of the trail so tightly that his head and right arm brushed the snowy slope.

He fought a childish urge to close his eyes, hoping, as a scared child may, that if he couldn't see the scary thing it wasn't really there and it couldn't hurt him. For one fleeting second, he was sure he wouldn't survive, plummeting helplessly down the ledge, flailing through the air. No roller coaster or amusement park ride would ever compete with the stomach wrenching, mind shattering fear he experienced in the Happy Valley Gorge. Someone had a hell of a good sense of humour, he thought fleetingly. They should have named it Death Valley Gorge, or Dirty Pants Gorge.

The dogs leapt down from the end of the last step, tugging the willing sled and its passenger freely through the air before stopping of their own accord a few seconds later on the frozen river. North realized he'd stopped breathing at some point during their wild, unchecked descent. He let out a shaky breath and tried to get his bearings, his eyes frozen wide like a deer caught in a headlight. Kia and Weasel grinned at him over the backs of their green jackets, pink tongues hanging from curled black lips. Somehow his two fearless lead dogs had unerringly guided them to the bottom of the gorge, and they appeared quite happy with themselves. And so they should; they'd conquered the steps with no help from their petrified leader.

His legs, North realized when he tried to step off the runners, were nothing more than limp noodles. He swayed and grappled for the sled bag to right himself. The dogs needed a break, and he needed to assess damages. He decided to snack the dogs and reassemble his nerves before carrying on to Rainy Pass. He thought about the small fifth of 'medicinal' brandy wrapped up in a thick sweater somewhere in his bag, and decided this might be a good time to find out where his medicine was.

Everything changed after the gorge. The Happy Canyon was North's wake-up call – it was that point in the race when he realized that just maybe he was in for more than he'd bargained on.

North Ruben knew without a doubt that from hereon in, he'd better be on his very best game.

TWELVE

Anchorage felt flat and cold after the hectic days preceding the start of the Iditarod. The colourful banners still fluttered along Fourth Avenue, but the sidewalks were devoid of the orange crowd-control fencing and masses of people. Bobcats scraped up all of the snow trucked in for the start of the race, and dump trucks carted it away. By Sunday afternoon, the downtown Anchorage streets were once again open to vehicle traffic.

After she'd seen Eddie and his friends on their way back to Inuvik the day before, Andi relocated herself and the remaining four dogs to Tom and Pat Shannon's house. She and North had visited with the Shannons several times during the week leading up to the start of the race, both in their own home and once when they'd met in town for dinner. The couple were exceptionally friendly and welcoming, and the two men had quickly slipped back into their comfortable, old friendship, but Andi wasn't completely pleased with the idea of staying with people she barely knew. Especially with her noisy, rambunctious sled dogs.

North had known Tom for almost twenty years and trusted him to ensure no harm came to his wife during her solitary stay in Anchorage. The two men had met during their first gruelling days at McGill University in Montreal, Quebec, where they were both enrolled in the Faculty of Law. They quickly found common ground in their love of the north, and immediately became fast friends as well as roommates. After they'd passed the bar, they had both, by some small miracle, been recruited by the same prestigious law firm in Toronto, Ontario. Over the course of two years and countless sleepless nights preparing briefs and doing endless hours of grunt work, they both developed an intense dislike for Toronto, which was often called Hogtown, or The Big Smoke, or simply 'TO'. It was the capital city of Ontario, and also one of the most populous cities in Canada. While North had stuck it out in TO for only two years, Tom lasted for over ten before meeting Pat through a mutual friend. Pat was a native Alaskan, and from the moment he'd met her, Tom was smitten. Twelve months later, Tom relocated to Anchorage, where he and Pat soon married and now ran a thriving book store.

Even with the Shannons' warmth and company, Andi was excruciatingly lonely. She felt like she was imposing on the childless couple's privacy, and couldn't shake a lingering feeling of unease. She slept badly the first night, and spent her first two solitary days doing little more than roaming the streets and trying to find alternate accommodation. Twice daily she took the dogs for a long walk, giving them all a chance to romp and run free in one of the city's many parks or greenbelts. The sled dogs were a handful – powerful, strong-minded and mischievous. And, of course, they loved to run. She couldn't handle all four of them at once, and was forced to walk them in pairs, but she didn't mind. Anything to take her mind off her absentee husband.

The Shannons' spacious home and fully fenced grounds were situated on Anchorage's outskirts, and the dogs were free to roam, run, and chase whatever wildlife made the mistake of crossing the fence line. The property's previous owner had built a large shop where Qannik and company slept, comfortable and warm on their padded beds.

If she wasn't walking the dogs, Andi either listened to the daily race reports on the local radio station, APRN, or scanned the few available television channels for race coverage. She knew that North had reached the Skwentna checkpoint late the night before, but hadn't heard an update since then. While the Shannons were at work, she spent hours sitting over extra-large cups of coffee at JavaGenie, scanning the local paper for temporary accommodation for herself and the dogs.

Late Monday afternoon, the day after North's departure, Andi was in the coffee shop for the third time that day. She loved the small café's relaxed, friendly atmosphere, high tables and padded leather stools, and the welcoming aroma of freshly brewed coffee and whatever happened to be baking. She felt more comfortable at JavaGenic than anywhere else in Anchorage, including the Shannons.

The afternoon coffee hour rush was over, and Andi was one of only two customers left in the small café. A familiar waitress around Andi's age stopped at her table and offered to collect her empty cup. "I've seen you in here quite often the past few days," the short, black-haired woman said, a tentative smile on her lips. Her dark eyes were warm but guarded, as though she was perhaps leery of invading her customer's privacy. "Are you here for the Iditarod?"

Andi smiled, welcoming the company and conversation. "Yes, my husband is running," she said. "His first time."

"Oh, my. That must be hard on you." The waitress picked up Andi's cup and gave the already clean table a perfunctory swipe.

Andi nodded vigorously and opened her green eyes dramatically wide. "You can say *that* again. I didn't realize I'd be so nervous about his being out there in the great beyond, all alone."

"Where are you from?"

"Canada. Inuvik, actually."

"Oh, okay. I heard there was someone from the Northwest Territories racing this year. So you're accustomed to the north, at least, and this bloody cold."

Andi laughed. "Oh, yes, we certainly are. We get much worse weather than this. How long have you lived here?"

"Um," the waitress rested her free hand on one ample hip and squinted in concentration for a moment or two. "I guess about thirty years now," she chuckled. "I came for one summer of adventure and never left."

Andi laughed, something she hadn't done for several days. Her face and laugh lines felt stiff and unused. "The north really has a way of growing on you, doesn't it?"

"It certainly does. My name is Rachel, by the way."

"Hi Rachel. I'm Andrea, but everyone calls me Andi."

"Nice to meet you, Andi. So I guess we'll be seeing you around for a few more days. Are you going to head over to Nome for the finish?"

"Yes, I'm only here for another week."

"Staying at the Alaska?"

Andi shook her head, and frowned. "No. My husband has an old friend in town. I'm staying at their place. With four sled dogs, if you can imagine."

"Ah. You don't seem too happy about that. Everything going okay for you?"

"Yes, but I'm trying to find another place to stay." Andi tapped her pen on the newspaper laying open before her, blue doodles next to several advertisements. "They're nice enough, but I just really feel like I'm imposing."

"Hmm. Have you tried the Green Aurora Guest House and Kennel?"

"No, I haven't heard of it. Do they board dogs, too?"

"Oh yes, they have a really nice kennel right next to the guest house. My husband's aunt and uncle own it, actually. I can give them a call if you want, see if they have a room open."

Andi's heart sped up, and she felt more alive than she'd had in days. "Oh yes, that would be wonderful! Thank you."

"I'll call them right now."

Rachel left to make her call. Andi tried not to get her hopes up; this was one of Anchorage's busiest times of the year, and the odds of finding a suitable empty room weren't in her favour. Too nervous to sit, she stood up and wandered to the frosted window, unconsciously twirling her silver AA ring while she peeked out at the street. The temperature had plunged during the day, and heavy, opaque exhaust plumed behind passing vehicles and those parked along the sidewalk, left idling while their drivers did their late afternoon errands.

"It's your lucky day!" Rachel sang from behind the counter. "They *were* fully booked, but had a cancellation a few days ago. They've got one room open."

Andi almost flew to where the waitress stood behind the counter, trying hard not to let her excitement show. "Really? That's wonderful!"

Rachel peered under the counter and came up with a sheet of paper. She pulled a pen from the pocket of her apron and scribbled briefly before handing the note to Andi. "Here's the address. Head south out of town and take your second left. You'll see the signs for the Green Aurora. It's about six miles out. I told Aunt Gert you'd likely come to see her."

"Rachel, how can I thank you?" Andi gushed, overwhelmed by the woman's kindness. "I'll drive out and talk to them right now."

Rachel laughed. "No thanks necessary, my dear. I just hope you like the place."

"I hope so too," Andi said. She put on her coat and gathered her purse, grinning broadly. "I'll be by for coffee first thing in the morning. Wish me luck!"

The Green Aurora Guest House was even more than Andi had hoped it would be. Gert and her husband Bill Gustafson both answered the door when she knocked, and offered to give her a tour of the entire premises. Andi was delightfully surprised; the elderly couple had, over the course of twenty or thirty years, built a small oasis in the middle of Alaska's pristine wilderness. The main house was an imposing two-storey log home, the kitchen and common rooms as well as the Gustafsons' small suite all on the main floor. The six second-floor guest rooms, two of which had a private bath, opened up left and right from the top of a wide central staircase adorned with thick, hand carved pine spindles. Six small log buildings clustered on either side of the main house and were available for larger parties or families, each having room for six guests, as well as a small kitchenette. The dog kennel was situated directly behind the main building and had a huge one-acre fenced yard and individual pens for up to twenty dogs. Andi's eyes lit up when they proudly showed her their latest addition – a traditional Swedish sauna in its own private log cabin.

"I'll take it!" Andi grinned when Gert showed her the available bedroom. It was a large, bright corner room with windows on both outside walls, a queen size bed and its own bathroom. Only seven other dogs were housed in the kennel, so there was plenty of room for her four.

"Will you be staying with us tonight, then, dear?" Gert asked, pushing her horn-rimmed glasses a big higher on her long hose, a habit Andi would become accustomed to. "We're having Shepherd's Pie for dinner, and Sticky Pudding for dessert."

Andi hesitated. "I'd love to, it smells divine, but I think it would be better if I came tomorrow morning. I'd better say good-bye to the people I'm staying with."

"I understand. Well, you come by whenever you're ready. Bill and I will be here all day."

"Thanks so much, Gert. I'll be back in the morning. Do you want me to give you my credit card information right now?"

"No, no. We can do all of that in the morning. I'll have a fresh batch of blueberry muffins and my special double chocolate brownies out of the oven by the time you get here. We can get acquainted over a nice cup of coffee." Gert winked, her faded blue eyes kind behind her old-fashioned glasses. "Bill picks wild blueberries every summer, and grinds his own coffee beans, you know. We get them from Rachel."

Andi laughed. "I'm looking forward to the morning already. See you tomorrow."

It was after six by the time Andi returned to the Shannons, and Pat and Tom were already home from the bookstore, sitting on the sofa in front of a blazing fireplace and sipping on a pre-dinner cocktail. She thought she smelled pizza, and suspected they'd picked one up from the local pizza parlour and left it warming in the oven. "Hi! You're just in time," Pat smiled, holding up a huge glass. She had changed from her dressy work clothes into a dark blue track suit, her shoulder length bottle-blond hair swinging freely around her shoulders. "Tom made gin martinis tonight. My favourite. Would you like one?"

Andi hesitated, taken by surprise at the offer and riveted by the frosted glass in Pat's hand. A row of small green olives jutted over the rim, pierced on a bright yellow pick. She took a deep breath and steadied herself. "Oh. Um, no thanks."

"Are you sure?" Tom asked, pushing an unruly shock of slightly overgrown, greying hair behind his ear. He set his own glass on the coffee table and stood up. "We have more in the shaker."

Andi shook her head and forced a weak smile. *Don't they know I'm a recovering alcoholic?*

"A glass of wine, then? A beer?"

"No," she said, a bit too sharply. "No, thanks." Tom looked at her curiously, then sat down and reached for his glass.

"It was just one of those days at the store. Nothing seemed to go right," Pat continued, totally oblivious to Andi's discomfort. "How was your day?"

"Well, nothing too exciting. I walked the dogs. Went for coffee." Andi shed her boots and coat by the door and padded on stockinged feet to stand before the fireplace, holding her cold hands to its warmth.

Pat took a deep sip of her chilled martini and closed her eyes. "Mmmm. This is pure heaven, Tom."

Andi stared at the graceful, long-stemmed glass in Pat's hand. Condensation had formed on the outside of its wide mouth. Andi's nostrils flared slightly. She licked her parched lips; she could smell the gin, taste the vermouth. The olives taunted her, perched in the drink, soaking in gin. She walked across the living room to the open kitchen and guzzled a full glass of cold water, then refilled it. She didn't really want to have the conversation with the Shannons, telling them she was leaving. She especially didn't want to tell them after they'd had a few drinks. She grasped the cold glass and sat down in a deep armchair facing the fireplace, then took a shallow, shaky breath. "I ... I'm going to be leaving in the morning," she finally blurted out.

"What?" Tom croaked, choking on the sip he'd been about to swallow. He jumped up, sloshing gin on his denim shirt. "You can't leave. I promised North we'd look after you."

Pat raised one plucked eyebrow and took another sip from her martini glass.

"I know you did, Tom, and I'm so very grateful to you both, but I've found a room at a guest house. It's also a dog boarding kennel, so will be perfect for us. I'll be able to board the dogs there when I go to Nome, and you'll get us all out of your hair."

"No, no, no. You can't," Tom sputtered. "Ruben will never forgive me."

"It will be fine, really. I'll call and check in with you every day if that will make you feel better," Andi volunteered.

"No. Absolutely not. You'll stay right here. With us," Tom said firmly. He drained his martini in one gulp, strode to the fridge and returned with the entire frozen shaker. Andi tried hard not to laugh. It had been a long time since she'd driven a man to drink, but it appeared that she might be in for a long closing argument with the retired councillor.

THIRTEEN

The next ten days of North's life passed by in an indistinct blur. Most sane people would call it a waking nightmare. Minutes and hours and days blended seamlessly, but far from monotonously, together.

Running, checkpoints, sign in, sign out.

Numbing cold, biting wind, blinding whiteouts, darkness.

Fatigue, hunger, aching muscles.

Rest the dogs, feed the dogs, check lines, check paws and replace little green booties.

When he'd left Finger Lake, North had not planned on stopping, other than two short breaks, until they arrived at Rainy Pass. It didn't work out that way. Of necessity, he rested for two hours near the bottom of the Happy Valley Steps. His nerves were raw, his confidence shattered. Two teams caught up to him, experienced Iditarod mushers who were familiar with the steps' hidden dangers. North watched them drop down to the river in a slow, measured descent, quite unlike his own out-of-control plunge. Both mushers, one of them a woman, carried on to the next checkpoint after stopping briefly to check on the rookie's welfare.

At 11:15 pm, after a run that taxed him both physically and mentally, North said a silent prayer of thanks when he arrived at Rainy Pass Lodge. After the usual check in routine he found his drop bag and replenished his supplies, then filled the cooler with another batch of warm dog food. Hunger had become a constant companion and gnawed at his belly, but exhaustion overrode any desire to heat up one of the frozen meals in his bag, and the lodge kitchen wouldn't open again until breakfast. The checker told him there were a few cots available for mushers who wanted to grab a few hours of sleep, and when North peeked into the darkened checkpoint cabin sometime past midnight he found two of the small beds unoccupied. A pot-bellied woodstove stood in a corner of the cabin and the room was a great deal warmer than the frigid outside air. North shed his boots then rolled up his green parka and placed it at the head of an empty cot. His eyes were closed before his head hit the lumpy makeshift pillow.

He should have slept the deep sleep of the dead, but dreams invaded North's restless slumber. Visions of emerald green eyes and long, burnished brown hair somehow transformed into a white, snow-covered trail that suddenly vanished over the edge of a cliff, leaving him staring helplessly at a dark blue sky. He was plunging over the precipice, his flailing arms unable to break his wild freefall. He tried again and again to scream, but not so much as a whisper came from his tight, straining throat. He started awake, gasping for air; his heart fought to escape the grip of a steel hand that threated to squeeze the life out of him. Sweat beaded his face, and he lay in the warm, slightly smoky darkness, listening to the reassuring human sound of gentle snoring until the painful pounding in his chest subsided. When he was finally able to draw a painless breath, he checked his watch and cursed softly; he'd overslept, his planned three-hour rest had stretched to five. He slowly crawled from the low cot, his protesting body responding like that of a man thirty or forty years his senior, all aches and stiff joints.

When he left the Rainy Pass checkpoint at 5:30 am with sunrise still three hours distant, the lodge was silent, and North abandoned his hopes of a warm breakfast and hot coffee. As soon as he stepped from the relative warmth of the cabin he knew the temperature had once again plummeted during the night. A north wind had risen, pushing a cold front ahead of it and whipping loose snow over the trail. The dogs at times disappeared in a cloud of swirling dark snow, the sled and driver following in a whiteout, blind and trusting.

The trail soon began to climb up the slope of the vast Alaska Range in earnest. This was the part of the trail North had been dreading the most – he knew he was at a definite disadvantage over all of the other racers. Although the trail was relatively easy for an hour or two, it soon became a steady climb and grew steeper by the mile. His Canadian Eskimo Dogs weren't built the same as the Siberian and Alaskan Huskies, and neither had they been trained and conditioned to the steep terrain. North watched resolutely and powerless to do anything about it as team after team and musher after musher overtook him. The trail continued to climb, weaving across frozen creeks and in and out of clumps of willow bushes. His teeth clenched in helpless frustration as he saw his position drop steadily. He thought he was now somewhere around the middle of the pack.

His team strained, pulling valiantly and throwing their muscular shoulders into their work, but the steep climb up the pass was more than they could handle. North became frustrated but was helpless – there was nothing he could do to improve his standing at this point in the race. He would have to bide his time, and make up for the setback later. There were still many days and miles to win back some of the trail he was losing, and he was confident that he would do so.

The landscape changed quickly, and soon they were above the tree line, running in murky pre-dawn light and whipped by the unrelenting, icy wind. Some unknown traveller possessed a good sense of humour; a three-foot high inukshuk, constructed of large chunks of wind hardened snow instead of rock, had been erected at a rest area. North knew the history of inuksuit well. The mysterious stone figures could be found throughout the circumpolar world. *Inukshuk* meant 'in the likeness of a human' in his native Inuit language, and with their two stone foundations resembling legs, a solid stone body, two stone 'arms' and a rock for a head, the figures did, indeed, resemble a human form. The traditional monuments had been used by his people for communication and survival for generations, and served a variety of purposes – as navigation or directional aids, to mark a place of respect or memorial for a beloved person, or to indicate migration routes or places where fish can be found. Today the long arm on this particular frozen inukshuk fittingly pointed toward Nome. North grinned at the familiar symbol; it restored his energy and gave him more hope than he'd felt in days.

As dawn approached the sky steadily lightened, unveiling the high, snow-covered mountains before them. White, shining peaks towered all around, some reaching 5000 feet or more, their pristine, shining caps of snow reflecting ever-changing, stunning shades of pink, violet and peach as the sun quickly and steadily rose. The mountains' lurking presence made everything below appear diminutive and humble. The landscape was pristine – an endless white blanket of deep, fluffy snow that softened and smoothed the rugged land that lay beneath it. When he finally reached the range's 3200-foot summit, North said a silent prayer of thanks.

Later, he realized that he should have been praying about what lay before him, not for what he'd already left behind. It wasn't the up part that was hard – it was the down.

The Iditarod trail, North was quickly learning, was fraught with danger – danger and treacherous gorges. From the range's high divide, the trail followed a twenty mile stretch out of the foothills, through the notorious Dalzell Gorge and into Alaska's vast interior 1000 feet below. Rohn Roadhouse, the next checkpoint, was a mere twenty miles away, but some mushers regarded the short stretch as the worst part of the trail because of the gorge. Even Rebecca Singleton had regaled himself and rookie Mats Pederson about her first nerve-racking encounter with the gorge. North had been too keyed up at the Musher's Banquet to give her tale much attention, but now he fervently hoped that at least Mats had been paying close attention to the petite, blond woman clad in shocking pink.

Now that he'd had an encounter with one of the trail's infamous gorges, North wished he'd also paid more attention to Bill Wrightway when the old timer had shared several tidbits of wisdom about Dalzell Gorge and some of the other trickier spots on the long trail. At the time, though, he'd focused only upon what he thought would be his team's most challenging part of the race – the high climb over the Alaska Range. Now, after barely surviving the Happy River Gorge, he wondered exactly *what* the infamous, feared Dalzell had to offer.

They'd made it up the mountain, though, and North steadfastly remained confident that going down would be child's play; he was determined to make up some lost time and hopefully gain a few positions in the race. The dogs were tired when they reached the summit after the long, taxing climb, but would have willingly continued to run had he not stopped to rest them. He gave them a well-earned snack, checked their feet and replaced several green booties that showed signs of wear, then massaged their shoulders and legs. He rummaged in his bag for anything that resembled human food, settling on two chocolate bars and a handful of peanuts to partially appease his hunger. His mouth watered for a plate of bacon, hash browns and eggs and about a gallon of strong, black coffee. He'd never been hungrier in his life, and swore he could feel his saliva hit his empty stomach. At the next long rest, he would take the time to warm some of the home cooked, frozen meals Andi had made him, and what he couldn't eat he'd store on top of the greasy, warm dogfood in the cooler, even if the thought of it made his stomach churn.

When they hit the trail again, Kia and Weasel set a fast pace, neither they nor the team showing any signs of exhaustion. They ran down a gentle grade for about two miles on good, packed trail and North's concern about the dreaded Dalzell Gorge faded. He and his team had survived the Happy River Gorge and its three wicked steps, and he was confident that nothing the Dalzell Gorge threw at them could be worse.

When the northerly wind finally diminished, it took the worst of the biting cold with it. The sky was a rare, brilliant shade of blue only seen in the most unpolluted of air, and the swiftly rising sun bore a measure of comforting warmth in its strong rays. North settled onto his makeshift chair on the back of the sled runners, relaxed and began to enjoy the ride. The team's familiar, smooth pace soothed and reassured him, and soon lured his sleep-deprived mind into a stupor. His thoughts wandered from sharp, cold air, blue skies, golden sunbeams and white-capped peaks to the heady, musky scent of his wife's warm body and the seductive glow of green eyes. His eyes drooped, then closed. His body rocked in a steady rhythm with the moving sled, swaying and rolling, the skis schussing quietly over the snow. His head drooped, his fingertips caressed warm, naked skin. His tongue tasted ...

The sled bounced hard, waking North from his sublime reverie. His heart was pounding. He licked cold, chapped lips and shook his head to clear the cobwebs that had grown there, more than a little disappointed to find himself clinging to the back of a bouncing sled instead of Andi's smooth buttocks. The first thing he became clearly aware of was the tip of Kia's black nose, held high and twitching as she sniffed the icy air. The big grey dog held her ears erect and forward; North sensed a warning in her alert bearing and felt an almost undetectable change in the team's pace. Both Kia and Weasel stared ahead with an unusual intensity.

North's dark eyes tracked the path of their gaze; his slightly groggy, daydream imbued mind refused to register what his eyes were seeing. Or, more accurately, what they *didn't* see. Almost exactly as it had appeared in his dream, twenty feet before him the expanse of empty white trail vanished into an endless, blue abyss of clear arctic sky.

The trail ceased to exist. It fell into oblivion, disappearing over the edge of a cliff in a familiar, stomach wrenching repetition of Happy River's deadly third step. *I've reached Dalzell Gorge,* North though stupidly, stunned at the horrifying sight. His body refused to respond to the fight or flight hormones racing through his bloodstream. Up until that moment, he hadn't really thought it possible to freeze in terror, but now he was a believer. Only his mind raced on, and he belatedly realized that everything he'd heard about Dalzell Gorge had been true. He'd been warned, but he hadn't listened. And that error in judgement may cost him everything he valued, including his life.

Within seconds he lost the opportunity to change the course of events; even if his mutinous muscles had been willing to respond, there was no time to slow the dogs or alter their path. The team was moving too fast, flying to the edge of oblivion. Either Kia or Weasel – North's befuddled brain couldn't distinguish which – howled just before the lead pair soared over the rim of the gorge, followed by their teammates, the sled and their screaming leader, who clung to the handlebar with one hand and the side of the chair with the other. They dropped down an impossibly steep chute, which was really no more than a narrow ice ledge, crashing around immense boulders and jagged rock outcroppings. North glimpsed a creek somewhere far below, and what looked like, but couldn't possibly be, open water. When the light sled bounced high into the air and sailed over a large boulder, North was sure it would flip, but it landed on one runner, hitting the frozen trail hard enough to snap his head back and teeth together. He tasted the metallic tang of blood in his mouth and swallowed hard. The sled slid and tottered on its right side for a few seconds, North scrabbling to balance himself against its cant, before it settled back on both runners again.

He knew they were tumbling down too fast. The sled pitched from side to side, careening out of control. He felt powerless, sitting on the seat instead of balancing on the back of the runners, where he might possibly have some control. It would be a pointless endeavour to try and stand now, he realized, and even more pointless to try and set the sled brake. The steep trail was cloaked in a sheet of ice, and the brake would fail to find purchase. With nothing to impede its plunging descent, the sled and its horrified passenger continued their chaotic run down the steep canyon wall, pummelled on every side by unyielding rock and jagged clumps of ice that ripped at the outer layer of his parka and beat against his shoulders and arms if he happened to lean too far left or right.

After what felt like a short lifetime North realized the sled had finally stopped lurching and dropping and had come to rest at a drunken slant. It was sitting on its right runner again, the left one jammed up against a long, low rock protruding from the snow. His stomach no longer felt like it was coming up his throat, though, which was a good thing. They'd reached the end of the steep, 200-foot plunge to the bottom of the Dalzell Gorge and by some small miracle, both of his hands were wrapped around the handlebar and his rear end was still planted on the seat. The creek he'd spotted only moments earlier ran nearby, its crystal-clear water gurgling and burbling over rocks and gravel. Even to North's traumatized mind it seemed incongruous and out of place to find open water in the middle of an Alaskan winter. He didn't spend much time pondering the fact that it was at least minus 20 and the shallow creek still ran freely. He had more important things to think about, like the fact that he now thought he knew what it felt like to have lived through a battle.

Although he was grateful to be alive, every inch of his body screamed in protest. He forced himself to release the handlebar, groaning when he attempted to stand. He fell back to the chair and rested for a minute to gather his senses, then carefully tested each of his limbs, stretching and bending them one by one. Relieved to discover everything appeared to be in working order, he stood on shaky legs. The dogs shook themselves out, each one shaking vigorously from the tip of its nose to the end of its fluffy tail. They once again appeared pleased with their death-defying plunge and grinned at their leader, unfazed and ready to continue their run.

North lifted the sled off the rock, relieved to see that there was no visible damage, but he would take a closer look at the stanchions and runners as soon as he could get the dogs and sled off the trail. He peered around to get his bearings; they were in the bottom of a narrow canyon studded with scrubby trees and willow bushes. The trail ran within a few yards of the creek, which appeared to be frozen further ahead. He stretched out his shoulders and cautiously rotated his head, testing his sore muscles. His left shoulder complained bitterly when he attempted to raise his arm and inspect the long rip in his parka. Another item to add to his list of repairs at the next stop.

The dogs appeared to be uncertain as to what to do next, and a couple of them had plopped down to rest while others sniffed the trail and shifted on their paws, ready to move again. North spoke to them for a moment, praising their fearless, surefooted plunge down the impossibly steep slope. He walked to the head of the gangline and grasped Kia's harness, tugging gently to get her moving. North walked the team along the trail until they were well away from trail's landing area and stopped for a break and a snack. He loosened the harness tugs, massaged shoulders and legs, checked paws and booties, and once again replaced several that had been shredded by either sharp rock or ice. Chica, his tan and black wheel dog, had a slightly raw spot on one foot, and he rubbed in a generous amount of ointment before bandaging it and replacing the bootie. He made a mental note to keep an eye on her foot. After wolfing down their snack the dogs settled on the snow, content to nap in the sun.

A quick inspection of the sled bag assured him that, in spite of ending up a jumbled mess, the contents of his basket seemed no worse for the wear. Even his bottle of medicinal brandy was still intact, and he helped himself to a generous swallow before stowing it back between layers of insulating wool clothing. The sled itself hadn't escaped so easily. One of the stanchions, the vertical pieces of wood between the runner and the top rails, was cracked. It wasn't completely broken, and could very likely survive until he reached the next checkpoint, but North decided to take a few minutes and repair it. He had several spare stanchions in his repair kit, along with some parts to do a temporary repair.

He set to work, glancing every now and then at the impossibly steep slope of the canyon wall, his eyes roaming from its base to the rim of the cliff 200 feet overhead. He snacked on some beef jerky while he repaired the sled, and his ragged nerves slowly settled. It probably hadn't been a pretty thing to watch, and he may be a bit shaky for the next few hours, but he'd survived the dreaded, infamous Dalzell Gorge.

He chuckled when he thought about it ... he'd cheated death twice in as many days. The only problem was, he still had another ten days and more than eight hundred miles to go before the damn race was over. When was his luck going to run out?

FOURTEEN

When he slid into the Rohn River checkpoint it was nearly noon; the repair job on the stanchion had ended up becoming a replacement and had cost him valuable time. He signed in and found a reasonably quiet, treed area to rest near the checkpoint cabin. He tied the sled to a stout tree trunk and unhooked the team from the gangline, then dry swallowed three aspirin to numb the pain in his aching shoulder. He didn't have quite enough food left to feed the dogs, so that task became the first thing on his never-ending 'to do' list. He pulled out the cooker and HEET and got to work on a new batch of dog food. While the snow melted he grabbed a chunk of straw from the supply next to the cabin and spread it for his dogs, who immediately began pawing it into comfortable beds.

With that done, he trudged to the cabin in search of the vet, who was already pulling his boots on when North walked in, having heard his arrival. He glanced at the notations in North's vet book, then followed him back to his team, where he proceeded to examine each dog's heart, hydration, attitude, appetite, weight, lungs and joints. He then checked for signs of foot and shoulder injuries, respiration problems, diarrhea and exhaustion. He declared North's team to be in excellent health, and made a note about Chica's sore paw in North's notebook. He advised North to keep an eye on it, but thought it posed no immediate risk to the dog.

As pain drugs are banned during the race, any musher caught administering drugs to his dog will be immediately disqualified. When a dog becomes injured or exhausted along the trail, it must be carried to the next checkpoint in the sled basket, where it will be attended to by the veterinarian. All dogs dropped along the race trail are flown back to Anchorage by the Iditarod Air Force, where they are safely housed and cared for by volunteers until they can be reunited with their owners or handlers. The safety, health and comfort of sled dogs is of paramount importance at all times. North appreciated this high level of care, and wouldn't have his loyal mutts treated any other way.

When the vet had finished his examination and the ravenous dogs had eaten, North fell into the sled basket for a nap, cocooned inside the warmth of his down sleeping bag. His last conscious thoughts as his eyes fell shut were that he was sure he wasn't meant to have survived Dalzell Gorge, and that he couldn't remember the last time he had eaten a decent meal. Two minutes later he slipped into a deep, dreamless sleep, oblivious to the barking dogs and hectic activity at the busy checkpoint.

Rohn River checkpoint, situated as it was immediately after the death-defying plunge down Dalzell Gorge, was often the racers' choice for a long rest. Many of them, especially the rookies, needed it to settle their nerves and possibly wash their long johns. Without planning to do so, Rohn River became a much longer rest than planned for North Ruben, Rookie #9.

He awoke from a deep sleep with a start and immediately raised his left hand to check the time, wincing at the stabbing pain in his shoulder. The illuminated green dials on his sturdy Timex cast a ghostly green glow inside the sled bag's murky interior, and he swore softly when he realized that his quick nap had somehow stretched into a long, five-hour snooze. He lifted his arms to unzip the bag and groaned, clenching his teeth to keep from crying out at the pain that erupted in the top half of his body. He collapsed back into the bottom of the basket until his nerve receptors quit shooting daggers through his upper back, shoulders, neck and arms, then spent a few minutes kneading and massaging his tortured, tight muscles. By the time he'd fought his way out of his sleeping bag and the sled basket and was on his feet, his muttered curses had escalated and roused the dogs. They immediately, and very loudly, demanded food.

A thick, ominous layer of cloud had moved in while he slept. He sniffed the air and detected the scent of fresh snow, much the same as a wild animal or dog would. Although sunset was still over an hour away the day had darkened considerably, and he slipped his headlamp on over his wool hat. He tested the light, checked his coat pocket for spare batteries, and then dragged his aching body to the nearest tree to relieve himself. After downing more aspirin, he opened the cooler and fed the complaining team. The insulated cooler kept cooked food warm for over twelve hours; he was thankful that he'd cooked an extra-large batch with his new supplies. With any luck he wouldn't have to cook again until the next morning.

His own stomach rumbled loudly, and his blood begged for coffee. After dishing out the dogs' meals, he trudged toward the checkpoint cabin, munching on a protein bar. He had wanted to leave Rohn at least an hour earlier; the first twenty miles out of the checkpoint were heralded to be fairly bad trail and he'd planned to run then in daylight. He resigned himself to the fact that that wasn't going to happen now, so he may as well take a few minutes and grab a coffee.

"North, is that you?" a deep, heavily accented voice called from somewhere nearby.

"Yeah, who's there?" North turned, his eyes sweeping the line of trees. He spotted a lone figure approaching from the shadows.

"It's Mats Pederson. From Norway."

"Oh, Mats, how are you doing? It's good to see you again," North said, overjoyed to have run into the other rookie. The burly Norwegian was the closest person he had for a friend among the group of mushers.

"I'm still alive, but just barely."

North grasped Mat's extended hand. "Yeah, I know what you mean. I was just going to see if I could grab a coffee at the cabin. You want to come along and we can exchange horror stories?" North asked.

"I had the same idea," Mats grinned and fell into step beside North. "I just woke up, but my dogs need to rest for another hour or so before we leave."

The rookies spent a few minutes visiting with the checker and vet while they filled tin cups from an old-fashioned coffee percolator bubbling on the wood stove. The small cabin was a basic one-room log affair with a wooden plank floor, a short bank of cupboards atop a counter built against one wall, a rickety wooden table with four chairs and no running water.

"So, what did you think about that Dalzell Gorge?" North smirked as he blew on the top of his steaming cup. He held it in both hands as he didn't trust his taxed muscles not to drop it. The two men had moved away from the woodstove and sat on a long wooden bench below one of the cabin's small, heavily frosted windows. It was covered both inside and out with heavy, clear polyethylene to shut out drafts, but did little to prevent Jack Frost from painting on the single pane of glass.

Mats grimaced and shook his head. "It was hell. I don't know which was worse – it or the Happy Valley Steps. Becky warned us about Dalzell, but I don't remember anyone saying the steps were that steep. How about you?"

"I've never seen anything like either of them. My team did well, though. Better than me, I was totally unprepared," he chuckled. "Guess it proves I'm really a flatlander." Now that the adrenalin rush associated with the horrifying brush with death had subsided, he couldn't really remember all of the terrifying details. His mind wandered for a moment while he speculated if it was the same way with childbirth . . . he'd heard his mother, aunts and sisters say that the pain of giving birth was excruciating, but they all agreed that a few days later they seemed to forget how bad it really was. Nature's defense mechanism, he guessed.

Whatever it was, he hoped to god he wouldn't have nightmares about the gorge for the rest of his life.

"Did you hear that three mushers have already scratched?" Mats asked.

"No, do you know who?"

Mats shook his head. "I just heard one of them was a rookie. Was wondering if it was you."

North laughed. "No, but I've thought about it a couple of times. Was anyone hurt?"

"I didn't hear. Don't think so."

The two rookies managed to down two cups of scorching hot, strong coffee each while they swapped stories and talked about what lay ahead. They both agreed that the worst must be behind them. When he'd drained his second cup, North rose from the wooden bench he'd shared with Mats. "I have to get moving," he said. "I'm going to drop a couple of my dogs here, so I'd better go get them sorted out."

"Yah, me too," said Mats. "Guess I'll meet up with you down the trail somewhere. Take it easy, North."

"Yeah, you too. Good luck, eh?"

During the race, drivers were allowed to 'drop' as many dogs as they wished, at any checkpoint, as long as they still had five dogs in harness and on the towline upon arriving at the finish line in Nome. Most mushers wanted the pulling power of a full team to cross the Alaska Range, then dropped one or more at the Rohn checkpoint. After crossing the range, extra dogs become more of a liability than an asset. The weight of extra food, as well as the additional time spent feeding, checking and cleaning their feet, replacing booties, and vet checks all slowed a racer down. However, once dropped, additional dogs could not be added to the team.

North knew which of his four mutts would be left behind, and quickly separated Togo, Ikkuma, Jinx and Lobo from the pack. Each of the dogs had done their part, putting their strength and shoulders to the heavy task of conquering the summit of the Alaska Range, but now their continued presence on the team would be more of a liability than an asset. None of the four were lead, swing or wheel dogs and their absence wouldn't affect the performance of the team, but they would still be missed.

North spent a minute or two with each dog, speaking to them in low, reassuring tones, praising them, scratching their necks and ears and stroking their silky ears. He double checked the fasteners on their green jackets, then chained them with a dozen other dropped dogs in the designated area behind the cabin. He had made arrangements with the volunteer on duty for their feeding, care and return to Anchorage, and they had already dropped a liberal amount of fresh, clean straw for the dogs to make their beds on. Although he knew they would be well cared for, it was hard to say goodbye to his loyal friends. They howled despondently at his retreating back. Their cries broke his heart.

North was determined to leave Rohn as soon as possible, hoping to make use of the last two hours of rapidly fading daylight. The jolt of caffeine had energized him and made him forget about his gnawing hunger. He quickly repacked the sled, adjusted the gangline to compensate for the four dropped dogs, and harnessed the remaining twelve dogs to the line. From behind the cabin, his dropped dogs continued to cry, their voices shrill, and their despair soul-wrenching.

Kia, Weasel and the rest of the team were restless and unhappy, reluctant to leave their pack mates behind. They stared at North with black-rimmed eyes full of reproach, then turned their snouts toward the cabin that shielded their mates from view; their mournful howl-growls were answered by their dropped teammates, and painful to listen to. Light snowflakes began to drift to the ground, the first of a possible heavy fall judging by the low, dark clouds.

North untied the sled, stood on the brake and pulled the snow hook. "Ready! Hike!" he shouted, calling the complaining team to action.

He had no time for long goodbyes with man nor beast.

The next leg of the race, from Rohn to Nikolai, was about ninety miles – one of the longer stretches between checkpoints, with some of the worst trails in the race. Some mushers had been known to run the stretch in as few as ten hours, others had required up to fifteen. The old timers were known to say, 'If you make it to Nikolai, you have a good chance to finish the race'.

When North started out from Rohn that evening his dogs were fresh and rested. He, on the other hand, didn't feel so great; almost every inch of his body ached despite frequent doses of aspirin, and he began to doubt the wisdom of entering the challenging race, whether it had been his lifelong dream or not.

Snow had started to fall in earnest and the wind had strengthened, further reducing North's vision in the rapidly failing light. The trail ran along rivers and creeks, skated over frozen overflow, around open water and hills and down and up gullies. They were back in a wooded area, slowly climbing up the saddle of a low hill on a trail that was becoming increasingly hard to follow, obliterated by fresh snow. He stopped after two hours to give the dogs a short rest and a snack, checking their paws and booties, and was relieved to find the abrasion on Chica's sore paw had gotten no worse. Another musher passed him and waved, but didn't stop.

It was just after midnight when North reached a heavily wooded area that he suspected was just before the Farewell Lakes. The dogs needed a meal and a rest, and being partially protected from the steadily blowing wind, the spot seemed just as good a place as any. He pulled off the trail and made camp, hurried through his routine but necessary tasks, then fed the dogs. They ate and immediately curled into round balls in the sheltering snow and straw cocoons they'd pawed together. Within minutes their backs and heads were covered in blankets of white. North zipped himself into his sleeping bag inside the sled bag and ate another protein bar and a few handfuls of peanuts. By the light of his headlamp he set the alarm on his watch to wake him in four hours. *Tomorrow,* he promised himself, *tomorrow I'll get a decent meal.*

By the time he reached the Farewell Burn, or simply 'The Burn' as it was called, the snow had finally stopped falling. The clouds continued to hang low and the night was blacker than the inside of a deserted coal mine. The Burn was a treacherous thirty-five mile stretch of land littered with debris left over from a massive wildfire that had ripped through the area twenty years earlier. For the first ten years after the fire, The Burn had been one of the most hazardous stretches on the trail and, according to some mushers, its dangers were on a par with the Dalzell Gorge. Since then The Bureau of Land Management had cleared out many of the snags and other obstructions, and the run through The Burn was now supposed to be significantly less hazardous.

It looked innocent enough in the beam of North's headlamp – a narrow trail meandering through copses of skinny, blackened tree trunks. Although the snow had stopped falling at some point during the night, a steady wind continued to blow from the north, drifting over the trail and exposing fallen logs, rocks and tufts of tall grass on both side of it. The team ran at a steady pace though, and they made good time. North wondered where Mats Pederson was, and if he had perhaps passed by while he slept.

An hour into The Burn, North realized that the wind was rapidly strengthening. Within minutes it reached gale-force, seeping into every vulnerable gap in his outerwear and biting the thin sliver of exposed skin between his cheeks and goggles. North knew the dogs needed their insulated jackets and belly warmers, and stopped only long enough to throw them a small frozen meat snack and dress them. He pulled off his goggles and headlamp and rolled his balaclava down over his face before replacing them, then tugged the zipper of his parka tighter before he set off again.

The temperature was plunging, the howling north wind pushing it down from the pole. North gathered the hood of his parka closer to his face and rolled out its wolf-trimmed rim in an attempt to block the biting wind from his face. He would later learn that the temperature recorded at Nikolai that day was minus 60 Fahrenheit, or minus 50 Celsius; with the wind chill it was estimated to have been around minus 75F, which worked out to around minus 60C. Whether in an Imperial or Metric reading, it was damn cold.

North hung on to the sled hour after endless hour, his cold hands molded to the handlebar and his eyes constantly scanning the shadows for moose, buffalo and wolves. They cleared the Farewell Burn without incident; his mind, dulled by the cold, sleep deprivation and lack of nutrition, became immune to anything around him. His hands, arms and shoulders ached, but he'd given up on aspirin; it didn't seem to help any more.

The last two-hour stretch into Nikolai was miraculously level, and the dogs, twelve on the gangline now, ran tirelessly. North wondered if they sensed they were on the homestretch to Nikolai, two hours ahead, or if they were just overjoyed at finding themselves on level ground. They seemed oblivious to the wind, protected from at least a little of its biting force by their quilted green jackets.

They'd been trailing a tiny speck of light for several miles, and as it gradually grew larger and brighter, North realized it was the light from a headlamp. It took his addled, cold brain several minutes to realize that he was slowly overtaking another team – the first one since the race began. He chuckled, a dry, croaking laugh, and when they finally overtook the other team North managed to unwrap one frozen hand from the handlebar and give the other racer a friendly wave as he passed by.

The adrenalin rush North experienced from his small achievement faded quickly. His mind soon began to drift again, and he sat huddled on the padded seat over the blue Coleman cooler while his mind wandered to warmer, gentler thoughts. Andi. Home. A warm, blazing fire. A hot meal. A cold beer. Regardless of his fantasies, though, his reality remained the same as it had for the past three brutal days, and would continue for another week or more.

Running, checkpoints, sign in, sign out.

Numbing cold, biting wind, blinding whiteouts, darkness.

Fatigue, hunger, aching muscles.

Rest the dogs, feed the dogs, check lines, check paws and replace little green booties.

FIFTEEN

Andi had spent only one night in the Shannons' home but was already anxious to escape its smothering atmosphere; she didn't feel the least bit comfortable and dreaded spending even one more night there. Throughout Monday evening Tom was persistent in his attempts to change her mind about leaving the next morning, his arguments grew louder and stronger with every passing minute and each martini, while Pat became increasingly silent and finally detached herself from the conversation entirely. Andi, however, remained equally adamant about moving and suspected that Tom's wife was not entirely unhappy to see her leave. As soon as their desultory, silent dinner was over – they shared the greasy pepperoni and canned mushroom pizza Pat eventually pulled from the oven – Andi immediately escaped to walk the dogs. When she returned hours later the Shannons had already retired for the night.

Their martini glasses and the empty cocktail shaker had been abandoned on the living room coffee table. The shaker had defrosted, and beads of moisture dripped down its smooth, silver sides to pool on the dark table's varnished surface. Andi stood with her back to the fireplace, staring at the remains of her hosts' private cocktail party, the forefinger of her left hand smoothing the familiar lines of her AA talisman, the silver triangle in a circle on her right-hand ring finger. She was barely aware of the heat still emanating from the dying fire's embers as her eyes, dark green and stormy, stared down at the remnants of the Shannons' drinks.

Her pulse sharpened, and she felt the familiar, dreaded pinch in her stomach; the old longing for alcohol, once imbedded in a person's blood, was a cruel and enduring companion. She clenched her teeth, picked up the glasses and shaker and set them in the kitchen sink. She dried the damp rings on the coffee table, then washed the long-stemmed glasses and set them on the drain board to dry. When she unscrewed the top of the martini shaker to rinse it out, she found a half inch of clear, gin-scented liquid left in the bottom. The gin and vermouth were diluted by melted ice cubes, but still carried the sharp, mouth-watering scent she was too familiar with ... the perfume that frequently haunted her dreams.

Andi's hand trembled when she lifted the shaker to her nose, unable to stop herself from pulling the tangy, piney scent of gin into her lungs. Her mouth watered, saliva pooling on her tongue. She put one hand on the edge of the sink to steady herself, too weak to stand on her own two legs. The longing that bolted through her body left her feeling helpless; she yearned for one little taste of the tempting alcohol. She craved just one small sip to soothe her ragged nerves and numb her mind. It had been eight years since Natalie died, but she remembered the wonderfully trusting look in her daughter's clear blue eyes and the clean, fresh scent of her blond curls as if it were yesterday. A knife still twisted somewhere deep in her heart every time she thought about the senseless waste of her child's young, lost life. The torture she continued to live with every day since her death sometimes seemed too much to bear.

And now she stood alone in the Shannons' kitchen with an aching heart and a half inch of watered-down gin in her hand. She thought about how easy it would be to just toss the few drops of alcohol down her throat. There were no witnesses; she had nobody to account to but herself. Her lips parted and her cold, trembling hand lifted the silver cocktail shaker to her lips. She closed her eyes, only to see a pair of chocolate brown, darkly lashed eyes regarding her with disappointment ... disappointment and something akin to reproach.

Andi started awake, her heart thudding painfully as she struggled to distinguish reality from nightmare. In her mind's eye, twisting, twirling strands of hot scarlet and pristine, cold white rose and fell, united together in a strange, macabre dance until, depleted of their energy, they finally merged and collapsed into a shimmering pink, wet pool.

Voices cried, a high-pitched keening. Were they human, or beast?

Her visions and dreams were getting worse. Blood. Snow. Snow and blood. White and red. She could still detect the coppery scent of the hot blood ... the crisp, sharp scent of cold, pristine snow.

Reality rushed back as her lucidity returned. She was still in Anchorage, laying alone on a strange bed, in a stranger's home. Her lover, husband and best friend had left days ago, determined to challenge himself and his dreams, intent on conquering a sometimes cruel and forbidding Mother Nature. Somewhere over Alaska's frozen, isolated expanse of land, ocean and mountain between Anchorage and Nome, the man she loved more than life itself was mushing in the Iditarod – living the adventure he'd dreamed about his entire life.

Her heart continued to throb. It missed a beat, then sped to catch up, thudding painfully against her rib cage. Outside her bedroom window, the wind howled and rattled the glass panes, taunting her jumpy nerves.

Sleep would be a stranger to her for the rest of the long, blustery winter night; she knew without a doubt – just as she knew that the sun would rise in the morning – that her husband's life was in peril. The signs were there, in her dreams, but she was powerless to help him.

She was out of bed and dressed before 6 am after a sleepless, nightmarish night, and crept out of the house before her hosts began to stir. The dogs, especially Qannik, were overjoyed to see her, whimpering and whining when she appeared. She fed them their daily meal of dry kibble mixed with a bit of warm water, then spent two chilly hours walking them. It was still dark out, the sun a good half hour away from rising, when she returned to the house for coffee. She was relieved to find that the Shannons had already left for their bookstore. Tom had written a short note and left it on the kitchen table, asking her to call and check in with them later in the day.

She showered quickly, blow-dried her hair and dressed in blue jeans and a heavy purple wool sweater layered over a light-weight black cotton turtleneck. After gulping down a cup of leftover, tepid coffee she loaded the dogs, their food and supplies and her and North's suitcases into North's big white truck. At 9:30, with a suitcase in each hand, she knocked on the front door of The Green Aurora Guest House. The wooden door was, quite unsurprisingly, painted an unusual shade of green that Andi suspected was meant to mimic the elusive, fickle green of the Aurora Borealis. When the door swung open, she was greeted by the luscious scent of rich, warm chocolate.

"Oh, you don't have to knock, dear," Gert said by way of greeting, surprising Andi with a warm, enveloping hug. "From now on, just walk right in. This is your home now." A large, paisley mauve apron was draped over Gert's green sweater and dark brown slacks; she had evidently fulfilled her promise of providing freshly baked double chocolate brownies and wild blueberry muffins for mid-morning coffee. The women chatted companionably while Gert quickly checked Andi in for a weeklong stay, urging her to get the dogs settled and come back to the kitchen for coffee and a good 'chin-wag' as soon as she could.

Bill Gustafson hovered beside the immense antique desk that acted as their guest reception area. He was, by Andi's best guess, somewhere around seventy years old, while Gert was likely five or six years younger. Bill was a soft-spoken, kindly man, balding and slightly stooped but still very mobile for his age. Gert was short and plump, but Bill carried not an ounce of extra weight on his tall frame. He helped

Andi lift the four sled dogs from their truck boxes and get them settled in the kennel. The new arrivals were met by loud, excited barks from the other dogs in residence, their greeting enthusiastically returned by the Rubens' four mutts who somehow got the entire group howling for several minutes. Each animal had their own comfortable pen, and Bill assured her that she could come and go as she pleased during her stay, and let her dogs roam free in the fenced grounds whenever she wished as long as there were no altercations with the other canine tenants.

Andi was impressed with the organized and well-equipped kennel. Bill showed her where to store her dog food and gave her a tour of the small but immaculately clean kitchen where she could prepare and cook the dogs' meals if she chose to. Bill was so enthralled by both the unique Canadian Eskimo Dog breed and Qannik's pure white coat that when Andi mentioned that Qannik was house-trained and spent most of the time with her and North in the house instead of the kennel, he insisted that she accompany them back to the house to visit Gert, who loved dogs as much as he did.

Gert showered the young dog with lavish attention and several Milk Bone dog biscuits, then Qannik promptly fell asleep on a rug by the back door of the kitchen, her black nose resting on big, white paws. Bill grabbed a warm blueberry muffin and tactfully vanished, leaving Andi and Gert sitting across from each other on the padded benches of the Gustafsons' cozy kitchen nook. Andi had a mug of fresh coffee in one hand and an immense blueberry muffin in the other. A plate of warm brownies sat in the middle of the table. "These muffins are delicious, Gert," Andi sighed and took another dainty bite.

"Try a brownie, dear," Gert urged, pushing the plate toward her. "You're much too thin."

Andi sighed. "I just haven't had much of an appetite lately. It seems like the past month has been so busy there hasn't been time to prepare a decent meal, much less eat it. And now that North is gone-"

Andi set the half-eaten muffin down on her plate and took another sip of the strong, richly flavoured coffee.

"I know it's hard on a woman when her man is gone," Gert nodded sympathetically. She got up and stirred the pot of beef-barley soup that simmered on the stove, filling the kitchen with a rich, meaty aroma. "There would sometimes be months go by when I didn't see my Bill. He worked on those big oil rigs, out at sea. There were times that I didn't know if he was dead or alive for weeks on end."

Andi picked at a few crumbs that had fallen on the white tablecloth. "How did you survive?" she asked, her voice barely a whisper.

"Oh, you get used to it, eventually. You keep busy and the time passes. And I had the children to keep me going," she said, pointing to a row of framed photographs hanging on the kitchen wall.

Andi looked up at the photos. "Four boys?"

Gert chuckled. "Yup. Four little terrors. How I wanted a little girl, but it just wasn't meant to be. Our boys have given us three beautiful granddaughters and two grandsons, though, and they aren't done yet. Do you have any children, dear?"

Andi hesitated, not sure how to respond. She'd struggled with the answer to this question for the past eight years. It was infinitely easier to take the coward's way out, and just say 'no'. She felt no obligation to tell a stranger the miserable, sad story of her life, and her loss. But for some reason the sweet, motherly woman sitting across the table from her compelled her to tell the truth. "I had a child," she said quietly, and raised her eyes to meet Gert's compassionate blue gaze. "A little girl. Her name was Natalie, and she was killed in a car accident when she was three years old."

Gert shook her grey head and reached across the table to squeeze Andi's hand gently. "I'm so very sorry, my dear. What a terrible, terrible thing to happen."

Andi shrugged. "It's been hard." There was really nothing else to say – no response that could easily convey the pain and sorrow and guilt and anger she felt. They sat in silence for a few minutes and sipped their cooling coffee, but it was a companionable, easy silence, unlike the strained, stuck-for-word muteness Andi had encountered in the past when she occasionally talked about her bereavement. "I'm really worried about my husband," she said, ending their private contemplations a few minutes later. "I've been having horrible dreams." She gazed out the frosty kitchen window at the picture-perfect mounds of soft snow and white-tipped evergreens, chickadees and redpolls flitting from branch to branch. It was a deceptively serene and calming scene, masking the deadly impact the sub-zero temperature has on all living things. "I can't even imagine what he's going through out there."

"Your husband will be just fine," Gert assured her with a smile. She got up and added some hot coffee to their cups. "The Iditarod hasn't lost a musher yet, and the race gets safer every year. I'm sure you'll hear from North when he reaches Nikolai. They have a satellite phone there now."

"Oh my God!" Andi cried, startling Gert.

"What is it?"

"North will call the Shannons' place," she moaned. "He doesn't know I've moved."

"Well, you call your friends right now and give them this number. Ask them to pass it on to your husband if he calls."

Andi nodded. "Thanks, I'll do that." She pushed her chair back from the table, suddenly exhausted. "I think I'll take Qannik back to the kennel and go unpack now."

"You just leave that beautiful pup sleeping right where she is," Gert said adamantly. "I love having a dog in the house again, and Bill will take her back for you later." She picked up Andi's plate and placed a couple of brownies next to the leftover muffin. "I'll just wrap this in some cellophane for you to take to your room. You might want a snack later. Lunch is at 12:30 in the big dining room."

"Okay. Thanks so much for everything, Gert," Andi said, accepting the wrapped plate. "I didn't notice, is there a phone in my room?"

"No, but you just help yourself to the one on the desk in the front hall. We just ask our guests not to make any long-distance calls without telling us," she winked.

Just then a bell dinged repeatedly from the reception area. It sounded like one of those small, round annoying contraptions that you tapped on when you wanted to get someone's attention. "Excuse me, dear. I'd better go tend to that."

Andi left her hostess talking in the front hall with a fortyish couple dressed in cross-country ski gear and ran up the wide staircase to the second floor, her room key clutched in her hand. She unpacked, placing her clothes in the cedar bureau and toiletries in the small but immaculate bathroom. Then she slipped back downstairs, relieved to find the reception area empty again. She left her new phone number with the Shannons, who promised to give it to North the moment he called.

Exhausted from her sleepless night, Andi drew the heavy, dark green curtains over both of the long windows and folded the duvet down on the queen-sized bed. She stripped down to her underwear and crawled under the heavy cover longing for a dreamless, undisturbed nap. She fell asleep within minutes, but her wishes didn't come true.

It seemed that not only would her nights be tormented by dreams of red-spattered snow and the scent of hot, coppery blood, but her days as well. Screams and shouts and strange, guttural grunts tormented her slumber, echoing through her mind long after she awoke and lay trembling in the darkened room. And there were always the colours – white and red, red and white – swirling before her eyes. She strained to recall the voices from her dreams, voices that screamed in terror, crying out for help. She thought one of them sounded like her husband, but was the other a woman?

Andi lay stiffly on the warm, soft bed, her limbs rigid and her shallow breaths barely raising her chest. She squeezed her eyes tightly closed and shut the world out, afraid to move for fear of losing her failing, tenuous hold on the dream. She willed herself to recall every detail, but the harder she tried the quicker the visions faded, until they were nothing but shadowy, distant memories.

White and red. White and red.

Snow and blood. Snow and blood.

SIXTEEN

Twelve long, miserable, cold hours after his departure from the Rohn checkpoint, North pulled into Nikolai. He ached from head to foot, but the intense pain in his left shoulder had thankfully diminished to a dull, lingering ache. He forgot about his misery for a few minutes when the checker who greeted him told him he was in fifteenth position; he thought he'd dropped to at least twentieth, and the good news bolstered his flagging spirits. North didn't want to merely *complete* the Iditarod ... he desperately wanted to finish within the top fifteen, and so far he was right on track to do so.

The arrival of the annual Iditarod racing teams in Nikolai, a small North American Indian village of no more than twenty dwellings deep in Alaska's vast interior, was cause for celebration in a community that had so little. The village was accessible only by air or water in the summer months, or snowmobile and dog sled during the winter. Any visitor to the isolated community gave the locals cause for celebration, and the village embraced the Iditarod racers every year.

North was greeted not only by the official checker, but also by a small party of friendly, enthusiastic residents, including a dozen children of varying ages who clamoured over his sled the minute he braked the team to a stop. Their excited, shrill laughter and youthful voices were music to his ears after days of solitude, and he spent several minutes answering their many questions and laughing at their antics before he shooed them away from his dogs, who were unfamiliar with the quick movements and unrestrained voices of children and had become overexcited and jumpy.

"When you've got yourself organized, there's a hot meal waiting for you at the community hall," the checker said, pointing to a small, weathered wooden building a few hundred feet away. His round face was ruddy, and both his plentiful facial hair and bits of curly hair jutting from beneath the rim of his hat were a bright coppery red, suggesting he was of Irish, or perhaps Scottish descent.

"I won't say no to that," North laughed. "I hear there might be a telephone around I can use to make a quick call to Anchorage."

"Yup. We have a sat phone in the cabin here. You're welcome to a few minutes on 'er if no one else is using it."

Two other teams were bedded down, taking a long rest, and North had pulled up behind them. After feeding and tending to his dogs, and spreading straw for their beds, North found his drop bag and cooked another batch of food for the cooler. As soon as it was done he made his way to the community hall, his mouth watering and stomach growling in anticipation of food and coffee, his one real addiction. He found a solitary musher, who introduced himself simply as '44', sitting at a long, plastic covered table, a cup of coffee and empty bowl on the table in front of him. North stopped to chat with 44 for a few minutes before the obviously exhausted man declared he needed to grab a couple hours of sleep and left the hall.

Clocks matter little on the trail when schedules cease to exist; one sleeps and eats whenever the opportunity arises. Although it was only 8 am, North accepted a large bowl of thick moose chili, a dish he wouldn't normally choose for breakfast, from the soft-spoken Native North American girl manning the facility. Her gleaming black hair was secured by a narrow leather thong at the nape of her neck, exactly like North's, but hung almost to her waist while North's skimmed his shoulders. She wore blue jeans and a flannel, green plaid shirt, with intricately beaded moccasins on her feet; her outfit bore an eerily similar resemblance to North's usual garb.

"Your moccasins are beautiful," he commented when she returned to the table to set a cup of coffee and what had to be half a loaf of sliced, buttered white bread before him. "Did you make them yourself?"

Her dark eyes lit up, and she turned one foot from side to side to display the pink, dark purple, mauve and white design that extended from the top of the soft leather shoe and around both sides. "Thank you. Yes, I just finished them."

North spooned a mouthful of chili into his mouth, chewed briefly and swallowed. "My mom and sisters all make moccasins and mukluks, but I've never seen such an intricate beading pattern on them. You've done a fabulous job."

The girl hung her head and shuffled her feet.

"What's your name?" North asked.

"Dakota," she said softly. "What's yours?"

"North Ruben, better known as Rookie #9 from Inuvik, Canada," North grinned. "This chili is amazing, by the way. Nice and spicy, just the way I like it. You didn't make it too, did you?"

Dakota nodded shyly. "And the bread. I baked it last night."

North shoved half a slice of bread in his mouth and pushed in another heaping spoonful of chili. "Mmmm," he moaned, his appreciation genuine, "everything is absolutely delicious. You're quite the talented young woman, Dakota."

She hung her head and smiled at her feet, her face glowing with pride.

North spooned in another mouthful of chili, then scrutinised Dakota with a speculative look in his dark eyes. "You wouldn't happen to have a pair of ladies moccasins in a size eight you'd be willing to sell, would you?" he asked, thinking the beautiful moccasins would make a nice present for Andi's birthday which was coming up on May 24.

Dakota's head popped up, and her dark brown eyes met his for the first time. "Really? You'd like to buy a pair from me?"

"Absolutely. I think my wife would love them."

She tilted her head to the side. "What's your wife's name?" she asked.

"Andi. Well, it's really Andrea but everyone calls her Andi."

"I have a few pairs I could show you. Are you leaving right after you eat?"

"No, I'm going to try and use the phone at the Iditarod checkers cabin, then grab a few hours of sleep."

"I live just down the street. I'll run home and get them, bring them to the cabin for you to look at after you're done eating," she said eagerly. She was smiling widely now, her eyes sparkling with newfound pride.

Dakota brought North another heaping bowl of chili without asking if he wanted a second helping, and he ate until his shrunken stomach ached in protest. It was the first hot food he'd had in over two days and he wasn't about to waste even a mouthful.

After his meal North returned to the checkers' cabin and pulled Tom Shannon's phone number from the inside pocket of his red plaid flannel shirt where he'd placed it next to Andi's picture for safekeeping. An adolescent, most likely the checker's son judging by the lad's fiery red hair and striking resemblance to the older man, sat in a creaking wooden rocking chair next to the warm woodstove, reading a well-thumbed *Sports Illustrated* magazine.

"Good morning," North said. "I'd like to use the phone for a few minutes if I can."

"You know how to operate a sat phone?" the lad asked.

"Absolutely. Got one of my own at home."

"Help yourself then. It's on the table over there." His eyes hadn't left the magazine even once during the short conversation.

North placed his call and waited patiently for the connection. He let the line ring ten times, his disappointment deepening with each additional ring. He was about to hang up when the Shannons' answering machine engaged and Pat's voice asked him to leave a message. "Hey, it's North. I'm in Nikolai and was just hoping to talk to my wife. Well, anyway, tell her everything is okay. I'm hungry and cold most of the time though. I wish you were here, Andi." He chuckled dryly. "Well, anyway. I guess that's it. I'll see you in Nome. Love you." He was just hanging up when there was a short knock on the door and Dakota walked in holding a large plastic bag.

"Hi, Dakota," North said dejectedly. He had been longing to hear Andi's voice again, and had looked forward to this phone call with anticipation for the past two days. A shuffling sound broke his dejected concentration, and he turned his head just in time to spot the teenage lad leap clumsily to his feet, his magazine lying face down on the wood plank floor and the empty chair rocking wildly.

"Dakota!" the lad, whose complexion now matched his hair, gasped.

"Hi, Liam," she said, turning her eyes to the floor.

North suppressed a grin, suddenly understanding why Dakota had been so eager to meet him at the checkers' cabin. "You got some mocs to show me?" he asked solemnly. He remembered only too clearly how embarrassing young love could be.

Dakota pulled out three pairs of mocs, two brown ones and one black. North picked up each shoe and inspected it carefully, admiring the tightly stitched, even seams. The beadwork on each pair was done in a unique, differing pattern and range of vivid or pastel colours. They all looked to be about the right fit for Andi. "How much for all three pairs?" he asked.

Dakota's mouth dropped and she blinked her large brown eyes several times. "Um. I don't know," she said hesitantly. "Thirty dollars?" Liam had sidled up to her side.

North frowned and shook his head. "Dakota, have you ever sold any of your mocs before?"

"No ..." she replied hesitantly, staring at the floor again.

"Well, sweetheart, people down south would likely pay that much for one pair of beautiful moccasins like this. "How about I give you sixty dollars for all three pairs?"

"Okay," she said, looking into North's eyes for the first time, her wide smile exposing perfectly straight, white teeth.

North dug out his wallet and peeled off three American twenty-dollar bills. He passed them to the beaming girl, along with his business card for the Qamutik Gallery. "I own a native art gallery in Inuvik," he said. "My phone number is there. If you ever want to start selling your moccasins or mukluks give me a call. I know I'd have a market for them. Your work is exquisite."

Dakota beamed and shuffled her feet. Liam peered over her shoulder at the business card she held in her hand. "Thank you, North."

North place the mocs back in the plastic bag and rolled it up into a compact ball. "Take care, kids," he said with a wave "and thanks again, Dakota. My wife is going to love these." He closed the cabin door to giggling voices and hushed, whispered conversation. *Good luck, Liam,* he grinned.

Four hours later, North was on the trail again. He and the dogs were fully rested and the majority of his aches and pains had faded to near non-existence. The former mining town of McGrath was forty-eight miles distant. He'd been forced to drop two more dogs in Nikolai; Chinook, one of his younger animals, was showing signs of fatigue, and Mika had a swollen ankle. He prayed that the ten dogs left on the gangline would get him to Nome.

From Nikolai the trail followed the south fork of the Kuskokwim River and crossed a series of identical lakes and swamps interspersed with wooden stretches. The sky was clear and the 3200-foot peak of Tatalina Mountain, southwest of McGrath, was clearly visible in the cold, dry air. He stopped only once for a short rest to snack the dogs and check their paws. The easy, uneventful leg took him just over five hours, but he neither overtook another musher nor was passed by one, and he was satisfied with that.

He arrived at the village of McGrath just after 5 pm. McGrath was a thriving and busy little community and boasted an airport, store, restaurant, and even had accommodation for travellers. The media staged themselves in McGrath for middle of the race reporting, further adding to the activity and festive feeling in the village.

North knew many mushers chose to make their '24-hour stop' in McGrath because of the many conveniences there. The Iditarod Race Committee had a few rules in place, mainly for the safety of both dogs and drivers. One of these rules required the mushers to make three mandatory rest stops: one 24-hour layover at any checkpoint, one 8-hour layover at any checkpoint on the Yukon River, and one 8-hour stop at White Mountain, ninety-nine miles from Nome.

He made his way to the checkpoint cabin and was met by an elderly, slight woman who greeted him warmly and introduced herself as Olga. "Are you staying for a short break or your long one?" she asked. Four or five teams were already bedded down at the checkpoint, drop bags and gear strewn around the sleds and cookpots bubbling. Three figures sat around a small fire, and their voices and laughter, one definitely feminine, carried loudly through the still air. North suspected they were all taking their 24-hour stop, and he'd heard the checkpoint could be noisy at times.

"Just a few hours so the dogs and I can have a nap," North replied. He wasn't tired, and he suspected the dogs weren't either, but Takotna was still two to three hours away; a little too far to go without a rest. North's strength had been restored after the good meal he'd had in Nikolai, and the pain in his left shoulder seemed a lot better. He planned to take his 24-hour rest at Takotna, where he'd been assured it would be much quieter than McGrath.

"Do you have time for a cup of tea or coffee, or are you afraid it will keep you awake?" Olga chuckled.

"I'll never pass up the offer of a good cup of coffee," North grinned. "It's never kept me awake yet." He scribbled his name to the check-in sheet she offered him, his cold, stiff hands making his signature barely legible.

Several strands of long, dark grey hair poked from the edge of the hood on Olga's faded blue, slightly tattered parka. The coat looked to be two sizes too large for her, making North wonder if it belonged to someone else. "The vet is inside," she said when he pulled out his vet book.

"I'll be up in a minute for that cup of coffee," North said. Olga returned to the cabin and left North to his tasks. It was bitterly cold and would get only colder when the sun set in two hours, so he spread some straw for the dogs, put on their jackets and moved them from the gangline to the tether line. He fed them from the cooler, which had more than enough food left for another meal now that he was down to only ten dogs, then headed for the cabin.

When he opened the log cabin's front door, a blast of heat hit him like the flame from a blow torch. A massive woodstove stood against one wall of the main room, leaping white and yellow flames visible through its heavy glass door. The room smelled strongly of wood smoke and burnt coffee. North stomped the snow from his boots and unzipped his parka. Olga was pouring two mugs of coffee, and several men were seated around a long wood table, stripped down to their pants and shirts.

"There he is!" Olga smiled. "North Ruben, come over here and grab a cup. This here is Hank, our vet. He's visiting us from Colorado." She smiled and squeezed the shoulder of a young, blond-haired man, no more than thirty years old, who sat at the end of the table. She moved to the next man in line and rested her hand on the broad shoulder of a senior whose facial features were all but hidden behind an unruly grey moustache and beard and waves of shoulder length white hair. "My husband Ray, he's been in charge of this checkpoint for the past twenty years. I'm just his slave," she laughed. Then she glanced at the two men at the end of the table. "And you likely know Bob and Johann since you're all in the same race."

North waved, said, "Hi," to the room in general, and accepted a mug of coffee and a couple of cookies from Olga. He sat next to Hank and presented his vet book. They all talked for a few minutes, mainly about the condition of the trail, the health of their dogs, what the weather was expected to be like and which mushers were where in the race standings. North had quickly come to realize that a great many of the Iditarod mushers were repeat racers; in fact most of them had run the race ten or twenty times or more, meaning they had a great advantage over the rookies like himself and Mats, who had absolutely no idea what the trail had in store for them. North recognized the other two mushers from the Banquet in Anchorage and knew they had run the race before, but hadn't exchanged more than a passing greeting with them before now. They were friendly enough, though, and seemed only too happy to spend some time chatting.

He finished his cup of exceedingly strong, black coffee, thanked his hosts, and escaped into the blessedly cool night, followed by Hank. The vet gave his dogs a quick check and signed them off as healthy and fit to continue the race. He looked at Chica's paw closely, shining a flashlight on her foot to get a better look, and agreed with North that there was barely any indication of rawness and she could continue in the race. North said he would keep an eye on it and continue applying ointment and bandaging her foot.

Hank returned to the cabin, and North crawled into his sleeping bag in the sled basket, his headlamp in hand. He set his watch alarm for three hours of what he hoped would be an undisturbed rest, free from the persistently dogged nightmares he'd been plagued with each time he laid his head to rest on the Iditarod trail.

SEVENTEEN

North slept through a great deal of his 24-hour stop in Takotna, as did the dogs. He fed them twice and filled the cooler with cooked dog food, enough for three meals on the trail. He fed himself too, heating up bags of the rich beef stew and meaty lasagna Andi had cooked for him. The meals were frozen in serving size, watertight bags that could be heated in hot water. Every time he warmed a meal, he saw her shining green eyes, felt the touch of her lips and smelled the lingering scent of the lavender that scented their sheets.

During his 24-hour stop in Takotna ten or more other mushers including Mats Pederson and Becky Singleton pulled into the checkpoint. Some stayed for their mandatory 24-hour stop, some for four or five hours to rest their dogs, and some merely long enough to sign the check-in sheet. He and Mats found they enjoyed each other's company and spent several hours talking over endless cups of coffee. They found common ground in their love of sled dogs and mushing, and laughed about their ignorance of the many hazards and hardships on the Iditarod trail. North served the burly Norwegian one of his bags of frozen lasagna, which Mats declared was of gourmet quality, despite being heated in a pot of questionably clean water. It was only what was inside the bag that counted, he declared with a toothy smile.

Becky Singleton, whose hot pink parka and matching dog jackets and booties were hard to miss, was one of the mushers who stopped for only a few hours to rest her dogs. She spent a few precious minutes visiting with the two rookies, and after they recounted their horrifying experiences with the Happy Valley Steps and Dalzell Gorge, she warned them to watch the weather closely during the next stretch of the race ... the beginning of the long battle to cross Alaska's vast, frigid interior. It would be a long and gruelling three to four day run, she said, mainly following the Yukon River over barren tundra. She told them of her own first-hand experience with devilishly strong winds that had pushed her dogs off course and whipped her and her team with a mind-numbing minus 100 Fahrenheit wind chill. If the first part of the race was fraught with danger from hidden, vertical gorges, she cautioned, then one of the biggest challenges in its middle was the horrific wind and weather they were sure to encounter.

Becky left a few hours before midnight, and Mats retired to grab a few more hours of sleep, leaving North to his own devices. He restocked his supplies from his drop bag and readied his team, anxious to get on the trail again the minute his 24-hour stop was over. He tried to estimate how many mushers had passed through Takotna since his arrival, which was really an impossible task as he had likely slept right through any number of arrival and departures. He finally concluded that he'd fallen back to at least twentieth position, which was a disheartening thought.

He began the short thirty-eight-mile leg to the Ophir checkpoint energized and optimistic, with a thermos full of hot, strong coffee in his bag. His left shoulder was still slightly sore but he hesitated to take any more aspirin. He'd already used up over half of his supply and still had a long, long road ahead of him. He was only about a third of the way through the race; the Bering Coast and the finish line in Nome were still almost 700 miles away.

North left Ophir, which turned out to be a checkpoint only, with no community, just past midnight on day six of the race. It was a moonless, calm though bitterly cold night, and the trail was generally easy to follow and maneuver. An hour out of Ophir the trail was following a creek when North noticed he had company. Six or seven rangy wolves, starving for more than just company, had slunk in a hundred yard behind him, their dark forms clearly visible against the white background of the frozen creek. The wolves' presence unsettled his dogs, making them cast furtive glances over their shoulders, whine softly and hang their heads and tails low. The wolves' presence unsettled North too, and he pulled his rifle from the sled bag and slung it over his shoulder in the unlikely event he would need it, but the lanky hunters disappeared as silently and stealthily as they had appeared. North remained alert for several more miles before he relaxed his vigilant watch.

From Ophir the trail led to the famous town of Iditarod, a long ninety miles away. An hour out of Ophir and about four hours before sunrise on day six of the race, the team started to tire and North began to search for a sheltered place to make camp. With no moon to relieve the black of night, he had to rely solely on his headlamp and instincts to find a good place to stop. Fifteen minutes later he spotted another trail branching away from the main run.

"*Come Gee! Come Gee!*" North shouted, simultaneously stomping on the brake to slow the team before they ran by the other trail. Kia and Weasel obediently followed his command to turn right, and veered onto the smaller trail. His two swing dogs, Nanuk and Suka, dutifully followed the leads, pulling the rest of the team behind them. North drew the dogs to a stop near a thin stand of small spruce trees. Other travellers had stopped there recently too, as evidenced by the remnants of a small campfire and circle of packed snow. It was far enough from the main trail to be out of the way and unobtrusive, and was a perfect spot to make camp.

A steady, increasingly strong north wind had blown away the previous days few scattered clouds, and the pre-dawn temperature had plummeted. The force of the wind was blocked slightly by the sheltering copse of trees, but still held the capacity to freeze exposed skin within minutes. North set the snow hook and tied the snub line to a sturdy tree. Before he did anything else he dug out the cooker and HEET and set some snow to melt, then unhooked the dogs from the gangline and put them on the long tether line, also secured to a tree. He examined each dog thoroughly, gently palpitating their shoulders and legs for signs of sore muscles before attaching their jackets. He removed forty little green booties, checked their feet, and refastened their boots. It was a time-consuming but necessary task.

North drank a cup of strong tea while the dogs ate their warm meal. He was hungry, but too exhausted to even warm a bag of food for himself. As soon as they were done eating, the dogs curled up in the small piles of straw North had packed from Ophir, tied to the top of his sled bag. North laid his sleeping bag out inside the sled bag and crawled in, squirming until he found a comfortable position before he zipped up against the wind.

To the haunting serenade of distant wolves, he gratefully slipped into dark, dreamless oblivion. The Aurora Borealis spread waves of dancing green, blue and red colour across the heavens, but he missed their glorious show.

Three hours later he was on the trail again. The run from Ophir to Iditarod was a long one, and North was forced to spend another night on the trail again. He began to fear he may have underestimated his dogs' appetites and may run out of food. Eighteen hours after departing from Ophir he pulled into the ghost town of Iditarod, which marked the mid-way point in the race. Founded during the gold rush in the early 1900's, the town's population exploded to over 10,000 souls for a few brief years. Over $35 million in gold was mined from the area, and the thriving town boasted hotels, cafés, brothels, a store and even a bank; all that remained now was one cabin and a handful of ruins, including the concrete bank vault.

North soon realized that he wasn't really mentally prepared for the days and nights that would meld together seamlessly, the transition from one to another so measured he wasn't aware of the passage of time. Night, day ... day, night. What did it really matter? One was long and cold, the other longer and colder. Time became meaningless, his struggle to survive more challenging with each passing mile and hour.

Checkpoints became an indistinct blur; Shageluk, Anvik, Grayling, Eagle Island.

Running, check points, sign in, sign out.

Cold, wind, blinding whiteouts, darkness.

Fatigue, hunger, aching muscles.

Rest the dogs, feed the dogs, check lines, check paws and replace little green booties.

Bone jarring terrain, hunger, fatigue, pain and desolation – they became his constant companions on the lonely trail for the next three days as he fought to conquer the Yukon River and vast, barren interior.

Along with the unrelenting cold, the mighty Yukon River sometimes offered up deadly suckholes – frozen, snow-covered whirlpools big enough to swallow a dog or a sled. *Three seconds.* At a full run, a musher usually had *three mere seconds* of notice that danger, and possible death, loomed ahead. Even through his yellow snow goggles, North's eyes burned from the concentrated effort of searching the frozen river for hours on end while praying he would spot the small telltale puff of steam seeping up through the snow, signalling open, marginally warmer water below. Either good fortune or The Lord was on his side, and he managed to avoid the Yukon River's deadliest hazard. He hoped that the rest of his fellow mushers would have the same good luck.

North spent countless hours gazing at the wide night sky from his padded seat on top of the battered blue Coleman cooler, a night sky emblazoned with more stars than he'd ever imagined existed. He spent countless hours dreaming of emerald green eyes and warm, soft lips.

The dogs usually needed no direction from their master. They ran, and North clung to the sled, along for the ride of his life, but there was nowhere to run to ... nowhere to escape from the cold, wind, hunger and pain. No way to escape the delusions that began to suffuse his waking hours and invade his restless dreams, turning them to hideous nightmares.

White and red, white and red.

Snow and blood, snow and blood.

He began to dread sleep, and the nightmares it would bring. He forced himself to stay awake until he was no more than a walking, mumbling zombie. He began to fear that there was a remote possibility that his nightmares weren't nightmares, after all, but a harbinger of something he didn't even want to acknowledge.

EIGHTEEN

"Hi, Dad, it's me," *Andi* replied to her father's curt 'Hello' on Sunday morning. "Just checking in from Anchorage like I promised." Her voice lacked its usual melodic vibrancy. A week of continual worry had taken its toll; her face had taken on an unaccustomed leanness that only served to accentuate her high cheekbones, a gift from her father's eastern European heritage. She had just finished feeding the dogs and had spent some time playing with them in the yard until the intense cold chased her back in. The outside temperature gauge read minus forty degrees.

"Hey, sweetheart, it's good to hear from you. How are you doing up there?" Alex Nowak detected a familiar, forlorn note in his only daughter's voice, one that immediately brought back worrisome memories. He was sitting in his Port Alberni, British Columbia, kitchen with a second cup of coffee and the remains of his solitary breakfast sitting on the old, gray Formica table before him. He was dressed in the same worn but clean work clothes he wore almost every day – dark green workpants and a matching button-down shirt layered over a light wool Stanfield's undershirt. Although he was semi-retired and had turned over the day-to-day operations of the family fishing boat to two of his sons, Bryan and Luke a few years ago, he couldn't quite shake the habit of preparing himself for work every morning.

A light but steady rain had started falling during the night, which wasn't uncommon for Vancouver Island in March. Outside the kitchen window the first early azaleas were blooming, their deep peach blossoms a bright spot of colour in the monotone green yard. Rows of rhododendrons and azaleas, planted by his dear, departed Mary years ago, would soon be in full bloom. Their large red, pink, fuchsia, orange, yellow and white blossoms lent a breathtaking riot of spring and early summer colour to the yard. Alex Nowak loved this time of year and the vibrant blooms' perpetual reminder of the deep love he and Mary shared for forty years. He still mourned her early departure from his life every single day.

"I'm okay," Andi replied apathetically. Snow had been falling for the past hour and had begun to accumulate in a soft, white layer on Bill's freshly shoveled sidewalks. She wondered if it was snowing where North was.

"I'm okay," Alex mimicked her words and monotone voice. "And what, exactly, does that mean?" He knew his daughter well; if he wanted to find out what was bothering her he'd have to dig a little. "Those friends of North's treating you well?"

"Um," Andi hesitated. "I moved out on Tuesday."

"You WHAT? What do you mean, you moved out?" Alex slammed his mug on the table, sloshing a bit of its cooling contents on the table. "Where the hell are you?"

"Don't worry, Dad! I found a really nice guest house about a mile outside of town. And it's got a great kennel so it's just perfect for the dogs. They'll look after them when I leave for Nome on Wednesday." She managed a weak laugh. "They even let Qannik in the house sometimes."

"Why did you move, or should I ask? And what did your husband say?"

"Well, I haven't exactly told North yet."

"Humph," Alex snorted. "When are you planning on telling him?"

"When I get to Nome."

"Jesus," Alex muttered. "So you're all alone up there, living in some kind of *guest house* with complete strangers. That doesn't sit well with me, baby girl."

"It's been wonderful, Dad. I'm fine. In fact Gert and Bill have been absolutely marvellous."

"Gert and Bill, eh?"

"Yes, the Gustafsons. They're an older couple. I guess Gert is in her late sixties and Bill is maybe in his seventies. You'd love Gert's cooking, Dad. She made Alaskan clam chowder last night that was just out of this world."

"Nothing can beat your mother's fresh clam chowder, Andrea, and you can't tell me otherwise," Alex said testily.

"I know," Andi sighed. "Anyway, I just wanted to call and tell you everything is going okay. North called on Wednesday. He was in Nikolai."

"Oh, so you were able to talk to him?"

"Uh, not exactly. He called his friend's house where I'd been staying, and left a message."

"Humph." Alex slurped coffee loud enough to let Andi know he was not impressed with her. "You have any idea when North will get to Nome?"

"No, but from what I've heard he's been doing alright. He's just past the halfway mark now but he's not anywhere near the front of the race, that's for sure."

"Ah shit, the poor guy. I know he really had his heart set on doing well in this race."

Andi sighed deeply. "I don't really care, Dad. As long as he comes back in one piece, I don't care if he comes in last."

Alex could hear his youngest child's laboured breathing, and knew she was trying hard to hold back her tears.

"I ... I know it's selfish of me," she continued uncertainly, "but since he left I sometimes wish I wouldn't have given him the money to buy those new sled dogs after what happened."

Only by a bizarre twist of fate had North been able to purchase new Canadian Eskimo Dogs to replace those that had died at the hand of an unknown murderer during the chaotic days of the Pivot Lake Diamond Mine fiasco two years ago. It was ironic that diamonds, those priceless, rare gems that had been responsible for the death of three of his precious dogs, were also so instrumental in restoring the strength of his kennel.

"Sweetheart, don't think like that. Whatever happens to North in Alaska is *not* of your doing," Alex said in a soft, sympathetic voice. "And besides, he's going to be just fine so quit your worrying. Your husband grew up in the Arctic and he's been mushing all his life. Not much different than what he's doing now, just a little longer race."

"Yeah, I know, but-"

"And besides," Alex continued, cutting Andi's reply short, "if it wasn't for you and that damn 'Sixth Sense' you inherited from your mother, those diamond thieves might still be syphoning diamonds off that mine. Everyone's damn proud of you for what you did."

Andi had been the only person who had suspected that something unusual was happening at the Pivot Lake Diamond Mine, 280 kilometers east of Inuvik. The mine was one of Tuktu Aviation's largest clients, and they held a contract to provide daily service with their DeHavilland Twin Otter, a workhorse of an aircraft large enough to carry up to nineteen passengers or about 3000 pounds of cargo, or a combination of both. Andi, as Tuktu's Flight Operations Manager, regularly reviewed all of the company's aircraft flight logs and billings, and noticed a pattern of unbilled Twin Otter flight hours.

She covertly investigated the discrepancies, and with the aid of her Assistant Dispatcher Ayame Saito, discovered over fifty unauthorized flight time hours that could be attributed to only one crew; Captain James O'Neill and his new co-pilot, Hank Brister. She calculated that over the span of four months, the pair's unbilled hours had cost Tuktu Aviation over $40,000 – a goodly chunk of change.

"Yeah, well I should have discovered the flight time discrepancies sooner," Andi lamented. The discovery had made her doubt her own competence, and the loss of revenue continued to feel like a personal affront, even two years later.

"Well, you exposed the crooks, my dear, and put the entire mess into the hands of the diamond mine, and that's all that matters now. You did the right thing," Alex said firmly, hoping to soothe his daughter's conscience. He knew she had enough to worry about right now without reopening old wounds, and that she was still fragile, even eight years after the death of her child, his beloved, sweet granddaughter Natalie. "I don't know why you're even thinking about all of that old business now."

After conducting her own damning and perilous internal investigation to unearth the reason for the unaccounted Twin Otter flight hours, Andi flew to Toronto and met with Sam Tavernese, Pivot Lake's Chief Executive Officer. She went unannounced and alone, but not empty handed. At first, her seemingly implausible story of missing flight hours, crooked employees and missing diamonds was met with disbelief. It was only when she reached into her leather briefcase and extracted proof – North's professional-quality photographs of Henrik Bruller's clandestine meetings with Jim O'Neill, and the gruesome pictures of his own murdered dogs – that she got the man's attention. Photos of blood-spattered snow, the lifeless bodies of the dogs, and a warning written in blood on the side of North's kennel to 'MIND YOUR OWN BUSINESS - NEXT TIME IT WILL BE YOU' were hard to dispute.

But when Andi pulled a small bag of raw, uncut diamonds from the depths of her briefcase, Tavernese finally became convinced that her accusations were valid. Sitting across from the CEO at his dark, gleaming wood desk, she held the stones that she, in a daring attempt to expose the diamond smuggling ring, had in turn stolen from the thieves. Reassured that they would act on her accusations, Andi gratefully left the entire mess in Tavernese's hands, including the bag of raw gems and photos, and returned to Inuvik.

A few weeks later Tavernese brought a private team of highly skilled men to Inuvik who North insisted on calling 'the hit men'. In a well-thought out and daring manoeuvre utilizing Tuktu's Twin Otter, a leased helicopter and several snowmobiles, Tavernese succeeded in catching the diamond smugglers red-handed and putting an end to their crime spree.

As much as she hated to admit it, it was just possible that North was right about the hit men. Henrik Bruller, the mine's Project Manager, lost his life, and Tuktu Aviation lost three of their employees: James O'Neill, Hank Brister, and Jessica Hartman had not only disappeared from Inuvik that fateful day, but their respective families had not heard from them in the ensuing two years.

As far as North and Andi knew, the entire fiasco was never made public, and the market value of the stolen diamonds never revealed to a soul, including the mine's shareholders. Andi's personal reward for exposing the diamond smuggling ring, one that she'd never expected nor asked for, was a handful of cut and polished Canadian diamonds. Each brilliant, perfect gem bore a serial number, a Certificate of Authenticity and a symbol of either a Canadian flag or a polar bear etched into its girdle. The appraised value of the stones was $100,000, but their market value had been substantially more.

At Andi's insistence, she sold all but one gem, the perfect half-carat princess cut diamond mounted in her platinum engagement ring, to fund the purchase of fourteen Canadian Eskimo Dogs to replenish and expand North's kennel. Because the ancient breed was relatively rare, their cost was astronomical and would have been impossible for North to fund entirely from his own savings. He was reluctant to accept Andi's generous gift, but she insisted. In his mind, the gems were tainted; they were Tavernese's way of assuring Andi's continued silence. To this day, North was positive there was a deep connection between Sam Tavernese and the Mafia. Andi thought his suspicions unfounded. The fact was, though, if not for 'Andi's diamonds', there would be no Iditarod for North Ruben. At least not this year.

It was a conundrum that continued to occupy Andi's mind for hours on end. There was no question that 'her' diamonds had made it possible for North to be competing in the 25th Anniversary running of the Iditarod, but if *not* for the precious gems they'd both be at home, safe and sound and warm. Instead, her solitary nights and long days were plagued by dreams and visions of impending disaster and scenes of bloody carnage.

"Leave me a phone number I can reach you at." Her father's voice broke Andi's reverie, and she became vaguely aware that he'd been talking to her for a while.

"Sure, Dad."

She was rattling off the number to him when Gert stomped from the kitchen to the reception desk. "Coffee and fresh pecan cinnamon buns are ready when you are," she smiled, her voice a loud whisper. Andi smiled and nodded energetically, mouthing, "I'll be right there."

"What's that?" she heard her dad ask. "Cinnamon buns? Does that woman bake, too?"

Andi laughed. "Yes, I think she's trying to fatten me up a little before I leave."

Alex sighed. "I do miss your mother's baking."

"Ah, Dad. I know you miss Mom. I miss her too, every single day. I'll bake you whatever you want when North and I come to visit next month."

"That honeymoon of yours is coming up quick. Got all your plans made already?"

"I'm letting North look after most of it. All I know is that we'll visit with you in Port for a week, pick up Bryan's motorhome, then meet up with some of our friends in Vancouver for the RV trip down Baja California. There's another couple coming too, but we don't meet them until San Diego. He's another old friend of North's from law school I think."

"Sounds exciting. From Alaska to Mexico; you sure do get around, girl."

Alex was rewarded with one of his daughter's genuine, sparkling laughs. "I'm looking forward to some nice relaxing time in the sun and on the beach," she admitted. "I've almost had enough of winter for one year."

"Well I'll let you get to your coffee and cinnamon bun," he said. "By the way, the peach azalea is in full bloom here."

"Oh, Dad! Don't rub it in, please," Andi laughed again. "I know Vancouver Island is the most beautiful place on earth. I just happen to live in the Arctic with the most handsome, wonderful man in the world, and that's the way it's going to stay for a while."

"I know, I know. Just teasing. You take care of yourself and phone me again before you leave for Nome, okay?"

"I will Dad. It's been nice talking to you. I miss you, you know."

"I miss you, too, baby girl."

They said their goodbyes and Andi retreated to the warm, cozy kitchen for a long visit and a luscious, warm bun. Gert's kitchen was one of the places she felt most comfortable ... it and at the JavaGenie, drinking coffee and visiting with Rachel. Bill kept insisting that Rachel's coffee beans were special. Maybe there was something to that theory after all.

NINETEEN

North's life for the next three days slipped into a habitual pattern: check in, present vet book and examine dogs, massage shoulders and legs, check feet, replace little green booties, feed the dogs, cook dog food and finally, when the animals were content and resting, attend to his own human needs. He was almost always hungry but too exhausted to eat more than a frozen candy bar or chunk of beef jerky. Most of the time he merely zipped himself into the sled bag and curled up in his down sleeping bag, happy to be out of the relentless, frigid wind.

He slept when his dogs slept – not the deep, restorative slumber he expected and longed for – but short, restless naps fraught with disturbing dreams. The screams of animals in pain, voices crying in the dark, and snow spattered with splashes of dark red blood became his constant, gruesome companions when he should have been dead to the world. He began to dread the few hours of sleep he managed to catch here or there, either at a checkpoint, or, more often than not, huddled beside the trail, and fought to stay awake, but always failed.

After almost three long, cold, energy draining days and nights on the awful Yukon River trail, North slid into the Kaltag checkpoint. He was taxed, both physically and mentally, and every muscle in his body ached. He no longer cared if he ever ate again, his toes and fingers were numb, and his cheeks dotted with patches of frostbite. He had begun to suffer hallucinations resulting from sleep deprivation, and called out to his father when the elder man passed him somewhere between Grayling and Eagle River, bundled in the old, tattered anorak North remembered from his childhood.

When he pulled into Kaltag he was cognizant enough, though, to realize that if he was so utterly exhausted then his dogs would be doubly so. They needed at least five hours of rest before tackling the treacherous Bering Sea ice – the next part of the seemingly endless race to Nome. He knew that neither he, nor the dogs, would make the long ninety-mile leg to the next checkpoint of Unalakleet in the condition they were in, and wisely decided to take his mandatory 8-hour Yukon River layover at Kaltag. He hated the thought that other mushers would surely pass him, and that he would fall further behind, but he had no choice.

On autopilot he unhooked the dogs, removed harnesses and booties, massaged their shoulders and legs and checked their paws. He fed them generous portions of warm, well-earned food and spread fresh straw for their beds. When he finally fell into his sled basket he was exhausted past the point of sleep. His restless dreams were plagued by indistinct images of dark shadows and blood-spattered snow.

Day ten on the trail, and North wondered, not for the first time, what in the *hell* he'd been thinking when he'd signed up for this hellish test of endurance called The Iditarod. His friends and family – everyone in his life except Andi, who seemed to possess an unlimited supply of faith in him – had told him he was mad. He was beginning to think they were all correct.

The ninety-mile leg from Kaltag to the village of Unalakleet, which name meant 'The Place Where The East Wind Blows' in the Iñupiaq language, should have been a piece of cake after his long rest in Kaltag. And it may have been, but for the persistent, debilitating winds that ripped across the barren land for the entire sixteen-hour ordeal. It seemed to North that the icy air even threaded its way into the seams of his heavy parka and snow pants, luring precious body heat from his core.

When the team finally skated across the glare ice of the large lagoon protecting the entrance to town, forty little green booties slipping and sliding over the lagoon's slippery, windswept surface, North almost

cried in relief. The town was the largest settlement between Wasilla and
Nome, and was also the base for the Iditarod Air Force during the
musher's race along the coast. It even boasted a few stores and a
restaurant.

Unalakleet was the last checkpoint before the treacherous run
along the Seward Peninsula; North arrived at noon on a clear and windy
minus 40 Fahrenheit day. He decided to rest for six or seven hours, a
little longer than he usually did, and treat himself to a hot meal at the
restaurant. He had managed to pass two teams while they rested beside
the trail, and thought he might be in about seventeenth position; still
close enough to reach his goal of placing within the top fifteen mushers.
He knew he had no hope of winning the race. His only consolation was
that Mats Pederson hadn't passed him – at least not that he was aware
of. The two rookies had made a bet as to who would finish first, and
North hated to lose a bet, especially when it involved a free steak dinner
and bottle of good red wine.

North dished out the last of the warm dogfood and bedded the
team down in piles of fresh straw, then located his drop bag. When the
dogs were comfortably settled, he made a dash to the restaurant, no
longer able to ignore the burning hollowness in his belly. The new batch
of dogfood would have to be cooked after he himself had been fed. And,
once again, his own rest, such as it was, would have to come last.

The sun was just setting when North released the sled brake and shouted
'*Mush!*' leaving the civilized community of Unalakleet behind. The
dogs seemed rested and ready to run, the cooler was full of cooked dog
food, and he felt more relaxed than he'd been since leaving Willow. The
next short leg to Shaktoolik was by all accounts a walk in the park and
he was confident that the worst part of the trail was behind him.
Nightfall brought a drop in the relentless wind, and although the
mercury pushed toward minus 45, it seemed warmer without the
debilitating wind chill. North left the dogs in their insulated green

jackets and belly wraps anyway, fearing they'd get chilled if he removed them.

Two hours into the leg a shooting star blazed across the indigo blue, star-studded sky, its brilliance unchallenged by civilization's artificial light. North made a wish on the falling star, tracking the meteoroid's path until it slowly faded from view. He pondered the question that had plagued him since childhood: *what lies beyond the stars?* His own wish, the very first thing that popped into his mind, surprised him; it had nothing to do with winning the Iditarod. What he *really* wanted was to be laying in the arms of his best friend ... the love of his life. *Andi would love this display of stars,* he thought. A powerful yearning, its bite as sharp as a blade, sliced through his heart. He missed his quirky, green-eyed bride and his calm, organized life back in Inuvik more than he realized. He shook his head impatiently and focused on the dark trail ahead.

Instead of following the windblown coast of The Norton Sound, the trail led slightly inland for a few miles before beginning a steady 850-foot climb around Blueberry Point, the first of three peaks in the Blueberry Hills. The last hill in the range would once again challenge his flatland-loving dogs: the climb was a brutal, steep four-mile rise to 1000 feet, and he wasn't looking forward to it one little bit.

The trail snaked around Blueberry Point, descended gradually before crossing a creek, and then followed the shoreline for a few miles before turning inland again. Once away from the coast, they entered the sheltering protection of a wooded valley. The moon hadn't made its nightly appearance yet; the night was totally devoid of light except for the faint glow from the mass of brilliant stars overhead and the narrow, wavering beam from his headlamp. Kia and Weasel didn't need artificial light to show them the way, though. Their sharp noses followed the scent of the dogs that had preceded them, and they ran surefooted along the narrow trail, weaving unerringly around scrubby trees and bush.

After looping around the second of the Blueberry Range's three high hills, the snow-covered trail once again returned to the Norton Sound's frozen shoreline. North pulled off the trail just before they tackled the last challenging mountain. He threw the dogs a small snack of frozen meat, checked tugs, lines and booties. He took a few minutes to give each animal a quick massage and was rewarded with soulful looks and the occasional swipe of a wet tongue.

Without the customary whistle and howl of wind overhead, the night was eerily silent. After the short break he hit the trail again, sled runners schussing over pristine snow. The team had one more peak to conquer, and it was going to be a tough one – a challenging four-mile long climb right up the spine of the range. It was the last climb before the Blueberry Hills released them to the barren coast and treacherous, constantly moving ice of the Norton Sound.

The dogs pulled slowly but steadily, Kia and Weasel setting the team's pace. After a while the trail levelled off and cut through a thick patch of evergreens before dipping down into a deep ravine. The dogs had to labour hard to climb out up the other side, straining, slipping back and straining again. At the top, the trail executed a sharp ninety degree turn before snaking through more scrubby spruce trees.

Ahead, North detected a faint lightening in the sky; he suspected the northern lights were lurking behind the thin curtain of clouds. The stand of fir and pine began to thin out, and North noticed a change in his team's demeanour – an infinitesimal altering of their carriage. They held their heads more erect and lifted their twitching noses higher to better capture whatever scent had caught their attention. Kia glanced over her shoulder, looking for guidance from her leader, her low whine barely audible.

"What's the matter, old girl?" North croaked, his voice rough and scratchy. His lead was trying to communicate something to him, but he was mystified as to what. He peered into the night intently, neither seeing nor hearing anything that alarmed him. "Northern lights got you spooked, old girl?" he laughed.

Kia whined louder and slowed her gait.

"Keep going, Kia," North called.

The dogs ran on, their ears alert and twisted forward, tuned in to a frequency only they could hear. A few minutes later Weasel suddenly lifted his snout skyward and howled. From somewhere up the trail, North heard the faint chords of an answering howl. One plaintive voice, followed by another and yet another, their eerie song louder with each passing second. North wondered if it was a pack of wolves, hunting for their dinner, or if he'd caught up to another team, resting in the woods alongside the trail. The howling and sound of crying canines disturbed him, though; the mere possibility of another encounter with hungry wolves spurred North to reach for his rifle. He tugged the sled bag's zipper open and reached for the rifle he'd left lying on top of his gear.

The trail seemed to be following a small watercourse created, perhaps, from mountain run-off during the short Alaskan summer. Small trees and shrub beds grew densely, forming an impenetrable wall and causing the trail to narrow to no more than a footpath. Kia and Weasel slowed to a trot when scraggly clumps of willow and stunted alder encroached on the twisting trail, brushing at the sides of the team's flanks and slapping at North's face. The canine voices ahead grew louder; it was becoming increasingly evident that the animals – either wolves or sled dogs – were in distress. His own team became more agitated with each step and began to whine continually.

North urged them on, their reluctance to continue growing with each passing minute. The cries ahead, sounding less and less like those of hunting wolves, continued to grow in intensity. North felt the first quiver of fear, which in turn released a flood of adrenalin to his veins.

His team's whining escalated to piteous, high-pitched keening.

North's focus cleared, his ears sharpened and his eyes bore through the blackness of the night. He cursed out loud when realization hit him. *"Those aren't wolves, goddam it! They're dogs ... someone is in trouble!"*

Kia, upon hearing the intensity of her master's words, began to howl plaintively. Her teammates immediately took up the cry, their collective voice loud and strident. They had reached the sloping outline of another hill and, with a frustrating slowness necessitated by the narrow, almost claustrophobic trail, made their way through riverine shrubs and around the base of the hill. With each passing second the cacophony ahead grew louder, pushing a fresh supply of adrenalin into North's bloodstream. His heart raced, pounding in his ears and behind his wide eyes. His exhaustion disappeared, as did every sore and aching muscle that had plagued him for days.

The next voice to split the night air was definitely not canine. A bloodcurdling, decidedly human scream drowned out the voices of the dogs. No sooner had the sickening scream died when North detected another noise – an unfamiliar, deep and forceful grunting. The strange noise quickly grew louder, then turned into an animal like, angry bellow.

North's blood ran cold. He swore in frustration at the team's pace, necessarily slow as they continued to weave through encumbering, dense willow. When they suddenly shot out of the shrubs and onto open land he shouted at his dogs, encouraging them to run like they'd never run before. They responded immediately, and began to run like their lives depended on it.

When North rounded the base of the hill, a scene that would haunt his dreams and awaken him in a cold sweat for months to come greeted his incredulous eyes. Years of hunting on the cruel Arctic tundra hadn't prepared him for the carnage that lay before him.

Even with only the dim glow from the stars overhead he knew what the dark splotches against pristine white snow were. He'd seen them before.

White and red. White and red.
Snow and blood. Snow and blood.

North Ruben's nightmares lay before him in a red and white tableau.

TWENTY

"Andi, telephone call for you," Gert called, knocking gently on Andi's closed bedroom door. "It's Rachel, dear."

"I'll be right there!" It was Tuesday evening and Andi was laying on her bed, reading a book and trying not to think about what her husband was doing every moment, which was an impossible task. Besides walking the dogs and tending to their needs, the only things that occupied her time in Anchorage were her daily trips to the JavaGenie and mid-morning coffee with Gert. Even with Rachel and Gert's lively conversation, Andi often had to ask them to repeat themselves when her mind repeatedly slipped to thoughts of North. Worry was her constant companion, and it showed in her increasingly dark and troubled eyes.

The cold, seemingly endless days also brought boredom, and with it that edgy, needy feeling that only an addict can relate to and that left her feeling empty and vulnerable. Her nights were relentlessly haunted by visions and nightmares, which left her mentally drained and physically exhausted every morning. She had no appetite and often skipped meals, but drank cup after cup of coffee which, in turn, made her hands shake and her stomach ache constantly.

In desperation she'd sought out the local chapter of Alcoholics Anonymous and had gone to the Wednesday, Saturday and Monday night meetings. The minute she walked through the door of the community hall she immediately felt the dark cloud of despondency lift. It helped to be in the same room with people who understood how she was feeling ... to be amongst people who didn't *judge* one another. The meetings worked their healing magic, as they always seemed to, quelling the need that continued to steadily grow inside her since North left over a week ago.

She trotted down the wide staircase to the main floor and picked up the handset from where Gert had laid it on the old antique desk. "Hello."

"Andi, its Rachel! What are you doing?"

"Hi, Rachel! I'm just relaxing and reading a book."

"I'm done my shift in an hour and my husband is at his regular Tuesday poker night. Why don't I pick you up and we can go out for a drink or something? I don't feel like going home yet and I'm sure you're bored to tears out there."

Andi paled. "Um, uh, I don't know," she stammered. Her heart sped up and she felt the first tingle of cold, clammy sweat on her body.

"Oh come on! It will be fun. We never really have a chance to talk when I'm at work. I'll be there by 9:30, okay?"

"Well, uh-"

"Oops, gotta run," Rachel whispered. "A bunch of customers just walked in. So see you in an hour or so." The phone went dead in Andi's hand. She stood by the desk, gripping the handset in her cold hand until the line's loud, annoying 'beep, beep, beep' spurred her to hang it up. The thought of entering a bar and sitting with Rachel while she sipped her wine, or beer, or cocktail or whatever it was she drank, fired the craving that never truly left her. But she truly enjoyed Rachel's company, and the opportunity to share an evening out and relieve her boredom was one she couldn't pass up.

Andi took a deep breath and turned to gaze out the large, uncovered windows. The distant peak of a high, snow-capped mountain that she didn't know the name of was just visible in the fading light. She would order a Club Soda with lime, she promised herself. It was the only thing she ever drank when she and North went out.

Andi ran up the stairs to shower and change from her tracksuit into something a little more presentable. *I can do this,* she whispered to herself. *I can do this.*

"We're going to the Arctic Bar," Rachel said. "It's one of my favourite places to unwind. Lots of the locals go here."

Andi drew a deep breath, murmured a noncommittal reply and forced herself to smile. They were cruising slowly down Fourth Avenue in Rachel's red GMC Suburban.

"Oh, there's a parking spot." Rachel pulled in between two pickup trucks and turned off the engine. "Looks busy tonight," she said. "I hope we don't have to sit up at the bar. That's a drag," she laughed. "The drunks keep hitting on you."

Tell her! Andi chastised herself as she followed Rachel through the bar's heavy, dark front door. *Just tell Rachel you are AA and that you don't drink! Show her your ring!*

The smells and sounds of the bar assailed Andi's senses the second she walked in the door. There was no mistaking the familiar odor of stale beer and cigarette smoke, and the underlying stench of damp, moldy, wall-to-wall carpeting. Tinkling glasses, low voices and a jukebox playing something slow and mournful in the corner of the dim room triggered a flood of memories, some good and some best forgotten. The Arctic Bar smelled and sounded like a hundred other bars in a hundred other cities, and was almost comforting in its familiarity.

"Oh, there's a booth," Rachel said, pointing to the corner of the room. "Let's grab it."

Andi followed helplessly and sat across from Rachel at the wide, wood-plank table. Before they had time to shed their coats a waitress appeared clad in skin-tight blue jeans and a thin, skinny white tank top that revealed every curve of her generously endowed, braless bosom. "Hi, Rach! What can I get for you ladies tonight?" she chirped, swiping a stained white bar cloth over the table.

Rachel's face screwed up and she pursed her coral lips. "I think I'll just have a beer, Steph. What was the name of that draft from the new brewery I liked last time?"

"Um, the Snowy Owl Pale Ale?"

"Yes, that was it. It was excellent." Rachel smiled at Andi, who sat rigid on the bench seat, following the exchange numbly. "Why don't you try one, too? I think you'll like it, and it's a local beer too."

Andi opened her mouth to refuse but couldn't get the words out. Her brain was stuck in neutral, her voice box frozen.

"Bring us two Snowy Owls please, Steph," Rachel ordered.

"Sure thing. Be right back."

Andi and Rachel shrugged out of their parkas. "This is great, isn't it?" Rachel smiled, fluffing the back of her short black pixie cut. "Thanks so much for coming. I'm glad we'll have a chance to visit before you have to leave for Nome. When are you going, anyway?"

"Wednesday afternoon," Andi croaked, clearing her throat before she could get the words out. Her mind raced, trying to formulate the right words and grasping at a way to tell Rachel she couldn't drink the beer that had just been ordered for her, and the reason why. Under the table, concealed from curious eyes, Andi twirled the worn silver ring on her finger feverishly, a corner of her mind praying that a miracle would happen and the talisman would provide her with the strength she knew she had lost.

"I love Nome," Rachel gushed, oblivious of Andi's distress, of the battle waging across the table from her. "It's so *quaint!* You ever been there before?"

"No, never," Andi replied softly, shaking her head. "This is my first visit to Alaska." *And probably my last,* she thought, but didn't voice.

"Really? Wow, you haven't missed much," she laughed. "You haven't lived in Inuvik all your life though, have you?"

"Oh, no. I was born and raised on Vancouver Island, then lived in Yellowknife for a few years before I moved to Inuvik."

"Vancouver Island? I hear that's a beautiful place. Like Seattle. I *love* Seattle," she sighed melodramatically. "It's so warm, and so green. And the ocean, I love it! How the hell did you get from Vancouver Island to Inuvik, anyway?"

"Um, it's a long story. Work, mainly." Andi felt edgy and uncomfortable and didn't want to get into the harsh details of her life in a dingy Anchorage bar. She felt out of control; pressure tightened her chest and her head felt dizzy. *Coming here was definitely a mistake,* she thought, thinking about how she could escape with her dignity intact.

"Here you go. Two Snowy Owls." The waitress dropped two cardboard coasters on the table and plunked down two pints of beer, their tall heads of foam dripping down the sides of the glasses. "Are you starting a tab?"

"Sure, might as well," Rachel laughed. "I'm sure we won't stop at just one." She pulled a pack of Player's Filter and a lighter from her purse, then lit a cigarette. She took a drag, inhaled deeply and blew a plume of smoke toward the ceiling. "I needed this," she smiled. She picked up her glass of beer and held it toward Andi. "Let's make a toast. *To new friends!*"

Helpless to stop the course of events, and too weak to change them, Andi wrapped a tingling hand around the cold, slippery glass of amber beer and lifted it to meet Rachel's. The heavy glasses clinked together. "To new friends," she whispered.

TWENTY-ONE

"WHOA! WHOA!" North screamed. He stomped on the sled brake with every ounce of strength he possessed. The dogs had become frenzied, wild things, their instincts incited by the pungent, coppery scent of fresh blood and screaming voices, both human and animal. They continued to strain against the plowing sled brake, dragging the metal bar through the deep, soft snow for several yards before they finally gave up pulling. Disturbed and anxious, they pranced on impatient paws and howled their protest. Long, gleaming fangs snapped at the air and each other while North hurried to set the snow hook, clumsy in his haste and alarm. He buried it as deeply as he could and said a brief, silent prayer that his beloved, priceless dogs would remain where they were ... that they would be safe.

"STAY," he shouted repeatedly. He ran to Kia and grasped the big dog's head in his hands. "Stay, Kia!" The lead dog whined pathetically and sat on her haunches, though she continued to tremble. Kia was the pack leader, and North trusted she would keep the rest of the team in control.

A hundred feet ahead lay what North would later describe as a war zone; it was a battlefield scene worse than any portrayed in the goriest horror movie he'd ever seen. The new moon's watery light shone on the most gruesome image he'd ever had the misfortune to witness: sled dogs' ravaged bodies lay splayed open on the trampled, bloody snow, some of the suffering animals still twitching in the final throws of painful death, their hot blood steaming as it met the frigid arctic air. Their team-mates, those still alive, screamed and howled in abject fear, desperately struggling to free themselves from their imprisoning harnesses and gangline, which was an impossible undertaking.

An enormous Alaskan bull moose, well over six feet tall at his dark shoulders and with hooves as large as snowshoes, bellowed and grunted in rage. He rose on long, muscular hind legs and pounded his sharp front hooves again and again into the helpless body of his current target, beating it to a gory, bloody mass of fur and guts.

Twenty feet away another moose, considerably smaller than his counterpart, stood with his legs wide and long head swinging low, bellowing over the inert body of another husky. Neither animal seemed unduly concerned with his presence.

North clutched his rifle and ran clumsily toward the chaotic scene, floundering in the deep snow and drawing in great gasps of icy air that burned his lungs. His eyes combed through the mass of dark, grisly shapes strewn on the ground for any trace of a human form, praying he wouldn't find one. Fifty feet ahead the musher's sled lay on its side, still attached to the gangline, and blocking his view of whatever lay behind it. The two maddened, murderous moose prevented him from venturing any closer.

"HELLO! ANYBODY THERE?" North shouted. A dark head immediately popped up over the edge of the sled, and a headlamp was flicked on.

"Help me!" screamed a thin, shrill voice. "Help me, please!"

"Get down!" North bellowed, raising his voice to be heard over the pandemonium of roaring moose and screaming dogs. "Get down and turn off your light! I'm going to shoot these bastards!"

The other musher's headlamp blinked off and his head dropped below the edge of the sled. North raised his rifle and turned toward the nearest beast, who was already focusing his attention on another helpless, panic-stricken dog. He knew he needed a clean head shot; his .22 calibre bullet would have little impact on an animal that probably weighted fifteen hundred pounds and had a carcass as tough as concrete.

From experience he knew, too, that shot placement was key in taking down large game. Even at a mere fifty feet, a head shot was his only hope of dropping the enraged moose.

There had been much discussion in Anchorage about guns on the trail, some of it fairly heated. A few mushers chose to race without one, taking their chances against the infrequent threat of encounters with marauding wolves, rabid foxes, or even the odd polar bear. Others carried only a small handgun, since extra weight in the sled was always a huge concern. North knew he would feel naked out on the land without a gun, and carried his old but trusty .22 Long Range Rimfire rifle. He hadn't expected to need it to drop an angry moose though; he'd been thinking about wolves, or a pesky fox, or even a hungry bear, but not a gigantic, maddened Alaskan moose.

North dropped to one knee and cleared his mind, willing his heaving chest to still and his breathing to slow. He took several deep, slow, frigid breaths and focused on one thing only – the head of the bull moose centered in the crosshairs of his sights, illumed by the light from his own headlamp. Today, more than ever before, he needed a steady hand. His old hunter's instincts kicked in – those learned on the Arctic tundra years ago, when his father had taught him how to hunt. He drew on the deep patience of his Inuvialuit forebears, those Arctic hunters whose survival depended solely on their honed hunting skills, and forced himself to wait for exactly the right moment to make his shot.

When the great beast suddenly stopped and turned to glare in his direction, seemingly aware of the intruder's presence for the first time, North slowly squeezed the trigger.

His rifle flashed, its explosive crack rending through the black night. North's bullet met its target, and he was already running toward it when the moose dropped to its knees, bellowing in rage and pain. North stopped several feet from the animal and aimed again. The second head shot silenced the huge beast, and it slumped heavily onto its side. Its long limbs twitched once or twice, then became still.

The shots had disrupted the other moose's attack, and it stood over its twitching target, bellowing and throwing its huge head from side to side as it pawed at the frozen ground. North ran toward it and raised his rifle. He knew he had only one chance – he stopped and dropped and took careful aim at the beast's head, then released another shot. This one easily found its mark, and the animal fell to the ground instantly.

North's euphoria was short-lived and dimmed quickly. He had to face another task now – a task for which he had little taste.

"Are you alright?" he yelled, rising from the ground.

"Yes, I'm okay," replied a weak, wavering voice. The cacophony had quietened somewhat, reduced now to a weak, keening whimper from at least one injured dog still clinging to life, and anxious, panic-stricken cries from the others. He searched for his own team, gratified to find them sitting on their haunches where he'd left them.

"Stay where you are," North called to the musher. "I'll take care of this for you."

He approached the grim scene, pausing just out of reach of the handful of frenzied huskies that had survived the attack. They snapped at each other and at nothing, growling in fear and frustration. It was evident that the poor creatures had been helpless when the vicious assault began – they were still in harness and strung together on the gangline. They had been sitting ducks.

North took a deep breath and willed himself to remain calm despite the burning stomach bile in his throat. He swallowed hard, and began a steady, slow examination of the scene. He focused the beam from his headlamp on each individual dog.

"How many dogs did you have in harness?" North shouted over the mournful barking and howling of not only the surviving dogs, but his own restless team, almost invisible in the dark night.

"Ten," came a choked reply. "How many are ... how many are gone?"

"I don't know yet. Just stay down." North thought the voice sounded familiar, but couldn't afford the time or energy to try to place it with a face or name.

Minutes ago there had been ten strong, beautiful Siberian huskies; North counted only six erect bodies now. Only six sets of panicked eyes and six sets of pointed, twitching ears followed his movements, snarling in fear as he drew closer. The dogs were traumatized, their black lips curled, baring long white incisors that gleamed in the dim light. Under normal circumstances most sled dogs are gentle and passive, and of no threat to humans or each other, but North knew better than to get within biting range of these distressed beasts.

Three dogs had been trampled and gouged to death. Their bodies were reduced to unrecognizable blotches of fur, blood and guts by the savage attack under the moose's hooves.

Only one poor beast, a magnificent male, clung to a weak thread of life. His thick, dark grey coat had once been mottled with patches of white fur but was now stained deep crimson red. From the dog's position at the front of the gangline, North surmised that he had been a lead dog. His partner stood rigidly beside him, wary of North when he knelt on the red, trampled snow next to the mortally injured animal to do a swift visual examination. The injured dog's hindquarters were crushed, exposing bloody muscle and shattered, sharp fragments of bone, and a coil of guts lay on the snow next to his belly, glistening and steaming in the frigid air.

The husky, sensing a human's presence, tried and failed to raise his big grey- and white-masked head from the ground. His beautiful blue eyes, once clear, sharp and intelligent, were clouded with pain and fear, and he whined softly when North laid a gentle hand on the confused, disoriented animal's neck. He didn't appear to be in pain, likely due to a severed spine, for which North was grateful. "I'm sorry, boy. I'm so, very, very sorry," he whispered.

Hot tears of anger and frustration ran freely from North's dark eyes as he stood and raised his rifle, surrounded by white and red. *Snow and blood.*

TWENTY-TWO

Moments later, silence ensued. The six surviving huskies, all wearing hot pink jackets and booties, quietened somewhat, as did North's team.

"It's over," he stated, his voice stronger and more controlled than the man himself felt.

"Can I stand up now?" the musher called, still crouched behind the sled.

North's eyes widened in surprise. It was a woman's voice, and one that he thought he knew. "Yes, you can come out," he answered, surprized by this unexpected turn of events. He knew that there were four female mushers entered in the race, but he'd never once considered that this unfortunate soul was one of them. But then again, the horrific event had unfolded so quickly, he hadn't had a spare moment to consider much of anything. His instincts had driven him to react as quickly as he could.

Light glowed softly behind the sled, wavering as a slight form clad in a hot pink parka rose slowly to her feet. "My God," she whispered. "Oh my good God."

"Becky, it's me, North Ruben," North called. He recognized Rebecca Singleton's trade-mark pink outfit instantly. He took a wide berth around her surviving, traumatized dogs and made his way to her side. The huskies continued to snarl and hang their heads low, suspicion and fear blazing in their blue eyes.

Becky had yet to look at North; her eyes were glued to the dark scene of carnage that lay before her. She was, North suspected, in shock. "Becky, it's all over now. There's nothing you can do for your dogs."

He would take charge of the situation until Becky came around ... *if* she recovered. He approached her cautiously, dimming his headlamp so the light wouldn't shine in her eyes. "Are you alright? Were you injured?" he asked.

"No. No, I'm fine. It's just ... just my dogs," she replied, her voice barely above a whisper, her eyes still riveted on the remains of her beloved team.

"I'm going to go get my dogs now, Becky," North said quietly. "I'll be back in a few minutes. Are you going to be okay while I'm gone?" She still hadn't looked at him.

"Sure. I'll be fine," she said tonelessly.

"Becky, look at me please," North asked. He wasn't happy about leaving the devastated woman alone for even a second, but neither was he happy about leaving his exposed, unprotected dogs alone. Where two insane moose had roamed, there could be more. North's dogs were his and Becky's only way out of this disastrous mess; it was imperative that he keep them safe and out of danger.

Becky slowly turned her head toward North's voice. Her right hand, drawing on the repetitive motion gleaned from years of mushing, reached up to dim her own headlamp's beam. Their eyes met, hers wide and staring. The light was too weak to see her pupils, but North guessed that they were dilated – a sign of mild shock. After a quick visual inspection, North was relieved to see no sign of injury on the woman.

"I'm going to be right back," he repeated. "Then I'm going to build a fire and make us some tea, okay?"

Becky just nodded her head, silent tears wetting her cold cheeks.

"I don't want you to do anything while I'm gone, okay? Just sit down right here by the sled and wait for me." He led her to the sled and urged her down onto the snow, settling her back against the wooden frame. "I'll be right back. Do you have a gun?" he asked.

Becky shook her head.

"I'll leave you mine," North said. "You know how to shoot?"

"No. Yes. I mean no, don't leave it. I don't like guns," she stammered.

North stared at her for a moment, then nodded once in acquiescence. He turned and ran clumsily in the deep snow to his waiting team. He released the snow hook from its bed of snow, gave the dogs a cursory check, and called his leads ahead to straighten out the gangline.

"READY! HIKE!" he shouted, releasing the restless team from their unwelcome restraint.

North ran beside the sled until it gained momentum, then hopped on its runners. To build a fire, he needed some wood, which meant backtracking to the riverine area.

"COME GEE! COME GEE!" he commanded. Kia and Weasel, their attention focused on Becky's team, hesitated in confusion. Kia turned her head, her gaze silently questioning North's command. "You heard me old girl, COME GEE!" he repeated. With a toss of her head, Kia swung into a sharp right turn, nipping at Weasel when he didn't immediately respond to North's repeated instruction.

When North called the team to a halt near the scrubby willows a few minutes later, they didn't question him again. He rummaged along the edge of the shrubs, hastily gathering dry, dead twigs and willow branches. He tossed two armfuls of tinder on top of his sled bag. Five minutes later, he was retracing the trail back to the scene of the attack.

When he rounded the corner of the hill a second time, North's stomach dropped. Where he had expected to see the soft glow of light from Becky's headlamp, there was only darkness. Fear gripped his heart once again, and he shouted at his dogs, urging them to even greater speed.

As they pulled nearer, a faint glimmer of light reflected from the snow; he breathed a sigh of relief when he saw Becky's headlamp. They drew closer and he saw that she had moved her surviving dogs, unhooking them from the gangline and holding them next to her behind the tipped sled to give them what she likely thought was a modicum of protection. North drove his team in a wide circle around the carnage and blood, calling them to a halt in front of Becky's sled, near enough to protect them from any further danger.

Becky was sitting on the ground, six Siberian Huskies encircling her body and forming a protective ring around their master. Each dog maintained physical contact with her, either sitting on their haunches, leaning into her or laying by her side. One animal had draped his sleek head over her outstretched legs.

"How are you doing, Becky?" he called as he buried the snow hook and began to release the harness tugs. He was relieved to see that she'd pulled herself out of her previously numb, almost unresponsive state.

"Oh God, North," she moaned, stroking a silky head. Her pink parka and wind pants were blotted with red patches of fresh, bright blood. "What have I done? My dogs are dead!"

"The first thing we're going to do is light a fire," North instructed. "And then we're going to melt some water for tea. Can you come over here and help me get these branches out of my sled?" he asked. Although he didn't need any help with the tasks, he wanted to keep Becky moving. He hoped that the simple chore would help her focus on the need to regain control of the situation.

"I need to secure these guys first," Becky said, rummaging for chains in her sled basket. "I don't think they'll take off, but you never know, after what they've been through. Those goddamn moose!" she swore softly, kicking out in anger at a lump of snow. "Those goddamn fucking moose killed my dogs!"

After a minute of fumbling she located the chains and hooked her dogs to the sled. North knew that it was only a token gesture. If the dogs wanted to run, they would run. They could easily drag the sled, even if it was lying on its side and heavy with equipment. But, exhausted from their harrowing ordeal, the six huskies had begun to calm down and were settling near each other on the snow. They continued to stay alert to Becky and North's every movement though.

Together the mushers built a small fire. The heat and glow from its blaze were a welcome relief from the penetrating cold and darkness and the chill that had settled into their bones. When the diminutive fire was burning steadily, North dug out his cooker and some HEET. He would feed all of the dogs from his supply of warm, cooked food, then cook another batch to replenish his cooler. He walked a good distance away to ensure the area was clean and uncontaminated by blood, scooped up snow into the pot and set in in the cooker to melt. The two mushers sat on the ground near the glowing fire and turned off their headlamps. Becky drew her knees to her chest, and wrapped her arms around them. Her head dropped to her knees.

North heard her soft sobs and agonized with her. He knew that there was a time for words . . . and there was a time for silence. He let Becky have her silence, respecting her need to mourn her dead comrades, if only in her thoughts.

After a few minutes he got up and went to check on his dogs. They were still restless, muttering and grumbling softly. He had unhooked their tugs, but kept them on the gangline and left their booties on, so they knew that the stop was intended to be a short rest only. When he dug out their food bowls and began dishing out portions of kibble and warm food from the cooler, they stirred restlessly, confused but still willing to eat.

He returned to Becky's side and slumped down by the fire, offering his companionship, comfort and support in silence. He fed an occasional small piece of wood from their shrinking supply to the fire. His rifle was never far from his side, and his eyes remained alert, constantly peering into the darkness surrounding their small circle of light.

"Should we try giving your dogs something to eat?" he asked.

Becky shook her head. "They won't eat. Not now."

After what seemed like a lifetime, the water in the cooker began to steam. North rose stiffly, grimacing as he brushed snow from his pants and massaged his aching knees through the heavy layers of warm clothing he wore. His joints had become cold and stiff, and now they burned and creaked in protest.

"I'll make us some tea," he said, and returned to his sled for tea bags and sugar. "I only have one mug. Where do you keep yours?"

"I'll get it." Becky rose and rummaged in her sled bag, then handed a dented tin cup to North. Her dogs remained clustered together, nervous and alert.

North filled the cups with hot water and threw two tea bags into each one. They could both use a strong brew and a jolt of caffeine. "Do you have any dog food made up?" he asked.

Becky's tears were slowly abating. She lifted her head and swiped the remaining moisture from her cheeks. "I do. I have food in the cooler. But I don't think they'll want to eat. Not yet."

"You know them best," North said, handing her a cup of strong, steaming tea, liberally laced with sugar. "Here, drink this. It'll warm you up."

She accepted his offering with a small nod, and clutched the tin mug tightly with both hands.

"I have some brandy. Do you want a shot?"

"No, thanks."

He poured a liberal amount into his own cup.

The scrap of a first quarter waxing moon had set for the night. North lifted his eyes to the wonders of the sky, to the stars sparkling brightly overhead, indifferent and impervious to the trauma and distress below them. Like the stroke of an unknown artist's brush, the trillion distant stars and planets of the Milky Way arched in a band across a black canvas. Stars always reminded him of the woman he loved more than life itself. Thinking about her now as he sat on the cold snow, miserable and disillusioned in the middle of a vast and harsh wilderness, sent a jolt of pain through his guts. Glittering stars always reminded him of Andi's sparkling emerald green eyes, and of the child she had lost but would love for eternity. Andi claimed that her beloved Natalie would forever be a star shining like a diamond in the sky.

North shook himself out of his reverie, suddenly becoming aware that the seemingly unrelenting wind had abated. Coupled with the additional warmth radiating from their fire, the night air had lost some of its bite. North loosened the zipper on his parka. He had lost track of time, and pulled the left-hand sleeve of his parka up to check his watch. The light green luminescent numbers told him it was just after 11:00. Only a few hours since he had left Unalakleet, but it seemed like a lifetime.

North drained the last of his brandy-laced tea. "Can I get you another cup?" he asked.

"Yes, please."

North made another cup of strong tea for Becky, again adding a generous amount of sugar. "Could you eat anything?" he asked, crouching beside her.

"No, thanks. Just the tea."

North handed her the cup, and was rewarded with a weak smile. *She's coming around,* he thought. The taut muscles in his neck and shoulders relaxed a little.

The fire flickered, its cheerful, bright flames somehow disrespectful and incongruous amid the wretched misery and loss laying in the nearby shadows. North took the opportunity to examine Becky more closely, noting the deep lines of grief on her heart-shaped face. Long curls of blond hair trailed from beneath the confines of her beaver hat. When she returned his gaze, the deep misery in her beautiful blue eyes made his stomach clench; without so much as a second thought he wrapped his arm around her shoulder and held her close. She leaned into him and snugged her head into the hollow between his neck and chest, seeming to welcome his closeness.

The distraught woman, survivor of one of the most vicious moose attacks North had ever had the misfortune of witnessing, was Alaska's own gem. Her fame was widespread in the racing world, and here she was next to him, bereft and in despair, her prize-winning dog team all but destroyed.

North knew they needed to get back on the trail as soon as possible, but he didn't have the heart to rush Becky, or her dogs, for that matter. It would take more than a few minutes to recover from a trauma such as this. He decided that the best course of action would be to gather the dead huskies himself and prepare them for transport to Shaktoolik. By his rough calculations, the next checkpoint lay about an hour up the trail – two at the most.

The rules of the Iditarod Dog Sled Race state that all deceased dogs MUST be taken to the next checkpoint, and there was no way in hell he was leaving any musher – neither man nor woman – to do that wretched task alone. He knew that all four corpses wouldn't fit into her sled; he would take at least one or two of the dead animals to Shaktoolik for her.

North gently disengaged himself from Becky and laid a gentle hand on her shoulder. "Call me if you need anything," he said. "I've got a few things to look after."

"Okay," she nodded, staring into the flames of the small fire.

He picked up his rifle, but had taken only two strides away from the fire when the first shrill warning bark erupted from one of Becky's dogs. The husky gazed into the darkness, growling low and deep in his throat. Her other dogs rose to their feet and began to whine, their distress mounting again. North's team, disrupted from their slumber, joined in. Within fifteen seconds, all of the dogs were on their feet, heads and ears pointed down the trail, back toward the riverine and its thick grove of willow – the willow that moose loved to feed on.

"Becky, get behind your sled and stay there!" North shouted, dropping to his knees. He pointed the barrel of his rifle into the dark night, prepared to protect himself, Becky and their dogs from whatever danger lurked outside his field of vision.

TWENTY-THREE

North peered through the veil of darkness, his sharp eyes probing the night for any sign of danger. Adrenaline burned through his veins, heightening his senses and making his heart rate jump. He forced himself to draw deep, measured breaths, purging the oxygen-depleted air from his lungs before drawing another. He ordered himself to focus: *You're a hunter, Ruben. Focus. Watch. Listen.* His heart slowed but continued its strong, rhythmic beat, sending blood rushing to his ears and a loud thudding to his brain ... *th-thump, th-thump, th-thump.*

Behind him, the strident cries of sixteen anxious sled dogs grew louder, the feverish pitch of their outcry mounting steadily. North tightened his grip on his trusty .22 and congratulated himself on his foresight to reload it after he'd made their tea.

Seconds passed, lengthening to one minute, then two. Each sixty seconds felt like an endless eternity. North remained motionless and alert, the rifle resting against his shoulder and his index finger caressing its trigger. Away from the yellow firelight his night vision gradually improved again, allowing his eyes to pierce another layer of night. He still detected nothing at all, and couldn't hear a thing except the dogs' feverish barking. There would be no advance warning of who or what the enemy was until it was upon them.

Dear God, please don't let it be a pack of wolves, North entreated to a God he seldom prayed to. He studied every shadow, his eyes so fixated on the nuances of the deep, velvety darkness that it took him a moment to register what didn't belong to the night; *a pinpoint of light!* He shook his head to clear his vision and squeezed his eyes shut for a second, not quite trusting the function of his sleep-deprived brain. When he opened his eyes again, the tiny dot of wavering light was still there.

It took his brain a moment to register the implication behind the dot of light. *It's moving, following the trail and approaching from the riverine,* he finally realized, groaning with relief. He rose to his feet and stretched his cramped, cold muscles, then slipped his mitts back onto his frozen hands. It appeared that help, instead of danger, had arrived in the form of a fellow musher.

North snapped on his headlamp and strode back to Becky's side behind her sled, where she crouched low to the ground and out of harm's way. "Becky," he shouted above the continuing clamour of the dogs, "it's okay. It's just another musher." The dogs sensed or smelled the approaching team and, realizing the newcomers posed no threat, their frenzied yapping slowly subsided to low, discontented rumbles. North offered Becky his hand and pulled her to her feet, inordinately pleased when she rewarded him with a weak smile.

"Thank God," she sighed.

With a modicum of peace restored again, Becky joined North beside their small fire to await the arrival of their unknown visitor.

The faint outline of the incoming team slowly loomed larger and clearer, illumed by the musher's headlamp. When the driver was close enough to discern the scene of tragedy that lay before him, he applied his sled brake and jumped off the runners. "Hello!" he shouted, his words heavily accented. "Is everyone alright here?"

North instantly recognized the deep, rumbling voice and accent of his young rookie friend. "Mats, it's me, North Ruben. I'm with Becky Singleton. We're okay," he yelled.

"I'll be right there!" Mats ran to the front of his team and attempted to guide his reluctant dogs through the slaughtered animals strewn on the trail. His dogs balked, growling and barring their teeth defensively, unwilling to approach the cooling carcasses. He finally capitulated and led them around the gory mess, giving it a wide berth. He drew his dogs to a halt thirty feet from North's sled, set the snow brake and ran to the campfire. "What the hell happened here, North?" he cried.

"Two moose attacked Becky and her team. Becky, you remember Mats Pederson, don't you?"

Becky merely nodded, her eyes never leaving the low fire.

"Hello, Becky," Mats said. "I'm so sorry. It looks like you've lost some of your dogs."

Becky nodded slowly, the bobbing, bright pink pom-pom on the top of her wool hat incongruously cheery. "Four of them," she said, her soft words almost lost beneath the rumbling of the dogs and crackling of the fire. "And my best lead dog, Alpha." Her voice broke and she turned her face away, swiping at her cheek with a gloved hand. "He ... he was my best friend."

Mats' eyes met North's. A single shared glance confirmed what they were each thinking. *It could have been me. It could have been my dogs lying there, mauled to death.*

"Looks like you two could use a hand here," Mats said decisively, the strain of the horrific situation thickening his accent. "I'll get my dogs settled and give them a snack. Be right back." He turned to leave, but Becky jumped up and reached for his arm with a small, narrow hand. His eyes registered his surprise at the strength of her grip, his bushy eyebrows rising almost comically.

"No!" she cried, showing more spark than she had since North came upon her an hour earlier. "I don't want to hold you back. This isn't your problem, Mats. Keep going while you still have a chance at this damn race."

The burly Norwegian hesitated for a moment, then turned to take in the full scene of devastation before him, his headlamp casting a parade of oscillating light and shadow over the grisly remains of mangled, bloodied sled dogs and the carcasses of two moose. Splattered and soaked in blood, the blanket of snow, once pristine and white, was now an appalling palette of darkening red, crimson and pink.

It was an ugly, disturbing picture. "No," he said firmly. "I will stay to help. Remember what Bill Wrightway said at the Musher's Banquet: 'Winning isn't everything'."

Becky opened her mouth to protest, then slowly closed it again when she saw the determined set of his jaw. She grimaced briefly, then shook her head in resolute acceptance before sitting back down on the ground to resume her study of the dwindling fire.

"Thanks, buddy," North said softly, thumping Mats on the back in a manly display of appreciation and camaraderie. "I'll fix you a cup of tea while you look after your dogs. Then we'll get started. Grab your gun when you come back. There may be more of these damn beasts roaming around out here."

Iditarod rules not only require that all dead dogs be taken to the next checkpoint, but they also mandate that any big game – deer, caribou, buffalo or moose – killed on the trail must be gutted and reported. In addition, any following teams must help gut the animal, when possible. No team may pass until the animal is gutted and the first musher has proceeded. North had been willing to turn a blind eye to the rule, to let Mats continue and have a shot at winning the race. He was pretty sure that Becky would have agreed. Deep down inside, though, he was relieved that he had insisted on staying. Not only would he appreciate the help and moral support, he knew that Mats was a crack shot with the rifle he carried; they had exchanged hunting stories the last time their paths had crossed at a checkpoint.

North tossed out the dregs of cold tea from his mug and refilled it with steaming hot water, adding a new tea bag and a dash of brandy. He dumped kibble and his special high fat, high protein dog food concoction into his cooler and added hot water. At least the dogs would have food on the trail.

Mats joined North and Becky at the fire a few minutes later and after tossing down his warm, brandy-laced tea, the trio began the gruesome task of separating the rapidly cooling corpses of the four dead sled dogs from the gangline. Becky took a moment to say goodbye to each precious dog, but only a moment; there would be time enough to linger over her grief and old memories when she was safely back home. Right now, though, it was the living animals that needed her attention, and her guidance.

They loaded the stiffening dogs onto the sleds – two on North's, one on Mats', and Alpha, the magnificent white and dark grey Siberian Husky lead dog onto Becky's, bringing a renewed and pitiful round of lamentation from her remaining six dogs. North wondered, as he often did, what went through a dog's highly intelligent and alert mind, especially under circumstances such as these, with the raw scent of fresh, coppery blood all around them? They grieved the loss of their brothers, their sisters and their pack mates – of that he was certain; it didn't seem right that the lucky survivors now had the grim task of hauling their downed comrades' bodies to Shaktoolik.

North pulled off a mitt and rubbed at his blurry, damp eyes; the events of the night had awakened vivid memories of the vicious attack on three of his own cherished Canadian Eskimo Dogs. He knew only too well the sharp pain and heartache Becky was experiencing right now. Over the past two years he'd often thought about the intense pain and anger he'd felt when he'd lost his dogs, and tried to imagine how a parent felt when he or she lost a child, but his mind couldn't comprehend or process that amount of grief. He gritted his teeth and shoved his hand back into his mitt, determinedly throwing his painful and self-indulgent memories aside. There was still work to do.

"Come on, Mats," he said when the bodies of the dogs were loaded. "Let's look after those goddamn moose so we can get out of here. Becky, see if you can get your team ready to hit the trail again."

When she began to protest, albeit weakly, that she would look after the moose herself, North shook his head. "No, we have this covered." Pushing all other thoughts aside, he turned and followed Mats' rapidly retreating back.

They still had two murderous moose to gut, and the night wasn't getting any younger.

TWENTY-FOUR

North and Mats gutted the moose quickly and efficiently, leaving their cooling carcasses exactly where they lay on the blood drenched snow. Scavengers would make quick and clean work of the remains within days.

While they tended to the grisly task, Becky righted her sled and repacked its jumbled contents. She shortened her gangline to hold six dogs instead of ten, pulling one from the team position to join her remaining lead dog at the front. Before she put the dogs back on the line she examined each one thoroughly for any sign of injury, talking and crooning to them softly, reassuring them as best she could. She made sure their pink jackets were straight and securely fastened, checked their paws and replaced pink booties, and gave the deep, thick fur on their necks a good scratch. She massaged their shoulders and legs and hand fed each animal a small chunk of warm, cooked caribou meat, which they eagerly accepted. The familiar, comforting tasks required little concentration on her part, and while she worked she silently prayed that they would all make it to Shaktoolik alive.

The incongruous quietude of the Alaskan night enveloped the three teams as they quietly glided away, leaving the scene of the bloodbath at their backs. Other mushers would soon pass this way, and there would surely be much drama and many questions exchanged at the next checkpoint. Becky's shrunken team of six dogs willingly followed North's departing sled, with Mats bringing up the rear. It was a subdued and solemn procession. The sled dogs, usually rambunctious and vocal and eager to get moving, were unusually quiet and passive. Did they feel the burden of their departed comrades, secured to the top of the sleds they willingly towed? Or were they merely so finely attuned to their humans' feelings ... to their sorrow?

North had estimated they were within two hours of the next checkpoint, the tiny village of Shaktoolik, or perhaps a bit longer depending on the condition of the trail and the wind. He would hold his dogs to a moderate pace to prevent Becky's smaller team from tiring, but by his calculations they should reach the safety of Shaktoolik around 3 am. Where he placed in the race's finish was no longer of any concern to him; getting Becky and what remained of her team to safety had become his only priority. He'd lost his drive and eagerness to even finish the race the moment he'd laid eyes on the gory remains of the pink-jacketed sled dogs.

The attack had occurred along the four-mile-long spine of the Blueberry Hills, and the trio continued to follow the dark trail, twisting, climbing, falling and climbing again until they finally broke out of the woods and onto the bleak and bare thousand-foot summit. No longer afforded the leeward protection of the mountain range, the vicious, howling winds the region was known for ripped at their clothing with a vengeance, stripping them of precious body heat.

North pulled his team to a brief stop, and waited for Becky and Mats to catch up. From the top of the summit they had an unobstructed view to the west, and although Shaktoolik was ten to fifteen miles away, the lights of civilization were clearly visible in the clear night. *We can do this*, North thought grimly. They took a short five-minute break, then with renewed resolve he called his team up and the procession set off along the trail again. North was determined to safely deliver Becky Singleton and the remains of her ravaged team to Shaktoolik.

The trail soon made a sharp left turn and within minutes they began the long drop off the mountain and to the beach. The beginning of the descent wasn't overly steep, as the trail continually curved and snaked back on itself, once again passing through wooded areas that North feared may harbour more murderous moose. Their pace was, of necessity, slow and steady. The trail, continually polished by near hurricane force winds, became treacherously icy. Trees loomed menacingly along each curve, waiting to claim a sled that may swing wide and out of control, and collide with an unyielding tree trunk.

The three mushers had agreed to stretch out on the trail, leaving enough distance between the teams to remain well out of each other's way and give their dogs a chance to settle back into a comfortable pace. Becky would remain between North and Mats, and North would stop every half hour for the trio to regroup.

North's team was running well, despite the strong arctic wind. He let Kia and Weasel have their head, fully trusting their judgement on the twisting trail. The muscles in his shoulders and neck were locked and rigid, and he forced himself to relax and try to ease the tension and pain. It worked, marginally, but he couldn't force the horrific sight of mangled bodies, trampled intestines and blood-spattered snow from his mind. His thoughts kept wandering back to a day he'd sooner forget – the day he'd found blood spattered snow and dead dogs in his own back yard. His despondent thoughts turned to his bride, his incredibly brave, beloved Andi whom he missed more and more with each passing hour. He thought about her continually, wondering what she was doing in Anchorage, and how she was filling the long hours of her days. He hadn't been parted from her since they'd married, and he'd had no idea that her absence would leave such a black, empty hole in his heart.

North absently noticed a gradual thinning in the trees alongside the trail, and realized that they must be nearing the beach on the wide and windy Norton Sound, which in turn opened up to the Bering Sea. His thoughts drifted back to Andi and the heartening knowledge that he would soon be wrapped within her soft and loving arms again. His tired, burning eyes drifted shut for a moment when some deep, obscure part of his brain suddenly brought the heady, familiar scent of lavender to his senses. Andi added fragrant lavender oil to her bath every evening, claiming the soothing scent calmed her thoughts and helped her sleep. He inhaled deeply, painfully aware of his loneliness but enjoying the soothing memory of his wife's scent.

Later, North would berate himself for his inattention. He knew better than to let his mind wander, especially on a trail as demanding as the one he was on that night. He'd even been forewarned of the treacherous descent to the Norton Sound beach, but later chalked his calamitous error in judgement down to sheer exhaustion and good old daydreaming. He would remember his blunder for the rest of his days, and had no-one to blame but himself.

He had begun to relax as they left the bloody mess at Blueberry Hill further and further behind. He thought they were, quite literally, out of the woods when suddenly the trail dipped sharply and his sled left the ground for the count of five. It was his wake-up call; North's mind snapped back to alertness. His body tensed, muscles strengthening instantly as another jolt of fear-induced adrenalin spread through his bloodstream. A fraction of a second later, in an incident uncannily and horrifyingly reminiscent of the Dalzell Gorge disaster, his team once again disappeared over the edge of an invisible ledge. There was no time to stomp on the brake ... no time to guide the lunging team away from the edge of the cliff ... no time to scream.

The last pair of dogs disappeared over the edge within seconds, sure-footed and fearless in their pursuit of the lead dogs. North and his overburdened sled, heavy with the added weight of two dogs, trailed behind in helpless freefall, and he experienced a brief, unsettling feeling of weightlessness as he dropped down into the black abyss. The heavens opened up around him, millions of brilliant, glowing stars shining above and below, while the beam from his headlamp was absorbed by the surrounding void of darkness. His comfortably padded seat fell away and his heavily booted feet lost their purchase on the sled runners, allowing his body to plummet through the night.

In whatever time North Ruben had left before he met his fate at the base of the cliff, his mind raced to comprehend his chances of survival. He knew that, regardless of whatever action he took now, the outcome wouldn't be good. It took every ounce of willpower he had, but he knew that he had to hang onto the plunging sled. His father's voice came to mind, his gruff words as clear as a bell and permanently ingrained in North's brain from long hours on the trail: '*Whatever you do, son, don't lose your team. Your dogs are your lifeline, and you will die without them'*. North knew he had to hang on with every last ounce of strength he had, then drop and roll when he hit the ground.

The impact of frozen terra firma crashing against soft flesh when he finally hit the ground at the base of the sheer rock cliff drove the air from his lungs in one deep, violent grunt. He had no time to drop and roll. It was only by sheer determination that his gloved hands remained wrapped around the sled's handle bar, and he landed hard on one side. He heard, rather than felt, the heavily laden sled hit the trail beside him with an ominous crack that his struggling brain couldn't quite identify.

North was dragged bouncing over the hard, frozen ground, disoriented and in pain that intensified with each passing second. He struggled to retain consciousness, drifting in and out of awareness. When he finally managed to open his mouth in a futile attempt to call his frenzied team to a halt, he found he couldn't breathe. His lungs were empty, his voice refusing to cooperate. He desperately tried to draw a breath, but his muscles and voice refused to cooperate; he couldn't breathe nor whisper nor shout at his dogs. White noise roared in his ears and his taut, rigid muscles began to soften. He felt himself slipping away into blissful, pain free unconsciousness. In a night already dark and shadowy, North lost what little vision he had as a heavy, black curtain fell over his eyes. He was gone for only seconds, but it was a blessed respite from the intense pain that wracked his body.

He awoke to the realization that he was still in motion, gripping the handlebar with his left hand while his brutalized body dragged alongside the sled, which was on its right side. He was being buffeted by rock hard snowdrifts and whatever lay beneath the thick layer of snow, and every inch of his body hurt like a bastard. "Whoa," he wheezed, forcing the single, incomprehensible word from his reluctant lungs. The dogs couldn't hear him and didn't respond, and North had no hope of reaching the sled brake.

Using every ounce of strength he could muster, he pulled a shallow, torturous breath of air into his straining lungs. "Whoa. Kia, Weasel, whoa." The hissed command was barely audible, his straining lungs still refusing to fully cooperate. "Whoa!" North called again, with slightly more success. The team slowed marginally. He called to them again, and they reluctantly drew to a halt beside a stand of evergreens.

North lay on the cold, frozen ground, breathing heavily. He dared not release his grip on the handlebar, and probably couldn't have even if he'd wanted to. After a moment he realized he was in total darkness; somewhere along the plunge down the precipice he'd either lost his headlamp, or damaged it. He was cognizant enough to realize his first order of business was to secure the sled. With his free hand he slowly and painfully groped for the snow hook. It was stored on a stanchion attached to the handle bar, and North almost cried in relief when he found it exactly where it was supposed to be. Designed to detach in a swift one-handed operation, he had it off the sled and in his hand in a moment. The metal hook was designed to be driven down into the snow so its two long, sharp tips embedded deeply, a process best accomplished when the sled was still slowly moving. He didn't have that option. He gripped the hook and drove it into the snow as hard as he could, praying that it would hold long enough for him to get back on his feet.

With the sled secured, he released his hold on the handlebar. His tortured, leaden arm fell heavily to the snow, sending fresh waves of hot pain ripping through his screaming deltoids. He squeezed his eyes tightly shut in a useless attempt to escape the agony, and lay on the frozen ground, afraid to move ... afraid to discover the extent of his inevitable injuries.

He may have dozed off – or more than likely passed out – for a moment, and was awakened by an unhappy and complaining 'woof'. *That would be Weasel,* he thought. He opened his eyes, wondering if he'd dreamt the entire harrowing ordeal, but immediately realized it had been a living nightmare. Weasel yipped again, protesting the delay, always ready to run. He heard another dog whine softly, then became aware of steady panting somewhere nearby. North's eyes fluttered closed again and his brain released him from a few more minutes of pain.

When he awoke again he was cold and disoriented. Panic clutched at his heart. His first unfocused and confused thoughts were for his team and their safety. *The dogs might be hurt, I have to check on the dogs, I have to warn the others, I have to get my rig off the trail.* He didn't know it at the time, but he wasn't even on the main trail. For some unknown reason, Kia and Weasel had departed from the Iditarod trail and followed an old path, possibly still used by deer and other wild animals, down the sheer face of the cliff.

It felt like hours had passed since his plunge over the ledge, but North guessed that, unless he'd been unconscious for longer than he suspected, only a matter of minutes had elapsed. He wasn't inclined to attempt to check his Timex. He was certain the others would be getting close; his biggest concern was to get off the trail and out of Becky and Mats' way, and to make sure his dogs were safe.

He sat up slowly and ran a check on his battered body. His legs and hands moved well, but his left shoulder felt wrenched again and he winced when he moved his left ankle. He took a deep breath, relieved that he could breathe normally again. He rolled to his knees, tried to stand and screamed in pain.

Even the slightest amount of weight on his left foot was sheer agony. He fell to the ground again, sweating beneath his heavy layers of clothing and breathing hard. His ankle was on fire, steady waves of pain radiating up the back of his calf. He panted and waited for the agony to subside. Getting back on his feet was going to be harder than he thought.

Dawn was still several hours away and he'd need some light if he were to assess the damages. He put a hand to his head, relieved to find his headlamp was still in place, strapped to his heavy felt hat. No amount of switch flicking restored the precious beam of light, though, and he concluded the bulb must have broken. He had a spare headlamp in his sled bag, of course, for all the good it did him at the moment.

Blocking out the pain in his leg and throbbing in his shoulder, he tried to focus on the bigger problem at hand; he needed to get himself, his sled and his team off the trail and out of Becky's way. He drew a deep breath, gritted his teeth and pulled himself upright, clinging to the sled for support. He balanced on one foot, holding his left leg uselessly in the air.

"Goddamn it!" he roared. His harsh words of anger, pain and frustration were absorbed by the uncaring, indifferent wilderness surrounding him.

"Becky!" he shouted, looking to the stars. He was completely disoriented and hoped he was at least facing the damn cliff. "Becky! Watch out below!" He wished he'd paid more attention to the heavens earlier and had noted his course in relation to the stars on this moonless night.

Still balanced on one leg, North peered into the night. His eyes were well-adapted to the darkness, and he was able to clearly discern the outline of his sled, still lying on its side. Even the corpses of Becky's two dogs had made the trip, and were still roped to the top of the sled bag. North's dogs were where they were supposed to be, on the towline.

North attempted to take a few short, one-legged hops, muttering and swearing fiercely before he dropped back down to his knees. He grasped the sled's wooden side and dragged himself upright again, wincing every time he jostled his injured ankle. Focused on his need to move further away from the cliff's edge and off the trail, he struggled to flip the light sled back onto its runners. He would check for damage and search for his spare headlamp only when he was safely out of the way.

"Kia, Weasel!" he called up his leads. By the dim, almost non-existent light of the stars, he could see his team lounging in various postures. A few of them had taken advantage of the break, and had curled up for a nap, but none of them seemed to be unduly distressed or exhibiting signs of injury or pain. Most of them were stretched out and relaxed, except for Kia, who sat alertly on her haunches, apparently assuming the position of lookout. Getting the team to move slowly, just a few feet up the trail, was not going to be an easy task. Weasel bounced up with a sharp yap, shook himself off and wagged his tail enthusiastically. The two leaders looked expectantly over their shoulders at their master, ready and willing to run again. Kia barked sharply twice, causing a stir amongst her teammates and rousing them back to work.

North hopped over to the snow hook and tugged it from the snow, then secured it back in its proper place. He eased himself onto the seat on the back of his sled, never as grateful for his little indulgence as he was at that moment. He grasped the handle bar with both hands. Ideally, he should inspect the gangline prior to setting his team in motion; their freefall plunge had undoubtedly tangled the lines or loosened the dogs' harnesses or tugs, but he had neither the time nor the physical ability to carry out the task. He let his injured left leg hang freely without touching the foot board on the runner, and stepped on the sled brake with his right.

"Kia, Weasel! Steady," North called. "Mush."

As expected, the team sprang ahead eagerly, pitting their strength and will against the drag of their burden. They were ready and willing to hit the trail, barking in joy at the prospect of another adventure. North grimaced when the sled jerked ahead a foot, jarring his shoulder. The brake appeared to be doing its job, though, and instead of surging ahead at full speed, the sled dragged slowly and heavily behind the team.

Kia turned her head and barked sharply at North, without a doubt telling him something was wrong. Something was holding her back, and she undoubtedly lay the blame on her master.

"Easy, Kia," North called, consoling his frustrated lead. He guided his straining dogs through the soft unmarked snow for about thirty feet, which he hoped would give him a wide enough safety zone when his companions made their descent.

The stand of evergreens he had spied from the base of the cliff would be a good place to stop and rest. North unclipped the snow hook again and stepped on the sled brake with his good foot while he dropped the hook beside the sled. When the team came to a stop he clumsily hopped to the nearest spruce tree. He floundered in the deep, unwieldly snow, falling and righting himself with difficulty. He bellowed and cursed in frustration before he was finally able to tie the snub line to the tree trunk. Daggers of hot pain shot up his left leg, and he screamed more than once. Not once did he consider giving up. The last thing he needed tonight was a runaway team.

North slowly made his way back to the sled, praying that his buddies would fare better than he had.

TWENTY FIVE

North's heavy mitts dangled at his side on their long idiot strings while he rummaged blindly inside his sled bag for his spare headlamp. When he'd loaded Becky's sixty-pound dogs on top of his sled, he hadn't anticipated the need to access his bag during what was supposed to be a two-hour trip to Shaktoolik. Getting the animals *off* his sled had been a hell of a lot harder than getting them *on.*

His cold, bare hand had just found the headlamp within the cavernous bag when North froze, suddenly sensing he was no longer alone. His hunter's instincts kicked in and he stilled his movements, becoming as rigid as the dark, snow-covered trees around him. His dogs had already settled down for a nap and seemed happily oblivious of danger or an unknown intruder. *Maybe my nerves are just shot,* North thought.

The wilderness seemed uncommonly quiet aside from an occasional snuffle from one of his resting dogs, or soughing of the light wind high in the tree tops. It was an isolated, tranquil spot, one that would normally soothe North's soul, but not tonight. He knew he was vulnerable and was happy that Mats and Becky weren't far behind him. He drew himself upright, the spare headlamp clutched in his hand, and tried his best to ignore the throbbing pain in his left foot. He turned the light on and breathed a sigh of relief to find it operational. He tugged the broken headlamp from his head and tossed it in his sled bag, then fit the new one on over his hat, the small task leaving him with an inordinate feeling of accomplishment.

He still felt uneasy, though, and reached back into the sled bag to find his rifle. The contents of his sled bag were a mess, tossed around when the sled had tipped to its side. The rifle wasn't where he always left it, and he was forced to delve into every corner of the bag before he felt the familiar shape of the smooth, walnut stock of his father's lovingly preserved rifle under his hand.

He swiftly checked the rifle for damage, released the safety catch and hobbled to the seat on the back of the sled. He snapped off his headlamp and waited for his eyes to adapt to the dark again, painfully aware that he was a sitting target. After a minute he could detect faint shadows against the brighter white snow under the tall spruce trees surrounding him. He began a slow, methodical search of the immediate area, and scanned the edge of the forest closely. The dark woods gave up no secrets, and North identified no threat. He relaxed marginally, his rifle resting across his knees.

Two or three more minutes passed and he saw nothing to alarm him, but the uneasy feeling of being watched, of unseen eyes piercing the night, remained. *Where are you? What are you?* His vision had improved, but another scan of the forest still revealed absolutely nothing. He twisted around to search the craggy cliff wall behind him. Grey and black boulders and the occasional struggling, scrawny tree were silhouetted against the rock face, but he spotted not a thing out of the ordinary. Still, the overwhelming sense of being watched ... of being something or *someone's* prey ... grew increasingly stronger.

North was so focused on his invisible stalker that he was only dimly aware of the burning in his left ankle. He thought it was either sprained or badly twisted, and wished he had a handful of anti-inflammatory drugs to combat the swelling and pain. He patted the pockets on his parka, found a bottle of aspirin and dry swallowed four tablets.

The feeling of being watched grew stronger. North combed the forest and immediate area again, his heavy black brows squeezed together in frustration. He'd left his mitts off, prepared to pull the trigger on his rifle, and his hands were becoming stiff. He blew on his fingers and flexed his hands repeatedly in an attempt to restore circulation and warmth to his frozen digits, fearing he'd end up with frostbite.

Where are you? I know you're out there! Show yourself, you bastard! He cursed at the invisible, unknown source of his dread.

It was nothing more than the faintest of sounds, no more than a whisper of wind, that made him lift his eyes skyward. He immediately berated himself for the oversight in his reconnaissance plan. He had overlooked the most obvious avenue of threat ... an attack from above.

An indistinct, although immediately recognizable shape was silhouetted against the black sky behind it. The wolf loomed sinister and menacing at the cliff's edge high above, and from what North could see, it was a massive beast. His stomach lurched when he realized the predator wasn't alone; another two dark, stealthy shapes slunk into view, flanking either side of their leader. *Night hunters.*

North reacted instinctively and instantly. He slid from his seat to the snow-covered ground, assuming his favoured firing position – kneeling on his left knee, his right foot flat on the ground. In his haste he forgot about his injury, and muffled a scream when his left foot connected with the ground. He hissed and panted until the worst of the pain subsided, then raised his rifle for the second time during what was turning out to be an immeasurably long and deadly night.

A low, menacing growl drifted down from above. Even as North attempted to bring the wolves' massive leader into the hairs of his gunsight, an almost impossible task on a dark night, he saw the beast drawing itself into a tight, powerful crouch, preparing to leap down the embankment to his prey. North's rifle cracked and a bullet ripped into the magnificent, lethal animal at the exact moment it sprang from the cliff's edge. By the time the beast hit the frozen ground at the base of the cliff, it was already dead. A spray of blood fanned out, dark against the pristine, white snow. The unsettling sight was once again uncannily similar to his dreams.

White and red. White and red.

Snow and blood. Snow and blood.

The wolves' presence hadn't gone undetected by North's dogs either. The team was in an uproar, every dog snarling and yelping in fear, the cacophony loud and jarring in the previously silent night. North glanced back at his dogs; they lunged against their restraints, throwing their muscular, strong bodies against their harnesses, desperately trying to free themselves. He prayed that the snub line and snow hook held against their powerful collective force.

North looked up to the top of the cliff again, astonished to see the two remaining wolves lingering at its edge. He was surprised that they hadn't fled, scared off by the sound of his rifle. He couldn't be sure that their leader's death would dissuade them from continuing their attack, and raised his rifle again. Although the night was frigidly cold, a drop of sweat trickled down North's brow and pooled in the inside crease of his eye, blurring his already challenged vision. He shook his head slightly to dislodge the drop of moisture and blinked a few times to clear his sight. He flexed the icy finger wrapped around the gun's cold metal trigger.

At his back, his team increased their efforts to escape, enraged by the smell and presence of the wolf thirty feet away. The other two wolves still lingered on the edge of the cliff, heads low, seemingly assessing the situation. North tightened his grip on the rifle and took aim at his next target. He started to squeeze the trigger, but before he released another bullet, a crack from another firearm pierced the night air and both of the dark figures above darted out of his sight.

North lowered his rifle and stared up at the rim of the rocky wall in surprise, and more than a little relief.

"North, you down there buddy?" shouted a familiar voice from above. A few seconds later Mats Peterson's bulky form loomed into view, his visage hidden behind the bright light beaming from his headlamp. Although North couldn't distinguish his friend's features, he recognized his booming voice.

North switched on his own headlamp. "I'm down here, Mats," he shouted back, raising his voice above the continuing wailing of his unhappy dogs. Mats peered over the edge, the beam from his headlamp just barely illuminating the dead wolf lying at the base of the cliff.

North aimed his headlamp at the wolf too, and by its bright light got his first clear look at his quarry – or was it his predator? His breath caught in his throat when he saw the surprisingly immense bulk of the animal. Judging from its size, it was an adult male Timber Wolf, likely weighing in at around 125 pounds. It was a beautiful specimen, and its thick, dark grey pelt shone with health. His head was immense, the large jaws powerful enough to snap the leg of an adult human or caribou with little effort. North felt a moment of intense sadness for the magnificent animal. The white and lighter grey markings on its exquisitely shaped head were so similar to those of today's Siberian husky; one could definitely see the evidence of ancestral markings. Its life ended much too soon, but in the wild one was either the hunted ... or the hunter. North had won this round.

"Kia! Weasel! That's enough! Be quiet," North roared impatiently. He was sitting on the ground now, still facing the rock wall, and as he attempted to turn toward his team he jarred his left foot. His shrill scream ripped through the night and he fell to his back, his rifle still clutched in his left hand.

"North! What's the matter? Are you okay, man?" Mats called, helpless to assist his new friend laying far below and in obvious pain.

"My ankle," North moaned. "I think it's sprained."

"Whatever you do, don't take your boot off," Mats yelled. "You'll never get it on again."

North lay on his back under the dark, star-studded sky, drawing short, hissing breaths through his clenched teeth and waiting for the worst of the pain to subside. He heard voices above, and a moment later Becky Singleton's hot pink parka, clearly distinguishable behind her headlamp, came into view. She stood next to Mats and leaned down over the edge of the cliff. "What in the *name of hell* are you doing down there, Rookie?"

North glared up the steep embankment and gritted his teeth. "I'm sure as hell not having a fucking picnic, Becky," he snarled.

"You okay?"

"Not really. My ankle's toast and I think my sled is busted."

"We'll find a safer route down and get to you as soon as we can," Mats said. Thankfully, North's team had quit their yelling, although they continued to occasionally yip and growl. They no longer strained to free themselves, but were still on full alert, ears and eyes glued to the body of the dead wolf.

"Becky, you've been on this trail before. What do you suggest?" Mats asked, keeping his voice loud for North's benefit. "This can't be the only route down to the coast."

"The trail follows this rim about another quarter of a mile, then makes a fairly sharp left down the mountain, but the slope is a lot less there. We'll be able to get down with no problem, but we're going to have to backtrack through the bush to get back to North."

Mats nodded. "Okay, let's get started. You lead and I'll stay close behind.

"Will do."

"North," Mats shouted, "we're on our way. Becky knows an easier way down but it will take us a while to get to you. Hang tight buddy!"

"I'm not going anywhere," North snapped, "but hurry, eh?"

TWENTY-SIX

It was just past midnight when Rachel dropped Andi off at the Green Aurora Guest House after their excursion to The Arctic Bar. She crept up to her room and crawled straight into bed.

At 3 am she awoke from a hellish nightmare. It's disturbing, graphic realism was sharp and horrifying, and infinitely more detailed than any vision or nightmare she'd ever had before. She saw her husband laying naked in a field of pristine, white snow, his arms and legs splayed wide in a perverse, erotic likeness to the snow angels she and her brothers had enjoyed making on those rare occasions when temperate Vancouver Island received a winter snowfall.

Ribbons of bright, crimson red spread out from beneath North's lifeless body, small rivulets that slowly grew longer and thicker until the landscape was awash in a sea of red and he floated in a pool of his own blood. In her dream Andi tried again and again to call out to him, desperate to awaken her lover from whatever force bound him there, away from her arms. As hard as she tried, though, she was unable to make even the smallest of sounds or utter a single word until, in a flash of awareness, she realized that she, herself, was without physical form ... she existed as merely a whisper, or a spirit, or a memory. She saw herself drift over the cold, silent field and float above the man she would love for eternity – the man who was her entire existence. She was desperate to hear his voice and talk with him just one more time. Without warning, North's eyes shot open and Andi stared into the lifeless, flat brown orbs, screaming his name.

In the safety of her warm Anchorage bedroom, Andi Ruben awoke with a strangled scream. The nightmare – was it a nightmare, or was it something real? – left her weak and utterly exhausted, her muscles uncooperative puddles of jelly. Her heart pounded wildly but her body, drenched in cold sweat, would not respond to her commands. She realized with a sickening jolt that her arms and legs were splayed wide under the bed's heavy down duvet, in an exact replica of her husband's pose. She knew without a doubt that the man who had healed her heart and taught her to love and live again was in danger, but she was helpless to do anything about it. While she lay warm and safe in a soft bed, her lover was battling for his life somewhere in Alaska, on a cold, unforgiving trail between Anchorage and Nome.

Andi wept for the man she loved, and prayed that her nightmares and premonitions were wrong, that for once in her life they were nothing but unfounded, insubstantial dreams. She could *not* lose her husband ... she *would not* live through another loss. She vowed that she would die before fighting the torment and demons of grief again.

Alone and afraid, Andi did the only thing she could think of to ease her pain and aching heart. She prayed.

Please, Natalie, my sweet baby girl, my shining star.

Please bring North home to me again.

At 4:30 she gave up on her useless attempt to fall asleep and silently crept back downstairs, her slippers in hand and fluffy pink housecoat draped over her thin shoulders. She made a cup of camomile tea and sat at the big kitchen table, her shaking, cold hands wrapped around the hot stoneware cup.

"What are you doing down here at this time of the morning?" Gert asked in a loud whisper when she swept into the kitchen wearing a long, green housecoat. Andi startled, then frowned at the small puddle of tea that had spilled onto the tabletop; somehow it had already grown cold. "Oh, I didn't mean to startle you, dear."

"I ... I didn't hear you," Andi whispered, discretely swiping a tear from her cheek. She grabbed a napkin from the holder in the middle of the table and mopped up the liquid. "I hope I didn't wake you?"

"Oh no, dear," Gert smiled and winked. "I'm always up by 5:00. Morning is my favourite time of the day, and I like to have something fresh out of the oven for my guests' breakfast." She filled the big coffee maker with water and scooped ground coffee into the basket, humming a soothing, melodic tune. "Bill grinds fresh coffee beans every evening before he goes to bed so I don't have to disturb him with all that noise in the morning," Gert explained. "That man does love his sleep." She started the coffee machine and sat down at the table. "And how about you, dear, did you have a good sleep? And how was your evening with Rachel? Did you girls have a good time?"

Andi sniffled and stared into the darkness outside the kitchen window for a long moment. When she looked into Gert's light blue eyes, she saw interest and concern, and what may have been a touch of sympathy behind the old-fashioned horn-rimmed glasses. Andi swallowed once, her throat tight and raw, then took a deep, steadying breath and squeezed her eyes tightly shut. "I ... I'm an alcoholic," she whispered, "and I almost made a terrible, terrible mistake last night." She forced herself to look at Gert then, and tears began to course freely down her cheeks; she no longer had the strength to contain them.

Gert rose, light and nimble for her age, and sat down next to Andi on the long wooden bench seat. She put her arm around the younger woman's shoulders and hugged her close. Andi hung her head and covered her eyes with one hand as deep, despairing sobs wracked her body. "Let it all out, my dear, let it all out," she murmured. Gert turned to Andi and gently, but firmly, drew her head down to her shoulder. She stroked Andi's long, glossy hair and patted her head until her tears subsided, much as one would a heartbroken child.

When Andi had no more tears to shed, she sat up, disengaging herself from the older woman's embrace. "I'm sorry. I don't know what came over me," she said softly. She reached for another napkin and blew her nose.

Gert gave Andi's shoulder a final, firm pat and slid off the bench. "We all need a good cry now and then, my dear," she smiled. "That's nature's way of clearing out all of the bad stuff in our soul and making room for better memories, you know. Now – how about a cup of coffee?"

Andi nodded and managed a wan smile. "I could definitely use a cup. It smells delicious."

Gert poured two mugs and set them on the table along with a pitcher of light cream, then dumped the rest of Andi's cold tea in the sink. After they'd both had one or two sips of the dark, rich brew, Gert cleared her throat. She toyed with her coffee spoon for a moment longer, then set it aside decisively. "You know, dear, there's no shame in admitting you have an addiction. Most of us do, in one way or another. Sometimes our weaknesses and addictions just aren't visible to the rest of the world."

Andi nodded her head and stared into the steaming green mug she held in her hands.

"And you said you 'almost' made a mistake last night. But you didn't, did you? That's the only thing you need to remember today. You *didn't* make a mistake, and that's all that matters."

Andi looked into Gert's blue eyes again, and suddenly realized that over the past three days she and the woman sitting across from her had somehow formed a deep, strong bond. She signed deeply. "You're right, but I came *so close*. Too close. Rachel ordered us both a glass of beer, and I just didn't know how to tell her." Andi frowned. "I think that deep down inside I really didn't want to tell her. But when I held that glass of beer in my hand and lifted it to my lips, something just broke inside of me."

When Andi smiled at her new friend again, it was warmer and stronger. "I knew I just couldn't go down that path again, but it was so tempting, Gert. It would have been so nice to just forget about the fear and pain for even a few hours." She shook her head and stared into her coffee. "Just a few hours of peace is all I was looking for."

"What is it you're so afraid of, dear?"

Andi pursed her lips. "I've been having these dreams. Visions, really. I have something like a 'Sixth Sense', and sometimes I just *know* things. And right now it's stronger than it's ever been in my life." She looked at Gert closely, trying to read the other woman's reaction, and saw nothing but empathy and understanding.

"And last night was the worst," she whispered. A lone tear ran down Andi's cold cheek.

"I think my husband is in danger. I ... I think he might be dead."

TWENTY-SEVEN

Almost five long, punishing hours after leaving the site of the moose attack in the Blueberry Hills, the welcoming lights of the tiny Inupiat village of Shaktoolik loomed ahead. Six teams had overtaken the much slower trio during the excruciatingly long night, shouting out questions regarding the gruesome event they had passed by on the trail. Understandably, then, the news of Becky's bizarre encounter with the incensed moose arrived at the next checkpoint before the survivors did.

North, fortified with a double dose of some kind of painkillers from Mats' first aid kit, gripped his sled's handle bar with resolute determination. He struggled to keep his left foot off the runners, and was more thankful than ever for the seat he'd built on the back of his sled. Almost every inch of his battered and bruised body hurt. Beads of perspiration dotted his brow, cooling instantly and leaving his skin cold and uncomfortable.

While Mats and Becky had been blazing new trail to reach him at the bottom of the rock wall, winding through scrubby forest along the base of the hill, North had succeeded in untangling and realigning the team on the gangline. He managed, albeit painfully, to check their harnesses and tugs, but nothing else. He could not right his sled or reload Becky's two dogs, which were now nearly frozen solid. By the time his rescuers arrived, North, exhausted from his efforts and the increasing, nearly debilitating pain in his foot, was sitting propped against the side of his sled. Both legs were stretched out on the snow, spread slightly apart, and his rifle lay across his knees. He was steadily and resolutely sipping from a rapidly dwindling fifth of brandy.

Misfortune had switched North and Becky's rolls; victim had become saviour, and saviour the victim. While Becky examined each of North's dogs for signs of injury or trauma, Mats righted his sled and jury-rigged a repair on a broken top rail, lashing it together with a length of rope. He seemed confident that it would hold until they reached Shaktoolik, where they could put together a better repair.

A cornucopia of stars still blazed in an inky sky when the travel worn trio finally limped into Shaktoolik in the early, pre-dawn hours of Wednesday, March 12, day eleven of *The Last Great Race.* Despite the early hour, a checker and a veterinarian appeared to be waiting for them and ran out of the checkpoint cabin only moments after the trio's arrival. They were still zipping up their parkas and tugging on hats and gloves in their haste to meet the mushers, but in deference to the newcomers' ordeal, the officials' greeting was restrained and without fanfare.

The checker was a slight man, barely taller than Becky. His face was so shrouded within the shadows of his parka's wolf fur trimmed hood that it was impossible to distinguish his features. His voice, though, was surprisingly deep, and bore distinct traces of a British accent when he introduced himself as Syd Blankenship. The second man was the veterinarian, who merely nodded grimly without introducing himself, too intent on giving the frozen corpses of the four dead Siberian Huskies a brief inspection. His long, thin face grew more pinched each time he trained his headlamp's bright beam on the gruesome remains of another animal.

After Syd checked the three mushers in, the two officials insisted on assisting a mostly incapacitated North with his tasks. Becky and Mats had already volunteered to look after their friend's team and get them settled and fed, but he had adamantly refused their offer, claiming that they had enough work to do looking after their own dogs. With a stubborn set to his jaw he unfastened his dogs from the gangline and hooked them to a long chain while the checker and vet spread fresh straw on the snow. Four other teams were already bedded down next to a line of scrubby pines on the leeward side of the small cabin, seeking the structures' protection from an increasing north wind which often reached hurricane force on the open, barren coast of the Norton Sound.

The checker and veterinarian worked in silence, seeming to respect the fact that before any questions were asked or stories told, North, Becky and Mats would need to attend to their precious sled dogs. After they had seen to their teams, the mushers and officials, with a cursing North leaning heavily on Mats arm, slowly made their way to the vet shack. It was a small, roughly built wooden building set twenty feet behind the checkpoint cabin. Metal fencing had been erected adjacent to its leeward side – holding pens for injured or dropped dogs.

"I'm Phil Barnsdale," the vet said, finally introducing himself when they were all inside his headquarters. He sat down at a small, scarred wooden table and set an official looking form with the Iditarod logo on it before him, then pointed to the only other two seats in the building, two cracked plastic stacking chairs. Becky and North both sat, while Mats and Syd leaned against the wall. Phil pulled a long hiss of air through his teeth, then exhaled noisily before he began the difficult interview. "I hear you ran into some trouble on the trail, Ms. Singleton."

"Yes, and please call me Becky," she said. Her lips were set in a thin, hard line and a spider web of wrinkles had grown around her sad blue eyes. She unzipped her pink parka and removed her wool hat, freeing her blond, disheveled curls. "I was attacked by two moose. They left four of my Siberians dead, as you saw." Without preamble, Becky recapped the events of her night, struggling to keep her raw emotions in check. Phil made careful notes, occasionally asking her to repeat a few words so he could ensure he recorded them correctly.

"Tragic," he said with a slow shake of his grey head when Becky had concluded her statement. "My sincere condolences, Becky. They looked like fine dogs. This kind of thing rarely happens, but I guess it's the chance you take when you're out in the wilderness."

Then he turned to North. "It looks like you've injured yourself as well?"

"Yeah, twisted my ankle I think," North said without elaborating further.

"Rough break. Maybe they can fix you up inside." He turned to Syd and Mats. "Well then, would you two mind giving me a hand, please? I'll need to examine the corpses more closely, so could you please get them off the sleds and lay them outside beside the shack for me?" He pointed to the far wall of the vet shack, away from the outside holding pens.

Both men nodded, their faces grim.

"Becky, why don't you and North go up to the cabin? I'm going to go out and examine your teams first, and then I'll start on the deceased. I don't think you want to be here while I do that. You've all had a rough ride, so go grab something to eat and get some sleep if you can. This is going to take a while, but I'll come get you when I'm done." It was the Iditarod veterinarian's duty to confirm that all dogs competing in the race remained in good health, and in this case that Becky's surviving animals had suffered no injuries during the attack. He was required to prepare a full, detailed report for the Iditarod committee.

"Nope. I'm staying," Becky said decisively. She had already handed her book to the vet, but Mats and North dug into their parka pockets and handed over their books. Phil promised to return them before the mushers hit the trail again.

While Becky helped North hobble to the cabin, Mats and Syd completed their task as quickly as they could, working as a team to retrieve each of the four frozen dogs. After Phil had given them a preliminary examination, he would seal each animal in a heavy plastic bag in preparation for transfer to Nome on an Iditarod Air Force aircraft. A full gross necropsy – a canine version of an autopsy – would be completed there.

When the task was completed, Syd and Becky disappeared back into the vet shack, and Mats trudged to the checkpoint cabin, exhaustion evident in his heavy footsteps as his boots crunched over the packed snow. North still sat on the top of the cabin's two steps where he'd insisted Becky leave him. "Why aren't you inside?" he asked.

North shrugged. "Thought I'd just catch my breath. It's been a rough night."

"Yah, it sure has." He held his hand out to North. "Come on, let's go in now. Get something to eat if we can."

North rose with some difficulty, the short rest having been long enough for his abused muscles to stiffen. Mats swung the wooden slat door open, releasing a blast of hot air and the enticing aroma of fresh coffee. The single room was lit by two large, hissing Coleman lanterns, which hung from the low roof beams. An immense black cook-stove dominated one corner of the small shack, its metal chimney snaking up and through the open beam ceiling. Extra split wood was piled neatly up against the wall on one side of the stove. The captivating aroma of perking coffee emanated from an old-fashioned coffeepot bubbling on the stove's metal cook top. Two huge covered pots sat on the other side of the stove, emitting the tantalizing, meaty aroma of stew. North hoped to God it wasn't moose meat. He didn't think he would ever be able to stomach moose again.

"Good morning, gentlemen," a middle aged, sturdily built woman smiled warmly, turning from her task at a worktop set against the length of another wall. Two rows of shelves constructed from rough twelve-inch-wide wood planking lay under the worktop, stacked with plates, cups, glasses and canned goods. A bucket of water sat on the floor next to it. The woman's steel-grey hair was pulled severely back from her weathered face and secured in a tight knot just above the nape of her neck. She wore a faded pair of blue jeans and a similarly worn and faded red checked flannel button-front shirt. On her feet were black fur mukluks, in deference to the chill that no amount of heating could prevent from seeping up into the bare wood floor. In her hand she held an enormous loaf of bread, its crust baked to a perfect dark golden brown. In spite of his pain and gloomy mood, North's mouth began to water. "I hear you all had a rough night," she said, her voice surprising soft and melodious, despite her rough appearance. "Can I interest you boys in some stew and fresh bread, or a coffee?"

"Just coffee for now, please," Mats said with a shy smile. He had removed his fur hat and hung it to dry on one of the hooks beside the cabin door, revealing a tangle of overgrown reddish blond hair. He was a big man, well over six feet tall and as broad as a barn door at the shoulder. With his full red beard and drooping moustache, he looked like a true mountain man, but his winsome smile and startling white, straight teeth seemed incongruous in the otherwise wild countenance. He stomped loose snow from his boots and hung his bulky parka on another hook. North had removed his parka and hat, but was struggling to reach a coat hook just out of his reach while balancing on one leg. Mats took his friend's clothes and hung them up next to his.

"Yeah, same for me," North concurred with a disgruntled sigh. "Just coffee, please. I'll take you up on the stew when we've sorted out whatever's going to happen next."

"Please, have a seat," their hostess said, indicating a large rectangular picnic-style table set against one wall and flanked by two long wooden benches. The table was covered in a red and white checked plastic cover and set under a small window adorned with a matching curtain, still drawn against the night.

Mats helped North hobble to the table, then peered around the room. "Do you have indoor facilities?" he asked cautiously.

"Just through there," the woman smiled, indicating the one interior door in the building. "There's two bedrooms with bunk beds back there if you want a nap, and also a bathroom. It's just a bucket system, but at least you don't have to freeze your ass off in the outhouse.

And I've put a basin of warm water there on the counter if you care to wash up."

Mats shuffled off quickly, a smile of delight at the surprising indoor convenience.

North slumped down heavily on the hard bench, grateful for the opportunity to finally get off his throbbing, aching ankle. After the adrenalin rush and trauma of the past several hours, insidious tendrils of exhaustion were threatening to render him immobile. He was looking forward to a cup or two of hot coffee and a caffeinated rush. And another dose of pain killers. He would need them to face the next part of his journey to Nome ... *if* he could make it to Nome. The thought of scratching from the race when he'd made it this far made his stomach lurch.

"I'm Linda Blankenship," the elderly woman said cheerfully, pulling two bright yellow mugs from the shelf and turning to the stove. She wrapped a small towel around her free hand and lifted the hot metal coffeepot by its curved handle, carrying the precious brew carefully to the table. "My husband, Syd, is one of the checkers here this year," she continued as she filled the big mugs with boiling hot coffee. "I help out wherever I can, mostly in the kitchen. Sugar and whitener are there if you need it." Linda tilted her head toward a cluster of condiments sitting on a round metal tray in the middle of the table. "Sorry, we don't have any cream or milk left."

"North Ruben," North offered, a wry smile creasing his exhausted countenance. "Rookie #9. From Inuvik, Canada. And I drink my coffee black, thanks."

"Pleased to meet you, Rookie #9 from Inuvik," Linda said, bright and chipper for such an ungodly time of the day. "I've had the honour of knowing Becky Singleton for some years now," she continued as she returned the coffeepot to the stove. "She's a fine musher. Placed in the top ten about four times, I believe. Came in second last year." There was a definite note of pride in her words, and her dark eyes reflected the sparkle in her voice.

Female solidarity, North wondered silently, or Alaskan pride? "Yeah, she's come pretty close to winning a few times," he said out loud, taking a big sip of coffee and scorching his tongue. "She runs an excellent kennel too. It's a real shame about her dogs – this is gonna set her back."

Whether it was the effects of the overpowering heat emanating from the crackling wood stove or the simple fact that his tortured body was finally stationary after so many long, gruelling hours, North felt the heaviness of total exhaustion settling into his limbs. He blew on his coffee's steaming surface a moment before taking another cautious sip. He needed to feel a caffeine jolt running through his veins more than he could ever remember.

Mats burst into the room looking remarkably refreshed and alert. His face glowed with health, his cheeks a shining vivid pink, and his red hair was wet and smoothed neatly back from his face. Even his full and bushy beard appeared to have a mini-makeover, and was no longer adorned with its previous sprinkling of crusty bits of dried food.

"Man, does it ever feel great to get washed up!" Mats exclaimed with a wide grin, white teeth vivid against the red of his beard and moustache. "Your turn, North."

"Nah, I'll wait a while. Going to enjoy this coffee while it's hot."

"Hey Linda, meet my friend Mats Pederson, Rookie #22 from Norway."

Mats frowned at North curiously, wondering if his racing buddy had gone mad.

"Mats, this is Linda, Syd's wife and brewer of a mean cup of coffee."

"Pleased to meet you, ma'am," Mats greeted Linda again in his heavily accented English, once again smiling shyly at the older woman.

"I'm pleased to meet you too, Mats," Linda said. She had removed the lid from one of the immense pots and was stirring its aromatic contents. "You're certainly a long way from home."

"I sure am. It's lovely country you have here."

"The most beautiful place in the world," Linda said with a gentle smile.

"How's your foot doing, North?" Mats asked, energetically stirring an amazing four heaping spoons of sugar into his coffee.

"Not too good." The savory aroma of Linda's stew was making North's mouth water, despite his lack of appetite.

"You're injured?" Linda asked sharply, turning from the stove. Her right hand clutched a long wooden spoon coated in dark brown gravy that threated to drip to the floor. "What's the matter?"

"Uh, just twisted my ankle, I think. Nothing to worry about," North muttered into his coffee, refusing to make eye contact with the woman.

"I think I'd better have a look at it for you," she said with authority, tapping the edge of the spoon sharply against the side of the pot before laying it back on the counter. She placed a lid on the pot, and marched determinedly to the table.

"No, really, I'm alright."

"North, you should let Linda look at it," Mats admonished. "You can't put any weight on that foot. Maybe she can help."

"I used to be an emergency room nurse before I became an Alaskan bush bunny," Linda said with a determined smile. She was already kneeling on the bare wooden floor beside North. "I do know something about anatomy and sprained ankles."

"Fine," North muttered, glaring at his fellow musher. "But just to shut my friend up." North wasn't anxious to succumb to the ministrations of a nurse again. He'd had too many encounters with them over the past few years, and they always resulted in some degree of pain.

Before her new patient could change his mind, Linda quickly and deftly unlaced North's boot. Her initial attempt to tug it from his foot met with firm resistance and a loud moan from North – the ankle was definitely swollen. Taking the next step, she removed the laces entirely, opened the boot wide and folded the tongue back to fully expose the foot within. Then she gently pulled the boot off his foot, coughing lightly when the stench of sweaty, dirty feet hit her nose.

"Uh, sorry," North muttered, embarrassed by his lack of personal hygiene. "Haven't had a shower in a week and I ran out of clean socks."

"Believe me, I've smelled worse in my time."

While attempting to jar the injured foot as little as possible, his nurse deftly removed the multiple layers of damp, odorous woolen socks from North's foot.

When she peeled the last thin layer from his foot, she gasped. North's ankle bone was invisible, camouflaged within an angry, swollen mass of skin that was already starting to turn blue. The foot was hot to touch, and the first sign of reddish bruising had already begun to creep up the calf of his leg.

North's black eyebrows shot up when he saw the full extent of his injury. His surprise rapidly turned to a grimace when she attempted to bend the swollen ankle.

"I think you have more than a sprained ankle going on here, my friend," Linda muttered, slowly shaking her grey head. "Much, much, more."

TWENTY-EIGHT

"Man, looks like you're not going anywhere soon," Mats said solemnly. North was laying on the lower bunk of one of the beds, Mats standing next to him, scrutinizing his friend's left foot. It was wrapped from his toes to mid-calf in multiple layers of flesh-toned elastic compression bandage, elevated on several pillows and topped with a sealed bag of snow.

North scowled and threw Mats a black look. The small, windowless room was bare except for two bunkbeds hewn from pine and topped with thin mattresses. A handmade pine table, similar to a nightstand but without a drawer, sat in the narrow space between the bunks and held another hissing lantern. The only colour in the room came from the handcrafted quilts that covered each mattress. The four quilts shared a common pattern, but different colour grouping. North's mother used to make quilts when he was young, and he recognized the familiar pattern his mother called 'Log Cabin'. Today the simple design and vivid colours went largely unappreciated; North's attention was focused on his hot, throbbing ankle. Even the smallest of movements made the stoic northerner wince, and the weight of the slowly melting bag of snow laying across his ankle caused more discomfort than he cared to admit.

"Here you go," Linda said cheerily, marching into the tiny bedroom bearing a glass of water in one hand and what appeared to be a foot brace in the other. She set the brace on the floor under the nightstand, then reached into the pocket of her jeans. She pulled out a small vial of pills. "These are nonsteroidal anti-inflammatory drugs."

She shook two round white tablets into North's hand and handed him the vial, which was three-quarters full. "Take two right now and two every six hours until you get to a doctor in Nome."

North sighed deeply but obediently tossed the proffered medication into his mouth, chasing it down with a few sips of ice-cold water.

"And no more brandy," Linda admonished sternly, shaking her finger at North. "Mixing drugs and alcohol is strictly a no-no."

North scowled at her, his black brows knitting together, then threw Mats another dirty look for sharing that bit of information with the nurse.

"Hey, buddy. It's not my fault you followed the wrong trail down that cliff!" Mats protested, unsuccessfully attempting to hide a dry smile. "There's always next year's race, you know."

North stared at Mats in disbelief. "I haven't called it quits yet, my friend."

"You'd be a fool to try and finish the race on THAT foot," Linda said, pointing at North's swollen appendage.

North harrumphed and averted his brooding black eyes. "What's going on outside?"

Mats filled him in on the events of the past hour. The veterinarian had examined North's and Mats' dogs and pronounced them all healthy and fit to continue the race. He'd done his preliminary exam on Becky's deceased sled dogs, and the animals' mutilated bodies had been zipped into heavy black body bags and laid out beside the vet shack. He confirmed that Alpha's wounds had been mortal, and that the big lead dog would not have survived more than a few minutes. North had been right to put him out of his suffering, although the Iditarod committee may still want to interview him to discuss his actions.

Becky was resting in the second bedroom, which had been opportunely vacated by two departing mushers. North wasn't surprised when Mats told him she had formally scratched from the race and that

Syd Blankenship was completing the necessary paperwork. Becky and her team would go on to Nome via the Iditarod Air Force. Phil had found her surviving six dogs in good physical health, although they were understandably traumatized. He recommended that the dogs be given a quiet, safe place to recover, and they had been moved to individual straw-lined dog crates in the holding pen pending their transfer to Nome within the next day or two. A volunteer would exercise and feed them, and ensure they received the attention and care they deserved.

"Where are my socks and boots?" North growled when Mats had finished updating him. "I need to get going." Two pairs of stunned eyes gaped at him in disbelief.

Linda recovered first. "Didn't I make it clear enough, North? You're not going anywhere except climbing on an airplane with Becky later today! Your ankle is either fractured or very badly sprained."

"Like hell!" North retorted. "I'm finishing this damn race, even if it kills me."

"Well it just might do that, if you insist on continuing with your foot in the shape it's in! That would be just plain crazy." Linda snapped. The formerly gentle and placid senior had transformed into the confident, professional nurse she formerly was. She crossed her arms over her bosom. "I can't let you leave. It would be paramount to suicide."

Mats had retreated to the doorway, ready to abandon ship if things got rough in the bedroom. North looked to his racing colleague for moral support. Mats shrugged quite eloquently for a man his size and muttered, "I'm going to go get some food now." He vanished through the open doorway.

"Mats Pederson! Come back here and help me," North roared. He attempted to sit up, then fell back to the bed with a muted cry. "Mats, you miserable coward, get back here!" The door separating the two halves of the cabin clicked shut, ending any further discussion on the matter.

Linda placed a firm hand on North's arm and gently pushed him back down to the mattress. "North, *please* listen to me. Be reasonable. If that ankle *is* broken, which I'm pretty sure it is, you could cause irreparable damage if you try to finish this race. And you'll be in a hell of a lot of pain while you're doing it, I might add."

North clamped his lips together and glared at the watermarks on the unfinished plywood ceiling above his head. He most definitely was *not* in a reasonable mood; he was downright miserable, and the knowledge that he had nobody to blame but himself made him angrier by the minute.

"Why don't you just rest for a while, hmm? Lord knows, you must be exhausted. I'll bring you a big bowl of stew and some nice fresh bread. I know it's hard to think straight on an empty stomach." Linda gave North's shoulder a motherly pat, transforming from authoritative nurse back to caring matron in the blink of an eye. She pulled a pillow from the top bunk and placed it behind North's head.

"It better not be moose stew," he grumbled to her retreating back.

Half an hour later, with a stomach full of rich caribou stew, warm bread, sweet apple pie and strong coffee, North felt marginally better. The NSAID drugs had taken the edge off his pain, giving him a modicum of relief.

Mats peered around the corner of the bedroom door, looking decidedly sheepish. "Hey, buddy. Feeling any better?"

"Yeah, good as new," North lied. "Sorry about before. I had no right to yell at you like that."

"Don't worry about it. It's forgotten," Mats smiled and stepped into the room. He pointed at the second bunk bed. "I'm just going to lie down and rest for a bit, if you don't mind the company."

"Help yourself. I was just about to shut my eyes too."

Mats removed his heavy boots and set them out in the hallway, then closed the bedroom door. He dropped down on top of the adjacent lower bunk fully clothed, a sigh of relief escaping his lips. "Can I turn off the light?"

"Sure, go ahead."

"How's Becky doing?" North asked after thirty seconds, his softly spoken words still loud in the dead silence of the small, black room. The absence of the lantern's steady hiss was only noticeable when it was gone, much like background noise nobody ever hears.

"She must be sleeping. Hasn't come out of the bedroom again." Mats stifled a yawn.

"Poor woman. I feel so sorry for her. Losing four dogs like that is going to set her back. I wonder if she'll enter the race again next year."

The only response was his roommate's deep, steady breathing. Mats Pederson had fallen dead asleep the second his head hit the pillow.

North desperately wished he could do the same.

His eyes snapped open, straining as they probed the black void before them but seeing only the continually twisting, twirling red and white bands of colour that seemed to be etched into his retinas. North's heart raced as he struggled to remember where he was, his drugged brain sluggish and unresponsive. He started to rise, but a sharp jab of pain in his left foot jarred him abruptly back to his senses. He fell back to the bed and forced himself to slow his laboured breathing. A few seconds later the memories rushed back – the incensed, plundering moose, the mangled, crushed sled dogs, Becky Singleton. A sea of blood and his own fateful, headlong plunge down that damn cliff, and then finally the long, slow, windy final twelve miles to Shaktoolik. To safety.

White and red, snow and blood. The ghastly images, permanently imbedded into his brain, continued to dance before his eyes.

North didn't know how long he'd been asleep, but by the sound of the snores beside him, Mats was still in la-la land. North was grateful for some time alone with his thoughts; he had a lot to process, and needed to come up with a good plan going forward.

Nothing stirred beyond the confines of the small, dark room – not a voice, not a sound. He felt like he'd awoken within a vast black hole, and closed his eyes against the unsettling darkness. He willed his taut muscles to soften, to relax. He needed to focus on the predicament that lay before him and find a way to prevent his lifelong dream from slipping from his grasp.

Andi's voice, as sweet and clear as if she were lying next to him on the narrow bed, the soft contours of her warm body molded to his, echoed through his head ... 'You gave it your best shot, North. You ran the Iditarod and it doesn't matter that you didn't finish the damn race. I'm proud of you. Be happy with your accomplishment.' Andi was always the more reasonable one in the family, and she was probably right. Maybe he should just accept the fact that he wouldn't be finishing the stupid race, and admit defeat. Maybe he should, but could he? He didn't think so.

North lay in the quiet comfort of darkness, reliving the wonders and hardships of the past eleven days, then contemplating his options. Several minutes passed before he reached a decision, and when he finally decided to sit up, it wasn't without a struggle; he felt groggy and slightly woozy, and was forced to pause frequently while his spinning head righted itself. He cautiously stretched out the muscles in his aching, tight shoulders and arms, then slowly rotated his neck from side to side and tried to knead out the hard kinks. Even the small movements made him feel stronger, got his blood flowing again and gave him hope. Now for the big test. He slowly swung his legs to the floor, right first, followed by the left. The first tentative pressure on his left foot sent an immediate jolt of red-hot pain up his leg. North swore softly and panted through the worst of the pain, much like a labouring mother through a contraction.

Still perched on the side of the bed, hunched over to prevent his head from colliding with the bunk above, he groped blindly for the foot brace Linda had left on the floor. His hand sent the plastic device skittering across the bare wood planking, the noise sharp and loud in the silence of the room. In the adjacent bunk, Mats' light snoring faltered. North froze, remaining motionless until the reassuring rhythm of deep, steady breathing resumed. He ran his hand along the floor again until he located the device, carefully picking it up when he made contact.

He definitely didn't want his new friend Mats awake for what he planned to do next.

The Shaktoolik checkpoint cabin remained quiet while North struggled to slip undetected from the bedroom, foot brace dangling from his hand. Another musher had crept into the room shortly after Mats had fallen asleep, and crawled up into the bunk above North where he still lay, smelling of wood smoke and snoring lightly. North breathed a sigh of relief when he finally reached the deserted kitchen area, where he downed two more of Linda's NSAIDs. He'd always boasted about his high threshold to pain, but North Ruben was already having serious doubts about his plan's chance of success. If there was one thing he knew about himself, though, it was that he wasn't a loser, and he wasn't a quitter. Not in life, and definitely not in a dog sled race.

He knew he had to act fast. Any moment Linda or Syd could pop into the room and make his life complicated. He had no idea what time it was, but judging from the bright, early morning sun outside the windows he estimated it was around 10 am, meaning he must have slept for almost four hours. He spotted his boots on the floor below his parka, and hopped on one leg to retrieve them. Halfway across the room he lost his balance and rested his left foot to the floor to steady himself. The pain was immediate and intense; he gnawed at his bottom lip to prevent himself from screaming out loud. He panted and cursed under his breath and kept going until he'd retrieved his boots and was seated on the bench.

Attaching the foot brace was a more complicated and painful task than he'd imagined. Luckily, Linda had tucked his socks into his boots,

228

but he struggled to fit them over his bandaged foot and ended up ripping one thick wool sock open in order to fit it around his bulky foot. It took him several more precious minutes before he was able to snap the unwieldly brace on, and then he was forced to remove his left boot's heavy felt liner and its laces before he could shove his foot inside. Every movement brought another jolt of searing agony. He couldn't remember ever experiencing such intense pain, not even from a bullet wound. The remains of his caribou stew threatened to rise from his stomach and he swallowed hard to push down the burn. He hoped like hell that Linda had given him enough pills to see him through to Nome, because Nome was where he was bound, and not courtesy of the Iditarod Air Force. Whether it killed him or not, he wasn't a quitter.

He quickly pulled on his socks and laced up the boot on his right foot. He was breathing hard, a sheen of sweat on his golden-brown skin. The enticing aroma of coffee drifted from the pot sitting on the edge of the woodstove and he yearned for a cup. Saliva pooled on his tongue, and he was almost desperate for at least a mouthful of the addictive, caffeine-laden brew, but he had no time to waste. At any moment Mats or – God help him, nurse Linda – could walk into the room and foil his escape plan. He suspected Linda and Syd may have laid down for a few hours of sleep in Becky's room. He had to get away, and now. His plan was tenuous, at best, even without the interference of others.

If there was a blessing in his wretched morning, it was that Phil had left their vet books laying on the table. North had already zipped his precious book inside his parka pocket. He was ready to leave, but he still had one small problem. His left boot gaped wide open; he had to find some way to close and secure it or his foot would freeze. He needed to find some way to protect it from the elements, to keep it dry and warm. His eyes darted around the room, finally alighting on a long, wide woolen scarf hanging on a hook by the door. It was a bright, hot pink. Without a moment's hesitation, he yanked the scarf down and wound it around his boot, overlapping the edges and tying the ends together securely. He had some heavy duct tape in his sled and would wrap it over the scarf to act as an additional wind and snow barrier when he was well away from Shaktoolik.

Away. He needed to focus on getting out of the cabin and away before anyone tried to stop him. With a lingering glance at the coffeepot, North opened the cabin door and hobbled onto the tiny landing. A quick glance at the yard told him he was still alone as he resolutely began the torturous, short trek to his sled. A new team was bedded down and the two that had been there when they arrived were gone. The new arrival must be the musher he'd shared a bunk with. North's dogs were still curled up and asleep, but stirred as he approached, and soon began to drag themselves from sleep, yawning and stretching out. When they began to whine and talk to their leader, he shushed them repeatedly, afraid they would draw attention to his departure. He did a double-take when he saw his sled. Somebody, and North was quite sure he knew who, had repaired his broken top rail. North was certainly racking up a long list of I.O.U.'s to his new buddy.

By the time the team was hitched to the sled North's body, beneath its heavy layers of winter clothing, was bathed in a sheen of sweat. For the sake of ensuring a speedy departure, North decided to delay feeding the dogs; if they were disappointed, they didn't show it. He suspected they sensed the urgency in his movements and demeanour, and most likely his pain. He scuffed their ears and made quiet promises of extra rations as soon as they were safely away from the checkpoint.

Despite the double dose of NSAIDs he'd taken, his ankle continued to radiate a continuous current of hot pain. He clenched his teeth and panted like one of his excited dogs through the worst of the spasms, resolution set in the hard line of his jaw. He untied the snub line, hobbled to the seat on the back of the sled, pulled the snow hook, and hung on to the handle bar.

"Mush!" he called softly. The dogs responded eagerly, but they hadn't quite cleared the dog lot when North heard shouts of alarm behind him. He recognized Linda's voice, and Syd's, but he stared stoically ahead, determined to ignore their increasingly frantic cries.

TWENTY-NINE

The dogs needed to eat. He knew that. They needed to eat, or neither they nor he would survive. He also knew that he'd forgotten to pick up his drop bag in his haste to leave Shaktoolik, and prayed that there was enough cooked dog food in his cooler to last them until they reached the next checkpoint. He had a small bag of frozen meat chunks for snacks; he could cook them up in a thin soup if he had to. At least it would give the dogs something warm to eat. Koyuk was fifty miles away across the treacherous, always windy 'make it or break it' Norton Sound. It was a five-hour trek on a perfect day, with a good strong team and a healthy driver, nine or more if the winds were hard.

It had been foolish of him to sneak out of Shaktoolik without making fresh food and feeding the dogs. But he also knew that he could be forced to scratch from the competition if the race officials at Shaktoolik deemed either he or his team was unfit to finish. If Linda Blankenship had had anything to say about it, North knew without a doubt that he would be heading to Nome by air, but there was no point in second-guessing his decision now. He'd finish the damn race.

He'd left the tiny village of Shaktoolik a few miles behind, thankful that the well-defined race route followed the shoreline for a few miles before heading out onto the frozen expanse of the Norton Sound. And thankful, too, that nobody appeared to be in immediate pursuit.

The coastline was a vista of barren and windswept tundra, the sky overhead a clear and brilliant azure blue. North searched for a good place to stop and feed the dogs before heading out on the ice and pulled up near a slight rock outcropping. There was little wind, but he knew it often died off during the morning hours, only to return with a vengeance in the late afternoon and night. With any luck he'd reach Koyuk by 6 pm.

The team slowed with a minimum of fuss, which told their master that they were either hungry or leery of the huge white expanse of ice looming off the coast. He threw the snow hook, stopping the sled and dogs. As many mushers did, North always carried a ski pole in his sled bag for those times the team needed a helping hand pushing through heavy snow. He slid off his chair and crawled the few feet to the bag to retrieve it, intending to use it as a crutch. After a few aborted tries he got the hang of wobbling around the sled without putting his full weight on his damaged ankle. Still, every movement was a tortuous ordeal.

He dug out the food bowls and stacked them up beside the cooler. The strangely subdued dogs sat on their haunches, peering at him with their inquisitive eyes and tilting their masked faces inquiringly from side to side, almost comical in their confusion. Never before had North fed them without at least releasing their tugs first, but today their routine had changed, and they were wary. One by one, North scooped out ten meager portions of food, ensuring there was enough at the bottom of the cooler to give them another small meal if he needed to. He hobbled back and forth between the cooler and the dogs, ski pole grasped in his left hand, bowl of dog food in his right. Back and forth, back and forth, ten times. It was a slow and labourious task that should have been completed within minutes, but instead took almost half an hour and left him weak and exhausted. He dug into his parka for the vial of NSAIDs and popped two more.

The dogs wolfed their food down within seconds, and when North delivered the last bowl he was able to immediately begin collecting the empty ones, wiping them out with handfuls of clean snow before nesting them together. He took a few moments to ensure each dog's booties were still in good condition, having been warned that the sharp sea ice was extremely hard on both booties and paws. He crawled from dog to dog, dragging the ski pole in one hand and holding his left ankle off the ground as best he could. Half expecting a rescue committee to show up, he glanced back down the trail often. How he would react if a race official loomed into sight on a snowmobile, or if Mats Pederson and his team of huskies came to retrieve him, he didn't know. He considered digging out his rifle, but decided that may be a bit drastic – he might be too tempted to use it.

North tossed the bowls back in his sled bag and rummaged around for his own package of human snacks. He was low on supplies, and would have to be satisfied with two chocolate bars; he stuffed them in his pocket to eat on the trail. The relatively short mile stretch of trail before him was often called one of the most treacherous segments of the race, and he knew he wasn't mentally prepared. To make it worse, the empty vastness of the Norton Sound was daunting not only to humans, but to many of the teams. Some dogs were put off by the vast white expanse of ice, and were hesitant to cross it. There wasn't as much as a bush in sight, only white, windswept ice and snow. The north wind would be his worst enemy today, and he prayed that the current calm skies stuck around for at least a few hours. He pulled the snow hook, called up his team, and set off on the forty-mile crossing across the Norton Sound to Koyuk.

North trusted that Kia and Weasel would keep their senses; where they led, the rest of his team would always willingly follow. From Koyuk it was another fifty miles to Elim, then another hundred to White Mountain, where every musher was required to take a mandatory 8-hour stop. Until then he would rest for only an hour or two when his dogs did, and catch up on his sleep in White Mountain. He knew he wouldn't win the race, but he was still determined to give it his best shot, crippled foot be damned. His tortured body was already looking forward to the long rest in White Mountain.

Mats Pederson caught up to North fifteen minutes into the run across the sound. The Norwegian was grievously upset with North, whether for leaving him behind, sleeping like a baby at Shaktoolik, or risking his own life to finish the race in his weakened condition. North didn't know for sure, because he wouldn't slow down long enough to have a long conversation with his rookie competitor, who refused to pass him and stayed on his tail for the duration of the run to Koyuk.

North's Canadian Eskimo Dogs were flatland dogs. They showed their true abilities and speed on the relatively flat tundra or frozen rivers and lakes around Inuvik, and North had been counting on gaining some time during this five-hour long Norton Sound crossing. He had even hoped, although he wouldn't admit it even to himself, to overtake a team or two and improve his race standings. He urged Kia and Weasel to push the team to their limits, and with each passing mile the distance between North and Mats widened.

Despite the winds starting out reasonably calm, the mushers' luck ran out halfway into the crossing. North pulled the team to a halt and threw them a snack, dug out the spare booties from his sled bag and crawled from dog to dog, replacing forty pair of little green booties, many of which had already been shredded by the razor-sharp sea ice. He inspected each foot thoroughly, and rubbed ointment onto chaffed paws. Mats caught up to him then, just as he was fastening the last bootie on Chica, his gentle brown and black female wheel dog. His team remained eager and ready to run, undaunted by the cold, or the wind, or the vastness and desolation of the land.

Mats' indignation had mellowed, and the two rookies agreed to stick together until they reached Koyuk. For the duration of the crossing they were brutalized by the onslaught of a howling gale. The legendary wind of Norton Sound was known to often reach hurricane velocity, and today blew out of the north, directly at their balaclava clad faces. The temperature plummeted with the arrival of the demonic wind, and North was thankful that his dogs were cloaked in their insulated green jackets.

It gave them a modicum of protection from the evil winds that ceaselessly whipped away precious body heat.

Although they were miles from land, the mountains and ridges of the Seward Peninsula were always visible, ringing the sound with white-capped peaks and slopes, picturesque against the intense azure sky. The buildings at Koyuk became visible from ten miles out, the sound's level ice surface allowing an unobstructed view of their destination. Having a visual bead on the end of the tortuous journey across the sound helped to keep North's mind focused on his destination, and not on his agony. To *not* focus on his pain became more and more difficult with each passing hour though, as every patch of rough ice and every flying bump over a concrete-hard snow drift jarred his entire body. Three hours after taking his last dose of NSAIDs, North reached into his pocket and dry swallowed two more, along with a Tylenol 3 for good measure. He tried not to think of the potential damage he was causing his internal organs. He had enough to worry about at the moment.

They reached Koyuk late in the afternoon, and North breathed a sigh of relief when the checker didn't react when he gave him his name. He'd been worried that Syd and Linda may have pronounced him unfit to complete the race and reported him to the Iditarod committee, even though in all likelihood he was.

The dogs needed warm food and a long rest of at least four hours, not necessarily in that order. North began his tasks, sometimes hopping around with his ski pole in one hand, sometimes crawling around on the snow on all fours. When Mats collected straw to bed down his dogs, he spread out straw for North's dogs too. When he went to get his drop bag, he lugged back North's too. When North protested, Mats refused to listen, claiming, "That's what friends do."

As quickly as his crippled, hurting body could manage, North scooped snow into his pot, poured HEET into the cooker, lit it and slid the pot in. He sorted through his dishevelled sled bag and explored his new drop bag. Besides being stocked with dog food and a few other items, such as clean socks, it was always thrilling to discover whatever food and treats he or Andi had packed inside. Today it was Andi's chewy, hearty Ranger cookies loaded with raisins, chocolate and nuts, and a large plastic container filled with bags of cooked beef and pasta casserole and chicken stew. He kept out enough food to warm for his supper, along with the cookies for dessert, and transferred the rest of the supplies into his sled basket. He selected a bag of beef and pasta casserole for dinner then, feeling rather guilty, dug out another and invited Mats to share a meal with him.

It was the least he could do for a total stranger who appeared to have a heart of gold.

Against Mat's protests, North convinced his fellow musher to carry on without him when he was ready to hit the trail again. North knew he wasn't a contender to finish in the top twenty, and he didn't intend to continue pushing himself or his team, but he saw no need for Mats to give up a chance at a cash prize.

With every hour that passed, the torturous pain in North's foot intensified and crept higher up his leg. He could barely move his left arm, and began to doubt whether he'd be able to make it to the finish line, but the idea of scratching from the race was more than disheartening – it was unthinkable. His competitive nature would drive him on until he crossed the finish line in Nome, or died trying to. It was, North realized glumly, looking more and more likely that he would have a shot at the dubious honour of earning the Red Lantern Award.

The Red Lantern Award, given to the last place finisher, began as a joke decades ago but was now perceived as a symbol of perseverance. The award had a long and interesting history dating back to the days of Alaska's gold rush, when sled dog teams hauled freight and mail over the Iditarod trail. Because the mushers often battled darkness and inclement weather, word would be relayed whenever a dog team was on the trail, and the roadhouses along the route would each light a kerosene lamp and hang it outside to help the musher find his way. It also signaled to others that a dog team was on the trail and people should look out for it. The lamp would not be extinguished until the musher and his team safely reached their destination.

Now each year a small gas lantern is lit on the first Sunday in March and hung on the 5000-pound Burled Arch. Called the Widow's Lamp, it remains lit until the last musher is off the Iditarod trail. The extinguishing of the lamp by the final musher signals the official end of the race, and he or she is presented with the Red Lantern Award.

North was only 170 miles from Nome, but he was still alive and he wasn't about to quit. He didn't care anymore if he finished first or last, as long as he slid under the Burled Arch.

The Red Lantern Award became more and more of a possibility with each passing hour, each passing mile, and each musher that called for trail.

THIRTY

Andi flew into Nome on Wednesday evening on a direct Alaskan Air flight from Anchorage. It had been hard to leave the security of The Green Aurora Guest House, where she'd become increasingly comfortable and had made a dear friend. Her early morning talk with Gert had assuaged her guilt about her near 'slip up' as the older woman called it, and calmed her fears for North's safety. Gert assured her that the Iditarod Trail Committee would have contacted her if North had been injured or was in trouble. Andi had even assisted with the morning baking, mixing up another batch of blueberry muffins while Gert made a mouth-watering coffee cake.

Leaving Qannik and the other three dogs behind had been hard, but Bill assured her that they would receive the best of care and get two walks a day, of which Andi was certain. Gert said she'd bring Qannik into the house for an hour or two every day and that Andi could call to check up on her whenever she wanted to. Bill even drove Andi to the Anchorage airport, so she wouldn't have to pay for expensive airport parking.

She took a cab from the Nome airport to the Nugget Inn, where she'd booked a room months in advance, shortly after North had registered for the race. It was race day eleven, and according to the headlines on the local television station the first musher, a man by the name of Marvin Boutillier from a small village near Anchorage, was leading the race. He was expected to cross the finish line within a matter of hours. The news neither saddened nor cheered her; she just wanted to lay eyes on her husband, and see for herself that he was alright.

She ordered room service for a late dinner, a clubhouse and fries that she barely touched, then put on her parka and boots and headed to Front Street. She wanted to see the great Burled Arch and familiarize herself with the area. She roamed up and down Front Street where bright flags waved from every building and storefront windows were plastered with congratulatory notes and advertising. On his or her way to the Burled Arch, each musher passes down Front Street and down the fenced-off, fifty-yard end stretch, or chute. Banners from advertisers, Iditarod supporters and sponsors lined the chute leading up to the famous arch.

Andi stood next to the great arch for several minutes, shivering slightly in the cold wind while she committed every detail of the huge monument to memory. She visualized North passing under it within the next day or two, his dark eyes flashing with pride and his familiar, wide grin exposing one overly long eyetooth. He would wave to the crowds, she knew, happy to entertain them for a few minutes. He would spot her in an instant, and give her that sultry wink that made her stomach flip. Her heart swelled with pride.

Andi smiled and turned away from the Burled Arch to retrace her steps back to the Nugget Inn. She and her lover would be reunited very, very soon, and she couldn't wait to lay her eyes on him, to taste the salty tang of his skin, and feel his strength beneath her hands.

She had a hot shower and crawled into her lonely bed at midnight. At 2 am she was still wide awake, fearful of sleep ... afraid to invite the nightmares that haunted her every night since North had left. Her exhausted body craved release, but she was terrified to close her eyes.

She flicked on the bedside light and rummaged in her purse until she found the small vial Gert had slipped into her hand when they stood in the front foyer of The Green Aurora Guesthouse saying good-bye. The plastic vial was an old Tylenol bottle, but what was inside was definitely not an over-the-counter drug. "Just take two before you go to bed," Gert said with her sweet smile. "These little blue pills will make sure you get a good night's sleep, dear."

Andi was never comfortable taking any kind of drugs, and rarely took even an aspirin. She slid two of the tiny round pills into her hand and contemplated them for several seconds before she popped them into her mouth, washing them down with a mouthful of water straight from the bathroom tap. She was ready to try anything that would free her from another night of terror.

THIRTY-ONE

The checkpoints of the Seward Peninsula blended seamlessly together – Elim, White Mountain and Safety became almost indistinguishable from one another within the recesses of North's struggling, sleep deprived mind. Several teams passed him during the night, running by when he stopped to rest or shouting out *'TRAIL!'* when they caught up to him, the mushers' way of asking a slower team to move aside and make way for them to pass if the trail was too narrow for two teams abreast. The mushers drove their dogs hard for the last hundred miles of the race, the lure of the Burled Arch drawing them to Nome much like the Siren's song of Greek mythology drew unwary sailors to their watery graves.

North slid into Elim, a tiny village of 300 souls on the shores of the Norton Sound, in the early morning hours, stopping there only long enough to feed his dogs and rest for a couple of hours in the well sheltered Native American community. He dished out the last of the cooked food, then let the dogs sleep for two hours while he cooked another batch for them. Every task, every movement, and each wobbly step he made took an inordinate amount of time and effort on his part. When the new batch of food was in the cooler North, crawling on all fours, dragged his sleeping bag onto the straw next to one of his dogs, crawled inside, pulled it over his head and dozed for an hour. He was too tired, too miserable, and in too much pain to eat anything or even seek a cup of coffee, despite his gnawing hunger. He knew his team needed a longer rest, but they would have to wait. The next stop on the trail was White Mountain, where he, along with every musher in the race, would make a mandatory 8-hour stop. There would be time enough to eat and sleep then.

He left Elim before dawn, his left foot causing substantially more agony than it had the day before. No longer restricted to the vicinity of his swollen ankle, searing fingers of pain shot up his left leg. He hadn't removed his boot since the painful experience of shoving his swollen foot into it when he snuck out of Shaktoolik, and he was deathly afraid to look at it again. Instead, he continued to take frequent doses of the NSAIDs. They seemed to help little, if at all, so he supplemented them with Tylenol 3 and the occasional slug of brandy, Linda's stern warning taking most of the pleasure out of each drop.

The trail to White Mountain crossed the Kwiktalik Mountains in a series of long grades, and proved to be the hardest and most challenging climb on the last half of the race. His willing Canadian Eskimo Dogs ran slowly but steadily until they eventually reached the 1000-foot summit called Little McKinley.

North's battle to stay upright and awake became a constant challenge as all he really wanted to do was curl up somewhere ... anywhere ... and close his gritty, tired eyes. He dozed off and on, jerking awake whenever he began to slip off his seat. Once, when the sled tilted at a steep angle traversing an incline, he couldn't catch himself and landed on the sled runners, still clinging to the handle bar with his right hand, his left arm laying uselessly at his side. He rolled onto the sled brake and applied as much pressure as he could with one hand, screaming for his team to stop. When the sled finally quit moving, he lay where he had fallen for another minute before he could muster the strength to pull himself upright again. After that close call he resorted to lashing himself into the chair with a length of spare line. He heard his father's gruff voice as clearly as though he was standing next to him: *'Whatever you do, son, don't lose your team. Your dogs are your lifeline, and you will die without them'.*

North wavered in and out of delirium throughout that long, cold morning, at times convinced that he lay within a circle of warm, soft arms, at others certain he was tumbling down an endless, icy abyss, falling and spinning until his overburdened lungs couldn't cope with the pressure and he started awake again, gasping for air.

During his periods of lucidity, his weary mind refused to rest. Memories looped through his head, the challenges and events of the past eleven days and nights rerunning in a continuous, Kodachrome loop.

Running, checkpoints, sign in, sign out.
Cold, wind, darkness.
Fatigue, hunger, aching muscles, throbbing foot.
Feed the dogs, rest the dogs, check lines, check paws and replace little green booties.

When North finally reached White Mountain on Thursday he pulled the exhausted team into the dog lot located below the sheltering banks of the Fish River. It was teeming with activity. A dozen other mushers were in various stages of their last mandatory 8-hour layover, some having just arrived, others preparing to depart. The mushers used the long break to cook, sleep or socialize. The tension and excitement in the air was tangible; they were only seventy-seven miles from Nome and the Burled Arch.

North had fantasized for days about the long rest at White Mountain, a tiny village of 200 that began as an Eskimo fish camp and later boomed for a few years during the Klondike gold rush. While he had steadfastly clung to the sled's wooden handle bar mile after torturous mile, slipping between reality and delusion, his wandering mind had conjured up a soft bed, a home cooked meal and a pair of gleaming emerald eyes waiting to greet him in White Mountain. He was sorely disappointed.

North's dampened spirits plummeted even further when the White Mountain checker informed him that he was currently in twenty-seventh position. It wasn't the outcome he'd dreamed of, but it was his reality. It was even more disheartening to hear that the winner of the 25th Silver Anniversary Iditarod Sled Dog Race, a seasoned repeat-winner from Alaska, had already crossed the finish line in Nome. He blew out a long, gusty breath, frustrated with his less than satisfactory personal performance.

North hobbled back and forth across the dog lot supported by his ski pole, dragging back his drop bag and armloads of straw to bed his team on. The dogs were exhausted, their endurance and strength having been pushed to the limit during the last climb. As he slowly and methodically spread the straw, he took the time to complete the other necessary tasks to save himself additional footsteps: he unhooked the dogs from the gangline and fastened them to the long tether line he'd attached to a stake driven into the snow, he massaged shoulders, hips and legs, he examined and massaged paws and replaced little green booties, and he spent a moment talking to and stroking each animal, ruffling and scratching their favourite spots. He owed his life to his team, and he owed it to them to keep them healthy and comfortable, regardless of his own miserable condition.

He fed the dogs the last of the warm food from the cooler, every clumsy step unleashing another wave of agony. His aching, exhausted body craved sleep, but before he could rest he needed to cook fresh dog food. He resolutely dug into his sled bag for the cooker and HEET and put snow to melt, then dug out the new supply of dog food from his drop bag, grateful beyond words that this was the last batch of food he should have to make before he reached Nome.

His mind wandered while he waited for the snow to melt, and his stomach rumbled in complaint – it wanted hot food too, preferably one of Andi's excellent home-cooked meals, a thick slice of her luscious lemon loaf and a massive mug of coffee, liberally laced with Southern

Comfort. Thoughts of his new bride brought instant pangs of remorse, and a new and unfamiliar ache in his heart called regret. What had he been thinking? Why was he here, in this great beyond alone with his pain and his fears? He should be at home, warm and content by his wife's side, curled up beside her on his old, immense polar bear rug before a blazing fire, laying on that expanse of soft, white, sensual fur on which they had spent so many pleasurable hours exploring each other's eager, naked bodies. He imagined his hungry hands running over her smooth skin. He felt his fingertips caressing the curve of her full, soft breasts, and tracing the long, lean sweep of her hips before slipping lower. North shook his head in frustration and sucked in a deep, cold breath, chasing his longing and all thoughts of his beautiful wife aside.

A small group of mushers had gathered at the edge of the dog lot, clustered around a low campfire. He decided he needed a better diversion than daydreams verging on eroticism while he waited for the hot water. He'd been hoping to see Mats again, but there was no sign of his rookie friend from Norway, and North didn't have the capability to search for him through the maze of bedded dogs, sleds and gear spread throughout the busy dog lot.

"So," one of the mushers said by way of greeting when North, supported by the ski pole, hobbled within the fire's welcoming circle of warmth. "You're a rookie, ain't ya? The one with them Eskimo Dogs?"

"Yes, I'm afraid I am." North replied with a wry smile. "I am most certainly that rookie."

"How are ya making out? Run into any problems?" His eyes, along with everyone else's, dropped down to North's leg, wrapped in silver duct tape, threads of hot pink wool peeking through the gaps. He shifted slightly, taking the pressure off his lame leg. He knew the mushers would have heard about Becky Singleton's ordeal by now, and wondered if they also knew about his part in her rescue, or about his stupid, crippling mistake in the Blueberry Mountains.

"No, no big problems, really," he said, lips pursed, shaking his head slowly. "Had a bit of an, uh, unexpected delay. But I tell you, this race has been a hell of a lot more gruelling than I ever thought it would be. It's been a real eye-opener, and I grew up in the Arctic."

His fellow competitors chuckled softly, and a few nodded their grizzled, unkempt heads, evidently satisfied with North's downplayed response. Nobody liked a braggart, especially these tough, hardened northerners. Each and every one of them faced imminent danger and his or her own life-threatening challenges every minute on the trail.

"You'll get used to it," a bearded, middle-aged man clad in a filthy dark blue parka said slowly. "Once the Iditarod gets in your blood, she's a demanding mistress. You'll be back, and you'll learn from your mistakes." He cracked a broad smile, exposing a gum line dotted with wide gaps and the odd yellow tooth. "We all come back for another shot at it. This is the fifteenth time I've ran the trail. Buddy over there," he said, pointing to a rugged, elderly man standing on the other side of the fire, "Buddy hasn't missed a race in the last twenty years. You'll be back," he laughed dryly before he turned away and shuffled back to his team.

North highly doubted it, but what did he know? He was just a rookie.

After a short visit with the group of seasoned mushers, North warmed a couple of small meat pies from his drop bag and made a mug of instant coffee, then dumped the rest of the steaming water into the cooler to thaw the dogs' food. There was food for the mushers available at one of the community buildings, as well as a warm spot to spread a sleeping bag, but the structure was two blocks away and would also entail a hike up the riverbank. Although it was tempting, North knew it would be an insurmountable ordeal for him to make his way there, and resigned himself to sleeping in his sled bag again.

Sometime during the afternoon, while North was dreaming about liquid emerald green eyes, naked skin, white polar bear rugs and Hershey's chocolate sauce, five or six other mushers, including a female driver, had pulled in for their 8-hour stop. There were four female drivers in the race this year, and all but one were veterans. After barely surviving the ordeals of the past few days, North felt a huge respect for the tough, determined women.

He slept fitfully at the busy checkpoint, and rose at 5 pm, two hours before his planned departure. He swallowed more NSAIDs and a Tylenol 3, ate another meat pie and drank three mugs of extra-strong instant black coffee, hoping the caffeine jolt would get his brain and blood moving again. There was still no sign of Mats Pederson, and North hoped Rookie #22 was well on his way to Nome. At 6:00 he began his slow, laborious preparations for departure. Every simple task now cost him an almost insurmountable amount of energy, and he tried to plan and economize each step he made.

Taking his cue from the more seasoned mushers, North decided to run the relatively short last dash to Nome with only six dogs in harness; there'd be fewer mouths to feed and fewer paws and booties to check. To lighten their load, he emptied his sled bag of everything but the bare minimum of essentials, including his rifle, enough food to last him to Nome, and the mandatory survival equipment. He separated four more of his beloved canine friends and left them with a volunteer at the dog lot. Weasel, who was favouring his right shoulder, had to stay behind, as well as Aurora, Chance and Duska, all of them howling and complaining bitterly when they were separated from their teammates.

While he worked, North tried to focus on the final stretch of the race laying before him, taking his mind off his pain and misery. When he left White Mountain, he would try to run the final seventy-seven miles to Nome within twelve hours. But, and this was a big but, there were still a few obstacles and *'ifs'* in his way. Namely, *if* the dogs could do it, *if* he, himself, could do it, and *if* the unpredictable arctic winds cooperated. The dogs could run for about five hours without resting, maybe a little longer with short breaks if conditions were good. At between eight to ten miles per hour, it should be possible to reach Safety, the second-to-last checkpoint fifty-five miles away, before 1 am. From there it was a mere twenty-two miles to Nome.

North had long ago resigned himself to the fact that he wasn't going to win the Iditarod, but he vowed that he wouldn't let the damn race get the best of him either.

THIRTY-TWO

Kia and Toffee were at the front of the gangline when North slid out of White Mountain an hour before sunset, exactly eight hours after he'd arrived. The six-dog team was well rested and edgy, but their master was almost as weary as when he'd arrived, and in considerably more pain. He was much more alert and cognizant, though, and realized that his delirium and stupor of the previous day may have had something to do with the rapidly diminishing supply of codeine-laced Tylenol 3 in his pocket.

North knew the condition of his ankle had deteriorated, and was sure it had doubled in size since he'd left Shaktoolik a day and a half before. The pressure inside his boot made him fear the thin skin holding the entire swollen mess of tissue, muscle, bone and blood together would rupture at any moment. What had hours ago been fingers of pain had grown into intense, hot waves that rose to his knee. He was beginning to suspect that the ankle was more than merely sprained, and that Linda Blankenship had been right; he was more than likely dealing with a fractured bone or two.

The trail leaving White Mountain followed the Fish River about three miles before cutting inland toward the southwest. In an attempt to draw his mind away from his pain and lagging spirits, North ran through his mental checklist: dogs were fed, cooked food was in the cooler, twenty-four paws were wrapped in new little green booties, and the harnesses and lines were secure. His spare headlamp batteries were in his pocket, tucked up with his drugs and the paltry remains of his medicinal brandy. He was all set.

The topography and geological makeup of the Seward Peninsula, which projects 200 miles into the Bering Sea and was purchased from Russia in 1867, is varied and dotted with towering mountain ranges, vast lakes, and wandering rivers. Reindeer, caribou and moose enjoy a thriving population, roaming the vast land unconstrained. North kept a vigilant eye on the trail ahead, terrified about the potential for another close encounter with Alaska's wildlife.

Although it could be a pleasant five- to six-hour run to Safety, the old-timers North had visited with around the campfire had warned him that the trail could become virtually impassable in bad weather, and had been known to be the downfall of many experienced racers, let alone first-time rookies with a bum leg. The wind and the weather were a huge consideration, and mushers were cautioned to always check the forecast before setting out for Safety.

He hadn't gone very many miles when it became evident to North that something was bothering his team. He wondered if it was the change of lead dogs, Toffee being a relatively new and very strongminded addition to his kennel, or perhaps the intuitive animals had picked up on the tenseness and pain emanating from North's aura; his wandering mind visualized himself enveloped in dark and muddy grey shadows of his own making. Whatever the problem was, it had disrupted the team's cohesiveness. They became short tempered with each other, growling and snapping at their teammates and sometimes reluctant to follow Kia and Toffee's lead, their unity as a team destroyed.

North struggled to keep his dogs on the trail as they ran through the gathering night, cutting over low, rolling tundra and several tree-rimmed creeks before reaching the Klokerblok River Valley. Lady Luck seemed to be on his side for a change, though, and as they dropped into the river valley the freshening wind subsided, soon becoming almost nonexistent. The trail snaked through the valley for a few miles before crossing the river and swinging away from it. A few miles later they dropped into the Topkok River Valley and the sudden end of the tree line. The shining, bluish-white expanse of crusty, wind-polished snow seemed to reflect the starlight from above, with nary a sapling nor a bush to darken the smooth, white landscape.

North stopped briefly to snack the dogs and check their booties. He reached for his vial of Tylenol 3, then shoved it back into his pocket, recalling what the drugs had done to him earlier in the day. He settled for a sip of brandy and a stale, crushed granola bar.

His luck ran out when they climbed out of the river valley and began a long, sloping ascent over a series of barren ridges topping out at 400 feet. The notorious wind he'd been warned about hit him with a force he'd never experienced before, hammering his body and lashing at his parka, threatening to tear it to shreds. It ripped at the dogs and their green jackets too, plastering the insulated fabric to the right side of their bodies and trying its evil best to rob them of their heat. The tremendous force of the wind took his breath away and the dogs struggled to stay on the trail as the overpowering gale beat them relentlessly. North realized he had reached the 'blow holes', an unusual series of natural wind tunnels that had been known to alter between hurricane-force winds to calm within a matter of feet. Passing through the 'blow holes' could be life threatening, especially for a rookie musher.

North's team lost the trail twice during their harrowing crossing through the blow holes, pushed off course by the violent, wicked wind. He spent several panicky minutes searching for trail, thankful that there wasn't as much blowing snow to obliterate the track as there might have been. He recalled Becky Singleton's almost unbelievable story of a musher who, just five years prior, had become stalled in the middle of one of the violent blow holes while attempting a night crossing, unable to either move forward or retrace his path. The hapless man was forced to wait out the blow, zipped into his sled bag. Overnight the relentless wind teased the zipper open and filled it with snow, enveloping the man.

He was rescued by another musher the next morning, already hypothermic and close to death.

Now that he'd had firsthand experience with the notorious blow holes, North berated himself for his lack of judgement. He realized that he had made two potentially fatal mistakes: he'd attempted the dangerous crossing at night, and he hadn't waited at the top of the valley for a more experienced Iditarod musher to follow through. And he wasn't through the blow holes yet; his carelessness could still cost him his and his dogs' their lives.

Between each of the ridges was a narrow valley with a stream running through it, lined with scrubby vegetation and somewhat protected from the debilitating wind. After fighting their way up several of the punishing ridges, North decided to take a short rest in one of the small valleys, praying that the next ridge would be the last one, the 500-foot Topkok Mountain. He threw the dogs a snack and they immediate curled up for a sleep. North heard the wind howling over his head, whistling above the edges of the ridges on either side. Down in the valley, though, it was fairly comfortable and he was able to catch his breath again. He reached into his pocket and downed two more NSAIDs and a Tylenol 3. He was lost without his Timex, which had been shattered during his dive over the cliff in the Blueberry Mountains. Judging from the intensity of his pain, though, he thought he was well justified to take another dose of medication.

North had let the dogs rest for about half an hour and was just about to call them up again when he saw the headlamp of an approaching musher. He waited, seated on his chair on the back of the sled, his own headlamp and the sharp barks of his team notifying the other musher of his presence.

The musher slowed his dogs and called for trail. North waved him by, but instead of passing, he pulled to a full stop just behind North's sled.

"Hey, Rookie," a familiar voice croaked.

North peered at the musher, squinting to see past the beam of the other man's headlamp. He couldn't quite see his face, or place the voice. "Yup, North Ruben. Rookie #9. And who are you?"

"Bruce Litman. We chatted a ways back. That damn coffee stand business."

"I remember. How are you doing, Bruce?"

"Better'n you, from the sounds of it."

"Yeah," North sighed heavily. "I've had a pretty rough go of it."

"See you made it through those blow holes alright."

"It was nip and tuck," North said. "Pretty scary shit up there. We got blown off the trail a couple times."

"Tell you what, Rookie. Why don't you follow me up Topkok and to the end of the beach? Don't know if you know it or not, but there's more of what you just went through up ahead. There's another good blow hole up the trail after Topkok, and when the wind's blowing this bad you can guarantee there'll be zero visibility along the driftwood line. You'd best stick close for a few miles if you don't want to end up in the Bering Sea."

North just about cried for joy. "I'll take you up on that, Bruce. That's the best offer I've had in a long time."

"Let's get a moving, then."

The two mushers called their dogs up and pulled out of the protection of the valley floor. The wind on the Topkok ridge was howling as hard as ever, making the crossing a challenge, but measurably easier for North with an experienced guide to lead the way. When they reached the mountain's 500-foot summit, North found himself looking out over the vast expanse of the Bering Sea. He peered down through the darkness for signs of the whiteout Bruce was so sure would envelop the beach, but the moonless night revealed no secrets.

Immediately after they reached the summit they began a steep, one-mile descent to the beach. As soon as they reached it, the visibility dropped to zero. Bruce had been right, and North was happier than ever that the taciturn musher had stopped to offer his assistance. They ran along the beach for almost an hour, the back of Bruce's sled sometimes disappearing right before North's eyes, even though he strove to keep his team as close as possible to their guide.

Eventually either the wind died down, or they drove out of it. They left the beach and ran along a narrow spit between the ocean and a lagoon, then across a wide river outlet that drained to the Bering Sea.

They ran on, Kia and Toffee following the barely visible team ahead of them. Night's darkness, pressing down in a seamless black blanket, was relieved only by the insignificant circles of yellowish light emanating from the mushers' headlamps. Overhead, yellow, red, and green bands of colour raced across the dark, moonless sky – the Aurora Borealis was putting on a breathtaking display for anyone who cared to enjoy the dazzling show.

Plans were made to be broken. That had always been North's motto, and he was somewhat proud of it, claiming that he was 'always up for a challenge'. Now his nonchalant attitude was coming back to bite him in the ass.

An hour before reaching the Safety checkpoint his wheel dog's harness broke. They had, only minutes before, reached a vehicle road that snaked from the Bonanza Ferry Bridge to Safety. North stomped on the sled brake with his right foot and shouted to get Bruce's attention.

Bruce threw his snow hook and walked back to North's sled. "What's the problem, Rookie?"

"Looks like my wheel dog's harness broke. I'll have to stop and repair it."

"I'll stay and give you a hand."

"No, Bruce," North shook his head adamantly, still seated on the sled chair. "I appreciate the offer but I can manage this alone. I think my dogs could use a rest anyway. You carry on without me and get to Nome."

Bruce pursed his lips and grumbled under his breath.

"I tell you what," North grinned. He dug into his parka pocket and pulled out the depleted bottle of brandy. "I think we could both use a shot of this right about now."

Bruce's short laugh sounded more like a dog's deep growl. North twisted the lid off the bottle and handed it to his guide. Bruce took a healthy slug, wiped off the top of the bottle with his grubby mitt and handed it back to North.

"You're okay, Rookie." He smiled for the first time since North met him. "The trail follows the road from here to Safety. You can't get lost. I'll help you get your team off the trail before I go." He walked to the front of North's gangline and grabbed Toffee's harness, calling to her softly. North climbed stiffly down from his seat and followed his sled with the new, excruciatingly slow hopping-hobbling gait he'd acquired. Bruce positioned the dogs and sled a few feet off the trail and imbedded the snow hook as best he could. There was nothing to tie the snub line to.

"Thanks, Bruce. Appreciate your help."

Bruce merely nodded and shuffled back to his sled. "See ya in Nome, Rookie," Bruce called back just before he called his team up again.

North's gloveless hands, exposed to minus 30-degree air while he struggled to repair Chica's harness, quickly became clumsy and uncooperative. Normally only an annoying task, the simple repair would prove to be a time-consuming challenge when conducted under the light of a headlamp by a cold, crippled musher.

Although he had planned to stop and rest the dogs in Safety, North decided to give them a long break right where they were. Since the wind had died down, they'd be no better off there than here; he could run right through Safety and continue on the last two-hour stretch to Nome. He abandoned the harness repair and dragged out the six remaining dog bowls, heartened by the fact he would only have to make six trips to feed the dogs instead of ten. He loosened their tugs and checked their paws when he brought each dog its food, and gave them each a quick massage.

He began to shiver uncontrollably, and decided he needed a mug of hot, sweet tea to warm him up. When the dogs had curled up and quietened, he scraped some snow into his pot and set it over the cooker then rummaged in his meager grub bag. He came up with a few tea bags but no sugar, two Oh Henry! bars and a forgotten bag of trail mix. He dropped his sleeping bag on the snow in the shelter of his sled and munched on his snack while he started the repair on Chica's harness. When his water was hot he drank two scalding mugs of strong, brandy-laced tea, warming his bare, freezing hands on the metal mug while he finished his task.

Despite the cold air and lingering traces of wind, he started to feel hot and wondered briefly if he were running a fever. He felt strangely detached from his surroundings, and surprisingly peaceful ... not at all like himself. And certainly not how he should be feeling after the most taxing, heartbreaking twelve days of his life. He'd lost *The Last Great Race*, but he felt almost *euphoric.*

Alone in the silent night, under a dark expanse of sky filled with a billion shining stars, North Ruben chuckled, then laughed out loud, an incongruous, misplaced sound considering his circumstances. "Keep that Red Lantern burning!" he shouted to the wind.

Kia raised her big grey head and gazed at her master for a moment with sympathetic eyes. It was after 1 am when rookie #9, unaware that he was more than a little delirious, crawled into his sled bag and the relative comfort of his cold sleeping bag.

North pulled into Safety, the last checkpoint before Nome, at 5:30 am on Friday, March 14, according to the weary checker. It was still dark at the early predawn hour, but the checkpoint was alive with activity.

Floodlights lit the area, and race officials as well as a television and radio crew milled around the checkpoint, sipping steaming beverages from large insulated mugs. Even though the winner of the 25th running of the Iditarod had crossed the finish line in Nome more than a day ago, race excitement was still tangible. Nome was only twenty-two miles away, and the Iditarod wouldn't officially end until the last contender crossed the finish line and claimed The Red Lantern. Then, and only then would the 1997 25th Silver Anniversary running of the Iditarod be over.

In Safety, all number bibs were returned to the mushers, to be worn for the last leg of the race. The winner was also required to wear his bib during the lead dog ceremony, but North knew he needn't worry about that event. When he thought about it, though, he wondered how he could have possibly expected a better outcome. His mushing experience, as extensive as it was, was really nothing compared to his competitors' whom, he'd come to realize, lived and breathed for the trail and the race. For them, mushing and dog sled racing was a determined lifestyle, not a hobby. He'd been a fool to think he could actually race, and win, against such fierce competition.

North felt feverish and weak when he arrived, and didn't even rise from his seat when he pulled up to the checker's station. Instead, he pointed to his duct-tape-wrapped leg and called for the race official to come to him, certain that if he got up, he'd fall flat on his face and never get up again. When the man passed him bib #9, North stoically tugged it over his head and tied it securely, smoothing the cold, white fabric over his bulky parka. He smiled and chatted with the checker briefly, declined an interview with an eager, pinched-faced reporter, and attempted to exude a calm and undeterred demeanour. He was determined to hide the full extent of his pain and misery from television cameras and curious eyes.

As he approached Nome a little more than two hours later, North heard a siren blare when he left the sea ice and hurtled up the long boat ramp. He wondered if the audible 'musher approaching the finish line' siren was for him, or another racer ahead of him. He didn't really care anymore; he just wanted the damn race to be over. He just wanted to *sleep* ... he wanted to sleep for a week and be free of the pain in his leg and his arm and the fogginess in his head.

Front Street was bare, any accumulation of snow long since swept away by the steady, prevailing wind and multitudes of traffic. North knew he should be running beside the sled and regretted the fact that he was adding his substantial weight to the team's burden. He called the leads to the side of the street, taking advantage of the occasional pocket of hardened snow and ice to move the sled a little easier.

They plummeted down the chute, the familiar orange crowd-control fencing lining both sides of the street to keep eager, noisy spectators at bay. North peered almost drunkenly down the final stretch of the course, squinting into the glare from the street lights, and spotted the famous Burled Arch beneath which the elusive finish line lay. Kia and Toffee picked up on the excitement in the air and ran like crazed fiends, barking and lunging toward whatever fate lay before them. Suka, Nanuk, Kodiak and Chica joined in, howling in anticipation.

Cameras flashed and excited bystanders cheered him along the final few feet of the race. North searched a multitude of blurry faces as they flashed by, his burning, unfocused eyes longing for a glimpse of his gorgeous wife. There were too many bright red parkas milling in the sidelines, though – too many false alarms. His weary, befuddled brain couldn't distinguish one face from another.

And then he was sliding under the Burled Arch. The celebrated finish line was finally, miraculously, at his back. North couldn't contain his tears ... he'd really done it. For North Edward Charles Ruben, rookie #9 from Canada, *The Last Great Race* was over. It was 8:14 am; the Iditarod committee declared North's official race time as eleven days, twenty-one hours and fifty-seven minutes. He'd finished the race in a very disappointing twenty-eighth place.

He'd had moments on the trail – many moments, as he would later recount to Andi – when he didn't think he would make it. Many long, cold, painful days when he'd been ready to accept defeat, to call an end to his ill-conceived dream. Many days when he would willingly have curled into a tight ball and drifted peacefully into a long, permanent sleep, if not for the thought of the loving woman waiting for him at home. Many times when he'd feared for his life.

North was barely aware of the unfamiliar press of people around him, the rush of activity invading his space. Bright eyed, strange faces with rosy cheeks loomed darkly in his rapidly shrinking field of vision; black shadows crowded in, blotting out his ability to see beyond a narrow field directly before him. Loud voices echoed distantly, miles from his humming ears: *Congratulations North! How does it feel North! Have you got anything to say to your fans, North Ruben?*

Heavy hands slapped him on the back and tried to grab his uncooperative hands; his fingers remained firmly wrapped around the sled's handle bar, glued to it, unable to relax and release. If he were to let go, North was sure he'd topple headlong to the ground, like a frozen Popsicle.

Then, all of a sudden, she was there. Two familiar, warm hands cupped his ravaged, frostbitten face, stroking the remnants of sweat and tears and frost from his cheeks. Bright emerald green eyes, etched with the accumulated fears and tears of too many long days and nights alone, probed his dark chocolate brown ones, inches from his face.

North felt the shift the instant his wife's mind linked with his ... a subtle, blurry wobble that should have been unsettling but wasn't. Everything else faded away – the noise, the fanfare, the voices surrounding him. Andi's eyes remained fastened on his, unblinking while she probed into his consciousness, delving into the recesses of his brain and retracing every second and every mile of his time away from her.

It was over within the blink of an eye, and North recognized shock and confusion in his wife's eyes when she realized that she had, for a very brief moment, united her mind with his. She'd just ran every step of the Iditarod with him, and experienced every harrowing and joyous moment of the past thirteen days. It was an unsettling, uncanny experience for them both. They needed no words to explain the knowledge and confusion in each other's eyes, slowly fading as the mayhem surrounding them slowly came back into focus.

North let out a long breath that he didn't realize he'd been holding. A smile creased his raw, cracked lips. "Babe."

"North, I thought you'd *never* get here! Don't you ever, ever do that to me again." Andi lowered her lips to his and, for a few precious seconds before his world went dark, made everything in his life right again.

THIRTY-THREE

Running, checkpoints, sign in, sign out.
Cold, wind, darkness.
Fatigue, hunger, aching muscles, throbbing foot.
Rest the dogs, feed the dogs, check lines, check paws and replace
little green booties.

White and red, white and red.
Snow and blood, snow and blood.

Running, checkpoints, sign in, sign out.
Cold, wind, darkness.
Fatigue, hunger, aching muscles, throbbing foot.
Rest the dogs, feed the dogs, check lines, check paws and replace
little green booties.

"North! North wake up!"

An insistent, demanding voice wove its way into his dreams. *I know that voice.*

A persistent hand shook him gently. *Go away ... let me be ... where am I?*

"You're having another nightmare, North. Wake up!"

He struggled to open his eyes, but they refused to cooperate.

"North, can you hear me? Wake up."

North's mind slowly released him from his dreams, and he reluctantly opened his crusty eyes, blinking several times to focus on the dimly lit room. It had been so very long since he'd been able to rest – to be warm and comfortable and free from hunger. To gently awaken to the musky, sweet scent of a woman laying by his side.

"Hey Babe, what time is it?" he croaked. His body felt leaden, still heavy with exhaustion. Lined, floor length curtains blocked the small room's one window, revealing neither light nor darkness beyond. His vocal cords were rusty from disuse and parched from the overheated, dry air of the hotel room.

A low, throbbing pain radiated from his left leg, now heavy and unwieldly within the confines of a rigid walking cast, a gift from one of Nome's orthopedic surgeons. Linda Blankenship had been right, god bless her soul. His left arm, suffering from a torn muscle, lay within a sling he'd have to wear for the next week or two.

"You've just about slept around the clock," Andi murmured softly, toying with the small silver Inukshuk that lay against her husband's chest, just below the hollow of his throat. "It's Saturday morning already." Her long, slim arm encircled his waist beneath the warm down duvet. "I've been waiting for you to wake up." Soft fingers trailed through the silky curls at his groin, pulling gently, teasing. "We should order room service for breakfast. You must be starving," she whispered. Her hand moved lower, cupping and squeezing.

North felt the warm tingle of blood rushing to meet his wife's arousing touch, his exhausted body still eagerly responding. He adjusted his legs to release the mass of his swelling manhood, moaning when she wrapped her hand around its length. His hand found her breast, soft and round, more than enough to fill his hand. He squeezed it gently and rolled her erect nipple between his fingers.

Andi sought his lips and kissed him softly at first, a series of gentle, quick brushes that soon grew hot and deep. Her lips moved down, tasting his chin, his neck, trailing along the length of his long, deep chest until she reached a taut nipple.

North moaned and threw his head back against the thick, down-filled pillows. "I've been dreaming about this," he panted, "every night while I was gone."

Andi turned her attention to the other side of his broad chest, her hand still busy beneath the covers.

"I want to touch you," North gasped. His hand slid down her side, over her hip.

"No," she whispered, releasing his rigid nipple from the ministration of her hot tongue. "Just lay there and let me take care of you. You've had a rough few days. This is my treat."

North grinned in the dim room. For once in his life, he was more than happy to follow instructions. *'Maybe I am a winner, after all'* was his last coherent thought before every muscle in his body tightened and the fireworks began.

He was starting to drift back to sleep a few minutes later, safe and warm and satisfied – at least for the moment – when Andi picked up the bedside telephone.

"Room service, I'd like to order breakfast for two," were the last words he heard before he slipped away into oblivion again.

Fifty-three mushers started the 25th Silvery Anniversary running of *The Last Great Race.* Only forty-four completed it.

Twenty-eighth place – I couldn't have done much worse, North thought glumly as he thumped his way through the expansive, crowded banquet room at the Nome Recreation Centre on Sunday, March 16. He trailed Andi and Mats as they searched for their designated table at the Iditarod Awards Banquet. His progress, hampered by his heavy walking cast and a cane, was clumsy and slow. On several occasions he was held up by fellow mushers who grasped his hand and wanted to exchange a few words. He was mystified by the number of strangers who acknowledged him. People he had never before seen in his life jumped up to shake his hand and wish him well, thumping him on the back. They were a friendly lot, North decided, these west-coast Alaskans.

Held on the Sunday immediately following the arrival of the first musher to cross the finish line in Nome, the banquet was a much anticipated gathering to congratulate the race contestants and honour the winner. Event tickets were usually a sell-out. The small, quiet northern city of Nome swelled by a thousand people during the race events, and hotels, motels and private accommodation burst at their seams. Savvy residents had been known to pad their pockets by renting out bedrooms, insulated garages and even sagging sofas to unprepared and desperate visitors.

The ten dogs North had dropped on the trail had all been flown safely back to Anchorage by the Iditarod Airforce, and waited for him in the loving care of the Iditarod veterinarians and volunteers.

"We should have tried to get a flight out to Anchorage yesterday," North mumbled after he dropped into a chair at their table. "We'd be on our way home by now."

"Tomorrow, sweetheart. Our reservations are for tomorrow."

"Won't come soon enough for me. Do they serve beer or do you have to go to the bar and get it?"

"You know you can't drink, North. You're on Tylenol 3. Don't mix drugs with alcohol. You know that." North looked at her through narrowed, dark eyes, wondering if she'd been talking to Linda Blankenship.

"I've just been through *hell* and back, and I'll have a damn beer if I want one. Where is the waitress? Hey Mats, why don't you go find us a couple of beers?" North's question sounded more like a demand as he threw twenty dollars on the table. "Better get me two. Canadian, if they have it." His new Norwegian friend scooped up the bill with a fearful glance at Andi, and dashed away before she could voice her dissent.

Mats had fared better than North in the race, crossing the finish line in twentieth place, almost dead centre of the pack. It was a stellar finish for the Iditarod rookie.

North's finish wasn't quite as memorable. In fact, he had no real recollection of it whatsoever. After passing beneath the elusive Burled Arch, his last memory was of Andi's warm, soft hands stroking his face. The next thing he clearly remembered was waking up in the Nome hospital, and he was furious. He felt like he'd been robbed, stripped of that glorious moment of victory and deprived of that once-in-a-lifetime thrilling moment of joy when you succeed in accomplishing something you've dreamed about all your life, even if you cross the finish line in twenty-eighth place.

"Come on, North! Cheer up," Andi scolded, frown lines marring her smooth brow. "One would think you've lost your best friend, not completed an amazing race."

North dragged his gaze away from the race officials gathering on the podium in preparation for the imminent commencement of the night's awards, not that he'd be winning one. His dark, brooding eyes skimmed over the crowded, noisy room, finally settling on the woman at his side. His wife was dressed casually in blue jeans and a sweater, as were most of the banquet attendees. Her lustrous, heavy hair was unbound and hung in loose waves around her shoulders, strands of dark brown, deep red and copper tones blended and shimmered, creating a rare, earthen colour many women yearned for. Andi caught him gazing at her, the love in his dark, chocolate brown eyes undeniable, and blew him a kiss.

North lifted a reddened hand to her sunken cheeks. "You've lost too much weight, Babe. You weren't eating while I was gone."

"I ate enough. You didn't fare so well yourself."

"We'll get fattened up on tacos and nachos and guacamole in Mexico, hmm?" North leaned over and pushed a strand of hair from her cheek, replacing it with a kiss.

"I can't wait."

Mats returned with a tray bearing four bottles of beer and one of Perrier. He carefully set the tray on their table, and had just reclaimed his seat when the microphone shrieked to life, announcing the commencement of the 1997 Iditarod Awards Banquet.

The winner of the 25th Silver Anniversary Race with a time of ten days, eleven hours and five minutes was Marvin Boutillier from Big Lake, Alaska. Marvin was a repeat winner, this being his twelfth running of the race, and his third win. He and the next nineteen mushers approached the podium in turn and accepted their sizeable cheques and the much-revered commemorative 'Iditarod 1997' silver belt buckle that each finisher receives. After he or she received their award, each musher was given a few minutes to make a short acceptance speech.

Only the first twenty mushers over the finish line received cash awards; Mats Pederson, his formerly ragged, bushy beard and mustache now neatly trimmed, grinned from ear to ear when he claimed his twentieth-place prize of $7,560. The funds would go a long way toward replenishing the Norwegian's empty wallet. As he was the first rookie to cross the finish line, he was also awarded the 'Rookie of the Year' award. He accepted his trophy and recognition with shy reverence and grace. When the crowd's raucous cheers had died, he gave an abbreviated and halting, though heartfelt acceptance speech that earned him another round of applause. Mats Pederson had obviously made many new friends, on and off the trail.

During the ceremony many other longstanding awards were given for various contributions and achievements during the race. The announcer and speakers droned on for what seemed like an eternity. North nursed his second beer slowly, not wanting to admit that he felt slightly woozy after downing the first cold one too fast.

Awards were presented and claimed: First to Yukon, First to Gold Coast, Fastest Time from Safety to Nome, Most Inspirational Musher,

Humanitarian Award, Race Champion. The list and the night seemed to drag on and on.

"And we've saved the best for last," the race official's booming voice finally said. "To North Ruben, Rookie musher #9 from Inuvik, Canada, the committee is pleased to present the Fred Meyer Sportsmanship Award!"

Applause thundered through the room, drowning out all else, deafening in its intensity. North was stunned beyond words. His aches and pains and general malaise vanished in an instant. Andi grasped his forearm, her fingernails digging into his skin in her excitement, and he turned to stare at her in disbelief. After a few heady seconds Andi wrapped her arms around his neck and kissed him long and hard. "Congratulations, darling!"

The entire assemblage stood, their echoing applause and cheers continuing while he slowly limped his way to the front of the room, cane in hand. Two burly mushers ran to his aid when North paused at the bottom of the low stage, supporting him while he navigated its three steps. When he reached the presenter's podium he clutched the corner of the tall wooden stand for support, woozy from either the combination of codeine and alcohol, or numb with wonder.

"Tonight we are pleased to present the Fred Meyer Sportsmanship Award to North Ruben," began the Iditarod Race Committee official when the applause subsided. "As you all know, the Sportsmanship Award is one of the most celebrated traditions in the Iditarod. Some winners of this award say it is their most treasured trophy. It's awarded to a musher whose actions help fellow competitors, and who is a role model for all racers ... someone who helps fellow mushers through tough situations."

Another round of applause echoed through the room.

"The recipient of this award," he continued, "is chosen by YOU. It's chosen by the racers, in recognition of the actions of one of your fellow mushers. Becky Singleton, can you come on up here for a minute, please?" The presenter skimmed the crowd for a glimpse of Becky, narrowing his eyes against the harsh neon lighting.

A quiet hush fell on the room as Becky's slight figure, still clad in hot pink but looking smaller than North remembered without her bulky parka, approached the podium. Without a moments' hesitation she strode directly to North's side and wrapped her arms around him, the top of her blond head barely skimming his shoulders. She kissed his cheek, leaving a hot-pink imprint of her lips, and whispered in his ear, "Thank you so very much North, I'll remember your kindness forever. You deserve this award more than anyone I've ever known. Congratulations."

Clinging to North's arm she turned to her friends and fellow Iditarod mushers, the people she'd known, loved and raced with for so many years. These tough, determined men and women were as much family to her as her own flesh and blood. Raising a hand to silence the crowd, her first public words since her harrowing event were brief, her bright, cobalt eyes brimmed with tears. "I wasn't sure if I'd survive this race. North Ruben saved my life. He saved the lives of six of my sled dogs. He is a true hero, and a great man, and I owe him a huge debt that I can never hope to repay."

The assemblage had reseated themselves but rose again, their applause deafening. Becky, having said everything she wanted to say, gave the microphone back to the committee official but remained next to North, her arm locked through his.

"North Ruben," the official began again, "you came to the aid of a fellow musher in distress. Becky Singleton and her team were attacked by moose on the trail, resulting in the death of four of her team. You came to her assistance and took measures to protect her and the rest of her team from further danger. At the risk of your own life, and at the inevitable expense of your placement at the finish line here in Nome, you saw Becky to safety. On behalf of the Iditarod Race Committee, it is with great pleasure that I present you with this plaque in honour of your unselfish and sportsmanlike behavior. Congratulations."

North shook the extended hand and accepted the small plaque, turning to the crowd before him. He waved it overhead with a sheepish grin before taking his place behind the microphone.

"Thank you all so very much. I'm overwhelmed." He pressed the plaque to his chest, his voice choked with emotion. "I didn't do anything that any one of you wouldn't have done, and by rights I should be sharing this award with Mats Pederson, too. He stopped, he helped look after the moose, and then," North grinned and pointed at his casted leg, "he helped look after me, too. He stuck with Becky and me until we reached Shaktoolik. When you see someone in trouble you stop and help them. That's what my father taught me, and that's the way I live my life. Life isn't about winning the race, it's about how you get to the finish line. And I hope I can teach my sons and daughters those same values. Thank you all again."

He turned from the podium and accepted the arm Becky offered. United by a bond that would last a lifetime, they threaded their way through the standing, cheering crowd. Andi was standing by her chair when North and Becky got to their table, but instead of the handshake she anticipated, Becky gave her a warm hug. "You've got a hell of a good man here, Andi," she said with a smile that was soft, and somehow sad. "He's a hero. Treasure him."

Andi's smile, when Becky released her, was genuine. After all, she'd seen what had transpired between her husband and the diminutive pink musher. "We have something for you, Becky," Andi said, resting a hand on her arm before she could turn away.

Becky looked at her with sad blue eyes. "For me?"

Andi reached down for a small white cardboard shopping bag, the name of one of the most prestigious Nome boutiques emblazoned in black on its side. She handed it to Becky with a rueful smile. "I think you're missing something. Go ahead, open it."

Becky pushed the royal purple tissue paper poking out of the bag aside and pulled out a long, plush cashmere wool scarf. It was, of course, hot pink. Tears sprang from her eyes, but she laughed. "I was wondering what happened to my scarf!"

Becoming someone's hero was not what North had anticipated when he'd commenced the gruelling eleven-hundred-mile Iditarod, but it was a gratifying way to conclude one of the most memorable events of his life. Dreams do come true, and he'd survived *The Last Great Race*, one harrowing and exhausting mile at a time.

North draped his arm around Andi's shoulders and grinned. "I think it's about time for us to get home, Babe. We have a honeymoon in Mexico to plan."

ACKNOWLEDGEMENTS

First I must give a big ***THANK YOU*** to my readers. When I finished writing my first novel, *Diamonds in an Arctic Sky*, I had no plans to write another book. It was only because of your encouragement and enthusiasm that I even considered it! Thank you from the bottom of my heart.

A huge thanks to Elisabeth Ratz, Kay Nicholson, and Amanda Pinkerton for your sharp eyes. I do appreciate the many hours you spent pouring over my manuscript. Your observations and comments did not go unheeded (most of them, anyway!). Any mistakes are entirely my fault.

To Krystal Tsuji, photographer extraordinaire, I cannot thank you enough for the privilege of having your award-winning, breathtaking Inukshuk photo on the front cover of my book. It makes my heart race every time I look at it.

And last, but not least, thank you to my husband, Heinz, who has put up with my less-than-social moods and hours locked away in my office. You can talk to me now!

I HOPE YOU ENJOYED

NORTH: The Last Great Race

PLEASE READ ON FOR
A SNEAK PREVIEW OF:

HONEYMOON BAY
(Andi & North, Book 3)

Available Now!

HONEYMOON BAY

ONE

After an hour-long delay due to high winds, the *Queen of Nanaimo* was finally underway on her two-hour sailing from Vancouver to Nanaimo. Newlyweds Andi and North Ruben were on their honeymoon, bound for Mexico after a short side trip to Vancouver Island, British Columbia.

Once on board the large ferry, Andi insisted that she and her new husband view the vessel's departure from the chilly vantage point of the upper deck. She looped her long purple scarf around her neck and dragged a slower and somewhat reluctant North up the stairs to the outside viewing deck. The icy wind was still strong, evermore so when they reached the open waters of the Strait of Georgia, a long, busy arm of the Pacific Ocean dividing British Columbia's lower mainland from Vancouver Island.

Andi gripped the chipped, white metal deck railing and leaned out to gaze at the churning waters far below, the wind whipping her long brown hair around her face. North stood guard at her back, his arms wrapped securely around her lithe frame, his weight a solid anchor against the unforeseen and unthinkable. They'd been married only three months, and he wasn't about to lose her to the waters of the deep and unforgiving Pacific.

She leaned into her husband's sheltering arms, the back of her tousled head resting against his collar bone, grateful for the warmth of his six-foot frame and broad shoulders. "I never get tired of looking at the ocean," she sighed. "I love living in Inuvik, but I really love the coast too."

"It *is* beautiful here," North agreed, leaning down to nuzzle a tiny white slice of exposed neck. "It must have been a great place to grow up."

"It was. I just love the smell of the sea," she murmured. "I've missed it, and all of this *green*. Have you noticed how green the coast is? It's like that all year long here." Her rather sad laugh carried a low, musical note. "The only thing I *don't* miss is four or five months of winter rain; it can get so depressing." She craned her neck and smiled up at her dark-eyed husband. He wore his shoulder length, jet black hair tied at the nape of his neck. His smooth, unblemished skin was the colour of dark honey, testament to his Inuvialuit heritage.

North chuckled. "Well, it might be dark for the better part of the winter up north, but at least it's not wet."

The earlier high winds had chased away any lingering clouds, but the water remained rough and the late afternoon sunshine danced and sparkled on the white-capped waves. The mainland lay well behind them now, thickly forested and, as Andi had noted, very, very green. Quite the opposite of the vast, white expanse of frozen terrain they were accustomed to above Canada's Arctic Circle. To the north the towering, snow-capped Coastal Rocky Mountains crawled along the mainland shore; Whistler and Blackcomb ski resorts were favourite weekend getaways for urban Vancouverites. To the west over a wide expanse of dark water a less imposing range of mountains marched along Vancouver Island's spine, slowly looming larger as the ferry left the bustling city of Vancouver in its wake.

Gulls and shorebirds tailed along behind the ferry, squawking and diving, while two majestic Bald Eagles soared high overhead. Although daylight was already waning, Andi was eager to give her northern husband a glimpse of the majestic local marine life. They kept a sharp lookout for Harbor seals and Orcas, those famous, graceful white and black killer whales, and were disappointed when none appeared.

It was mid-April. Andi and North had returned to Inuvik from Nome, Alaska, only a month earlier, after North had competed in the 25th Silver Anniversary running of The Iditarod, a world-famous sled dog race. The long, gruelling competition had been tougher and infinitely more dangerous than he'd expected, and he'd placed a dismal twenty-eighth in a field of forty-four finishers. He'd also come home with a trophy he'd just as soon not have received – a fractured ankle. His walking cast had been removed only yesterday, but his doctor had warned him to stay off his foot as much as possible. North had never been a good patient, and didn't intend to let a little thing like a broken bone stop him from doing whatever he pleased.

The Rubens had barely had enough time to reorganize their lives before it was time to leave on their honeymoon. Married on January 2, 1997, they'd foregone their honeymoon until the Iditarod was over. North's nephew Eddie Ruben, who had dreams of one day owning his own sled dog team, was staying in their home and would care for North's kennel of twenty-four Canadian Eskimo Dogs during their absence. North had promised him a pup from the next litter, although Eddie would have gladly taken on the responsibilities without the reward.

Andi still had a month of leave from her position as the Flight Operations Manager for Tuktu Aviation, the second largest flying company in Inuvik. Her boss, who was also the company's owner and CEO, had encouraged her to take off as much time as she needed to during the slower winter months, before their busy summer flying season began. Andi loved her job and missed the excitement and daily challenges of the aviation world.

North was a self-employed entrepreneur and owned a thriving art gallery in Inuvik, although most of his sales were made to private buyers, collectors and other galleries throughout Canada and the United States, as well as overseas. His gallery, The Qamutik, was a treasure trove of northern art work and handicrafts, from soapstone carvings, paintings and caribou-hair tuftings to handmade clothing and mukluks.

The newlyweds were heading to Vancouver Island to spend a week with Andi's family in Port Alberni before departing on their honeymoon – a much anticipated motorhome trip down Mexico's 1200-kilometer-long Baja Peninsula. They would stop in various villages and towns along the way, with a longer one-week stay in the famous resort city of Cabo San Lucas. Three other couples were going with them – old friends who each had their own recreational vehicle and were looking for some adventure. Andi still wasn't convinced that RV'ing was the ideal way to spend a honeymoon, especially in Mexico; she'd been pushing for a week or two at a Mayan Riviera Resort. Neither was she crazy about sharing her husband and her honeymoon with six other people but, for her husband's sake, she was willing to give it a try. He was almost as excited about the RV trip as he had been about running the Iditarod. Andi just hoped their tropical vacation would have a better outcome than the Iditarod had.

The Rubens had flown from Inuvik to Vancouver via Yellowknife and Edmonton. It was almost a two-day journey, with an overnight in Edmonton, Alberta. From the Vancouver airport they'd jumped into a cab to the Horseshoe Bay ferry terminal. Andi's father, Alex Nowak, had been ecstatic to hear they were coming home for a visit, and promised to be waiting for them at the Departure Bay ferry terminal in Nanaimo.

The late afternoon sun was rapidly losing its warmth, and the air was noticeably cooler. Andi felt North shiver in the biting wind, stronger now that the ferry had picked up speed. She turned in the circle of his embrace and entwined her arms around his neck. "Want to go down below now? We can grab a coffee and something to eat at the restaurant."

"Yeah, that would be great," North shivered. "I'm hungry." They turned toward the closest exit to the passenger decks below.

"You're *always* hungry!"

North grinned and wiggled his heavy, black eyebrows comically. "I'm always hungry for you, Babe. Do you want to go make out in the bathroom?"

"Oh my God!" Andi giggled. "You're forty-one years old, Ruben. Middle-aged men don't make out in public bathrooms!"

North signed dramatically. "Shot down again. Well, I'll settle for a burger and fries then, as long as you're buying."

An hour and a half and multiple cups of coffee later, they disembarked *The Queen of Nanaimo* and retrieved their suitcases from the baggage carousel. Alex Nowak was waiting for them in the passenger loading zone outside the ferry terminal. Andi dropped her suitcase and ran to her father with outstretched arms. "It's so good to see you, Dad!" she cried, hugging him fiercely.

Alex Nowak was the epitome of a weathered, rugged sailor. One's immediate impression of the man was that of strength and brawn, regardless of his seventy-plus years. He stood straight and tall at slightly over six feet and was still well-muscled. His lightly bronzed face was generously lined with deep furrows, thanks to decades of sun and sea air, and his deep-set eyes were a startling shade of cerulean blue. His cheeks and chin sported their customary two-days' growth of grizzled stubble, and curls of grey hair that were badly in need of a cut escaped from beneath the brim of a grimy ball cap. He hadn't dressed up for the occasion of their arrival; Alex was clad in faded work pants and a tattered, long-sleeved grey Stanfield's undershirt. The classic Canadian garment was often worn as a light sweater by many working men, and the warm, soft woolen pull-over was the practical base layer of any respectable Island man's wardrobe. Some Islanders joked that you could tell the might of a man by the condition of his Stanfield's; the more worn and shabbier his sweater, the more of a force to be reckoned with would be the man. Alex Nowak's Stanfield's had more seams than substance.

To Andi, though, her imposing father was, and always would be, a teddy bear. After Maria Nowak (whom everyone called Mary) gave birth to three boys, the Nowak family was blessed with a girl. From the moment she was born, Andi had been cherished and more than slightly spoiled by her close-knit, loving family. Even her three rowdy brothers, Luke, Bryan, and Malcolm, had always had a soft spot in their hearts for their little sister. The four siblings were inseparable when they were young.

When Andi was finally released from her father's grip, North and Alex shook hands and slapped each other's backs, their embrace just short of a hug. The two men had met only once before, on the occasion of Andi and North's wedding in Inuvik, but had bonded immediately and developed an instant mutual respect for each other. It took only a moment for the men to lift their luggage into the bed of Alex's old beat-up Chevy pickup, where the suitcases mingled with tangled fishing nets, crusty crab traps, and two rounds of heavy, blue dock line newly purchased at the Harbour Chandler in Nanaimo. The trio climbed into the cab of the truck and merged into heavy ferry traffic from the Departure Bay terminal and onto the Island Highway.

Heading north out of Nanaimo, the busy highway hugged Vancouver Island's green, scenic east coast until reaching the quaint, somewhat touristy seaside town of Parksville about thirty minutes later. There they turned west to follow the narrow, curvy Alberni Highway inland. They talked without pause, eager to catch up on each other's news.

Darkness had fallen during the crossing, somewhere between Vancouver and Nanaimo, but in the gleam of the Chevy's headlights they were able to catch glimpses of mystic, gargantuan Douglas fir and Western red cedar trees as they drove through the ancient forest called

Cathedral Grove, situated about thirty kilometers west of Parksville. When she was a child, Andi swore she could hear ancient voices murmuring amongst the huge old trees, their sighs and whispers there for anyone to hear, if you only really tried ... if you only really *believed*. Even now her ears tingled as they passed through the famous landmark and on past Cameron Lake, the narrow, two-lane highway winding and twisting its way westward.

Port Alberni, or 'Port', as it was commonly referred to by locals and Islanders, sat at the terminus of the Alberni Inlet. The Inlet was a narrow channel stretching from the Pacific Ocean on the wild, rugged west coast of Vancouver Island inland forty kilometers to its terminus at Port Alberni. Through the slightly open window, the unmistakable and unforgettable scent of salt marsh, fish, diesel fumes and rain assailed Andi's nose. Thirty minutes into their journey North had succumbed to his seemingly perpetual fatigue. Not fully recovered from his ordeal in Alaska, he was slumped against the passenger door, snoring intermittently.

"It's good to see you two," Alex said softly, his deeply timbered voice melodic. "You're living too far away from the family, you know."

Andi smiled, "I know, Dad. But I'm just so glad to be back for a visit. I've missed you a lot."

"I've missed you, too, princess," he said, patting her knee. "You have no idea how much."

Andi smiled and leaned her head on her father's shoulder. They'd always been close, and she missed him something fierce.

After a few moments Alex asked, "So how are you *really* doing, my love?"

She knew what he wanted to know, heard the unspoken question behind his words. In his soft, round-about way, her father was asking if she was finally getting her life back together. On the outside, of course, everything looked great – she had a new husband and a good job. But what he wanted to know was if she was okay on the *inside* ... if the inner

Andi was finally healing. Alex Nowak had good reason to be concerned for his only daughter.

Eight years earlier Andi and her first husband, a geologist, had lost their only child, three-year old Natalie, to a speeding truck on an icy Yellowknife road. Andi lost her marriage, and then she lost the will to live. Alcohol began to control and destroy her life until one day she realized she needed help, and turned to Alcoholics Anonymous. She was winning her ongoing battle with sobriety, but it was still a daily struggle, and always would be. Andi would never forget her sweet daughter and thought about her daily but, thanks to North's strength, love and support, she was healing and growing stronger every day.

"I'm doing fine, Dad. Really. You don't have to worry about me anymore," Andi replied with conviction. And she was.

They chatted quietly for the duration of the ninety-minute drive, catching up on her brothers' lives, the fishing business and general island gossip. The Nowak family home was situated on the west side of Port, and as they passed through town and the familiar streets of her childhood, Andi felt the tension acquired during the last few hectic days ease from her tired body.

"The kids are all looking forward to seeing you two. Do you think you're up to a family dinner tomorrow?" Alex asked. He was just pulling into the wide driveway of their home on Polly Point. Situated on two acres of grandfathered land, the Nowaks were one of the few families in Port Alberni that had the luxury and convenience of owning a private commercial fishing dock. Their land sat on a section of the Alberni Inlet that drew water deep enough to moor the Nowaks' large commercial fishing trawler.

"For sure. I'm dying to see everyone," Andi said, yawning as she elbowed North awake. "We're both too beat to do any visiting tonight, though."

"I hear ya," Alex acknowledged with a smile. "The little ones will be in bed by now anyway. You just go on up to the house while North and I see to the luggage. Sylvie's been locked in the house for a few hours now, and I'm sure she's heard us. She'll be glad to see you."

North opened the passenger door, the rusty door hinge squeaking in protest, attesting to the Chevy's long life in the salt air. North grimaced and rubbed the sleep from his eyes. "Man, I gotta fix that for you."

Andi gazed at the large, cedar plank house that had been her home for so many years. Tonight it sat dark and mysterious, high above the roadway. She slung her purse over her shoulder and began the long trudge up the wooden staircase. On either side of the stairs were terraced gardens, planted in a profusion of azaleas, rhododendrons, California lilacs, roses and ornamental evergreens. Native salal, ocean spray, dull Oregon-grape and profuse ferns bordered the plantings, providing a wide green zone between the carefully tended gardens and the wild, encroaching forest beyond.

The minute she opened the front door, a fury of black and tan burst onto the porch, leaping with joy. Andi knelt down to greet the eight-year-old Rotti-cross, who then ran nimbly down the steps barking joyfully at the sight of her master. Andi was pleased to see that Sylvie still had so much life left in her. She was still healthy and nimble for her age.

Flipping on lights in each room, Andi did a whirlwind tour of her old family home. She was glad to see that her father was keeping it clean and in good repair. Or perhaps the boys had hired a housekeeper for him, she thought, making a mental note to ask them about it.

By the time the men had finished lugging the suitcases up the impossibly long steps, she had put the kettle on to boil and taken her mother's large Brown Betty teapot out of the cupboard. In spite of their fatigue, they talked over cups of tea until midnight, when with a huge yawn Andi declared she couldn't keep her eyes open another second.

North and Andi slept in her old room, in the close and unaccustomed confines of a double bed. Nothing had changed since she'd left home all those years ago ... the furniture looked a little shabbier, the quilt and curtains faded. In the closet hung her abandoned high school jacket and prom dress, too good to throw away, but never to be worn again. Through the open bedroom window, the sound of distant waves lapped at the shore of the Alberni Inlet and lulled them to sleep.

Andi woke only once during the night, when her mother's voice stole into her dreams. Her eyes flew open, but of course her mother wasn't there. North lay against her side, his deep breaths long and even and his naked skin warm against her body.

While she waited for her racing heart to slow, Andi struggled to recall her mother's words. As it is with dreams, though, she couldn't quite remember what they were, but was sure they were important.

ABOUT THE AUTHOR

Joan Mettauer grew up in Alberta's heartland. Her love affair with aviation was sparked at an early age, and she dedicated most of her working years to the flying business in Edmonton, Alberta, Yellowknife, N.W.T. and La Ronge, Saskatchewan. Her final years in the aviation industry were spent in Inuvik, N.W.T., from where she bid farewell to Canada's North.

Now retired, she returned to her Alberta roots and lives in Medicine Hat with her husband. Her greatest joy is spending time with her eight grandchildren, who are scattered around the world in Canada, Switzerland and Australia.

You can find her at:
Facebook: Joan Mettauer, Author
Instagram: Joan Mettauer, @joanmettauer
www.goodreads.com
Amazon worldwide

40931406R00171